FIJI 1970
THE NEW WEST SERIES, BOOK ONE

TOM TATUM

Published by Wolfpack Publishing
6101 S. Rainbow Road, Suite 1350
Las Vegas, Nevada 89118

WOLFPACK
PUBLISHING
— EST 2013 —

WOLFPACK
PUBLISHING
— EST 2013 —

Text copyright © 2021 Tom Tatum

Published by Wolfpack Publishing
5130 S. Fort Apache Road, 215-380
Las Vegas, NV 89148

Paperback IBSN 978-1-64734-927-1
eBook ISBN 978-1-64734-926-4

FIJI 1970

CHAPTER ONE

MEMOIRS OF A PEACE CORPS VOLUNTEER

I was lying face down in front of a new Pioneer speaker. It was wired to a shiny Sony reel to reel tape deck fresh from a duty-free shop in Suva run by Fiji's ubiquitous Hindu business 'guerrillas '. The Japanese had allied with the colony's Indian merchants to take over every market in Fiji. The American Peace Corps volunteers were unwitting allies in this effort. They bought the best available duty-free tape machines for rock and roll easy listening pleasure. Stereo sound like this was almost better than sex. The band's music seeped into every opening of my body and aroused my passion. My dirty blond long hair was swept to one side.

The warm, smothering South Pacific night breeze wafted the acrid smell of pot or 'ganja' through the living room. I lived in a small yellow wooden-framed beach house on the south coast of Fiji. The house was a piece of leftover colonial beachfront junk. The neo-colonialist lived in these 'hand me down' houses.

I was vaguely aware that my very romantic PCV (Peace Corps Volunteer), 24-year-old girlfriend lay sprawled on her stomach next to me. She was also stoned. Her waist length auburn hair was fanned over her head. It was almost touching an over-amped speaker. Dianne had a pair of long, perfectly tanned, second generation Finnish legs. They were completely exposed by a green Australian mini-mini skirt which revealed her white silk panties.

A third PCV faced the other speaker headfirst. He was semi-stoned, too. It seemed lately, when impromptu sex with Dianne was desirable, another PCV had camped in my two-room house. Fiji's-PCVs were nourished with food and conversation with other volunteers. Otherwise, most of them would have been victims of tropical disease, loneliness induced psychosis, or murdered by irate husbands, wives, or brothers of 'local' lovers. I decided to pass out. My hand reached for the open bottle of Fiji Rum. I took a last strong swig.

The sun—the boiling, direct, always hot tropical morning sun woke me up. I raised my head from the hard pine floor. I was one of three bodies pointed toward the madly flapping tape. The reel-to-reel machine spun endlessly on its way to wearing out. The auburn head moved next. One hand mustered the long strands of hair back toward their home on the bared tan shoulders. The other hand popped a white silk panty seam back over a slightly exposed vagina lip. It tugged the mini skirt that necessary inch lower. A blue eye looked at my brown eye and Dianne said, "Cooper, if you'll crush some coffee beans in the mortar, I'll fire up the kerosene burner and boil some water."

Life and reality as a PCV came into focus. My unfulfilled sexual tension collided with the reality of day 926 in the tropics with one foot in America and one foot in a neo-colonial primitive Peace Corps Volunteer experience. I rose and stepped over a sleeping athletic male figure. I knew my exile from America was nearing its end. My escape from Fiji must be quickly plotted before it was too late.

I had long observed the colonies' lost sailors and burned-out English expatriates who never quite exited Fiji. Too many bridge games, too much gin, local beer and dark rum produced dazed "Europeans", as the Fijian's called them. Their long-term scorecard was kept-up by not-so-secret affairs with Fijian house girls and other "mates'" wives on the reef-locked white sand beaches of these tiny South Pacific islands. It was at once a paradise found and a paradise lost, whether you landed at its smelly ports or the spic and span international airport with its modern hotel, where inter-national pilots and their flight attendants made their steamy homes on the jet set highways before the 747s turned them into bus stops.

If I stayed much longer my life would become too intertwined into this dying colonial scene of casual sex, high octane dark rum, cheap pot, and my ongoing affair with the Peace Corps staff nurse in the capital city of Suva. She was always willing to lock her office door while she gave me a checkup.

I remembered the first time Nurse Williams said, "Take your shirt off, Cooper." Then she rubbed the cold stethoscope back and forth against my nipples until I was aroused. She said, "After I check your prostate, roll over so I can make sure there is no swelling of your testicles from the antibiotics." I rolled over on the examination table on my back. My khaki shorts were down around my ankles and my hardening dick was up in the air. She climbed onto the table with knees against the side of my chest. Her white full nurse's skirt made a tent. Her hands-free entry was followed by a dozen or so precise deep contractions that rocketed me to a quick orgasm in sync with her deep tight spasms.

When the boiling aromatic local coffee was ready, Tab, the party spoiler but now awake friend, ambled into the kitchen for his free breakfast. We all discussed his current plight—how to save him from both expulsion from the Peace Corps and a lifetime ban from Fiji.

Tab's rapidly escalating problem was with the recently unchained Fiji government which, after 90 years of British Colonial rule, was exploring the "I'm Boss" syndrome full throttle. Tab, who still could not take his dark brown eyes off Dianne's legs as he drank the hot, rich local coffee that grew wild on long ago abandoned jungle coffee plantations, had just managed to piss off the minister for co-operatives. He was our "Super Boss".

Tab, while running around the capital city trying to set an all-time Peace Corps record for bedding local girls during his tour of duty, ended up under the prime minister's niece's sulu (skirt). She then involved him through her outer island royal family in helping the Fijian handicraftsmen. They made all the 'arts and crafts' for the tourists to buy on rainy days. They never seemed to receive much of the money. This problem existed in all societies. Minds like Mill, Keynes, Marx, John L. Lewis, and now Tab, were attracted to solving it.

Tab, armed with part of the royal family's blessing but without the prime minister's direct knowledge, whom the niece failed to inform, solved the problem quickly using his USC Business School mind. His incentive was to keep his draft deferment a third year, therefore avoiding a quick trip from Fiji to 'Nam, to help the Johnson-McNamara team.

Tab formed a handicraft co-operative for the native craftsmen. It was like an ESOP in the USA which allows the employees to own the company. It's Marxism with the rules set up by Wall Street corporate lawyers and accountants or, in this case, the fading British Empire. This co-operative worked splendidly for a while. Tab was allowed to re-up in the Peace Corps an additional year. This gave him the all-time local girl record in the capital city by a foreign male from any country. This included the American GIs who ran the place during WWII and produced Suva's "colored" population. The prime minister's niece kept her sulu pulled up over her beautiful chocolate thighs for Tab when she was in town. The craftsmen made "big bucks" and turned out more wood carvings, tapa cloth, shell bead necklaces, and straw hats than ever, which allowed the tourists to spend more hard currency. Marx and Jefferson would both have accepted board of directors' slots in this tropical enterprise.

Then, suddenly, a big black cloud appeared on the horizon. It turned out the Super Boss, the Minister of Co-ops, R.K. Patel, went straight for Tab's balls by firing him and asking the Peace Corps director to put him on the first plane from Nadi Airport to the USA. A little sleuth work by Dr. Joe, a PCV who had gone to Harvard Business School where they taught the down and dirty street politics of the New England industrialists, figured out the play. Dr. Joe's office was on the main wharf at the Suva Port where the handicrafts arrived from the outer islands by boat. A customs inspector who Dr. Joe plied with Fiji beer knew the game and it was a hot potato. The minister of Co-ops' brother was the middleman or wholesaler for the island handicrafts to the tourist hotels. He made a fat profit, some of which it was rumored went to the "ol'" minister himself, our "Super Boss".

Racism now entered in a big way, because Tab was white, the Fijian craftsmen were black (Melanesians), and as fate would have it, the Super Boss was a card-carrying Hindu Indian. Super Boss' political party was part of the fragile newly formed Alliance Party coalition government led by the prime minister whose niece started this with Ho Chi Minh, anyway. The prime minister wanted to avoid this brawl since most Fijians hated the Indians big time. He also needed their votes in the parliament style government, so he dodged the exploding bomb after the Super Boss told him Tab was under his niece's sulu nightly. He barred her from seeing Tab immediately. Then, he sat on his hands when Super Boss fired Tab, even though the craftsmen on the prime minister's home island village in Lau were headed back to non-union Colorado mine workers' wages again.

My kitchen had become the bunker for saving Tab from the jungles of Southeast Asia while proving socialism could work in a world driven by greed, politics, and one man, one vote. I watched Dianne's backlit long auburn hair as she brushed it again and again. The key was to get some dirt on our Super Boss, the minister of Co-ops. This would force the prime minister to fire him, therefore moving up his deputy who was a Fijian. I hoped the deputy would be sympathetic to the island craftsmen and save Tab in the process.

Tab was scrambling to pack his faded brown leather shoulder bag and catch the Saturday Suva Express bus on the coast highway. I suggested that I come to the capital in my beat-up gray Land Rover and join up with Dr. Joe. We would peruse the Co-op Dept. files in the guise of doing some research for our fruit wine co-op that Dr. Joe and I were attempting to sell to some Aussie businessmen who didn't believe in socialism.

With a long last glance at Dianne, who had now emerged from the bedroom, wearing an Australian bikini which signaled she wanted beachtime, Tab disappeared through the screen door. He walked toward the coast highway to the bus stop for our quaint little expatriate beach village. That left me on a hot summer tropical Saturday morning alone with Dianne for the first time since I could remember. My mind raced through a check list that concluded the house girl was off. The Aussie couple next door had left ahead of us for the beach. The Fijian handyman had macheted the grass on Friday, and Fiji had no home delivery mail service, or any services.

CHAPTER TWO

THE BEACH

Two hours later, my brown eyes raked the tanned back of my Aussie neighbor's wife Jill who lay face down on her blanket in the searing noon tropical sun at Natadola beach. Shocking what passed for beach clothing in Australia. Her bottom appeared to be totally exposed from my sight line. As I approached from behind, I could see a thin strip of cloth between her tanned hips. I wondered when American designers would copy these great swimsuits. It was wonderful to experience the future first.

Suddenly, I was looking at Jill's beautifully endowed Aussie breasts. They hung bare as she rolled over. She sat up and casually put on her bikini top in slow motion. She looked me straight in the eyes with a wonderfully teasing lusty smirk. "Hi, you good-looking Yank!" she said. "Paul's snorkeling about one-half kilometer out and I've been sleeping, you see."

Dianne emerged from the brush, PCV style. She had a full sulu and a long-sleeved white cotton shirt covering her bikini. PCV cover-up rules applied since she had to walk by a Fijian village. It overlooked the pristine white sand horse-shoe beach. As Dianne untied her sulu, it dropped to the white sand. I wondered if it would always be my fate to spend Saturdays with a bikini clad, dark tanned women on a deserted tropical beach where we could make up the rules.

The beach was so isolated that Dianne and I invented a game. We often played it in shallow warm tidal pools that were left by the ebbing tide. We could sit in one of the pools, chest to chest with our bathing suit bottoms off under the blue water. We made love to the beat of the surf as we watched the shoreline at eye level. The pleasure of orgasm in the warm South Pacific Ocean water mixed with the visuals of a pristine, palm tree rimmed white sand beach is etched in my mind forever.

I collapsed on the sand, still fighting a hangover, and debating Tab's plight in my mind. Dr. Joe's help was his only salvation, but it was also risky to me personally. I wanted to hang around Fiji through December when my draft deferment expired. I hoped the draft lottery, or a truce would save me from Vietnam, or I planned exile to cold Sweden or Canada. However, I couldn't decline to help my friend. I also needed an excuse to go to the capital city.

Nurse Williams had called me at the Co-op office in Sigatoka while I worked on Friday. She wanted to see me in Suva. She was leaving the colony secretly. So, I would drive the muddy, dangerous, unpaved coast road in my aging Land Rover early Monday morning. I would visit the minister of Co-ops' office and audit my co-op's latest New Zealand banana shipment receipts, say goodbye to Nurse Williams, and test destiny.

I watched Paul's snorkel bob as he worked the dying inter-reef line for rare shells, then sleep came again—that wonderful beach sleep to the rhythm of the shore break. It is so deep it extinguishes all desire, all ambition, all greed, and all memory.

The rest of the weekend was routine Fiji. More beach sleep followed by snorkeling, cold Aussie beers, a bumpy washboard-gravel-road ride back home, bridge games with the Aussies, local gossip, lots of passionfruit rum drinks, and local take-out Indian curry with popcorn size Fiji rice.

Monday dawn came early. I checked the Land Rover's engine fluid levels. I visually checked the Dunlop all terrain tires. I "kicked the tires and lit the fire" with a flip of the ignition key. Dianne was still asleep as dawn broke over the central mountains. I was capital city bound on a dry winter day.

CHAPTER THREE

QUEEN'S ROAD TO SUVA

The Land Rover lunged, bounced, screamed on the muddy, rain forest surrounded two-lane dirt road to Suva. I had no time for sexual fantasies as I fought the wildly spinning steering wheel from blind corner to blind corner. I drove on the right-hand side of the British colonial-built dirt road. One lapse of habit back to the left-hand side of the road USA style and it was head-on into a speeding 7-ton Toyota cargo truck or a packed-to-the-roof Fijian style bus. They had a frontal steel bumper like a small bull-dozer blade. I always wondered, after being confronted by a bus speeding toward me in my lane around a narrow muddy blind corner, whether I would someday reflexively steer right to avoid the collision and die hard in the Crown Colony with a hot Land Rover engine in my lap. Fortunately, in three years I never swerved the wrong way.

The trip to the capital in a Land Rover on moderately dry roads on the southern side of the main island of Viti Levu usually took four hours with no breakdowns, mud slides, giant fallen trees, or rocks crashing through the Land Rover windshield from speeding trucks and buses.

It was the third world game of chicken as Indian and Fijian drivers pushed the buses and overloaded 7-ton trucks through Grand Prix-style maneuvers. Australian and American tourists in little Japanese rental cars were regularly splattered against mountain walls or run off the road into the ocean. Most of them lived, but they never returned to Fiji to spend badly needed hard currency during future vacations. Everything has a natural predator. The third world bus and truck drivers are the natural predators of first world tourists. Adam Smith probably deduced this first when he wrote "The Wealth of Nations". He hypothesized the third world would always have a trade deficit. Fiji's cheap prices would always attract tourists.

The coastal flats near Suva were a welcome sight after crossing the long concrete one lane bridge at Navua on the eastern side of the mountains. My gasoline was running low and a minor repair was needed for the Co-op Department Land Rover. I whipped the gray Land Rover along the newly graded dusty road at fifty miles an hour, dodging chickens. The rule was to never stop for an animal or chicken you hit and killed while driving in Fiji. The price was exorbitant if you were American, and villagers ate them anyway. Of course, the tourists didn't know this "roadkill rule". They generously subsidized the village farmers when they stopped. I believed some villagers trained chickens to run in front of rental cars.

The road near the capital was always well graded past the prime minister's beach house to the Suva city limit. I sped to 65 mph. I kept hoping he would move his weekend beach house to the drier windward side of the island where I lived. He never did. He probably feared the blind corners and speeding buses and trucks too.

I checked into a Suva tourist harbor hotel where I sometimes stayed. I charged it to my Co-op travel account. I hated Peace Corps Volunteer capital city apartment floors. I read "Catch 22" in PC training. I deduced that like in wartime you could live hard and poor in the Peace Corps or you could live comfortably with extra hard work and common sense. Living well had always appealed to me, so a harbor front hotel at ten dollars Fijian a night was a luxury I treated myself to when in the capital city on expenses from the Valley Co-op which I managed in Sigatoka for the government and its development bank.

After the cruel, bone jarring ride to Suva, a quick call from my hotel room to the PC national office produced the soft-voiced nurse on the line. Her boss, the Peace Corps doctor, was out on an agricultural department patrol boat for a week. She was available for early drinks and dinner at my hotel. She agreed to bring a little something from the medicine cabinet to rejuvenate my tired, aching body. Nurse Williams always had a veritable drug cabinet in her purse. She liked to prescribe for friends.

I finished my shower and wrapped a bright orange flowered print sulu around my 34" waist. Nurse Williams walked into my beachside room dressed in her splendid white uniform the PC doctor made her wear. It recreated America for the ill or homesick volunteers who tried to wimp out of the Corps. All it did was make them miss home even more when they saw the tight-waisted, white, full long skirt with the full-busted, starched blouse and the white net stockings Nurse Williams wore. Some of them probably saw their mother through their high-fevered, frenzied tropical sweats as they lay sick from tropical diseases no one had ever heard of or cared about in the USA.

Nurse Williams really turned me on from the first day I met her when she was touring my province with the PC doc in a United States embassy loaner jeep. She was straight from Motown. She had dark brunette, short hair with a pretty, oval face. It featured one slightly crossed brown eye that always wandered faster and faster as she approached orgasm. It was easy to time a mutual climax with her, based solely on her crossed-eye speed. Her chin was weak. Below it was a pair of 36C breasts with a perfect pair of smooth, dark brown, half-dollar sized nipples. The left one was inverted and only popped out in full heat. I visualized them and I started to stir underneath my sulu. My eyes proceeded downward toward the woven reed-matted floor. They found a tight waist which filled out into 36-inch hips with milk white thighs and athletic calves. Nurse Williams was tight where it counted and full round where it counted.

I walked toward Nurse Williams, who dropped her native woven shoulder-carry basket to the floor. She licked her red lipsticked lips with her magic pink tongue that curled at the tip. My right hand unsnapped her four-button blouse and released the front-snap, full metal-rimmed bra she wore when on duty. Her brown nipples and perfect milk white breasts spilled into my right hand. My left hand finished pushing up her long skirt. My middle finger plunged into her pantiless, already wet vagina which had a unique sweet scent like a French perfume. Her hand moved with the deft, easy speed of a professional nurse as it slid in between the folds of my sulu and started its caressing motion. Easy, eager, wonderful young sex with lust in the tropics followed—while "serving" our country.

This time it was standing up Hindu style since I was six-two, and she was a foot shorter. As I entered her, she wrapped her legs around my hips while we leaned into a woven bamboo reed wall covering, which gave with each surge of our sweating bodies. The inverted nipple suddenly went hard against my moist chest. The slightly crossed eye went to orgasm speed. Our mutual orgasms came swiftly and loud, Fijian style. This was going to be a trip to remember if the intrigue with Tab played as well as the opening night of sex with Nurse Williams. The Tales of the South Pacific were wrong. These islands are beyond Paradise.

It was time to take a vacation from sex, which was a difficult thought as Nurse Williams' thighs loosened. Her ankles slowly slid down the back of my legs. I made a slow exit from her to reality—a tropical reality. The late '60s and early '70s unleashed legal sexual freedom as never known before for American females and males. If the '40s were the war years, and the '50s America's years, the '60s were the first sexual freedom years. There was no limit to fucking worldwide. When the Rolling Stones fired up their guitars and every other friend became a dope dealer, it was the California Gold Rush. As Nurse Williams' special scent drifted into the dark tropical night, my mind turned to the only real game I knew. It was politics, money, and power. My southwestern ranching heritage had instilled it in me since babyhood.

The Super Boss' big brown nose and fat, greedy face flickered in the lamp light of the beach hotel room. Nurse Williams' breasts heaved slowly up and down as her curled toes with bright red nail polish touched the floor and flexed slowly but deliberately. She rubbed her hard brown nipples against my taut stomach muscles, making ski runs through the sweat of my body. As she transferred her energy to me, she knew that she had a mission, only her final role still needed to be discussed. It would be a "whiz banger", as they say in New England. Nothing Nurse Williams had studied, fantasized, or thought of in her Midwest mind could have prepared her for it.

Tonight, we would make love again, in a mutual hypnotic state aided by pharmaceutical grade opium. She would pledge the loyalty to Tab that I needed. She would faithfully agree to carry out the mission. Her assignment would be revealed in a letter she would find in my Land Rover glove compartment at 6:00 PM Tuesday night. If she failed, Dr. Joe and I could die.

CHAPTER FOUR

AFTER NURSE WILLIAMS—THE SUPER BOSS

Sunrise came early in the tropical warm, muggy morning air with the scent of Nurse Williams still lingering in the damp sweat-drenched sheets. Nurse Williams' soft, nude, listless body lingered in the room, collapsed face down on a Fijian sleeping mat where last night's reveling had been consummated.

I stepped over her comatose body. I pulled on a pair of colonial khaki dress shorts; a hand ironed, white safari, Indian tailored British short-sleeved shirt complete with epaulets and my dress black leather sandals; brushed my teeth; splashed water on my face; sprayed on a little precious Right Guard. I wrote a note: "Remember, Tab, six o'clock, my Land Rover glove compartment in front of the national botanical garden. It's been cool—see you Stateside or in our next lifetime."

I folded the note and looked down at Nurse Williams. I decided the best place for it was between the cheeks of her beautiful round bottom. I softly pushed it into the bare cleavage, not waking her. As I left the room the note quivered in the breeze from the slowly rotating ceiling fan as Nurse Williams breathed rhythmically to a dream in the guerrilla theater of her mind.

I would never see Nurse Williams again except in fantasy. Her plane to Hawaii was scheduled for Wednesday and she said she would never return to Fiji or reveal her Stateside address. She did not discuss her reason for leaving Fiji.

My Land Rover rattled through the nearly empty, early morning streets of the capital city. The smells from the huge, sprawling national market filled the air. Reef fish, fresh butchered meat, wild tropical fruit, flowers, coffee, and charcoal fires for boiling tea water filled the tropical breeze. I downshifted as the Land Rover rounded a sweeping curve. Suva's main drag came into view with its drab gray stone government buildings along the coral reef-locked harbor's beachfront. The white gloved hand of an immaculately blue uniformed, bronzed giant Fijian policeman moved traffic through the city center.

Tab was waiting at our favorite tea shop, the Banana Cafe. He sat at a small street-side table as I swung the Land Rover into a parallel parking place, front end first in one try. He looked tired. Clearly, he wasn't sleeping much.

I swung open the light aluminum door of the Land Rover too hard and its aging hinges groaned. I sat down at the sidewalk table and Tab greeted me with a "Bula" (Fijian Hello) and a Fijian handshake. It meant we could talk freely. He knew the capital city spies. Apparently, none were at a nearby table this morning, just early rising tourists off to see the parliament building or the botanical gardens a block down the street. I watched the sporadic early morning traffic descend from Laulau Heights where Tab lived.

I outlined the plan quickly over fresh fruit, coffee, and horrible English white bread with butter and jelly. A Fijian 10-year-old shoeshine boy polished our leather sandals. I would meet Dr. Joe at the wharf in an hour. We would go to the First Australian Bank where key government officials kept large deposits. We would use the good ol' anglo boy network to trace the suspected fund transfers between the Indian handicraft middlemen at the wharf and the Super Boss.

We were sure they existed because the Indians loved banks; unlike the Chinese and the Fijians who operated in cash. The Indians had learned their banking lessons about interest well from their former colonial masters, the English. The Chinese, if necessary, just wanted to be able to depart quickly without a stop at the bank. The Fijians, who lived in a communal society, had no word or concept for interest. Marx would have been proud to be a Fijian.

The banking mission would take all day since the ledgers were kept by hand by the mostly colored clerks the Australian managers relied upon to run things while they lunched at the Suva Yacht Club, or played grass court tennis at the botanical gardens, or lawn bowled. They saved golf and sailing for weekend diversion. They would get it done today for Dr. Joe who kept his Co-op account there. Everyone was aware Bank of America had just opened down the street with an IBM computer in the window.

Tab would go about his normal activities while suspended from his job, then have a nocturnal secret rendezvous with the prime minister's niece. This would throw the capital city spies off our track since they were following Tab.

Dr. Joe and I then would carry out the final part of the plan with Nurse Williams. Tab didn't need to know its details in case he was interrogated. He was curious. I wondered if he knew about Nurse Williams' and my liaison. It was absolutely vital she not be connected to this operation before she left Fiji.

The shoeshine boy finished ,and we gave him a Fijian dime with some breakfast and sent him off to school, we hoped. I said my goodbyes. I drove off to the National Wharf to see Dr. Joe at his shed-like office in the main banana export area.

The shabby, rust-covered, steel hulled inter-island freighters were off loading copra, bananas, and coconut oil as I wheeled the Land Rover up a concrete ramp onto the main wharf. I parked at Dr. Joe's front screen door under the high-beamed sheet-tin roof that blocked the already searing morning sun. Heavy-muscled, bare to the waist Fijian laborers manhandled the 55-gallon drums of coconut oil as they hauled them up from the freighter holds and swung them onto the dock with ancient, hand-operated winches which the New England whalers probably left. The rhythm of the work was exhilarating as the NFL tackle-sized gang chanted some ancient Fijian song while they stacked the steel drums into neat rows in the main export wharf area.

I pushed open the American-made screen door left by the American Seabee command which had built the dock in 1942 as MacArthur fell back from the Philippines. The shed was still painted peeling Army brown-green thirty years later. Dr. Joe was at his desk with a long white adding machine tape flopping off its side.

Dr. Joe loved numbers, and his wire-rimmed glasses on his skinny nose were his tools. He would trace the banking path we needed to stop the Super Boss. It would be deadly accurate work as always. Harvard had taught him well, as had his dad who made his living selling carloads of watermelon at a fraction of a cent markup. I was southwestern and had no real concept of his world. I only knew you used cheap land which you owned or leased with cowboy labor to graze cattle to make money. You always were prepared for the essence of life which was water politics and the resulting warfare.

Today was one of the best days of my young life. Dr. Joe offered me the obligatory cup of kava which was always available on the wharf. When the latest shipment came in from Fiji's outer islands, the boat captains and wharf middlemen passed out samples of their kava. Today's batch was from Tavanui, the national favorite. It quickly numbed my tongue, cooled my system, and gave me a lift like the Coke we drank in the drug-store soda fountains in my youth. All tropical cultures ran on some mild throat-quenching semi-narcotic drink.

Dr. Joe immediately reviewed the plan with me. He owed me and Tab a big favor for bailing his co-op out when he tried to "corner" the "kava market" and ran out of cash. He was happy to join the effort to save Tab. He was intrigued by a day of crunching numbers in the bank's back office. He had absolutely nothing to do at the wharf lately since his co-op was also being slowly "iced" by the Super Boss after it started to raise the price of Fiji kava. This threatened to end the time-honored tradition of Indian middlemen cheating outer island Fijian kava growers after they landed at the main wharf. The Fijians often sold their kava for quick cash so they could get to the nearest pub for endless rounds of strong, warm Fiji beer.

We jumped into my Land Rover and drove off the wharf, back past the national market to the Australian National Bank. We parked in the rear and both entered a private door to the managing-general partner's office. I followed the lanky Dr. Joe in his mismatched Bermuda shorts and short sleeve shirt his mom sent him from Atlanta. The colored (or part-Europe-an) back room bank clerks practically saluted him. They knew something big was up and his legend as a numbers whiz was well known in the trop-ical capital city sandbox. The year before he had hand reconciled their an-nual report to Sydney after they had given up hope of a true trial balance. Most of the colored clerks were also hip to the great "kava corner" play since they had watched the dollars ebb and flow from our three co-ops' accounts at its peak.

If the colonial government civil servants had ever figured out Dr. Joe had cornered the lucrative Christmas kava market, Tab, Dr. Joe, and I would now be doing hard time in Fiji or serving in Vietnam. The colonial, colored bank clerks had kept their mouths shut because they hated all the parties. Their mismatched parents condemned them to a life of no-man's-land in this racially divided tropical paradise. Their only way out was to marry an unattractive unmarried daughter of the Aussies and New Zealanders who ran Fiji for the British to get an exit visa.

A quick meeting with Jonathan Lightfoot, the bank general manager, in his tropical tailored shorts, long white socks with polished loafers, tailored dress shirt, and school tie provided the desired results. Dr. Joe would oversee the audit of the suspect bank accounts under the guise of looking for some misplaced co-op kava funds. This would give him access to all the appropriate ledgers. We had the help of a colored bank clerk named Tom Sambika, whose dad was an American GI and mom a Fijian princess, and whose wife happened to be Mr. Jonathan Lightfoot's sister.

I left Dr. Joe around noon, crunching numbers in the board of directors' room. I went over to the Fruit Wine Co-op headquarters to establish my principal alibi for the capital city trip.

The wine co-op had been founded out of necessity by Allen, a graduate Cal Tech chemist, Tab, Dr. Joe and myself to make bathtub fruit wine. We couldn't afford much booze on our $52.00 a month Peace Corps stipend. My co-op's fruit processing factory supplied the purees in large plastic garbage cans, which we had the PC office import for us from Hawaii under the guise of an agricultural experiment. Allen did the wine making and chemistry. Dr. Joe did the bookkeeping, banking, and ordering. We used real glass bottles from Australia and corks from Spain. Tab marketed the wine to the hotel restaurants that bought his co-op's handicrafts. Our nominal Fijian partner, Chief Sululu, and his friends drank all the excess product to keep prices up.

From small volunteer bottling and corking parties in Dr. Joe's living room on Sundays, the co-op grew to a bottled annual production level of 50,000 units. The fruit wine was on every formal hotel menu and in every co-op grocery store on the island. Then a mysterious round of exploding bottles occurred shortly after Sululu and his Fijian friends took over the bottling and corking operations.

I was trying to help solve this problem. It basically meant kicking Sululu's ass to make sure the corks were being properly pounded into the bottles. Also, that they were dry—not wet or damp—when they went in the thin necks. Nuances were not Sululu's strong point, but my mission proved easier than anticipated.

Kicking Sululu's ass was impossible because an old aunt had died on his home island of Lau. He was away for the month. His sidekick, Keo, let me into a crumbling rented store front warehouse, and the problem resolved itself. The roof was leaking onto our wooden crates of precious Spanish corks. I showed Keo how to dry them in the sun in between the winter rains. Then we covered the cork cases with plastic sheeting we purchased at a nearby lumber yard.

Getting the roof fixed would take three to five years, even if the landlord were inclined. Besides, our operation was under a loophole in the co-op law which allowed us to produce "spirits" without a distiller's license, which took an act of Parliament to obtain. The Fiji Beer Co., which was a monopoly, was trying to close us down but couldn't find our clandestine production site to serve the papers on our fifty plastic garbage cans of silently fermenting fruit wine. In real English common law, you have to find a body. No Elliot Ness-style raids were going to be allowed within the sight of the Fiji national court building.

By four o'clock, Keo was bored with the drill, so I left to find Dr. Joe. First, I parked my Land Rover in front of the botanical gardens across from the Grand Pacific Hotel, a relic where Michener had written stories at the hand-carved monkey wood bar while smashed on gin and tonic, the prevailing European drink of the Islands.

I wrote Nurse Williams a brief note which concisely provided her instructions. It was unsigned on plain brown paper, printed, and left in the unlocked, watertight glove compartment. It had begun to rain Fiji-style in sheets of water from a black sky. I grabbed a British made umbrella from one of the back bench-seats of the Land Rover. I eased into the rain with a deft, well-practiced explosive pop, and headed to the back door of the bank two blocks away.

When I arrived, Dr. Joe briefed me on his findings, which were startling. Large sums of money routinely moved from several wharf handicraft trader accounts to the Super Boss' wife's account. Then, on a delayed basis, to his account with exactly half of each of that amount going back into his brother's account, who ran the wharf operation. However, all these cheques had been written for "Co-op consultation services" which might be a gray area under the rapidly eroding civil service regulations of the almost independent Fijian government.

What we needed to support this smoking gun was some hard evidence in the form of an accounting ledger in a certain Super Boss' handwriting. We hoped it might be in his locked private files at the co-op headquarters, which meant a break-in of sorts, pre-Watergate-style.

Indians always kept good ledgers, as trained by the British. I had already figured this foray might be needed. Nurse Williams was the decoy. She would strike terror simultaneously like Jeb Stuart's cavalry did when they started their now famous rebel yells at the battle of Bull Run.

Dr. Joe and I had free run of the co-op building in daytime office hours. We would have to sign in with the Fijian police guard after six o'clock, which we wanted to avoid. American PC volunteers often worked at night; a custom no local understood. Once past the guard, no one would question our presence in or near Dr. Joe's Kava Co-op's other office on the Super Boss' floor. We left the bank at five and went to our favorite Chinese restaurant for a long dinner and a couple of beers which would cost us two Fiji dollars. The rain from the black clouds continued unabated at one inch per hour.

At six o'clock, as Nurse Williams would recount in her letter to me from Hawaii, she arrived at the Land Rover, as planned. She was very wet from a ten-block walk from the Peace Corps office. Fortunately, she had brought a dry change of civilian clothes. She stripped down in the back of the Land Rover and dried off with my beach towel.

Then, she laughed, as she pulled out a pair of red nylon Valentine's Day panties her college boyfriend had given her at Iowa State. She had picked them up by accident from a dark drawer at her house in her early morning stupor. The heart-shaped hole exposed her vagina perfectly as she squatted, putting on her wire-rimmed bra next, and a dry skirt and blouse. She packed the wet clothing in her straw shoulder bag, climbed back into the passenger seat and opened the Land Rover glove box.

She read the note, cried, then laughed hysterically. She got ready to cross the street, when the rain abated, to the bar at the Grand Pacific Hotel. The note read:

Super Boss R.K. Patel always goes to the bar at the Grand
Pacific Hotel at 7:00 PM on Tuesday to hustle tourist women
while his wife is at the National Red Cross board meetings.
He knows Kevin, your boyfriend, is on a fisheries dept. boat
trip. He expressed his desire to have sex with you at the Co-op
headquarters when Dr. Joe's office door was open last month.

We need to make sure he does not go to his office to-
night. Take him to your house, please promise him a blow
job which will satisfy him but put one of your sedatives in
his Scotch to be safe.

While he is asleep, perform minor surgery on him . . .

Then she started to cry as she read through tears. The instructions were
clear and performable.

At six o'clock, Nurse Williams walked across to the Grand Pacific Hotel bar on her last night in Paradise. She sat at the tourist end of the bar and
waited for Super Boss to arrive, as she sipped the requisite gin and tonic.
The bar chair was uncomfortable because it failed to support her aching
thighs, putting pressure on her sore hip muscles, so, she took a quarter of a
Quaalude and one small morphine pill with her first drink.

By seven, Super Boss had not arrived, and Nurse Williams was on her
third gin and tonic. She was getting drowsy. So, she took some high-grade
speed to lift her energy level.

At seven o'clock, Dr. Joe led me through a co-op building basement
storeroom window he always left unlocked, to work late at night because
the night guard locked the main door at ten o'clock and slept until dawn. A
quick trip up the brand-new elevator in Fiji's first pre-independence high-
rise office building put us on the Co-op HQ floor. We worked for an hour
in Dr. Joe's eighth-floor office, at fake number crunching. Then I scouted
Super Boss' office, which was empty. At eight o'clock I figured Super
Boss was safely at the bar with Nurse Williams, so we went to work.

The outer secretarial office was open as usual; a Shell credit card they
mailed me the last week of college took care of the feeble inner door lock.

Dr. Joe and I went to work in the private file cabinet. The folders were
a mixture of Hindi, Fijian, and English, making it slow going. Dr. Joe read
Hindi and I read Fijian. We split the English files.

Meanwhile, at the Royal Yacht Club, Tab met the prime minister's niece. He made a grand exit with the forbidden fruit. A plainclothes Interior Ministry operative followed them in a not-so-secret new government Land Rover to Tab's house. Tab was delighted his alibi was established, as he watched from a window as the Land Rover parked in front. The Fijian security operative settled in for the night.

Visions of sugarplums danced in Tab's head as he watched through the open door of his bedroom as one of the island's most stunning princesses removed all her western clothing. She wrapped herself in a traditional Fijian sulu which hung from her full, free floating breasts to the tip of her toes with a slight drape as it cleared her full bottom. She was smiling as she entered the room and put an orchid lei around Tab's neck. Tab silently thought, the fountain of youth is all that it's reputed to be. The Spanish Conquistadors were wise to search so long for it in the New World. If they had found Fiji instead, history would be different.

Meanwhile, at the Grand Pacific Hotel it was 8:30 and Super Boss had not appeared. Nurse Williams was getting dizzy with her vision starting to blur. She fended off an Aussie paper supplies salesman, but the edge of the bar chair had put her bottom and legs to sleep. Her bladder started to ache from the fourth gin and tonic. She hoped Super Boss would show. Nurse Williams was in danger of over-dosing in her bar chair if Super Boss didn't appear soon. She held her position bravely.

Dr. Joe and I continued our search with no luck. Maybe our hunch was wrong. Maybe the public-school trained Patel hadn't kept a proper British ledger to check his partners' payments. Maybe years of booze and colonial service under Australian contract officers had made him sloppy. We needed the code to find the file fast before the guard made his last round at 9:30 PM...

The bed springs rattled the quiet house in Tab's middle-class "European" neighborhood. The Lau princess could do it all night, in Fijian timeless island style. Tab wasn't going anywhere for the night, as the nineteen-year-old phenom from Lau taught him the tropical secrets of a thousand years of island village days and nights.

The government Land Rover stayed parked outside his apartment to note the activity. By Sunday, the agent mentally noted, Tab would be off to America. The princess off to a Medicine Woman on the island of Tavanui to make sure no little colored Tab arrived in the prime minister's royal household. No American husbands were welcomed by the royal family.

For tonight, nothing to do but watch the house, take notes, and make sure the princess was safe.

As Nurse Williams' bladder started to explode, she paid her check, bolted dizzily for the door, and crashed into the Super Boss who grabbed her before she toppled to the floor. Her off-white cotton short skirt stuck to her hips. She squeezed her bladder muscles one more time and tried to compose herself as everything from her knees to her chest cramped.

Patel was delighted by this accidental knockdown. Mrs. Patel was at her sister's in Nadi, so he had the whole night off. That's why he was late. He was drinking at a Hindi political club with some local merchants. Someday he wanted to be deputy prime minister and getting rid of Tab for the prime minister certainly helped his career path.

Now he had Nurse Williams, his secretly long desired Peace Corps conquest, in hand. First, he thought, get her out of the bar quickly to avoid being seen by the PC headquarters and American embassy staff which frequented the bar after ten o'clock. He gambled and he said, "Let's go from here before the rain comes again. I will make sure you get home safely. There are drunken village toughs running about tonight."

He was blown away when Nurse Williams said, "Let's go, you're right"...figuring her bladder would only hold five more minutes at best or it was squat Fijian village style in the middle of downtown Suva. He turned, she followed, while the ancient Fijian bartender watched with an amused smile. American women, he thought.

Patel's government black sedan was waiting, driverless on Monday night, in front of the hotel. Nurse Williams was pushed into the passenger seat by a heavy hand. Patel closed her door, walked past the government plates, CO-OP I. He climbed behind the wheel and asked directions. He pulled away, never noticing the eighth-floor lights were on in his office as he shifted the gear lever on the steering column. He ogled Nurse Williams' exposed thighs.

At nine o'clock, Dr. Joe had found a file named in Hindi: "Market Forces of Fijian Handicraft: A Study." The back-folder page with government staples contained six ledger pages in Patel's Hindi handwriting. They matched the bank transfers one to one precisely. He had remembered his British school master's lessons well. We took the pages from the file down the hall to the building's only Xerox machine. The PC staff had donated it to the Co-op Department when they received a newer model. Six pages later our work was complete. We would retrace our steps, exiting through the unlocked window, then walk to the Grand Pacific Hotel for two hours of late-night drinking with the hard-core bored PC HQ staff to establish our alibi. Nurse Williams would be long gone when we arrived at the bar. I had planned carefully.

I was shocked when Patel's car roared past us as we walked the block to the hotel. He never looked up as he shifted gears because his eyes were locked on Nurse Williams. Fate walked with us on the sidewalk that night. Maybe the Octopus God which protected my province and who killed the mighty Shark God's army in a legendary battle had saved me again. I hoped he would protect Nurse Williams, too. I prayed to him silently since Dr. Joe did not believe in magic.

I had performed a quickie ceremony with the witch doctor in the village near my house for Nurse Williams the night before I left for Suva. It invoked the Octopus God's protection in our battle to save Tab and the Handicraft Co-op. We had used a pair of panties she left in my Land Rover on a previous trip to Suva. The witch doctor and chief were reasonably sure the spell would work to protect someone through an article of clothing they had worn. The witch doctor gave it his best shot with the panties since Nurse Williams was in Suva and not physically available. He was the best witch doctor our province could provide...and his chief owed me a favor.

Nurse Williams arrived at her apartment with Patel on her last night in Fiji. She would go AWOL to the mainland, returning to her secret Stateside life.

The alcohol and drugs blurred her mind, and her body was still numb after the longest pee of her young life. Patel ambushed her as she exited the bathroom. She surrendered without a struggle. His hand shot up her skirt and hit the heart-shaped panty opening. He went into shock. She didn't and guided him to the couch where she poured a drink into a glass with a prescription sedative already in its bottom.

He gulped it without a thought as she unzipped his tropical wool tailored pants, pulled out his dick, and started to give him a hand job. She wasn't sure if he passed out before or after orgasm—it didn't matter. He was on the couch, out cold for at least 12-15 hours. She popped another cocaine pill and washed her hands for minor surgery. From her extensive medical kit, she took out a small scalpel and a micro torch to cauterize wounds. She pulled out the note and read it once more. It said:

*Surgically remove his right testicle and put it in a jar of pre-
servative and leave it in the glove compartment of the Land
Rover on your way to the airport. Destroy this note by fire.*

Nurse Williams pulled down Patel's pants and white boxer shorts and
rubbed his testicles until they dropped and enlarged. She then deftly cut a
small slit in his scrotum. She slid out his right testicle, clipped it off with
a pair of surgical scissors, and cauterized the severed tube. She stitched up
the incision and put the testicle in a peanut butter jar of preservative. She
burned the note.

I found the jar in the Land Rover's glove compartment at noon the next
day when I recovered from a massive hangover. I was the life of the Grand
Pacific Hotel bar until 12:00 AM closing time.

CHAPTER FIVE

THE WEEK AFTER NURSE WILLIAMS

The jar was in the Land Rover glove compartment, peeking through the Valentine shaped hole of cheap red nylon panties. Nurse Williams wisely left no note, but I didn't need one. I remembered my surprise in her office a few months before when my finger traced their pattern while she was checking an ear infection. She claimed they were her only clean pair, and besides, it was 100° in the shade.

I stashed the jar in a semi-secret compartment. It had been welded behind the left rear bumper of the Land Rover to hide spare keys and money in a communal society with no locks. I dropped the panties at Tab's mailbox at PC HQ in the standard thin brown paper Fijian envelope. It was a good hiding place for them, since Tab never picked up his mail from the USA.

It had already been agreed that Tab, Dr. Joe, and I should avoid each other, indefinitely. The Three Musketeers had played the Fiji theater. Dr. Joe had already relayed the Xeroxed copies of the purloined documents to Tab.

The prime minister had wasted no time in summoning Tab to meet with the First Secretary, his hatchet man. Chief Levu, the First Secretary, actually liked Tab and delayed the meeting for three days, seeking another solution. Simultaneously, a new buzz was making the rounds in the capital city on Wednesday afternoon. Super Boss was absent without leave and missing. In her letter from Hawaii, Nurse Williams had reported that before she left him, Super Boss had stirred a little and moaned loudly. So, in the interest of humanitarianism she gave him a little injection that zonked him for a full 24 hours.

I split town after a quick stop at the Wine Co-op to make sure Keo put the newly purchased heavy plastic covering on the cardboard cases of corks from Spain. World trade was truly wonderful. I mused the cork makers never thought they would be shipping duty free corks as medical supplies to the American Peace Corps office in Suva, Fiji. With Nurse Williams gone it was even more important to protect the dwindling cork supplies until our own escapes from Fiji were consummated.

The plastic sheeting was in place, Fijian style. I tucked it tightly, American style. I put a few rocks on it so the ceiling fan wouldn't blow it off. I picked up a couple of reserve cases of passionfruit ginger wine for the coming weekend. I signed it out on the warehouse ledger and headed back to Sigatoka.

As I drove past the national market, I pulled into the area where the villagers from my province sold their crops and handicrafts. Five minutes later, after two bowls of kava, two women and one man from the village of Nato near my house, loaded in for a free limo ride home. They brought enough smoked barracuda and fresh fruit for a five-day trip. This was the real Peace Corps. The Fijians were our personal friends. Once you knew them, nothing was impossible.

Hopefully, we had just bought 2,500 Island Handicraft Co-op members a brighter future. My already slightly cynical mind wondered if they would ultimately fare well under their own chiefs, who would run the co-op after independence. Historically, the British colonial government used the Council of Chiefs to steal for it, the same way the U.S. Government had used the Bureau of Indian Affairs in the western USA.

Tab arrived at Ratu Levu's office and listened to the drill. He was out of Fiji immediately, and the princess had already left for Tuvanui on the morning boat. Ratu Levu loved him and everyone appreciated his work for the Island Handicraft Co-ops. He would be made an honorary chief before he left at the royal bungalow on nearby Bau island. The PC Country Director had already agreed to the plan. He would be on the next regular Saturday Pan Am flight to Honolulu where the Peace Corps would debrief him for two weeks with all expenses paid. Ratu (Chief) Levu finished and Tab handed him a thin, plain brown envelope labeled with a special Fijian provincial word that meant "the sky is falling". Tab signed the note, "Chicken Little". Levu, who had an English nanny for his children, went into a private anteroom while Tab admired the museum quality Fijian handicrafts that graced his walls. The collection included some pieces Tab's co-op had presented to the prime minister.

A half hour later, Ratu Levu emerged from a door that led directly to the prime minister's office. He was carrying a small, exquisitely carved kava bowl. Ratu Levu performed step by step a private royal, chiefly kava ceremony. First, he changed from his western tailored wool sulu to a tighter wrapped native style print cotton sulu. Fijians were always changing their sulus in public. This drove westerners slightly nuts.

Next, he pounded the kava to dust and tied it neatly in a porous cloth. He dipped it in the water and chanted a welcome not even Tab had heard in dozens of ceremonies on dozens of islands. He presented Tab the polished, carved coconut kava cup and Tab gulped it down. Tab then served Ratu Levu, then the new deal went down almost as we hoped.

Tab got to stay in Fiji for his last six months in the Peace Corps, ending December 15th. This solved his draft lottery problem since the last Vietnam lottery winners got called on December One. If he won, he became a free man. If he lost, he skipped straight to Canada from Fiji on Air Canada. He could take his PC Pan Am non-refundable air ticket at face value plus 100 US dollars to their agent at Nadi airport with some hand-picked handicrafts for his supervisors.

Second, the Fijian Deputy Co-op Minister moved up one notch. Also, the prime minister's grandson who just arrived from Cambridge and the London School of Economics took over as Chairman of the Handicraft Co-op with Tab as his special advisor. Tab was stationed in the capital city. Therefore, no island travel for Tab for the duration of his tour. Third, as a personal gift in the chiefly tradition, the prime minister was immediately returning the princess to the capital city until December for additional schooling. Ratu Levu's aunt from Tavanui, who was a medicine woman, would chaperone her.

Next, Tab would still be made an honorary chief but not until December. He would have no traditional right to a house site since he would be made chief of an abandoned village site now under the new National Co-op building. Finally, Tab would not return to Fiji. His name would be entered in the secret log at the Interior Department as an undesirable as long as the prime minister lived.

Then Ratu Levu pulled Tab into the anteroom, gravely smiled, told him to watch his back. Super Boss had been relieved of duty by the prime minister, because of the ledger and also because of a secret report from the royal physician at the National Hospital. A morphine-dazed Super Boss had been found by a Fijian cleaning lady in a certain missing Peace Corps nurse's apartment. He had participated in a bizarre sexual act practiced by a Hindu Kali Tantric Yoga cult in the capital city. His right testicle was missing, and he was under sedation at the National Hospital. He was awaiting the return of his wife from Nadi.

In the apartment police found three Polaroids from a standard issue Peace Corps camera. One photo of the Super Boss passed out on the couch with his pants off in full erection. The second photo was a large, brown inverted nipple in a close-up shot. The final blurred photo appeared to be a close-up shot of a white female's red heart-shaped panty-surrounded vagina lips.

A certain Nurse Williams, the apartment's occupant, had cleared Fijian customs at Nadi International Airport's regular Saturday afternoon Pan Am flight and U.S. customs in Hawaii later that night. She had disappeared into Honolulu.

Ratu Levu added, "Her re-entry visa has been terminated but it is rumored by our sources in the capital city, that your friend, Cooper, knows her intimately. Therefore, MISS (the Ministry of Interior Secret Service) will be assigned to tail you throughout the local police investigation of this matter, so none of Patel's friends interfere or pose a threat to royal family members or their friends.

Tab showed no emotion because that was his style. He was under house arrest with private security for six months with the most beautiful playmate in Fiji while the co-op was being transferred to the royal family's control.

Ratu Levu looked straight at Tab, then touched an ancient Fijian sacred whale's tooth with his left hand. He grasped Tab's right hand in the male Fijian handhold, hugged Tab in the warrior tradition, smiled once ear to ear, and then exited.

Tab exited through the anteroom's other door, directly to the hall outside the prime minister's suite of offices. He would never speak to Ratu Levu or the prime minister again. As Tab descended the New Zealand quarried marble steps, a six-foot, well-muscled Fijian MISS officer in village civilian clothes moved quietly behind Tab—jungle style, feet never quite touching the floor. He could have been stalking a wild boar with a machete or a bamboo spear.

Tab made a rare stop at PC HQ on his way to his apartment. The PC country director pretended he was not there. He checked his private mail cubicle and found the mushy brown envelope. He locked himself in the men's room. He opened it, laughed as a faint scent wafted up to his nostrils. He knew Cooper had been Nurse Williams' Lover. He smiled to himself. He then took the standard flip top sterling silver Zippo lighter all male PCVs carried from his khaki pants pocket and set the cheap red nylon panties on fire.

Sixty seconds later, the last trace of Nurse Williams' Fijian life was turned to ashes. He washed them down the old wooden sink's drain as the ceiling fan cleared the remnants of the pungent nylon smoke. Tab then lit up an unfiltered Fijian cigarette and smoked it. He exited the men's room and strolled through the PC office without a care in the world.

Tab saw a uniformed Hindu Indian police inspector checking the mail in the private open mail cubicles of the capital city PC volunteers. A couple of minutes later, he searched Tab's empty cubicle. The investigation of the sex cult was underway. In the ensuing days, all close associates of Nurse Williams would be interrogated at the PC HQ in the director's office with a deputy U.S. consular officer present.

It was determined, I heard from a volunteer who hung out with the country director, that Nurse Williams had gone crazy treating depressed, homesick, or diseased volunteers. She used drugs and had been invited to join the Hindu sex cult in a weak moment. This was possibly arranged by an unknown PCV. She was terminated while away at a medical conference in Hawaii. She could not return and be interrogated by the Fijian police and charged with a sex crime. This would have embarrassed the embassy, the Peace Corps, the USA, the host country government, and her chosen profession.

Washington chose only the most predictable clean-jean ex-PC volunteers to return and run in-country field operations. The director's handling of the sex cult affair was exemplary, tidy, and quick. I loved disinformation campaigns which cleverly used most of the facts. Even Fiji's few remaining Oxford and Cambridge trained British ex-pats were amazed this time. The Yanks might finally get on with running their world empire in an orderly, courteous, and pragmatic manner.

As Tab left the PC office, his Fijian Army MISS shadow quietly picked up the chase. He was smoking a cigarette, unfiltered like Tab's. Years of training with the Gurkha troops as a Fijian commando in the rain forest had taught him to smell a burning nylon jungle parachute at three miles distance downwind. Years of fucking bored Australian and New Zealand tourist ladies at the Fijian beach hotels had taught him about cheap nylon panties. The smell from the men's room exhaust fan told him all he needed to know. He would report to Ratu Levu that Tab and Nurse Williams had set up the Super Boss, case closed. The red panties in the Polaroid had gone up in smoke. There was no evidence. My plan accidentally worked perfectly as the loop closed between Nurse Williams' and Tab.

The Indian police inspector who was nosing around the PC office walked right into the men's room for a whiz after his inspection. He noticed a very pungent odd cigarette and nylon smell, but Indian women always wore cotton, if anything, under their silk saris. The smells from the cremation fires were of fresh cotton or silk in Fiji. Life turns often on the small coincidences, traditions, and jungle training.

I was anxious to see my friendly village Chief Kavula and his witch doctor. As I neared home, I had brought them a special gift in a jar to perform an ancient cleansing rite. The Land Rover plowed up a quarter mile of choking dust as it roared through a seaside village on the island's dry, southwestern windward side. Tomorrow Patipati, my Fijian assistant, and I would go to the village in late afternoon to start the cycle of hope, expunge an evil spirit from my life, and arrange for a curse.

CHAPTER SIX
THE VILLAGE WITCH DOCTOR

The witch doctor looked at the human testicle in the jar with wide eyes. No white boy had ever handed him a fresh testicle in a jar before. He and Chief Kavula knew not to question its origin because they owed me a big favor. After a long Kava Ceremony during which I presented them the amazing jar, the witch doctor started to chant some ancient curse. I said my goodbyes. The curse, which was about to be applied to the testicle in the jar and therefore its owner, was out of my league. Black magic in its purest form is horrific, deadly, ancient stuff. Even being in a room where an ancient ceremonial curse is levied can change your life forever and irreversibly. I was cleansed of all evil spirits from Suva by the Kava Ceremony. I was ready for routine work at the co-op office.

I was a short timer in the Peace Corps and Fiji. No risk was necessary for a story that was almost over except for the curse and Super Boss' final fate. I wondered what fate the witch doctor would assign Super Boss as I drove back to my house in the Land Rover, dodging village chickens, kids, and cows. I thought about Super Boss. Would he be eaten by a shark, hit by a falling coconut in a windstorm, or run over by a Land Rover... Suddenly, a big bang occurred, and my Land Rover skidded vertically. I couldn't see anything as the windshield went brown and imploded slowly. While thinking about the curse I had hit a village horse who now straddled the hood of the Land Rover. I slowed from 10 miles an hour. The Land Rover came to a halt, baying horse and all.

Patipati, my assistant, and I gingerly brushed windshield glass off our legs, chests, arms, and faces with our eyes closed. I had experienced this occurrence once before when a large rock from a passing truck hit my windshield on the coast road.

Once I was sure no jagged bits of glass were around my eyes, I slowly opened them to make sure I was not blind. Light returned, my eyes worked, as the horse came slowly into soft focus. The horse kicked his hooves in the air. Then he rolled right over and off the hood. He landed on all fours looking slightly dazed but bellowing.

Village horses cost $45.00 Fijian. That was a month's pay for a Peace Corps volunteer. He was standing on all four legs, a good sign. I honked the horn and he reared. After a final quick look at the Land Rover, he ran pell-mell through the village. I remembered vaguely from detective novels that if there was no corpse then no murder had occurred. If the horse died, it would now be in the "bush". He would be eaten by the tropical scavenger birds before dark. I looked at Patipati and he was already laughing.

Villagers came running from all directions, hoping to claim ownership of the horse. Forty-five dollars was six months' cash income. The horse was gone before the first "owner" could reach the Land Rover. I was very happy he was alive and well. The villager was stuck with helping me assess the Land Rover's body damage. It was superficial except for the left fender which had to be bent back from an all-terrain balding tire, with a large tree branch. The British made Land Rovers out of aluminum which was always easy to bend or hammer back into shape. They were impossible, of course, to weld without special equipment. After a roadside chat with the village chief, I gave him two dollars for the villagers' help. I lowered the remnants of my detachable windshield and locked it down on the hood. We were off in a cloud of dust. I wondered if the curse had anything to do with a horse. A mile down the road, I dropped Patipati off at his village. He gave me the usual "Bula Tale" (goodbye).

Dark came over the land as my headlights penetrated the bedroom windows of my house. Dianne, who was still enjoying a beach vacation, was startled by the explosion of high beam lights. She jumped up to look out the window. The lights revealed her nipples under the thin cotton top she was wearing. It was usually anchored by Australian bikini panties which accented her long legs.

I was happy to be home and 25 years old. At 25, sex is always magical. Tonight's was immediate. In youth, the physical part of life dominates the memory mental part of life. You arrive in a slightly bashed Land Rover from a business trip out of a political thriller, then you make love all night in the tropics with waves crashing on the reef under a full moon.

The move from the Land Rover to the bedroom was in milliseconds. I will remember each step all of my life. My feet moved across the dull gray aluminum door frame of the Land Rover to the moonlit tropical dark green grass to the rotting blue wood porch. The ancient screen door swung open. It slapped shut as I moved across the painted rough-hewn, hardwood floor of the beach cottage. My hand pushed away the hanging shell beaded strings that guarded the bedroom. Dianne stood in the moonlit layers of brown and white. Her tanned brown legs met white cotton bikini panties. They met a tanned, flat brown stomach. It met a white, native sheer cotton top draped over her breasts. It met a bronze-tanned face with golden, sun-bleached auburn hair.

The visual impact was instant. The sexual impact was explosive...I dropped my khaki shorts in mid-stride. She dropped her bikini briefs simultaneously. I entered her in a standing position. She was already very wet. I had caught her masturbating. The Peace Corps women were all experimenting. Her body started to rock, sway and surge with mine. The beat of the crashing waves and the sound of the wind through palm trees were our music.

The morning sun's light shaft, diffused by mosquito netting, played on my naked leg. Our bodies stirred. I watched Dianne as she rose from the straw mattress. She pushed the mosquito netting open. She stepped naked and lightly on the floor. She stretched ballerina style for a long moment before shaking her hair. It touched the cheeks of her bottom. They tensed as she raised up on her ballet trained toes. She spun on her toes 180°. I watched the performance. She stayed on her toes. Her arms and hands raised to a point near the low, silent ceiling fan. This stance from some childhood ballet class tilted her breasts slightly up while her tensed thighs thrust her golden triangle of auburn hair forward. It was too provocative, too early to remain passive.

My hand led my arm through the draped opening in the mosquito netting. I touched the magic triangle at its tip. So much for another routine morning at the office in the tropics. The resulting romp, followed by a cold shower and a slow breakfast, consumed the entire morning.

I went to the co-op's passionfruit factory at noon. After checking on things there, I planned to go upcountry for a couple of days with Patipati to check crop production. With a late start upcountry, we would spend the night in an interior village. This always led to an adventure. The higher upcountry was pleasant this time of year with nights much cooler than the coast. Sometimes you could imagine frost on the grass in Mikimiki. It was at a 3,000-foot altitude in the mountains.

Late in the afternoon the Land Rover churned through the loose river rock as it left a small wake. We drove slowly up the narrow shallow river 40 miles from the coast. The village of Mikimiki was built on a mountain river ledge, 3,100 feet above sea level. About two miles from the village, the steep switchback logging road ended. We were fording the Land Rover upriver until just below the falls. The water sloshed into the high floorboards. The engine whined in low four-wheel drive. All the electronics were high and shielded on the Land Rover. They had been built for colonial Africa where there were few roads. I had never drowned a Land Rover engine in Fiji, even when I had water in the passenger compartment.

I carefully forded upstream. I hoped for no deep hidden holes or newly formed sandbars from the last rainy season. The wheels constantly searched and found solid river rock for traction.

It had been six months since I had made the trip to Mikimiki. It had been by horse on the rain-soaked trails with dangerous crossings over flooded fords. Only in the dry winter season could I risk a Land Rover trip upriver.

I loved Peace Corps adventures. I had a fully rigged, government owned Land Rover for an expedition to Mikimiki on a $52.00 a month salary. My Fijian assistant, Patipati, who always traveled upcountry upriver with me, clung to his hand bar. The Land Rover lurched as it moved forward over the submerged river rocks. He thought this was insane. He preferred the horses that were offered at the co-op office near Keikei five miles downriver.

Suddenly, the left front wheel spun wildly out of control. It signaled the edge of a deep sand bar. The Land Rover tilted sideways. I snapped the steering wheel to the right a whole turn and hit the gas. It was river quicksand which could be a foot deep or bottomless. The Land Rover strained to go right but kept tilting left. Water started into Patipati's door. He realized the water pressure could seal him in this rapidly sinking aluminum tomb. He madly hand cranked the narrow, left window down. At the last possible moment, I reached for my door handle. It was now tilted toward the sky. The left rear wheel hit something solid for a second. The two right wheels freed the Land Rover from the gripping, invisible hands of the sandbar.

Patipati, now soaking wet, displayed a rare frown. As a Fijian warrior, he was committed to the entire adventure—even if it meant death at my side, even if my western stupidity caused his death. Retreat was loss of manhood and honor. Losing a chief in battle was unthinkable. I had been made an honorary chief. I had a house site at the provincial village capital where Chief Kavula and the witch doctor ruled.

It was agreed as soon as we were about 50 yards upriver that Patipati would find a stick, then walk barefooted. He would probe the river in front of the Land Rover for the final half-mile to Mikimiki. In this manner the Land Rover progressed upriver with Patipati like a leadsman on some ancient Mississippi river boat. This boat had a maniac at the wheel.

I saw Mikimiki on the eastern bluff about 600 feet above the river. A steep, washed out logging path led almost straight down to the river. I intended to shoot up it in one monstrous rush in low four-wheel drive. Patipati would walk up in case the Land Rover rolled backward with me on the ascent. I would leave him by the river to recover my body if I failed to jump free in time. Jumping free was difficult from this model Land Rover because it had an aluminum top with fixed place doors. I wished for a Colorado ranch soft top Jeep with no doors for the ride. Wishing in Fiji only wasted time.

CHAPTER SEVEN
THE ASSAULT ON MIKIMIKI

Patipati gazed in sheer wonderment tempered with horror. I gunned the four-cylinder aluminum head, cast iron block, under-carbed Land Rover engine. I popped the clutch at 4,000-plus RPM. It catapulted in low four-wheel drive straight up the sheer river path to Mikimiki. All I could see was blue sky and the tops of trees as the Land Rover screamed and clawed uphill defying gravity.

I had a deal with Patipati to take my body back to Sigatoka for shipment home. He was to burn the Land Rover if it didn't explode. The government could collect the insurance. This Land Rover was an amazing machine. It was perfectly balanced, with wheels that stuck to the muddy river path. It groaned. It slid backward. It lurched to the left. It hit a rock and spun hard right. I whipped the very old-fashioned, wide rimmed steering wheel from side to side. My sandaled feet worked the gas pedal like a ballerina's. I prayed that on the ascent I would not have to double clutch shift to the high four-wheel range. I prayed the engine would not stall forcing a reverse jump start double clutch to first in a half-second or less.

Halfway up the road, the first disaster struck. The Land Rover hit a large, partially hidden boulder. It tore the muffler hinge loose causing the rear muffler pipe to act like the rudder on a boat. It plowed into the muddy path on each dip of the suspension. The Land Rover now roared like a ship from hell. Sparks flew as the aluminum exhaust pipe hit rocks.

I did not think. Every move was pure reaction to live another second. The G-forces pinned me to my seat. It was better than any meditation, except maybe my out-of-body experience during a Kundalini Yoga lesson. Thought was precise. I was like a man caught in an avalanche with a snow-mobile. It was a pure blend of instinctive mind, machine, and physical strength. The experience was in the black and white light bar, with colors, only a clear, sharp instant slow-motion image.

Two-thirds of the way up the steep muddy path, the slide backward started. The left front wheel lifted and lost traction. A millisecond later the right front wheel started to spin dangerously almost losing its traction. One final chess move; live or die. Make the move. Regain traction. Go up the hill to a hero's welcome and the rest of my life. Screw up the move, then explode and die. Tumble tail first down the road into the riverbed, almost 400 feet below. Don't make the move and die.

The move was to feather the accelerator, drop the RPM's for a split second, then hope the right front wheel held its traction. This would pull the front end of the Land Rover down so the left front wheel regained traction. In one final surge accelerate all the way to the top of the bluff on the quickly hardening, higher, drier roadbed. If I backed off the gas too long, the rear wheels would sink too far into the vertical mud bank and it was goodnight. The big problem was that the time for the move to the gas pedal took away my last opportunity to open the door and jump free of the machine.

I made the move. The engine roar sagged a millisecond. The Land Rover tires slipped backward in a short lurch. They hit rock and the front wheels came down. After one slow-motion whirl they both regained traction. I hit the gas. I shot up the remaining 200 feet in one enormous uphill slide. The Land Rover lurched over the rim of the trail. I slammed on the brakes, but it was too late. I slid into the side of a village bure (house). The Land Rover came to a stop in its empty main room.

I climbed out of the Land Rover and the villagers were cheering. They waved machetes and iron fishing spears in the air. No Land Rover had ever entered Mikimiki in its thousand years of existence.

For a few minutes, I experienced what Lindbergh must have felt in France. One man and one machine in a place where neither had ever been together. Mystified villagers touched the machine to make sure I was not a ghost. They had seen Land Rovers. They had all seen white men. No one had ever seen a Land Rover climb the ancient water trail from the river to the village. They had seen horses and riders plunge to their deaths when they lost their footing in the mud on the trail during rainy season. Everyone had seen village women slip backward on the muddy path and roll into the river with their heavy pots of water. But no one had ever thought a Land Rover could make the ascent.

The village chief immediately ordered a ceremonial dance and feast honoring our visit. It would take a day to prepare and three days to celebrate. The chief of the whole region had ordered a full-dress dance and feast with men and women from ten mountain villages. He ordered the slaughter of two cows, five domestic pigs, plus all the wild pigs, river prawns, river fish and coconuts that could be rounded up in a day.

Patipati enjoyed his role as translator-sidekick to the warrior hero of the hour. He perched on the Land Rover's bumper. It was parked in front of the village's co-op office which was a 10x20 bamboo-sided shed with a sloping, corrugated aluminum roof to catch water for its rain tank. Patipati held court to a bevy of bare-breasted, sulued mountain girls. Patipati was in heaven. Once he finished his bookkeeping chores at the co-op office, he would have his choice of eligible unmarried mountain girls.

Patipati would make a great catch for one of these back-woods village girls. He had been educated in the capital city through secondary school by the Jesuit priests. He was on the rise in the co-op department. Someday, a co-op Land Rover would be his, plus, a downriver government house and a government salary. Mikimiki was only 41 miles upriver from the Pacific Ocean, but the younger school children thought tide was a soap. Some of them had never seen the ocean. To an upriver, unmarried girl, Patipati was like a Pacific Northwest salmon sushi spread in Tokyo. The next three days would be a test for Patipati.

As for me, I planned a good old fashioned homecoming weekend romp with the blessings of the village's chief. The witch doctor had been instructed to figure out how to turn me Fijian after the Mikimiki hill climb. The chief knew a good replacement when he saw one. I had one major flaw. The decline of the empire launched by Norman the Conqueror in 1066 on that gray, rainy English day had started. Even the chief of Mikimiki knew it. I would be feted but not asked to stay like the early lost, white-skinned whalers who had washed up on the Fijian village beaches 200 years ago. They had been mistaken for gods.

CHAPTER EIGHT
THE VILLAGE NYMPH

I woke up the next day at Mikimiki with a massive kava "jag". I vaguely remembered kava hallucinations starting around midnight. That meant I drank a gallon in two hours. I spent a lot of time dashing out of the ceremonial bure where all the men of the village were drinking, to find a tree to pee on just like Boy Scout camp.

On my fourth or fifth trip to a tree, the hallucinations started. I was peeing on a palm tree. I was looking at the Big Dipper, enjoying the mountains of Fiji on a clear, cool moonlit night. After I stopped peeing, my tree trunk turned into a smiling face of a beautiful young Fijian girl. Her smiling eyes guided me to full, bare light mahogany breasts with dark erect nipples. They were pushed up by her light-skinned palms as her elbows rested on her hard, flat stomach muscles developed from hauling water daily from the river 600 feet below.

Her blue flowered print sulu was knotted perfectly on the right hip bone. The cloth pulled taut across her brown stomach just above the slightly bulging triangle of her thick, curly black pubic hair. The sulu dropped straight to hide the full thighs and strong calves of a mountain girl.

I zipped up my khaki shorts. I reached to touch the hallucination, which was like a life-size hologram. My hands passed through her warm nipple as my fingers touched each other in the middle of a vapor breast.

She laughed and dropped her hands. Her breasts sagged to her stomach. Suddenly my fingers felt the cool mountain night air. I touched the now-flattened nipple again. Once again, my hand passed through it and felt the warmth of her full breast.

She laughed again. Her right hand pulled the knot of her sulu and it danced down her thighs. It fell on the thin grass beneath the giant coconut palm. She tensed her stomach muscles as she opened her thighs. She bent her knees and appeared to lean against the old palm tree although they seemed one. She parted her opening with the thumb and forefinger of her left hand. She beckoned to me to enter her with her right hand.

I reached to touch her opening with my middle fingers. I felt the warmth of her passageway, but my hand passed through vapor. I could see my hand. She laughed again and unzipped my beltless khaki shorts. They fell to the ground. She passed her dark pink palms through my penis several times, which erotically woke it. As her hands disappeared through my skin, I felt them touch my testicles, but could not see them. It was the most erotic moment of my life. It triggered desire. I entered her as she braced her widely spread thighs by pushing her broad, flat village feet against the base of the coconut palm. She looped her strong arms and hands around the tree to suspend her body. I penetrated her in a rocking standing motion.

The effect was dazzling as my body mingled with hers. I could always see mine but only feel hers. It was the only ejaculation I would ever view backlit by moonlight during a tropical hallucination with a village ghost girl from Mikimiki on a night when the ancient winds of the Fijian gods rewarded me for saving Tab. Then she disappeared. I could only see a palm tree trunk as I zipped up my khaki shorts. The light breeze rustled the palm leaves and the moment vanished.

I picked up the blue, print sulu from the ground. I looped it around my neck as I walked back to the bure to talk to the men and drink more kava. When I reached the circle, the village chief stared at me. He fingered the blue sulu as the other men stared into the kava bowl in silence. He started a long, rambling story about his sister. She had died in the 1920's from an epidemic of measles brought to the village by British soldiers and prospectors looking for gold. She loved a young British soldier from whom she caught the spotted disease from which few Fijians recovered that year.

At 16, she was buried in a blue sulu beneath a young palm tree over-looking the head waters of the Sigatoka river 600 feet below the village. She faced the eternally setting sun of western Viti Levu.

The chief smiled as he fingered the blue flowered cotton sulu. He of-fered me another bowl of kava which he dipped from the giant hand carved monkey wood bowl. It cooled my dry mouth. It relaxed my muscles as its pungent smell mingled with her memory.

A month later, I wore the sulu in Sigatoka at a function of the Fijian National Museum sponsored by Tab's Handicraft Co-op. The curator ap-proached me and astounded, asked where I had found a perfect 1920's East Indian Trading Co. royal flowered blue, print sulu. He knew of them, but none had survived Fiji's tropical rot intact. He had only seen them in old village black and white photos in the museum archives.

CHAPTER NINE
THE CATHEDRAL

The final morning, I woke up in Mikimiki with a massive but survivable kava hangover. I slowly started to move my legs and arms. I lay on a triple-thick nest of straw mats under a mosquito net. It was suspended from the center beam of a bure. Through the gauze effect of the mosquito netting, I could see Patipati. He was already up. He was heating water for tea on a one burner kerosene stove we traveled with in the provinces. Sitting next to Patipati was the chief's nineteen-year-old niece. A sulu barely covered her full breasts while she chopped up a small fresh wild pineapple with a machete.

Everyone in Fiji carried some version of a machete. They served as the multi-purpose tool of choice by all the islanders for chores ranging from cutting the grass to murder—which rarely occurred.

It was time to rise and drink some hot tea. Then eat some fresh wild pineapple from a forgotten British plantation. Then tease the chief's niece, and get myself and Patipati out of Mikimiki before we encountered any more kava, nymphs, or chief's nieces. Another night in Mikimiki and the two of us might be required to take permanent residence. The chief was growing too fond of our company 40 miles up a river valley of this isolated island nation. The village and the chief had jarred the weak grip western civilization had imprinted on my young mind.

Days of kava or ganja, and the tropical sun created an illusion of paradise found far from the maddening crowds of US cities shattered by race riots and demonstrations against the Vietnam War. Illusion melded with reality and reality melded with illusion. The setting sun painted the mirrored silent water of quiet tropical bays on windless days with a perfect orange image that dared you to choose between the matte and the matter. At Mikimiki, I had pushed the limits after having risked all with Nurse Williams in the Suva adventure.

From recent past memory, Hobbes entered my mind from some college philosophy course. He pushed away the dream and forced me to see the matte. He told me to leave these people alone, let them live without my window to the west...for a moment longer in their eternity. Let them enjoy this island mountain village which was not yet on any AAA map given to tourists in Ohio as they boarded Pan Am for their South Pacific vacation.

Patipati disappeared into the bush one more time with the niece. Then, while the chief was taking his late morning nap, we roared out of Mikimiki in the mud-splattered Land Rover. The descent down the path to the river was less exhilarating than our arrival. It required low four-wheel drive plus a foot on the brake. We hit the water to start our long ford downriver, bump by bump over its rocky bed.

I had already decided to take a small detour to the village of Katiti on the way back down to the coast. It was two miles inland from the river on a richly soiled, broad, alluvial flood plain. Two objects of obsession propelled me to Katiti, both equally alluring. First, there was the magnificent stone cathedral sitting in the middle of the village. It had been built by a crazed Jesuit priest over a forty-year period from 1880 to 1920.

The church represented the only solid building in the river valley's sea of bamboo thatched roof structures. It was the equal of any church in the world. The large gray stone had been brought upriver on bamboo rafts for 25 miles to build the edifice. It was a marvel of determination and engineering unparalleled in the entire province and maybe the entire country. The village of Katiti was Catholic. It still supported the province's only interior secondary school. It was run by a rapidly aging Jesuit priest named Father Mone' and a dozen Fijian nuns.

I always loved to visit Father Mone' whom I had first met two years before at Mikimiki when he passed me, hiking in by foot before I had the Land Rover, on his equally old gray horse. He rode side-saddle on an ancient French leather saddle that must have been donated to the church by a rich patron.

The second reason to visit Katiti was Sarah. The petite blonde Peace Corps teacher from Stanford had come straight from Haight-Ashbury to the Peace Corps a year after I arrived in Fiji. I liked this five-foot-two, blue-eyed blonde woman. She had drawn a rigid line which I called the bamboo curtain because I dated Dianne. Every three or four months I dropped in to Katiti to make a half-hearted attempt at setting the bamboo curtain on fire. I really stopped to make sure she was still sane. Maybe it was the influence of the nuns, or maybe the woman really could survive month after month in Katiti with no known boyfriend.

I was once again motoring full speed toward the village on an empty gas tank. We saved the last emergency five-gallon-can to reach the coast where British Petroleum could refill the Land Rover with expensive imported Indonesian gasoline.

It was two in the afternoon when we pulled up in front of Sarah's small two-room wooden house next to the cathedral. It was probably 95° with humidity near 100 percent as a mid-afternoon tropical rainstorm threatened. The cathedral's weathered gray stone and silver gray tin roof was set off against massive black cumulus clouds. It produced a study Goya would have loved to paint. I wished for the camera that I never bothered to carry.

I raced from the Land Rover to Sarah's door to beg her Pentax camera, but no one answered the knock. Then a black-robed, black-faced nun appeared. She explained in Fijian-style English that Sarah and Father Mone' had gone to the interior to interview village girls for the next school term. They would not return for a day or two. However, we were welcome to stay at Sarah's house until their return.

Patipati had just unloaded the Land Rover as the storm, with massive lightning strikes, showered the village with afternoon walls of cooling water. The temperature plunged 20° as nature created its own air conditioning system. The rain finally lightened as I heard the roar of heavy trucks—not one, but four or five, with a Land Rover in the lead. I went to Sarah's front door. I opened it and exited onto the verandah. It was covered by a tin roof.

Slowly coming up the muddy road was a convoy of military trucks and jeeps. They flew the Fijian flag and the British army flag. The Gurkhas had arrived with a Fiji battalion for their annual winter war games in the Crown Colony. I knew an adventure was at hand if I could hang out with the Gurkhas for a day or two while I waited for Father Mone' and Sarah to return.

The Peace Corps left the Sarah's of the world in their third world outposts vulnerable to long, lonely, sexless existences. She lived under the forever prying eyes of the villagers, and the black-faced Fijian Catholic nuns. It was time to make sure Sarah was OK. She was too good to be squandered on the stone cathedral in the jungle, so some Australian cardinal could maintain a pin in the map on his wall for the Sigatoka river valley on Fiji's main island.

CHAPTER TEN
DANCE WITH KALI

An hour later, a very tired Patipati and I were having dinner with a Gurkha captain in a quarter-acre canvas camouflage campaign tent left over from some forgotten war on the plains of India. The captain spoke perfect Oxford English. He had a difficult time understanding my southwestern mountain version of English. He was interested in picking my mind on America's civilian position on the war in Vietnam and its effect on the American military tradition of kicking the hell out of everybody from the Sioux Indians to Rommel's Elite armored units. I was dining with boys who were the world's best modern alley fighters in uniform, under western control—or kind of western control.

The man I was sharing a polished silver tray of potato knishes with was an expert in yoga and light infantry tactics. He spoke five languages, including ancient Sanskrit, shot par 76 golf, and skied at St. Moritz. He still carried a hand-carved, ivory-handled dagger in his boot. Its blade was forged from a sword tip broken by Alexander the Great on his passage through Afghanistan. It was presented to him by a Pakistani heroin warlord he captured while on patrol in 1949 in the Khyber Pass in desperate bid for freedom. My dinner companion, the captain, cut the heroin lord's right hand off at the wrist for this moral offense. However, he kept the dagger for that fateful time when he would use it as his last line of defense.

Dinner proceeded pleasantly as short-skirted Gurkha privates served the officers' mess with awesome platters of exotic curry prepared with fresh Fiji vegetables. Eggplant curry with fresh river prawns came first followed by yellow rice the size of movie house popcorn. The wealthy, light-skinned Sikh farming community of the upper mountainous river valley made sure the army boys ate well on their annual training exercise in Fiji. It was their only link with a similar mountain homeland they left fifty years ago to seek a better life in the coastal sugar cane fields of Fiji. Now they were prosperous mountain village farmers on land leased from the Fijian Native Land Trust Board. They had replicated their former homeland. They again feuded with the poorer dark-skinned Hindus downriver who had migrated from Bombay's slums to Fiji.

Talk progressed to the Vietnam War. My position was clear and to the point. First, it was historically a Chinese vassal state. Secondly, it was a wasted effort in a decadent French Asian colonial castoff with no significant strategic or economic importance to the USA. It was a big macho joyride for the Washington cocktail party circuit, the defense contractors, and colonels looking to make general. Worse, there was no commitment to win from the politicians at home.

Historically, I said, I would have volunteered to go as a 1st lieutenant in the Army or as a Navy pilot. That's how western born private school educated southern college boys behaved. They had commanded every winning effort by the U.S. since the revolution when George Washington left his Potomac plantation and kicked ass against the world's best regular army. I had been raised in the southwest and educated in the south. It was a tradition in my family.

I made it clear to the colonel that if we had really wanted to hold ground in this region, we would have nuked or fire-bombed Hanoi a long time ago. Nobody that counted in the USA gave a shit about how many yellow faces died in North Vietnam. No, this one was a theoretical war, like the ill-conceived disastrous British plunge into Afghanistan a century before. Better to miss this one in some offbeat jungle like Fiji rather than be grenaded in your sleep by a black ex-big city gang member who had been drafted and hated sunbelt ROTC white boys with silver bars on their lean shoulders. In Vietnam, you couldn't have shot enough of the troublemakers in your platoon by firing squad or in their back to make a difference. It was every man for himself.

This time, the real smart men were sitting it out while the brass and the politicians took a beating. They could not win without the best and the brightest in the officers' corps. They did not have it in this weird war game. Plenty of cheap Asian teenage prostitutes, but not American military honor or victory.

After five curry courses and several sterling silver cups of 12-year-old Black Label Scotch, the collapsible field tables were stripped of their hand-woven white linen Indian tablecloths. The monogrammed sterling silver field-ware was placed in its polished teak field chest. I liked these guys. I could have fought with them. They were winners. They had beaten the hell out of the communist Malaysian rebels for the Brits a decade before. Substituting Koreans for them in Vietnam was like sending the National Pony League Champions against the NY Yankees. The Koreans were losers. Korea had always been the bad doormat peninsula for feuds between Japan and China once every century. In the haze of the Scotch, my thoughts drifted.

Suddenly, but subtly erotic Indian music began from a quartet of Gurkha musicians sitting on the Oriental carpets which had been spread over the swept dirt floor of the officers' mess tent. Patipati had disappeared after two Scotches. He could not drink the white man's firewater without falling asleep. Patipati, the leader of late night all out "kava" parties was like Little Red Riding Hood in the presence of a fifth of hard liquor. He was usually smart enough not to push the envelope. I was routinely dropped to my knees halfway through an average Fijian kava ceremony. Patipati disappeared just as the Sikh girl arrived.

She was approximately 14. This was marriage age for a Sikh Indian village girl. She was perfectly full-figured. She had long, braided black hair. She wore a festive dancer's sari accented with circular donut-holed brass breast cups. They exposed her large brown nipples which protruded through the upper wrap of the sheer silk sari. I thought, maybe this was the fabled night. I had heard rumors of the secret night dances of the mountain village Sikh Indian girls who had lost their virginity. Therefore, they were no longer suitable for marriage. Hindu and Sikh farm girls married between 12 and 16, but they had to be virgins for their family to arrange a marriage. Both Sikh and Hindu schoolgirls who got pregnant before marriage regularly hung themselves in our province. They simply failed to appear at school the next day. Girls who only lost their cherry and got caught became dancers. This sort of ritual prostitution was managed by a relative until they could be married off to a non-Sikh foreigner. Worse, in bad economic times, they were sold as slave girls to an Arab freighter captain at the Port of Suva. They were transported back to the Middle East for duty in a secret royal brothel. Finally, they were dropped down an abandoned desert well during a religious crackdown by the fanatic Muslim priests from Mecca. Portland, Oregon had the same problem in the USA with kidnapped girls, I had read.

Tonight, I sensed that a dance of the rumored cult of Kali mixed with drug-assisted Tantric black yoga was about to begin. A sterling silver pipe with a perfectly carved Meerschaum body of a nude Hindu goddess was passed from hand to hand. I inhaled and was hit by a Bruce Brown film quality forty-foot big wave. Frat house hashish had not prepared me for the exotic sexual uplift that this ancient Himalayan grown drug packed.

Black Label Scotch, hashish, and the driving Sikh Indian music created a mental thermal effect. My mind saw the bright yellow aspens at Gold Hill near Telluride, Colorado in a foot of pure white snow at 12,000 feet. She began to dance. She used perfect hand and body moves mastered only with years of training in yoga. The yoga emphasized the Tantric sexual positions she would bring to her husband's house. The flowing sheer layers of the silk sari accented the body of this light-skinned Sikh girl. The dance was Balinese in grace but alluringly sexual, like the belly dancers of the Middle East.

My senses burst as her full thighs thrust through the seamless folds of the sheer silk dance sari. She passed from one exotic position to another, always with the beat of the drummer accenting the move. I froze as she passed in front of me. The revolving motion of the brass breast plates, and her brown-eyed stare began to hypnotize me. She thrust her thighs forward. Her breast plates seem to whirl until the brown nipples seemed to burst through the sheer silk. Could this be the last rational thought of my western mind, a meeting with Kali? Was this my final moment on the frontier of western civilization as I perceived it until tonight?

The sari functioned only as an airy veil as her fully nude body danced in front of me. One exotic motion followed by another. Each move displaying sexual positions I never had dreamed or experienced. Yet we never touched as my senses exploded in bright colors hotter than fire.

Then suddenly, as my body ached for orgasm, a Gurkha soldier with a razor-sharp sword appeared in the dim, hazy light of the kerosene-lit dance floor. He began to twirl it at speeds which made the blade disappear like ceiling paddle fan blades on a hot tropical night. The sword flashed and the girl's head disappeared. Her body danced on faster and faster to the music's frenzied beat. The sword flashed and her right arm was gone. The sword flashed and her other arm was gone. The music quickened and the sword flashed again, and her legs disappeared. The swordsman vanished. The nude torso with only the spinning brass breast cups danced the grotesque dance of Kali. She began to beckon me to say goodbye to earth and enter the lurid world of perverse sexual deviation and destruction forever. I was moving irresistibly toward the pure, pulsating opening of the dancing torso. My body heaved to the music. My mind screamed for mercy. I felt soft hands way back in space restraining my heaves, closing my lips.

Through the reflection of the whirl of the spinning brass breast plates came the beautiful blonde hair-framed face of Sarah the almost nun. I felt Sarah's right hand quietly restraining my chest. Her left hand softly kept my lips together to stop the scream from within my soul as Kali began to lose her grip on my psyche. The whirling sword, the music, the dancing torso, the dim light, the smell of hashish all receded. Sarah pulled my mind slowly back from the dream frontiers of tribalism to the Hobbesian jungle of logic with its rule of law. But on my journey of journeys, more deadly than physical death, Kali fought back. She sought to trap a portion of my metaphysical mind forever, then leave me mentally stranded between the two worlds. Forever a dead man in both lands, no better than the shell-shocked, mindless bodies that litter so many V.A. mental hospital wards.

The dancing torso whirled again, closer. Kali's full breasts and flaming open vagina more alluring than ever. The sword swung closer and faster over my head. The fiery torso moved to satisfy the carnal void of my gray-blue industrialized mind. Sarah's dreamlike image began to become dimmer as my body temperature plunged. My breathing began to slow.

Sarah took swift action as this drug hypnotically induced hypothermia began to destroy the oxygen trying to flow to my brain. A tiny leftover guard camera in my mind saw the snapshots. Her warm hands stroked my chest in a slow rhythmic motion to awaken it. Kali fought for my brain.

"Come," she said. "Come forever, no pain, no more reason, no more travel; enter me and the sword will sever you forever from the screaming lepers outside the tent..."

Then a blazing fire back-lit the dancing torso exposing the hedonistic scars of a thousand fingernail claw marks of its dead victims. The golden light burned brighter. I realized Sarah cradled my head in the dim candlelit room, in the shadow of the stone-gray cathedral. The rhythm of my life began to return. The spinning sword obliterated the dancing torso until only the glint of the reflected light from the brass breast plates remained. Then it flickered, disappeared like a firefly.

In the early morning pastel river valley light, I emerged from a hazy dream state to the knock of a black-faced nun. She told me Sarah had stayed in one of the other church compound's vacant houses near where the Gurkha soldiers were camped. She had left suddenly an hour before daybreak when a police messenger had arrived by Land Rover from Sigatoka with a telegram.

Sarah's younger brother had been killed by a person named Devil's Angel, the nun said, at a village called Altamont in California. He was listening to music by a rolling stone. She quietly sobbed for the fallen friend's brother. She also knew she would never see Sarah again.

CHAPTER ELEVEN
CALIFORNIA GIRLS

I was confused, saddened, but happy to be alive as I finished packing Sarah's few belongings into a wooden banana crate. I would send them by bus to Peace Corps HQ in Suva. Neither the nuns nor I had a forwarding address for Sarah. Like so many acquaintances and PCVs who passed through my life in the late sixties and early seventies, she was from someplace in California. In her case, it was Northern California. Some days it seemed like everybody under 25 years old from California was on the road someplace in the world. Hawaii and Fiji were already hangouts for the perpetually tanned blonde girls and long-haired surf riders from the West Coast. The girls had taught me about sex and drugs. The boys had taught me to surf.

France had sent its Jesuit priests out to bring religion to its New World empire. It seemed that California in the late 1960s had sent its blonde girls out to foster the drug enhanced sexual rock and roll revolution worldwide. Their mere presence changed the dynamic of any gathering. I had even learned to distinguish the girls from the north from the girls of the south over time. From the north of California came the well-spoken sensual women with long, straight, natural blonde hair. They carried key-locked diaries to record their pleasures. They traveled like their pioneer great grandmothers who crossed the "prairies" or sailed "the Horn". From the south came the genetically perfect "blonde" girls whose pubic hair never matched their dyed, sun-bleached hair. They lived for the moment, always pushing to expand the physical experience regardless of the emotional or mental consequences.

I packed a small, engraved, leather key-locked diary on top of Sarah's belongings. I wrapped it in a simple, red-flowered print sulu. I closed the wooden banana crate top and nailed it shut. I carried it out into the bright, hot, late morning sun. I found Patipati at the Land Rover, waiting in silence.

He had just washed it. Without a week of caked river mud, its gray aluminum shell tried to sparkle in the bright tropical sun. When Patipati washed the Land Rover, it was a signal that he was ready to return to his village. I was also ready to go downriver and check on the co-op's central office clerical staff. I had had enough of tree spirits, dope, Sikh dancing, ghosts, kava, Kali dreams, and a California tragedy to last for the remainder of the winter.

Patipati had reminded me the potato crop was ready for harvest. That meant good hard honest co-op marketing and sales work for the both of us. It was time to quit spreading the gospel according to the Co-op Department and market Fiji's first ever large-scale homegrown potato crop.

Patipati loaded the banana crate into the back of the Land Rover. Our dirty clothes and various burlap bags of fruit and vegetables almost filled it. With a twist of its key, the Land Rover roared to life. Patipati wheeled it into a tight U-turn. We drove down the rutted, muddy dirt road from the cathedral to the main valley gravel road back to town. I could see the black-faced nuns waving goodbye in my side mirror.

The Land Rover screamed as Patipati overtook the express bus to Suva on the coastal highway. I waved it to stop. Patipati exited and pulled Sarah's banana crate from the back of the Land Rover. I gave the bus driver four Fijian dollars to make sure he personally delivered it to the Peace Corps HQ in Suva. That was two days' pay for him. I insured the deal by telling him he would get another dollar from Patipati when he dropped off a signed receipt at the co-op passionfruit factory office on his return trip. Whatever comfort I could provide Sarah was my only goal.

As the bus moved away, my mind searched for an answer to the riddle. Was Kali a dream? Had Sarah been a dream? What had really happened near the forgotten cathedral on the river plain of the middle valley? Was it drugs? Had I scraped up against a powerful force outside of my normal perception and western education? Had death lurked that night as a most dangerous game at the edge of the world beyond the reach of western intellectual or medical power?

I was happy potato season was here because it meant long hours of mind-numbing hard work, like roundup at my family's ranch. There was no time for white sand deserted beaches with my neighbor's Australian low-cut bikinis. There was no time for travel to Suva with political intrigue in mind. There would be no travel to upriver missions or to the edge of the universe where man still lived with only himself and the spirits of yesterday, today, and tomorrow in nature. It was great to be within five miles of my house with a safe, sane return to the missionary position if Dianne happened by to visit. Back to listening to the anti-Vietnam rock and roll groups fight the war for me and everybody else in the Peace Corps. Back to two-week-old international editions of Time Magazine, and the three-month-old Sports Illustrateds my mom still sent in care packages. She also sent aunt's home-canned blackberry jam, even though the co-op factory I managed made half the passionfruit jam in the world.

The news of me making thousands of little jars of jam for people to eat had scared my elderly aunt half to death. That's how the Peace Corps operated in the late sixties. Economic, business, or political science majors managed the third world's co-ops and factories. The factories tried to turn out consumer products. Making passionfruit jam was a hell of a lot easier than college chemistry, and a lot more fun. I had no reports of death from our customers, so everything seemed to be working fine. Fiji also had no product liability laws. If you ate a fatal meal, that was it for this lifetime. Karma ruled.

Patipati dropped me off at my house in the late afternoon. He drove back to his village near the co-op's passionfruit factory. I walked across the grassy lawn and through the always unlocked door of my house. It was empty. Dianne was at the upriver village medical center where she worked. I headed for a shower. A shower would feel good after the trip up valley with only river baths.

I dropped my shorts. I peeled off my bula shirt and entered the makeshift shower which was fed by a tank with a hand pump from a saline coastal well. The pump worked and the salty cold water cascaded against my body. I noticed rouge droplets on my chest, they quickly rinsed away. Upon close inspection, my skin was not cut or scraped. Another mystery left over from the journey upriver. Now, potatoes were on my mind. Potatoes would be good work for a while.

CHAPTER TWELVE

"MO BETTER POTATOES"

I slid out of bed at first light. I glanced once more at the sleeping long-limbed nude form in the shadows of another tropical winter day. Abstinence, I counseled myself. The urge to return to bed and play with Dianne lingered in my mind. Abstinence because it was potato season. Not just any potato season—Fiji's first full-scale attempt at a major potato harvest in its short written and long oral history. I had no attachment to the brown skinned dirty little vegetables, but the government did. I was suspicious of any vegetable that grew underground.

I liked the exotics the co-op marketed like watermelons, bananas, guava, and passionfruit. I particularly liked planning the ad campaign and helping write the copy for our co-op's passionfruit products. I often leaned back in my co-op office chair and imagined that after I finished the Peace Corps, I would build a worldwide business empire anchored by passionfruit juice distribution. It was the natural third wave replacement drink for orange juice which everybody would tire of in the new dawn of the seventies. I would be surrounded by beautiful sun-tanned models as my high-octane marketing campaign careened through the known world selling passion-fruit to the masses. Passionfruit juice drinks were the only choice for the chorus in the sexual revolution we were responsible to preach worldwide.

Potatoes brought other images to my mind—none of them were much fun. The politics of potatoes in Fiji were terrible. The government allowed millions of guavas to rot on trees or be eaten by fruit bats. However, it carefully prepared an Import Substitution Plan of the Crown Colony of Fiji which called for the elimination of seasonally imported crops like the Australian and New Zealand potatoes. They would be replaced by local Fijian potatoes grown by the co-op I managed. The plan failed, of course, to take into account that native Fijians did not eat potatoes. Therefore, they saw the effort as a misguided attempt to enrich their hated Indian rivals who ate potatoes in curry.

The plan also overlooked the fact that new potatoes grew from seed potatoes. They had to be supplied to the co-op farmers by the same Australian or New Zealand potato farmers that we were about to be forced out of the Fiji market after 50 years. Also, the plan failed to account for a local virus called "tropical wilt", which in hot weather caused potatoes to rot from the inside out. It also "infested" nearby potatoes in the ground or their hot burlap shipping bag homes. It was the plague of the veggie world with a six-week timeline to a rotting, stinking death.

Finally, and most importantly, the plan failed to realize there was no cold storage for potatoes anywhere in the tropical island paradise of Fiji at any price. Potatoes died fast in a tropical climate without cold storage. Everybody in this tiny country needed to eat lots of maturing potatoes quickly or the co-op's farmers were going to be bankrupted big time.

I sped along the coastal highway to the potato packing shed to view the new electrical-powered sorting machine. It was imported to wash and pack the potatoes by size or grade. The Fijian co-op farmers refused to engage in this task for any reasonable amount of money on any regular schedule. It was clear that giant task of digging, washing, bagging, shipping, and selling some 200,000 tons of the rapidly maturing potatoes would be war for the next six months.

As I drove, a fantasy about Nurse Williams called to me like the famed sirens of ancient Greece. Nurse Williams was back in America, lost in its vast engine of post-World War II industrial trivia. Nurse Williams was in the sack with some midwestern industrialist, blowing his mind for a piece of some beer bottle plant in the barren reaches of the American economic engine.

Once Nurse Williams got control of the beer bottle plant, I would use it exclusively as the worldwide container manufacturer for my passionfruit empire. Nurse Williams' beer bottle plant would make the containers for every ounce of the premium drink of the third wave sold worldwide. Nurse Williams would be a very important industrial captain. When our private planes met at supermarket chain trade shows, Nurse Williams and I would be reunited again in my plane, Passion One USA. No golf or tennis tournaments for us, just good clean corporate jet age American fun. Nurse Williams had always been an important ally in the co-op fight. She would be rewarded.

My mind snapped back to reality as thousands of dirty light brown tropical potatoes arrived by seven-ton truck loads at the co-op sorting shed near Sigatoka, Fiji. They marched down trays, were washed, sorted, separated into 112 lb. burlap bags to wait their turn to be eaten, or rot to death from tropical wilt. After the first trial run of the sorter, it was back to zero. The sorter if misaligned, sometimes nicked the thin, underdeveloped skin of the tropical potatoes, accelerating the potential for the spread of the dreaded wilt. It was back to sorting by hand, a job everyone hated.

But bigger trouble was brewing. It turned out to be real dynamite big time triple trouble. When I hung-up the battery-powered World War II issue shortwave phone, I had to sit down. I explained it to my staff, including Patipati.

Two tramp freighters, one from Australia and one from New Zealand, had arrived at the Port of Suva in the capital city. Their holds were filled with cheap potatoes from the same potato growers who had sold our co-op the seed potatoes. They had timed our crop's harvest perfectly since they sold us the seeds. They were planning to wipe us out because we had to sell our potatoes for at least double their asking price to pay off the co-op's potato seed loan to the Fiji Development Bank and return a profit for our member farmers. Naked capitalism had struck my ship for the first time in my life. All my college economics courses were worthless. This was ranch polo with no refs, winner take all.

If a major Suva Indian merchant wholesaler bought these ship-borne potatoes and unloaded them at the national wharf, it was disaster. The colony, by my calculations, had 24 weeks' of potatoes counting our co-op's rapidly maturing supply to eat in 12 weeks. With no cold storage available and constant hot weather in Suva, the main market prices would plunge as the potatoes rotted. It was time to consult the Paramount Provincial Chief

Kavula and make a plan.

I met the province's highest ranking Paramount Chief Kavula at his coastal village. He was a much-decorated war hero. It was decided I would go immediately to the capital city and meet with the new Minister of the Co-op Department, Ratu Sili, a Fijian from the eastern province. I would request him to ask the prime minister to have Parliament pass a temporary law banning the importation of foreign potatoes retroactively for three months. This would give our co-op enough time to sell the Fiji-grown potatoes before they rotted.

This legislation was not Chief Kavula's idea, but he agreed to it anyway since he believed in the co-op. He particularly liked me, plus Dianne's long legs, which he ogled at every ceremonial opportunity. The chief, however, had another idea which he really liked better, if mine failed. To guarantee that Parliament passed the necessary legislation fast enough to stop the foreign potatoes from being unloaded and sold at the main Suva customs wharf, he would bring 100 ceremonial battle-dressed warriors with ancient hand-carved wooden war clubs the size of baseball bats to Suva. They would ride on the next convoy of trucks carrying the co-op potatoes to the capital city's marketplace. He and the warriors would pow-wow with the prime minister and Parliament, old style. Their war clubs, war paint, and spears would be with them.

This idea made me extremely nervous because while the chief cared nothing about legislation, he loved war. He had been decorated by the British army for bravery in the Malaysian insurrection where he fought against the communist guerrillas. He had been decorated in his youth by the U.S. Marines as their chief scout in the World War II fight against the Japs at Iwo Jima. If Chief Kavula attacked the about to be independent Crown Colony Parliament with 100 warriors dressed in sulus, bula shirts with shields, spears, and ancient wooden war clubs, then I would be the first known U.S. Peace Corps volunteer to be hanged for starting a civil war in a Crown Colony in the now faded British empire. I would be the last footnote in a 500-year parade of adventurers eliminated from the empire by grown men in white wigs. They carried out the law of Her Majesty's courts throughout the known world.

The Chief was deadly serious. He gave me 48 hours to get to the capital city and solve this problem before the next fleet of potato trucks to Suva went with Chief Kavula and his village warriors on the eve of

Fiji's independence.

I jumped in my Land Rover and Patipati almost fell out of his still open door. We roared down the valley highway back to my hardline national telephone service at the coastal passionfruit factory. The plan was simple. After I called Manu, Ratu Sili's deputy, I would call Dr. Joe at the Customs wharf in Suva. He would freeze the top Indian wholesale potato buyers in place. He would tell them the Fijian co-op members intended to torch the Indian farmers in the Sigatoka valley if they dealt with the foreign potato sellers. Also, the very famous Chief Kavula would bring his best men to Suva to visit their warehouses with torches.

This ploy had been used in every western movie I had seen. It would probably work here because no one watched western movies, except the Fijians. I reasoned the move would freeze the key potential buyers of the cut-rate priced foreign potatoes for at least 2-3 days. Then the New Zealand and Aussie potato sellers would cut the price again. Greed would attract back the buyers. The sellers would cut the price to the floor as the shipping costs mounted. They also realized the potatoes would rot in the ships' unrefrigerated holds. They would take a loss to destroy the Fiji crop to protect their long-term market. The co-op's gamble was that the hodge-podge of burned-out colonials that still controlled the pre-independence Parliament would pass the prime minister's emergency legislation fast. This would prevent the cheap potatoes from being unloaded at port and sold to the capital city merchants.

There was always the chance someone in New Zealand or Australia had paid off the colonials. Then they would stall the legislative process. This would bring the chief and his boys to town to meet with the Parliament, ancient war clubs and all. The Fijian village potato crop was already dug out of the ground. The old chief and his boys were ready for a trip to the big city anyway to party in the legendary pubs at the national marketplace.

I completed the calls to Manu and Dr. Joe from the co-op passionfruit factory. They both agreed to help the co-op farmers. I kept Chief Kavula's plan to myself. I fished from my desk drawer a nude color Polaroid picture of Nurse Williams with her inverted nipple, and a pint of Fiji dark rum. It was like being on a destroyer in a World War II movie in the dim light of my office. I patted Nurse Williams' famous nipple which represented an erotic button for good luck. I downed two swigs of dark rum chased by a glass of fresh passionfruit juice. I started to slide the photo back into its hiding place, but I decided Patipati and I needed her luck and energy for the trip, so I slipped it in my shirt pocket and ran to the Land Rover.

Patipati drove. He gunned the engine, spraying the tin-sided factory administrative office building with loose, wet gravel. He accelerated onto the coast road. We sped down the coast road to my house to pick up a few clothes for the all-night trip from hell to Suva on the black, rain-soaked mountain road. Suddenly, a 7-ton "outlaw" potato laden truck roared past the Land Rover with its headlights turned off. One of the co-op's Hindu Indian farmers had just broken ranks with a big-time end run. The co-op members had borrowed the co-op's seed potatoes with a promise-to-pay note that required them to sell their potatoes back to the co-op to pay off their potato seed loan as well as profit share. The bamboo wireless had probably reached the valley's Indian farmers. Their relatives who worked for the wholesalers in Suva knew that the foreign potatoes were sitting in the harbor. They knew their impending sale would destroy the market for local Fijian grown potatoes. Better to sell illegally than gamble a total loss.

If Patipati and I didn't stop this renegade freighter of contraband potatoes, the dam would break. The late planting Indian farmers in the valley still had unharvested potatoes in the ground. They would end run the co-op and help crash the market. They would fail to pay off their loans for seed potatoes. This would start a second war front as the Fijian village farmers burned them out for destroying the co-op and devaluing the potatoes they had already dug and delivered to the co-op. This was the classic case of a really bad day getting worse very fast. It was still only 9:00 PM.

I knew the "X" signed seed potato co-op marketing agreements were useless in this situation. A year from now a civil court would give us a judgment against a judgment-proof Indian farmer with 13 hungry kids on five acres of subleased river plain land with a one-room hut. If this truck reached the capital, then a 1,000-farmer biracial co-op which was the pride of this racially fragile developing country would blow apart. The co-op had bet its entire capital pool on the first crop of Fiji potatoes. Also bet was a big chunk of Fiji Development Bank's agriculture loan capital. There was no choice but to stop the truck and seize the potatoes, at machete point if necessary.

The word "hi-jacking" crossed my mind as Patipati wheeled into the front yard of my house so I could grab a machete. The truck roared on toward Suva. It would soon slow on a very steep mountain climb five miles up the road. There we could easily catch it and force it off the road on the upgrade. I ran into the house and found my dull-edged, cheap, rusted tin machete in the kitchen closet.

Dianne, semi-asleep and nude, stumbled into the kitchen, carrying a candle lantern. She had been awakened by the commotion. She startled when the candlelight gleamed across the machete in my right hand. She gasped and dropped the candle.

The candle landed on the top of my flip-flop clad foot. I reflexively flinched as the hot wax singed the top of my right foot. That caused the flat-sided blade of the machete to graze her hard, flat, bare stomach. She screamed, fully awake now. She realized it was me. She asked what the hell was happening.

I explained in three sentences the day's events. I said goodbye. She threw her arms around my neck. She stretched high to kiss me goodbye. She rubbed her soft brown nipples up the open front of my bula shirt. I remembered Patipati was waiting in the Land Rover. The clandestine potato truck would now be approaching the nearby mountains. If it cleared the first mountain ascent, it was out of our home province and the potential legal stakes for stopping it rose dramatically.

Her tongue touched my throat. I realized she had decided to disarm me with plain old-fashioned sex in the kitchen. Patipati by custom would never enter the house to find me without first being invited. Thousands of potatoes marched through my head as the rum and a juvenile sense of danger pulled my body away with a sharp bolt toward the door. I glanced back for good luck. I lunged through the door with the machete.

Patipati was still at the wheel. I signaled him to the left passenger side of the Land Rover. I jumped into the driver's side to start the nighttime chase. I knew Dianne wouldn't chase me into the yard with Patipati in the Land Rover. It was strictly against Peace Corps rules to be nude in public. She always obeyed the rules. I fleetingly wondered if the Peace Corps manual had a rule against hi-jacking trucks on national highways in third world countries. If this para-police maneuver failed, I would soon know the answer.

With a potential potato civil war brewing, it seemed logical to stop the outlaw potato truck on the main road to Suva as it climbed into the central mountains that separated eastern and western Viti Levu. I had Nurse Williams riding in my pocket for extra good luck. This could be one of those nights to remember when real life imitates fiction. I could cross a line which never let me cross back.

CHAPTER THIRTEEN
MIDNIGHT FREIGHTER

The Land Rover whined in reverse gear. It slithered backwards over the dew-wet freshly macheted grass. I spun it onto the graveled main road to the capital city. I caught the silhouette of a sulued figure peering through the screen door of the yellow wooden-sided cottage. It was a startlingly beautiful female silhouette with a solid gold top backlit by a flickering candle lantern. Then the image was gone forever. I shifted the Land Rover from first to second. The race to catch the fugitive freighter with the contraband potatoes moved into high gear. Winner take all was the game on the main road to Suva, Fiji.

Patipati opened the glove box. He retrieved the half-empty pint of Fijian dark rum. He passed it to me. I hit fourth gear on the flats along the reef-rimmed coastal highway east of Sigatoka. A quick pull on the pint bottle sent 160 proof fire across the top of my tongue, then down the back of my throat. The effect on my empty stomach was instantaneous. It convulsed, burned, and sent the cheap liquid straight into my bloodstream. I jolted awake. I refocused my eyes on the edge of the head lamps. We sped through the still moonless night on a rough gravel road in the middle of the South Pacific at a breathtaking 60 miles an hour.

I calculated we would catch the potato laden freighter which was maxed out at five miles an hour on the three-mile steep climb through the first coastal mountain range pass in about 20 minutes. Roadside palm tree trunks cut the Land Rover lights like disco strobes. We fish-tailed around the long curve of Nama Bay with a mountain on one side and the ocean on the other.

I could hear the crash of surf on the rocks below. It surged at high tide with an onshore western breeze. We arched around the bay on a half-mile, 180° curve. The fresh, warm wind blew through the Land Rover's open front air vents that allowed air to enter but kept dust out of the vehicle.

Patipati's eyes were wide open as he rode shotgun to my left. He watched for animals and other possible road hazards at the edge of our high beams. The road ate our headlight beams in milliseconds as they searched the continuing black hole which seemed to pull us toward the edge of the universe. Single frame images of Nurse Williams whip-sawed through my mind. I down-shifted to second to begin the climb to Wonka Pass from sea level some 2,700 feet above. We would catch the freighter in two- and one-half miles, if my mental calculations were right. We closed at 1,000 feet per minute.

I asked Patipati to translate when we stopped the fugitive truck. I would carry the machete. I would officially seize the truck. If this scheme backfired, I could always skip the country. He would have witnesses who could testify that he was under my control in his role as a Fijian Co-op Dept. junior officer and translator. Tension permeated the stark Land Rover cab. It slid from corner to corner on the deserted road. I hoped I knew the driver and the farmer personally. Then I could turn the truck back to the Co-op HQ with a conversation. However, I did not recognize the truck as a local one when it roared past us a half hour ago, but its burlap bags bore the co-op mark.

It was a new blue, 7-ton Toyota semitruck. The locally owner-operated trucks were all red or yellow, but new trucks were arriving from the Japanese factories monthly in our region. Backed by easy Toyota financing, they were overtaking British Leyland (the historic provider of semitrucks in the Fiji market) as independence neared. Most of Fiji's agricultural transport semitrucks were owned by burly, pot-bellied Hindu Indian owner/operators with lead feet the equal of A.J. Foyt. Most had naked girl profile-silhouetted mudflaps, white on black, over their rear double tired axles. The tits on these girls were amazing in size and shape.

My mind focused on a 30 mph slide through a switchback turn as the headlights caught an infamous 50-double-C titted mud flap. I knew we had our freighter in sight. It labored uphill carrying nine or ten tons of recently harvested potatoes at 7 mph. The driver and passenger side doors were open. The drivers kept their doors open on the steep mountain grades. If they missed a double clutch shift to low first gear and the drive shaft twisted from the torque of the climb and the weight of their always over-loaded trucks, then the truck rolled backwards, and they could jump free. They would have five seconds before the truck reached terminal velocity and rolled backwards into a black hole off a 1,500-foot drop at the top of a rain-forested pass.

With my left hand I patted for good luck the secret nude Polaroid of Nurse Williams in my shirt pocket. The tropical rain forest fragrant night smells were like Nurse Williams' perfumed natural scent. Life in Fiji was definitely not as much fun since Nurse Williams had skipped for Hawaii.

I wondered what Patipati did for good luck. It was clear to me after countless late night kava sessions with Fijians that the western concept of good luck had no meaning in this tropical paradise. Every day was a perfect 10.

The immediate work was to stop the truck before it reached the flat half-mile ridge line stretch of road along the top of the pass and was able to accelerate. The blue monster closed in on the top of the pass. He knew I was behind him as the Land Rover's high beams hit his left side, outboard rearview mirror. I flicked my dimmer switch on and off. This signaled I was going to pass going uphill. I swung to the left into the open downhill lane with gravel spewing from my rear wheels. As I shifted from high first to second, I gunned the engine into the black nothingness. The driver slowed, not realizing he was really the game being hunted. Suddenly, his companion riding shotgun saw the Co-op Department seal on the Land Rover door. We pulled even at 6 mph, fifty yards from the top of the pass.

Bad luck was on our side, I looked up into the lighted cab. I saw one of V.J. Singh's henchmen from Suva next to an unknown, dark-skinned Southern Indian driver with a scar down his right cheek. V.J. Singh was my hated enemy in Suva. He was the brother-in-law of the hated ex-Super

Boss, Patel. He controlled the wharf's wholesale food imports, including potato shipments. He had opposed the importation of seed potatoes by the Valley Co-op member farmers in an early, violent meeting a year before in Suva. He had the thug in the passenger seat throw me out of his office after I had refused a bribe to sabotage the co-op's plan to borrow money from the Fiji Development Bank and start the home-grown potato business in the Sigatoka Valley.

Their plan flashed through my mind in two seconds flat, faster than a teletype printer. V.J. Singh had ordered the two shiploads of potatoes from his pals in Australia and New Zealand to panic the co-op's farmers. He was attempting to panic them into selling for rock bottom prices to him while bankrupting the Valley Co-op. The men in the truck would not surrender easily. This was not simply stopping a local truck driver with an embarrassed, frightened co-op farmer. These boys had a paid in cash bill of lading for the potatoes. They were Suva bound.

Fifty yards from the top, I was door-to-door with the overloaded Japanese semitruck. Suddenly, the thug passenger whipped out an illegal sawed-off shotgun. He fired. He blew out the Land Rover's front windshield in a brutal blast. I went blind as the windshield imploded backwards into my face in a thousand pieces, mixed with buckshot. Patipati slumped forward, face into his lap. The Land Rover veered right into the slow-moving truck's frame. It locked into its slow uphill climb.

My eyes opened from the shock. I saw Patipati move. He had only been stunned from the shock of the wall of glass. The buckshot seemed to have been absorbed by the windshield as it hit in a glancing blow. Neither of us was wounded from the blast. We had small cuts on our faces, exposed arms and legs from the flying safety glass. It was our second imploded windshield in a month.

I was pissed, because now we would have to drive all night with no windshield. That meant one million tropical rain forest night bugs in our mouths and nostrils during the 100-mile drive. The potato raid still had to be stopped. If this truck reached Suva, word would reach the remaining panicked Valley Hindu farmers. They would jump ship quickly.

My decision was final, brash, and instant, like those long dead Southern confederate cavalry commanders in my family. They had fought for Lee and died or moved to Colorado during reconstruction to escape Yankee government. I ordered Patipati to get a spare 5-gallon gasoline can from the space behind the driver's seat. It was strapped there for the all-night Suva trip to augment the two mounted on the Land Rover's back bumper. Unlike the Penn Turnpike, there were no 24-hour gas stations on Fiji roads. Traveling here was like in the wild, wild west. We were a moving mini-gas tank farm for this high speed, gasoline guzzling chuck wagon race.

Patipati leaned over the seat and grappled with the gas can straps. The truck picked up speed. The clinging Land Rover churned to the top of the pass.

I slid the Land Rover carefully back down the left side of the semitruck, out of view. Patipati put the gas can in my seat. He steered with his right hand at 10 mph in second gear. I opened my door, stood on the Land Rover's running board, wind in my face. I splashed gasoline over the tarp that secreted the load of potatoes on the flatbed blue semitruck from hell. The truck started to pick up speed on the flat road of the ridge line. I flicked my unfiltered lit Fiji cigarette at the tarp. Patipati veered the Land Rover to the left to disengage from the truck.

The effect was instantaneous as the tarp ignited in a 10-mph wind-fanned sheet of flames. I took control of the big Land Rover steering wheel. I downshifted into first and braked to get completely clear of the now vigorously flaming truck.

We drifted back 25 yards behind the truck. The driver and his shotgun rider jumped free. We braked as we approached the jump site. The truck, now driverless like a reinless buckboard, veered left with its sudden freedom. It plunged over the 1,500-foot ridge line drop into the thick rain forest below. It exploded in a mushroom 1,000-foot fireball of instantly baked potatoes. Its nearly full twin gasoline tanks had both ignited. It was a beautiful, stunningly red stark fireball of man-made hell against the dark green canopy of dense rain forest. The truck burned in a grove of hundred-year-old monkey wood trees. It had ignited near a rushing stream of brown runoff water at the base of a 300-foot waterfall.

The scar-faced, dark-complected Hindu driver lay face down in a muddy ditch on the ridge side of the mountain road. We stopped. Patipati climbed out. He crossed in front of the Land Rover cutting its headlight beams. He turned the driver over to make sure he didn't drown in the mud. The driver whimpered and begged for mercy at the sight of a real Fijian warrior. I told Patipati to stuff a half-baked potato (they littered the road making a trail over the steep edge) into the driver's mouth so we wouldn't have to listen to him. Patipati was a kinder soul. He just told him to shut up or he would eat him. This was an old Fijian cannibal village joke. The capital city Indian truck driver shut up instantly.

I climbed out with an electric torch (flashlight). I swept the far-left roadside with its beam until I found the thug shotgun rider. He had broken or sprained his left ankle in his jump for life. He was dragging his leg toward me, using the shotgun as a cane. I ran toward him and kicked the shotgun out from under him. I grabbed it as he toppled forward. I tossed it over the cliff side of the road into the now small forest fire. Civilian guns were illegal in Fiji, so it never existed anyway.

Patipati and I dragged the creepy, stocky Indian thug over to his driver friend. We sat them beside the road in their muddy clothes. Patipati splinted the thug's ankle with our Peace Corps first-aid kit from the Land Rover. It was probably only badly sprained. I made a white flag with a piece of roadside bamboo and a bandana from my stash in the glove compartment which I carried for dust protection on long dry drives. The next bus or truck to Suva would pick them up. We gave them a bottle of water and some bananas for their dinner, since it was now 10:30 PM in the middle of a rainforest in central Viti Levu.

I reached into my pocket and pulled out the self-portrait Polaroid of Nurse Williams. I shined my flashlight on it one last time. I gave it to them for entertainment, as well as a message to V.J. Singh assuming the Super Boss was still lurking on the sidelines. Nurse Williams was touching her inverted nipple while sitting on a wooden chair in only a pair of ripped off Pan Am issue black high heels. Her head of black hair was thrown back, her face to the camera and knees a couple of feet apart. Her smooth white inner thighs formed a vee. Her lipsticked red lips were highlighted by-droplets of moisture which glinted from the Polaroid flash. It gave me an instant hard-on standing silently in the center of the muddy road, backlit with 200-foot flames from the rain forest below on the heels of a near death experience.

My concentration on the Polaroid was broken as Patipati gunned the Land Rover engine back to life. This Polaroid was my last secret physical connection to Nurse Williams' life in Fiji. I needed to send a message with my two roadside captives. I walked over to the pathetic potato thieves. I handed the shaking driver the Polaroid. He gasped. He barely heard me tell him to give it to V.J. Singh. I handed the almost empty pint of Fiji dark rum to his injured associate to help deaden pain. I walked behind the Land Rover's passenger side.

It was Patipati's turn to drive for an hour. I crossed behind the taillights. I saw a torn piece of the blue truck's mudflaps with the 50-triple-C chest. I picked it up as a gift for Mr. V.J. Singh, if we needed to meet again. I sure hoped he had lots of insurance or needed a lot of crispy baked potatoes. I tossed the muddy, mutilated mudflap into the back of the Land Rover with the empty gas can. I climbed into the passenger seat. I closed the light-weight aluminum door with a dull thud.

Patipati gunned the Land Rover off in high first. He sprayed our victims with a well-deserved coat of mud. It began to rain in buckets. The white flag disappeared from the red glow of our taillights. As we accelerated to second gear and Suva, visions of Nurse Williams danced in my head. I rested now. My eyes closed. Nurse Williams was the best good luck a PCV could obtain in the middle of the Southern Pacific Ocean.

CHAPTER FOURTEEN
THE POTATO WARRIORS

It was dawn when I wheeled the mud-spattered Land Rover into Suva. My face was wind burned from the all-night drive with no windshield. I looked like a wild, wild west outlaw with a red bandana pulled over my mouth and nose to block the bugs. They could have suffocated me as the windshieldless Land Rover whined through the night at reduced speed on the coast road. Patipati slept contentedly behind me in the Land Rover's cargo compartment. The seat tops blocked the wind from his crumpled body. They gave him some relief from the wind and bugs.

I slowed to city speed. I motored toward the co-op's main potato warehouse. It was across the road in a long-ago abandoned World War II U.S. Army Quonset hut from the tourist hotel where Nurse Williams and I met that last wonderful night.

The Valley Co-op leased this one-of-a-kind heat trap from the Co-op Department for $1.00 a week. No large cold storage facilities existed on the island at any price. The British trained Fijians didn't even serve mixed drinks at bars with ice. The concept of storing large quantities of potatoes in anything but burlap bags was a mystery to the locals. At least this metal-roofed monster kept our potatoes dry from the capital's torrential rains, and also safe from the roving bands of out of work village boys. They scavenged the streets for free food in between unloading tramp freighters and playing endless games of pickup (bare-footed rugby). The national sport was rugby.

I drove up to the crumbling concrete loading dock. I couldn't help looking across the main coast road to bungalow #5, home of the Nurse Williams party two months ago. Instinctively, I knew the potato revolution would not go as well or be as much fun without her.

I was rocketed back to reality as a soft, warm, pre-sunrise tropical breeze blew the slight stench of rotting, wilt-riddled potatoes through the missing windshield of the Co-op Department Land Rover. It caused me to almost gag as Patipati stirred in the cargo compartment. These potatoes wouldn't last another ten days in the midday 100° tropical heat of their home. It was time for action. Once the word leaked that "wilt" and heat were halving the life of the Sigatoka Valley potatoes, then V.J. Singh and his allies would have an excuse to buy the foreign potatoes that sat a quarter mile offshore.

The warehouse stocked to the ceiling with 112 lb. bags of potatoes constituted eight times the net worth of the co-op. If they weren't sold it was all over for the agricultural marketing experiment I had been sent to supervise by the co-op department. There was no reason to even go inside the hut and check the inventory sheet with the co-op guard/warehouseman. It was time to go straight to the Peace Corps headquarters. There, I could get a private phone line back to the Sigatoka Post Office. I could dispatch Patipati's cousin Nio to find the Paramount Provincial Chief Kavula. I would have him bring 100 ceremonial battle-dressed warriors to Suva aboard the Tuesday night caravan of 10 co-op trucks loaded with burlap-bagged potatoes. It was time to gamble.

The plan that flashed through my mind was simple. It was drawn from my experience in anti-Vietnam demonstrations in college. I outlined it to Patipati as he landed with a thud in the passenger seat of the Land Rover as I nosed it onto the coast highway. I followed the early morning sporadic traffic into the capital's central district, past the national marketplace as the sun rose.

The chief would lead the potato laden trucks and warriors to the steps of the National Parliament Building where I would meet them. I would give the order to dump the 77 tons of Fijian home grown, fresh potatoes on the

Parliament steps while he would deploy the battle-dressed warriors with shields and spears to guard them until Parliament banned the importation of all foreign potatoes for three months to keep the native potatoes from being exposed to diseases like wilt. This turned weakness into strength.

Three months would force the tramp freighters to turn back to Australia and New Zealand with their potatoes or their cargo would rot in rapidly heating, unrefrigerated airtight holds. I calculated in six weeks the embargo would cause an absolute potato shortage in Fiji, with panic buying of the last third of the co-op crop. The co-op could jack the price into the sky then to cover its loss on the first two-thirds of the potato crop.

Parliament would have to act fast because this was a media event of worldwide scope. Newspapers would carry pre-independence Reuters wire service pictures of 100 ancient battle-dressed warriors with a dark-tanned, dirty-blond, long-haired, American Peace Corps volunteer. They would be sitting on their home-grown potatoes on the steps of the National Parliament Building in sight of a tramp freighter full of foreign potatoes. My emotions surged. They reminded me of anti-war marches before Kent State.

The white frame, tropical Victorian house which headquartered the Peace Corps Fiji in-country staff, came into view. I pulled the Land Rover into a parallel space marked "Country Director". I knew he was out of the country orienting the next batch of boys and girls in a training camp on Hilo, Hawaii. They were dubbed Fiji Seven—meaning, they were the seventh group in order of arrival. Mine was Fiji Four. Your group number created immediate superiority over each succeeding group of volunteers. Homage was always to godlike Fiji One. They had pioneered life in this isolated island paradise, little visited by Americans since World War II.

Parking in the Director's spot would piss off the Deputy Director. He was a beer drinking, overweight midwestern type who was working his way up the Peace Corps bureaucracy to country director. He could never figure out what my co-op was doing until he read it in the national newspaper. Two days from now, the headlines would be about me and the potato warriors barricading the parliament building. He would be sitting on the shitter in the headquarters building with the morning paper. He would freeze, because with the country director in Hawaii, he would be responsible for my activities in the potato war. If he mishandled it, no more advances up the ladder to one of the sixty or so cherished country director jobs worldwide.

Parking in the director's space started my day with a smile. It would get me a mandatory penalty night in a T-group encounter session while I was in the bustling capital city. The Peace Corps solved every problem with staff led T-group encounter sessions. Everyone on the headquarters staff was a Berkeley trained T-group therapist. Always ready to lead us in a discussion of our innermost sensitive thoughts on a moment's notice while we explored the deviant behavior of our friends' minds. I loved T-group. I specialized in making grown men cry with a whipsaw macho mind game of T-group rat fuck. Tab, Dr. Joe, and I invented it at the training camp in Hilo, Hawaii.

T-groups were mental masturbation for upper middle class university graduates. I thought it would be great if Chief Kavula and the Fijian warriors arriving on the potato truck convoy were assigned to Peace Corps T-groups by the Fiji government for their stunt. The Peace Corps might consult on T-groups for the chief and his trusty fighters who happily massacred the guerrilla communists in the jungles of Malaysia for the Brits as the sun set on their empire.

I shoved the half-asleep Patipati out the other side of the mud-spattered, windshield-less Land Rover. I told him to distract the Peace Corps recently arrived receptionist who drooled at the sight of his muscular body. This would allow me to call his cousin at the Sigatoka Post Office to get a message for action to Kavula with no fear of being overheard. I would make the call from Nurse Williams' vacant office. The new Nurse Williams was being trained with Fiji Seven and personally flown to Fiji with the country director. I presumed he would warn her away from me, Tab, and Dr. Joe. He now disliked us all on sight.

With our hair matted from the wind and dirt, Patipati and I looked like raccoons who had just been let out of prison. One bronze-black and one sun-tanned young outlaw.

The bored Washington-trained G-6 receptionist-secretary to the director and the deputy director gasped at the sight of Patipati. We walked up to her desk at 7:30 AM as unexpected as Lassie would have been on this rare, blue-skied day in the capital city.

I said, "Hello, Katie, I need to call my co-op office at the passionfruit factory. I'll be on the nurse's phone. Thanks a bunch, dear," as I walked through the lobby to the empty office. The Peace Corps HQ had an unlimited phone bill provided by the U.S. taxpayers.

Patipati stopped and whispered in her ear. The windshield-less ride had at last triggered some primitive urge in him to finally fuck Katie. She had eyeballed him for nine months since she arrived in the capital city. I heard her turn the switchboard off. She and Patipati headed into the director's empty office with a slam of the door. She could not listen from the switchboard to my call west to the potato warriors. Their convoy was now being loaded for tonight's shipment to Suva. We always shipped at night when it was cooler, to preserve the potatoes during transport. Heat accelerated wilt.

I tapped my foot to the rhythmic banging of the country director's desk against the outer wall of Nurse Williams' office. I whistled and dialed a capital city operator to place the fatal call to Sigatoka. No turning back for me, Patipati, or even Katie whose panties were now probably around her ankles, with her pleated gray skirt bunched above her waist. I knew I would always miss Patipati after I left Fiji. This young highwayman rode with me for adventure and justice. Life would never be this simple or pure again.

It was with great pride and clarity I said in Fijian, "Please put me through to Nio at the Sigatoka Post Office Customs section, operator." I tapped my foot in time with Katie as her shoulder banged against the thin wood wall that separated the two offices.

CHAPTER FIFTEEN
NIGHTTIME CONVOY

Patipati and I sat with the Land Rover engine idling in front of the co-op potato shed. Our headlights were turned off. We faced the coast highway. We had a newly installed windshield. It was so hot we had it swiveled down so we could let in the light breeze from Suva Bay. We were doused in "OFF" which I had sent parcel post from my mom every six months. It kept the ever present, jumbo, bloodsucking tropical mosquitoes off our young unblemished skin. The blue exhaust smoke from the well-worn engine also helped screen them out of the Land Rover.

Patipati was snoozing in the passenger seat. He was probably dreaming of his morning rendezvous with Katie in the country director's office. Their fling ended when the deputy director arrived about ten o'clock. He bellowed, "Who the hell is in the director's parking space?!" Of course, he knew it was my co-op Land Rover. He clearly wanted me to be publicly chastised as well as accrue a T-group encounter session.

I emerged from Nurse Williams' empty office to provide a decoy for the two lovebirds. Katie simultaneously exited the country director's office with a file folder in her hand. Her clothes looked like she had slept in them for a week. Most capital city volunteers had house-girls who dried their clothes on a large smooth river rock in the sun, so no one noticed her condition except me. I was assigned to T-group by the "Acting Director".

Katie slid back into her chair and scooted tightly against her desk in the reception area behind the 1950's-looking English switchboard.

I knew Patipati would climb out the director's open office window into the side yard of the Peace Corps headquarters. He would meet me in the Land Rover. Once I was scheduled for T-group, we could depart. As I left, I saw Katie's still elongated nipple peaking from an unbuttoned seam in her fluffy-fronted Washington, DC-type white blouse. Her bra must have been around her waist, or it was still in the country director's office. I wondered how she would solve that problem. I stopped at her desk, reached down, and buttoned her blouse, as the deputy director turned to enter his office.

With that final humanitarian act, I walked out the front door toward eight hours of sleep at Nurse Williams' still empty Peace Corps provided apartment. The potato warriors would arrive sunup the next morning.

Fourteen hours later, we were on stakeout duty. I glanced down at my watch. I calculated the potato convoy should arrive soon, barring no major road or mechanical problems, which always had a high probability in Fiji. I figured maybe another two hours. I cut the Land Rover engine to save petrol. I continued to watch the road. I listened for the new lead yellow Toyota truck the co-op had just purchased with a friendly Japanese financing plan.

An hour later, I was jolted alert. I heard the whine of the 10-truck convoy on the coast road. The trucks upshifted on the level capital city pavement after eight hours of torture on the rutted gravel national coast highway. The heavily-loaded trucks sounded great. I jabbed Patipati's arm to wake him up. I fired up the Land Rover and pulled the headlight knob. I accelerated onto the paved highway to lead the convoy into the capital city center.

I saw the first truck roar into view. It was followed by nine others. Sitting on top of the canvas covered loads of potatoes were ten ancient battle-dressed, upcountry Fijian warriors per truck. They had spears, shields, paint, and war clubs. Riding shotgun next to the co-op's number one driver, Raja, was Chief Kavula. He had a big fucking smile on his bronze-black war painted face.

He probably hadn't had this much fun since he was with the U.S. Marines as a lead scout at Iwo Jima in 1945 at the age of 16. He was carrying his favorite hand carved war club. It had been used by his grandfather who had been a cannibal for the first half of his life. Later, the British hanged his grandfather with 16 other chiefs in 1922 for failing to convert to Methodist imposed Christianity. The Brits insisted they quit their animist native religion. Their religion taught them to respect children, elders, nature, and all living things except captured enemy warriors. They regularly ate their captives after cooking them in above ground log-fired stone/earth ovens.

So, almost 50 years after the British Empire took control of Fiji's 300-plus idyllic islands, a "do-gooder" English Methodist missionary made a hit list in which the province's chiefs who hadn't publicly converted to the Methodist church were named. The missionary presented it to a British civil service officer in charge of the region. He promptly ordered a horse-mounted squadron of British army light cavalry up the Sigatoka River Valley to round up the refusenik chiefs. The army brought them to a remote village. They were bound in leg irons and wrist chains. They were given one last public chance for a baptismal dip in the river.

They refused the magnanimous British public offering en masse. After a summary kangaroo court, they were convicted of treason against the Crown for inciting rebellion. They were sentenced by a wig-head. They were hanged by the neck en masse in fall chiefly garb in the village center with half the province watching, including their multiple wives, children, and even grandchildren in some cases.

After that very religious experience, the masses of Fijians in my province attended church regularly each Sunday. They quietly practiced animism under the guidance of witch doctors and secret cult leaders. They made sure they did it at night. They used the most obscure provincial dialects so no one could decipher their activities. With independence on the way, Chief Kavula and his boys were ready to turn up the heat in the civil rights department. There was even talk of a monument to the 17 hanged chiefs at the still inhabited village where they met their savior and were admitted to heaven. Chief Kavula secretly planned to use his village's share of the co-op's potato profits to build a memorial statue for the slain chiefs.

The chief flashed a wave as my Land Rover pulled onto the coast road in front of the lead truck. The convoy slowed to a 15-mph crawl on the paved urban highway. It produced the familiar low rumble of under revving over-loaded truck engines in low gear.

It was 6:00 in the morning on a bright, almost full moon night. It was 85° with the wind about five mph off Suva Bay. It was pleasant work in shorts, a tee-shirt and flip-flops. They were the standard dress of all PCVs in the country night or day. The temperature was perfect for a potato revolution.

The Land Rover pulled smartly in front of the line of trucks. Patipati leaned out the left passenger side window. He shouted the salutation to the paramount chief required of every Fijian. He also shouted the appropriate greeting for me to the high chief and his warriors. He apologized that I was busy driving.

I did not want the convoy to stop. That would mean 100 warriors plus 10 truck drivers and one high chief would then need to be formally welcomed in a kava ceremony. This might give one of the co-op's hired Indian truck drivers time to call V.J. Singh and alert him the convoy had not stopped to unload the potatoes at the co-op shed. I knew we had potential if not active spies among the seven Indian truck drivers. They were under contract to the co-op to supplement the three trucks we owned. Some of the contract drivers drove for V.J. Singh regularly. Some were probably relatives.

Almost all the low caste Hindus on Fiji's main island had intermarried every 14 years during the past 70 years. Their eyes were definitely moving closer together with each decade of newly arranged marriages between second cousins. If the convoy stopped now, we could lose the element of surprise, and maybe the game.

I intended to run the police traffic check point two blocks north of the parliament building, if it was manned. I did not want an early morning capital city police force trainee, Fijian or Indian, to phone Suva police HQ. A report that had a convoy of 10 tarped trucks with a high chief from the southern mountain province, and 100 ceremonial battle-dressed warriors at his station would sound an alarm. We were rolling through Suva in third gear with 77 tons of potatoes to back us up as ballast.

We rounded the turn to the national market. Suva's large sleeping harbor burst in to view on the right with the national market straight ahead. The convoy drove at 25 mph. It made a loud racket in third gear on the dark, pre-sunrise empty streets. Suddenly, an empty 2-ton British Leyland delivery truck burst into view from around the backside of the paved bus parking area at the national market. It drove at high-speed ramming rate, headlights off, toward the chief's lead truck.

V.J. Singh had been tipped which I quietly computed must have occurred during the hour delay the trucks had stopped along the coast road to Suva. I would get the facts later. This maneuver demanded quick action, or my operation was lost. If Singh's truck clobbered the high chief's truck, then warfare would break out at the deserted national marketplace. We would never make it to the parliament building for our hopefully peaceful lobbying effort to block the unloading of the foreign potatoes.

My only hope was to clobber the on-rushing British Leyland delivery truck with the speedier, quicker turning little British bulldog I was driving. They would never risk guns in the capital. It was bumper car time. I had grown up driving them at every annual San Miguel, Colorado County Fair. I pulled the steering wheel hard right. I yelled at Patipati to jump clear of the Land Rover. I slowed to 10 mph on the turn. He jumped instantly as I cornered slowly.

The convoy rolled forward, oblivious to the dark headlight-less hunter that closed to 100 yards of the lead truck on a 90° intercept at 30 mph. It had two five-gallon gasoline cans strapped to its front bumper. Clever, I thought, a second baked potato recipe in just 48 hours.

The Land Rover skidded out of the slow turn. I slammed it into second gear. I accelerated toward the smaller truck's back tandem axle wheels at ramming speed to avoid the gasoline cans and spin it away from the chief's truck. The driver looked at me sideways like I was a white devil from hell the instant before I hit my high beams to blind him. I rammed my solid-steel front bumper into his back tire. He went into an instant hard right spin toward my tail. Then, with a quick downshift and stab at the brake, I disengaged and spun hard left for ten feet. I accelerated past the revolving cab of the small Leyland delivery truck. The frenzied young Indian driver fought the madly spinning wheel to regain control.

The convoy was through safely. Patipati had leapt onto the running board of the chief's lead truck. Except for a bloody left elbow and torn khaki shorts, he was fine. He was gesturing to the chief's driver, Raja, to keep rolling toward the nearby target. It was the National Parliament building's front steps. No one was going to hang these Fijian villagers again for their religious, economic, or political beliefs. Anyone who stepped in front of the potato juggernaut physically or politically would be a casualty.

I definitely wasn't in the mood to take prisoners after this latest challenge. The capital city boys had better be ready to send the foreign potatoes packing or run for election next year in a newly independent country with the ire of the Western Viti Levu Fijian village farmers. Elective democracy was a lot more fair than colonial rule with its inside deals in the capital city hotel bars. This morning was a step forward for elective democracy in Fiji.

CHAPTER SIXTEEN

THE CAPITAL STEPS

The convoy surged forward as my Land Rover regained the lead. It turned into Suva's main drag, heading for the parliament building. At 20 mph, we drove past the empty traffic control stand which was our last possible hurdle at 6:00 in the morning. We raced past the co-op department headquarters which would go ballistic in two hours. We passed the Grand Pacific Hotel where Nurse Williams last worked her occult magic on behalf of the natives. Parliament was in sight as we rolled past the National Botanical Gardens with their perfectly groomed, empty lawn tennis courts and grass bowling greens.

Suddenly, a Suva police Land Rover knifed in front of the convoy 100 yards from the parliament steps. Bad luck, I thought. I slowly braked the Land Rover to stop the column of trucks which finally came to a noisy halt 25 yards from our objective.

Two full-dressed police officers, both Fijians, climbed out of their now stopped royal blue police Land Rover. They looked over the column of tarped covered trucks with 10 warriors on each truck. One was a sergeant and the other a corporal. They were unarmed as always except for their perfectly-polished, dark hardwood nightsticks. They wore dress-blue sulus and perfectly pressed, white military style shirts. They weren't smiling as they walked past the Land Rover. After a quick glance, they approached the lead truck with Patipati on the passenger side running board. The chief was sitting inside holding a war club. His truck's 10 battle-dressed warriors were climbing from the top of the tarp-covered load of potatoes. They were preparing to defend him.

I rolled down my window to listen. It was better for me to keep out of these matters with a paramount provincial chief present. But visions of an unairconditioned, stinking Suva prison cell danced in my mind. If this encounter at 6:05 AM on the empty streets of Suva went badly and the boys decided to fight their way through, I was toast.

The corporal held a walkie-talkie in his right hand. He had not radioed headquarters, which was only a quarter mile away, for backup or to alert them of the mystery convoy. Headquarters had guns available. I prayed silently that we did not have any illegal village hunting guns hidden in potato sacks. They could be used to counterattack if armed police barracks reinforcements were brought out to turn back the potato convoy or seize it once its goal was fully understood.

Patipati was now off the truck's running board. He was standing between the ten warriors and the two Fijian policemen. All three had dropped to one knee to acknowledge that they were in the presence of a provincial paramount chief. They could only address him from a kneeling position and only when invited. The sergeant was asking permission to address Chief Kavula. The sergeant was speaking coastal dialect from our province with the right accent. This was a good omen. If this Suva police officer were from our province, or even married to a woman from our province, there was a good chance the chief could finesse him. A Fijian villager, regardless of his governmental westernized role, could never oppose a paramount chief on a provincial mission of honor.

The conversation continued between the kneeling policeman and the old chief in the cab of the new Japanese truck. Patipati now kept the gathering mob of warriors, who had descended from the other ten trucks, from advancing past him. Tension mounted minute by minute. The stalled convoy became more and more opposed to being turned back to the potato graveyard at the co-op's rented shed on the coast highway.

I could see the Aussie tramp freighter riding on its anchor in Suva harbor, waiting for orders from shore to unload. Two years' work with the co-op's potato farmers hung in the balance. A walkie-talkie call to police headquarters would be total disaster.

The chief continued to talk in provincial dialect as the two police officers continued to listen. They were getting edgy as the throng of battle-dressed warriors moved in closer with their ceremonial war clubs, shields and spears which had only been intended for our worldwide media event. I didn't have Nurse Williams' good luck Polaroid when I needed it. I had stupidly given it to the thug driver on the coast road. Fourth down and one inch from the goal line, her luck was deserting us.

So, with eyes closed, I visualized Nurse Williams one more time as the chief continued to drone in an almost ceremonial chant. The policemen couldn't speak or walkie-talkie because no one could interrupt a speaking paramount chief by custom and provincial law until he stopped talking again.

The roar of 10 truck engines broke my Nurse Williams visualization. The chief and Nurse Williams had pulled us through. I opened my eyes as the policemen mounted the running board of the chief's truck and prepared to escort it to the parliament steps.

Patipati ran to the passenger side of our Land Rover. He opened the dented, squeaky gray aluminum door. He landed with a thud safely in the passenger seat. I turned the ignition key and the Land Rover roared to life.

Patipati explained what the chief had negotiated. I shifted into first gear and prepared to lead the convoy the last 25 yards. In essence, the conversation had gone favorably. The chief ascertained, after the necessary opening salutations, that the sergeant, a commoner, but the ranking civilian police officer, was from the coastal village of Maki. It bordered our province but was technically not in it by official government mapping.

The mapping was carried out by the Brits, who didn't speak the language, but they drew the lines. However, Maki had always traded salt deposited from trapping sea water in ocean side tidal ponds for Riku style fired water pots which were made in the chief's village. Once the chief established that linkage, he ascertained that sergeant's grandmother had come from the chief's village. Fijian men by custom married outside of their native villages and often provinces to avoid genetic problems.

Fijians, unlike Westerners, trace their genealogy from their mothers. It turned out the key grandmother was the chief's mother's sister. She was also the sister of the dead "wood nymph" who I had encountered during my trip upriver to the village of Mikimiki.

Mikimiki was both the home village of the chief's mother and also the grandmother of the middle-aged sergeant. He did not live in our province by map or political jurisdiction but did by custom and tribal jurisdiction. The basic rules of the 240,000 surviving Fijians were those of one small city scattered over 300 islands.

The sergeant had asked for physical proof of the relationship. He was allowed to by custom. There were no birth certificates in Fiji, historically. The chief provided him with a distinguishing physical trait of the sergeant's grandmother in question. This was the oral tradition of proof of identity for all Fijians. The physical trait also had to be well known and visible. The chief provided a knockout from his hazy boyhood memory. The sergeant's grandmother had an inverted nipple. They were rare in Fiji, but visible since women went bare breasted in the villages. Maybe Nurse Williams was the chief's aunt reincarnated. It was a mind-blowing concept.

With this proof, the sergeant accepted the chief's command. He escorted the potato convoy to the parliament building steps before radioing Suva national police headquarters. The Fijian corporal had no other choice but to follow orders. The crisis ended as suddenly as it began—Fiji style.

CHAPTER SEVENTEEN

POTATOES FOR PEACE

During the night, while the potato convoy rolled toward the capital city, I would later learn of a secret midnight meeting which had taken place in the co-op department's conference room between the new Minister of Co-ops, Ratu Sili, a minor relative of the prime minister, and V.J. Singh, Suva's leading importer of foreign potatoes. Patipati and I had vanquished his henchmen on the trip to Suva two nights ago.

Dr. Joe was working late to prepare the annual report for his wharf-based kava co-op. It had to be typed manually before delivery to a local printer. We all did our annual reports on the department's new IBM correctable typewriter at night after the minister of co-op's male executive secretary left work.

It was also quiet at night. We could always go next door to the Grand Pacific Hotel for refreshment, then go dancing in the capital city's only late-night disco. Dr. Joe was just finishing the last section of his co-op's annual report when in walked V.J. Singh and Ratu Sili. They ducked into the main conference room after they saw him in Ratu Sili's secretary's office typing. They closed the door.

Dr. Joe remembered that the co-op minister's executive secretary had

an intercom system. It went to every room on the top floor. It also happened that the last time Dr. Joe had a meeting in the conference room, the
intercom on-off button was broken when it was activated. The executive
secretary could take notes for the co-op minister over it. It had broken with
the button stuck in the "on" position. That was two weeks ago. However,
nothing was ever repaired in Fiji on a timely basis, if at all, mainly due to
a lack of spare parts. There was an even chance the ancient British-made
intercom was still stuck in the "on" position.

Dr. Joe continued typing and flipped on the executive secretary's intercom's power switch. He listened in on the most amazing conversation. He
proceeded to transcribe it word for word. While a mile away Patipati and I
waited in the Land Rover at the co-op shed for the potato convoy to reach
the capital city.

Dr. Joe knew about the co-op's problems with the wilt-ridden potatoes
that were slowly rotting in the tropical heat at the co-op shed. After my
request by phone from Nurse Williams' apartment, he had helped persuade
the Fijian longshoremen to strike if they were forced to unload the imported potatoes from the tramp hulls in Suva Harbor. This had brought me
extra time for my plan to work.

When the conversation between V.J. Singh and Ratu Sili turned from
the usual polite Fijian style salutation to the potatoes in the tramp freighters in the harbor, Dr. Joe began to type the most remarkable off the record, totally deniable conversation. It forever colored my judgment of
business-government relationships. It ended my naiveness about politics,
money, and honor among high government officials. It was better than any
chapter in The Prince.

The engines of the convoy went silent as the 10 trucks and co-op Land
Rover semi-circled the steps of the National Parliament like a wagon train.
The two capital city policemen stepped off their respective running boards
of the chief's lead truck. They both knelt in a final salutation, then rose to
call police headquarters on the corporal's walkie-talkie. The warriors were
already on the concrete steps. They removed the tarps from the 10 trucks
and prepared to unload 77 tons of potatoes in 1,500 burlap bags onto the
Parliament steps. They planned to man this barricade night and day until
Parliament passed a ban on the importation of foreign potatoes while a Fiji
Agriculture Department study on foreign potato wilt was completed.

Ten warriors per truck began to chant ancient war songs. They were led by Paramount Chief Kavula. Detachable wooden side rails came off the semi flatbed transport trucks. The Fijian-style rhythmic unloading, always to a chanted song, began as 112 lb. bags of potatoes were tossed man to man. They could unload the 10 trucks in 15 minutes at this rate. Police headquarters reinforcements could reach the scene in two or three minutes. This presented the last real problem. Chief Kavula had used up his favors to reach the Parliament steps.

The corporal pushed the "send" button on the walkie-talkie as Patipati and I exited our Land Rover. We joined the line of Fijian warriors to help unload the chief's truck. It was all hands-on deck to save the ship. Every second counted. The corporal started to talk into his walkie-talkie, but nothing transmitted. It was business as usual in Fiji. Probably a headquarters policeman on the day shift had forgotten to recharge the walkie-talkie for the night shift.

Electricity still remained a mystery to everyone in this third world country. Storage batteries were even a bigger mystery to Fijians who simply used them up like bananas.

Fate had intervened again. The two police officers would now have to walk back to their Land Rover and drive to Suva police headquarters to make their report to the lieutenant who commanded their shift. He would then have to drive over to the Parliament steps to check out their report before he took action. That was exactly the 15 minutes the 100 ancient, battle-dressed warriors needed to unload the potato convoy and to build a barricade around the steps of the National Parliament building. Then the warriors would take up their position until the embargo legislation was enacted. Infant democracy at work was a wonderful thing.

I was happy to be in the line of warriors at 6:30 AM helping toss 112 lb. bags of potatoes from hand to hand as the tropical sunrise broke at the eastern most point of Suva Harbor. It produced an electric, multi-colored glory in the partly cloudy tropical sky. The subtle red-orange early morning hues trumpeted the arrival of the brave village potato warriors into the Byzantine complex ways of the capital city with its competing economic and political agendas. I knew the system was designed to enrich a small circle of urban players at the expense of the rural, straightforward village working masses. They lacked the same educational and social privileges. This urban class, which was led by Oxford educated Fijian Lau Paramount Chiefs with the help of Cambridge educated bureaucrats was already working to disenfranchise its own rural population in the name of economic development or greed.

The potato bag barricade was completed. The warriors moved into a defensive position. The convoy of trucks, their tarps rolled and their wood-railed sides back into place started their diesel engines. They rolled away empty in unison for their next assignment. I felt naked standing by the co-op Land Rover with Patipati after the trucks departed. I was happy to see the 1,500-plus bags of potatoes neatly stacked in zig-zag rows, forming an eight-foot wall. It blocked the steps to the main arched stone entrance of the National Parliament building.

The warriors stood on the ascending steps behind the barricade. They were picture perfect with big smiles, war clubs, spears, and shields. The chief sat cross-legged, Fiji-style, behind a large hand carved wooden kava bowl. He prepared a special mixture of highlands kava from the mountain region of our province to present to the prime minister and the capital city's other high chiefs. Since they had not invited him to the capital city, this ceremony of presenting kava to them was necessary. It covered his ass for barricading the government building.

Fortunately, the English had built the parliament building outside of any existing village site boundaries, so, technically, no one really cared anyway whether the chief had an invitation. If Parliament had been located in a village, however, we would have been already at war.

Sirens abruptly wailed as three capital city police royal blue Land Rovers cruised into view and stopped in front of the potato barricade. A senior gray-haired Fijian lieutenant, followed by the sergeant and the corporal, exited his Land Rover looking at the scene in disbelief. Chief Kavula continued to prepare the sacred kava. Patipati and I climbed into our dusty, dry-mud-caked gray Land Rover. We drove away to find breakfast at the Banana Cafe.

The chief could handle the situation which involved hours of ceremonial welcomes and discussions with other ranking chiefs. Some were high ranking government officials and Parliament members. He had two clean typed copies of the legislation the co-op wanted enacted in his sulu pocket. Katie had stayed late at the Peace Corps HQ office to type it under the supervision of Patipati after Manu, Ratu Sili's deputy at the co-op department, "failed" to submit the legislation to the Parliament.

Patipati and I pulled up in front of the Banana Cafe. The hip capital city single male Peace Corps volunteers met there for breakfast each morning. The Peace Corps doctor claimed these Suva based volunteers had a higher incidence of gonorrhea than any unit in the U.S. military. Some of these guys had butts that looked like pin cushions from the constant barrage of shots. The sailors from the constantly docking tramp freighters brought in new epidemics which spread through the capital city party girls and amateur prostitutes like wildfire. The same capital city party girls hung out with the poorer but friendlier PCVs when the docks were empty.

Dr. Joe was sitting at his favorite table. He had a giant smile on his white, thin face. Dr. Joe was a number-crunching loner who did not hang with capital city party girls. I knew something big had happened. It had to do with business, hopefully, the potato business. It was off-season for the kava business which his co-op controlled.

I sat down next to him in the outdoor sidewalk seating of the Banana Cafe. Patipati continued past us to a table occupied by Katie and a junior Peace Corps staffer named, James Smith III, from Denison, Ohio, in the heartland of the Midwest. This would piss off James, whose single goal in life was to bed Katie. He would have to sit and be polite. Otherwise, the rest of his paperwork tour as our administrative payroll aide would be in T-groups learning how to be sensitive to natives like Patipati. Sensitivity training, I believed, was vital for not only Peace Corps volunteers but for staffers. It reminded us who was in charge here as we rampaged through a third world society anchored by tribal custom and oral history.

After the usual polite jive bullshit greeting, Dr. Joe looked me in the eye once more and said, "You'd better read this now and then eat, Sundance."

My code name was Sundance, after a popular western movie of the era. Some PCVs kept waiting for me to drive a co-op Land Rover over a river bluff into the Sigatoka river ala the big screen Sundance with his horse. My exploits with the Land Rover upriver were legendary in the capital city. They had caused the country director to turn down my co-op's request for a US AID surplus V-8 Jeep. It could have extended my activities substantially.

I took the brown envelope, unlooping the string while ordering my favorite capital city breakfast from a teenage mini skirted Chinese waitress. She was a favorite of the entire breakfast group, morning, or evening. I read it quickly. I was amazed. This eight-page transcript would prove invaluable if things went badly at the Parliament steps with the chief and his boys. Dr. Joe had assisted again like a Boston Celtics guard.

I put the magic transcript back into the string-tied envelope. I stuck it in the waistband of my khaki shorts under my droopy, dusty, sweat-stained white cotton short-sleeved shirt for safe keeping. They would have to strip search me to find this prize before I surrendered it. This was the final trump card in a finesse grand slam bid bridge game.

Trouble loomed as I took my first bite of a half-peeled, fresh organic pineapple. The country director's blue Jeep with its embassy plates and American flag on the front bumper pulled into the open parking space in front of the Banana Cafe's outdoor patio. The deputy director was driving the country director. The director was supposed to be in Hawaii. They both looked pissed. The Banana Cafe was definitely not one of their breakfast hangouts.

He seemed to be looking at a Polaroid picture as he jumped from the left-hand drive American-made Jeep. He landed on the sidewalk five feet away from our table. The deputy director turned off the Jeep. It "ran on" because it hated Fiji regular gasoline. These guys would have more fun if they drove a Land Rover, I thought silently.

The director walked straight toward me. I knew he didn't have a good luck Polaroid of Nurse Williams. It probably was a picture of Chief Kavula and the warriors down at the Parliament building. I was the Peace Corps volunteer executive in charge of the chief's province's co-op, therefore, the King of Potato Land. The Polaroid was evidence against me. I wanted the photo. I had destroyed my co-op's Polaroid camera accidentally. Dianne and I had smoked a joint and done some Polaroid poses one night. We had accidentally melted down the black plastic Polaroid camera while baking some of the artistic, partially developed shots in our kerosene oven while stoned.

The director sat down. He tossed the Polaroid in front of me and a squirming Dr. Joe. He said, "What the fuck are you doing, Cooper? The co-op minister's office wants the Peace Corps out of Fiji tomorrow morning, lock, stock and barrel."

I replied, "I'm eating breakfast with Dr. Joe on the way with Patipati to the co-op's potato shed to supervise the sorting of the Valley Co-op's rapidly rotting, wilt infected potato crop. The co-op can't sell it because of the looming threat of the cheap foreign potatoes that are on the tramp freighters in Suva Harbor."

We could both see them from the Banana Cafe's outdoor terrace.

I added, "After Patipati and I finish at the shed, my boss, the chief, wants me for a press conference photo opportunity at the potato barricade with the warriors in the Polaroid. The chief plans to give Parliament his legislation for temporarily banning the importation of foreign potatoes to make sure they don't spread wilt in the future to our homegrown potatoes from the Valley Co-op."

"The chief has ordered me to back this legislation as the Co-op's Senior Operating Officer assigned to it by the Co-op Department of Fiji. I'll help explain the foreign-induced wilt problem to the English-speaking press, since the chief can only speak Fijian in public."

The director and the now-seated deputy director gazed simultaneously at me in shock. Both reached for my water glass to regain control in stunned silence. PCVs and natives playing at democracy was a new game for these guys. They mostly wanted PCVs to give shots, teach school and count fish. Their greatest fear was political involvement by a volunteer. It could lead to Washington Headquarters or local embassy involvement.

The Nixon State Department and its worldwide network of embassies considered the anti-war Peace Corps volunteers a nuisance and an embarrassment to Washington. They wanted the Peace Corps reined in fast. This was supported by the Republican political operations crooks around Nixon who wanted the Kennedy-inspired kid volunteers put to sleep in gas chambers.

I asked the director if I could keep the Polaroid for my scrapbook as I rose. Dr. Joe tried not to burst into laughter. I reminded him the press conference would be at 12 noon Fiji time. That meant the chief would be ready by one o'clock when the sun was hot and high for nice photo opportunities. Then, Patipati who had Katie in tow, joined me. We said our goodbyes as we headed for the co-op Land Rover.

The deputy director yelled to Katie and offered her a ride to the office. She yelled back that she had cramps and was taking a medical day off per U.S. Government Foreign Service Hardship Post Rules. He turned red and then gulped down Dr. Joe's half empty glass of water in one motion. We climbed in the Land Rover. As I backed up, it pinged the American flag on the front bumper of the Jeep by accident. I pulled away. I saw it dip down at half-mast in a solemn gesture to the potato warriors and the old Fijian ex-Marine chief from Iwo Jima who was too tough to surrender.

CHAPTER EIGHTEEN
THE SHED

Patipati and I arrived at the shed ten minutes later. We quickly put Katie to work typing a press release on co-op mimeograph carbon paper. I wanted to hand out copies at the press conference. It was just like Vietnam anti-war demonstrations all over again. In college, makeup-less, hairy-legged, braless freshman coeds typed press releases in the fraternity house basement for Xeroxing at the campus library. In Suva, Fiji, we worked in a leftover World War II Quonset hut built by the WW II Seabees. Now they were in South Vietnam building new port facilities as the war effort crumbled under the advancing, mindless army ants from North Vietnam. The ants had been ordered to victory or death by Ho Chi Minh and the headmen in Hanoi. This was clear to everyone in the world, except Nixon and the Pentagon.

Those poor North Vietnam stiffs routinely died in stinking, rat-infested tunnels with a carbine, a pair of shorts, and one day's rice supply. They didn't even have a dog tag to mark their passing. Lenin must be up in heaven crying at his experiment in economics gone mad in a rice-paddied vassal state of ancient China. Neither the armies of imperialism nor the zealots of Asian communism were clear headed.

This was as close as Patipati would ever get to experiencing an anti-war demonstration. I felt like a proud frat brother watching him turn the crank of the ancient British mimeo machine. Katie had clean typed the co-op's press release for the chief's press conference on USA sick pay.

The phone was ringing regularly at the potato shed selling desk. Mano, our trusted Suva clerk answered the calls. I ducked all calls. Two came in from the deputy country director. Then, bingo, V.J. Singh was on the line. The import potato king of Suva, Fiji had called me. I took it as I patted the manila folder tucked in my short's waistband under my shirt.

I wondered what V.J. Singh would say as I walked through the neat, brown burlap-bagged rows of potatoes on the way to the seller's desk. The black, brittle, ancient plastic British phone was off its hook. There were no "hold" buttons in Fiji. A caller listened to background noise or conversation until someone took the call. It was always amazing, as an English-speaking caller, what you heard if you could translate the background Fijian or Hindustani.

V.J. Singh greeted me with the usual "Nameshai," which means "hello" in Hindustani. He moved straight to the point with just a hint of veiled threat in his voice. He did not mention his burned truck. The deal was simple. He offered to buy all our co-op's potatoes at three cents a pound (which was our cost of production), if I would stop the potato war. That meant the co-op farmers would have no incentive to grow potatoes next year.

If Singh had the co-op potatoes plus the foreign ones on the ships, then he controlled all the colony's potatoes for three months. Until another shipment arrived from New Zealand or Australia, he could systematically raise the price from the prevailing wholesale level of four cents a pound to twelve cents a pound over a ten-week period. The supplies would run low and the grocers would hedge their stocks in Suva. The co-op broke even; Singh made a fat profit. I said no. He offered three and one-half cents a pound. I said no again. He hung up abruptly without even a goodbye. I knew his tactics well. His next move was going to be political and straight to my gut. He knew without me to advise Chief Kavula, the capital city Fijian chiefs could handle Chief Kavula. Singh could still win all the marbles and eliminate large scale Fijian potato farming forever.

V.J. Singh was one tough customer. He wanted to maximize his personal profit and knock his opponent out forever. I suspected I would see his mailed fist in the capital city government office. It would be straight to my jugular. I wanted to take that chance for the chief and the Valley Co-op farmers. They deserved a fair rate of return on the potato harvest from their about-to-be-independent country. Independence meant it wasn't colonial business as usual with the rural villagers be damned when they interfered with capital city deal making.

CHAPTER NINETEEN

POTATOES FOR PICTURES

The press conference was the first one in the history of the country held on the Parliament steps. The ancient battle dressed warriors manned the burlap potato bag barricade. They provided an impressive and photogenic backdrop for the chief. He stood 6'6" tall in his sandals. He spoke through a 12-volt, car battery powered mike and portable amp provided by one of his grandchildren. The grandchild, educated at the University of Hawaii, played in a Suva rock and roll island band. The car battery provided power through the entire press conference. This was a surprise. Its country cousin batteries usually died at village functions, plunging the cheap electric guitars into silence.

There was no television in Fiji. The press corps consisted of the usual suspects. They included not only newspaper, magazine, and government owned radio reporters, but also, freelance photographers. The photographers doubled as wire service reporters for Reuters, AP, and UPI worldwide telephone picture feeds.

One 16mm film crew showed up for Australian and New Zealand government TV. Both countries had an interest in the first ever revolt by their long dominated small neighbor, colonial Fiji. The noon sun appeared. It was 102° in the shade. The sun was a better alternative than the average 4-inch afternoon rainstorm.

The chief opened the press conference with a unique twist which was a Fiji style kava ceremony. He welcomed the capital city press corps to the potato barricade. This event added 15 minutes. But it established the good manners and dignity of the villagers from the province. Bowls of kava were passed out to the reporters, photographers and 200 plus onlookers. They included capital city policemen, bureaucrats from various interested government departments and the Peace Corps Deputy Country Director.

Then Chief Kavula rose from his hand-woven straw mat. He had been sitting cross-legged during the welcome ceremony behind a great hand carved, monkey wood four-legged kava bowl with a whale's tooth attached ceremonial style to its front lip. He faced the crowd.

He began to speak: "We have journeyed from the coastal mountain province of Nagoga by the Great River of God. It is our home from the beginning of man in Fiji after the ancient ones crossed the great King of Waters with the coconut palm and the pig as their only friends. The stars were their only guides in passage from the Dark Continent many call East Africa today. The ancient spirit warriors rowed the long boats—called dugout canoes today—while the women nursed their baby children and suckled the pigs. The ancient ones lived only on the fish they caught, and the cassava roots they brought from the Darkland.

"A great storm washed them naked onto the shores of Fiji. I am descended from the ancient ones. I am the Paramount Chief of my people. This government must stop the unloading of the foreign potatoes. They bring a disease to Fiji. It will ruin the Valley potato farmers on the eve of our independence from the British Empire. I want this government to stop the harm by the white colonial foreigners to my people now."

Chief Kavula stopped speaking as the reporters scribbled on their note pads. Flash bulbs popped and the potato war rose to the center of Fiji's attention. Chief Kavula was winning the war from the potato barricade on the steps of the Parliament building. He called for governmental intervention to help the ancient and hardworking village farmers from Sigatoka Valley. They were being victimized by the bullies from Australia.

One picture, as they say, is worth a thousand words. It hit the front page of the national newspaper and the wire services worldwide. The Fiji colonial government was backed into a corner when the first picture of the chief and the potato warriors was snapped. It was handed to the Fiji Times newspaper courier for quick developing for the late afternoon capital city edition. Capital city maneuvering could not get the foreign potatoes unloaded at this point. The government wouldn't dare move the chief and his warriors from the front steps of Parliament by force. They couldn't serve the Australian-led colonial business interests in the capital on the eve of independence.

I mused to myself. The Australian embassy, which was the most racist bastion of colonial bigotry on the island, must be enraged. A hick provincial grandfatherly Fijian chief just turned back a shipload of dumped export potatoes with some other old guys carrying ceremonial dance spears and shields. They couldn't touch the chief today. They would be after me when they received word of my involvement. They hated the American PCVs. They considered them dangerous hippie drug users who meddled in neo-colonial politics to the detriment of Aussie interests in this transitional colony.

They were under attack by the Japanese trading companies on one flank and the forces of Fijian independence on the other. Old and stable economic interests were in transition. The usually too drunk to think Aussies were on the way out the door in Fiji. The Aussie contingent had worn out its welcome in Fiji. Their mediocre work for excessive economic benefit was about to disappear with their Royal Yacht Club memberships.

The press conference ended when the chief finished speaking. He sat down cross-legged once again behind the great kava bowl. Chiefs didn't answer questions. This part of the press conference was directed to me. I was the co-op's executive director of field operations. I kept my answers aimed at one target, which was the embargo. The co-op wanted three months to dig and sell off the Sigatoka potato crop. I assured everyone it was ample to supply the country. This was technically true, but really a white potato lie. The tropical wilt disease was consuming the stored potatoes at an alarming rate.

I gave no signal to the bastards in capital city. Our secret plan to end the potato war would drive prices from four cents a pound retail to twelve cents a pound retail. Even with 50% loss in storage, the co-op would make a 50% profit for its member farmers after their loans, transportation and marketing costs were recouped.

I had learned in anti-Vietnam War demonstrations and debates to hang tight on the emotional and correct rhetoric. Say it over and over until everyone believed it.

A voice in my mind said: "The Aussie bastards are dumping potatoes to wipe out the local farmers. Just keep chanting, 'No more neocolonial potatoes in our homeland. Support the hardworking, patriotic, soon to be independent, hometown farmers.'"

It was easy, too easy. I said it in fifty different ways to the capital city press corps. They all finally bought it. There was no way they could reasonably disprove the negative I had established.

The negative was simple: "Foreign potatoes are bad business for Fiji." Whomever tried to prove that foreign potatoes were good business for Fiji had to hurdle the photos of the chief and his warrior farmers behind their unsold barricade of bagged potatoes in front of the Parliament building.

The Aussies who lived in the colony in their all-white residential enclaves and clubs played into the co-op's hands. If the arms merchants in the USA had been this easy to corner, the Vietnam War would have lasted about six months after the first demonstrations started on the college campuses.

As the press corps dwindled, Patipati relieved me. He answered last minute technical questions about the co-op, its members, and the potato crop. I walked to the side of the small crowd where I felt a jostle, definitely not a tap. It was a B-level Indian administrator who said the new Co-op Minister, Ratu Sili, wanted to see me in the Secretary to the Prime Minister's office at 3:30. Manu, his Deputy, was too chicken to deliver the message himself.

The first bullet struck my back as V.J. Singh went to work. He knew the pre-independence Parliament would approve the embargo on foreign potatoes for three months, retroactive a week, to keep the ships from being unloaded. If he offed me as the co-op's point man on potatoes, he might still be able to panic the farmers. He could still gain control of the potato market. The game never stopped in the capital city. Greed was king of the port city streets. Wholesale fortunes were won and lost with each arriving ship or export seasonal crop. Greed was the grease of capital city politicians. Money changed hands in brown envelopes and post-dated checks for the independence election campaign coffers of the islands' newly emerging political elite.

The press conference took an hour and fifteen minutes. The prime minister's secretary's office was in the Parliament building. I had time to kill. Fortunately, I saw Peggy Sue Moss, a Peace Corps volunteer from Key West, Florida. She was half Cuban and half Irish.

Peggy Sue worked in the National Parliament Library as a consultant on archives storage and research. She was bored most of the time. Independence was still three months away so there wasn't much to store or retrieve. Today she was wearing a blue skirt slit up the side, Hong Kong-style. It was broken by a panty line. Covering her heavy, drooping breasts was a flowered print blouse, unbuttoned to the magic cleavage line. She smiled. Her eyes locked onto me like radar as I advanced to say hello.

I said, "Hi, Peggy Sue, let's skip the sun to someplace cool and private, away from the press, and I'll tell all."

She touched my hand, winked, and led me off to the side of the Parliament building. We entered an "Employee Only" door to the New National Archives storage area. It was cool and empty, with hundreds of metal gray shelves soon to be filled with legislation. We entered her windowless office. She slammed its fire door which self-locked.

Peggy Sue said, "You and the Chief really have pulled off the event of the year. This is what the Peace Corps is supposed to be about, Cooper. I really admire you."

I thought to myself. It was getting crazier in the capital city each new trip I made from the rural river valley. Once the potato war was won, it was time for some quiet R & R on one of the island's pristine surfing beaches. Then it was time to close the Fiji chapter of my life.

CHAPTER TWENTY
POTATO STATESMANSHIP

Peggy Sue held a Zippo lighter in her right hand and lit a cigarette. I exited her windowless office in the empty archives sub-basement of the National Parliament building after a short nap. I hoped she didn't set the archives on fire. I rode one of the capital city's only elevators to the top floor of the Parliament building. The potato meeting was about to begin in the Prime Minister's Secretary's office. After my nap in Peggy Sue's office, I was on full alert. She warned me not to assume the potato war was over. She knew the building's politics.

It was time to concentrate. I patted the brown manila folder I had stuck in my waistband when I knocked on the Prime Minister's Secretary's door. It opened. The trap had been perfectly set. Ratu Levu, the Prime Minister's Secretary, the Minister of Co-ops, Ratu Sili, and V.J. Singh were in attendance. I was the expendable man. V.J. Singh had made his deal. Ratu Levu explained it to me, after the usual salutatory Fijian greetings. The co-op and its potato farmers would get one and a half months only of emergency embargo legislation. V.J. Singh would be designated as the co-op's selling agent for its potatoes in the capital city. He would also buy the Aussie and New Zealand potatoes riding anchor in Suva harbor. They would be unloaded and held in a bonded customs shed for four weeks. Then Singh could distribute them with the co-op's remaining potatoes.

Patipati and I would be reassigned to Co-op Headquarters in the capital city under the direct supervision of the new Minister of Co-ops, Ratu Sili. We would work with V.J. Singh to expedite the co-op's paperwork and shipment of the potatoes farmer by farmer as they were harvested. V.J. Singh would set the price weekly with approval of the Co-op Department. He would pay the Co-op Department, not the Valley Co-op, the farmer's proceeds as they accrued. The Co-op Department would deduct the farmers' loans for the Valley Co-op and repay the Fiji Development Bank. It would then remit the balance to the Valley Co-op less administrative fees to be distributed as profits to the member farmers.

The capital city boys had covered all the bases. V.J. Singh would help finance their campaigns next year from his profits. He had cornered the potato market until independence. The minister of co-ops could also skim money guised as administrative fees from the potato sales proceeds. The net proceeds would now pass through the unaudited co-op department bank account to the Valley Co-op's bank account for its profit distribution to the member potato farmers. Under this plan, the profits could be slim. Patipati and I would shuffle paperwork under watchful eyes at the department headquarters. We had no hope of reassignment to the Valley Co-op. The farmers would assume we had sold them out for comfortable jobs at headquarters in the capital city.

I looked at Ratu Levu, Ratu Sili, and V.J. Singh. I said, "No. This is what's going to happen, you all. Patipati and I will continue to administer the Valley Co-op's potato sales. Parliament will pass tomorrow a 3-month embargo on all foreign potatoes, including the ones in the harbor. They will not be unloaded onto Fijian soil. You can trans-ship them to American Samoa if you need a deal to save face for the Aussies and the New Zealanders. Call the American embassy. I believe they will arrange this for Fiji on the eve of independence.

"V.J. Singh is on equal footing with every other merchant in the capital city. He is now on a COD basis for the delivery of the Valley potatoes to his enterprises. The Valley Co-op will set the price for its potatoes each Monday at 9:00 AM, based on market conditions in the colony. The co-op will not raise prices more than 20% a week without consulting the prime minister's office. The chief and his warriors will stay here until the deal is concrete, just like the floor of your archives."

I felt Peggy Sue's support beaming from five floors down. I continued, "That's the deal, with all due respect to the prime minister and the Nation of Fiji."

Their reaction was quick and well-rehearsed. Ratu Levu pulled the Polaroid of Nursed Williams out of his sulu pocket. He laid it on the table for all of us to view.

He said, "We have been investigating a capital city deviant sex ring. Ratu Sili's predecessor, V.J. Singh's brother-in-law was recruited by your associate, Peace Corps staff nurse, Sheila Williams. Mr. V.J. Singh's chief driver will testify that you and Patipati ran him off the main road to Suva two nights ago. You caused him to lose control of his empty truck, which burned. Then you and Patipati sold him this pornographic picture for one-dollar Fijian, a felony in the Crown Colony. We will not arrest you. The Peace Corps country director will terminate you for return to the USA on the Pan Am Saturday flight from Nadi International Airport. Patipati will go to jail."

Every single island male set his clock around the twice a week Pan Am flights into the international airport at Nadi. Flight attendants and women tourists with American Express travelers' checks arrived in the Crown Colony. Pan Am supplied a twice-weekly fresh contingent of off-duty flight attendants who spent three days, until the Saturday flight. The party was year-round at the Nadi Sky Lodge.

I didn't want to take the Saturday flight to Honolulu, so I replied, "No deal."

I pulled out the transcript of the conversation between V.J. Singh and Ratu Sili at the co-op headquarters the night before. "Read this, gentlemen. Call me in Peggy Sue's office when you are finished. Dr. Joe has a copy, and he is sitting at the Fiji Times office with both the written transcript and a tape he made on his Sony cassette recorder. He had brought it to listen to The Band while he typed his annual co-op report last night at the co-op department headquarters."

"Ratu Sili and Mr. V.J. Singh, remember you both walked past him into the conference room. Ratu Sili, you should get your executive secretary's intercom for the conference room fixed if you want to have secret meetings. If you guys are going to control the country and fuck the rural village people, at least master the technology. Call me in Peggy Sue's office. I will wait out of the hot afternoon sun there. Call before 3:00 PM, or Dr. Joe will give the transcript to the Fiji Times for the 5:00 PM capital city final edition. You'll never find the master of the tape or transcripts. No funny business, you all."

The prime minister's secretary, Ratu Levu, was not amused. He started reading as I left. V.J. Singh and Ratu Sili were in abject shock. They stared at me with hatred in their eyes.

I picked up the Polaroid. I stood for a moment and said, "Thanks for returning this to me. I'll get you a Xerox of it for your next business trip. Like the U.S. Navy's famous Mae West poster of World War II, it's great luck."

The door slammed as I left at 2:25 PM. They had 35 minutes to play ball. Then Dr. Joe and I would expose a scandal that would rock the foundations of this about-to-be-independent Crown Colony. If the rural Fijian warrior-farmers found out the capital city Fijian chiefs were selling them out to the Indian merchants for campaign contributions, then they would burn the capital city to the ground after they ransacked it.

I exited the elevator. I knocked twice before entering the unlocked door of Peggy Sue's office. She was sitting in a yoga position. Her eyes closed while she chanted. Her blouse partially open, exposing her massive breast which hung toward her stomach. Her skirt split widely. Her knees protruded awkwardly in an almost 180° line. I locked the door. I stood facing her. I picked up her lighter which was cold. I lit a Fiji cigarette to break the silent tension.

I handed her the Polaroid of Nurse Williams. She observed with a shy sudden familiar smile. She grabbed the lighter with a sudden flick of her left hand. She lit the Zippo lighter. She set the Polaroid on fire. As its flames crackled, I felt the heat. Nurse Williams' inverted nipple disappeared forever. She sat the Zippo lighter on the cool gray concrete floor. I wondered if she would set me on fire next like Nurse Williams. Maybe there really was a bizarre secret capital city PCV led sex cult.

The phone rang. The Prime Minister's Secretary Ratu Levu's answer was swift and decisive. I held the old-fashioned telephone receiver between myself and Peggy Sue so she could share the news from the fifth floor.

He said, "Your deal is accepted by all parties. When your current tour of duty with the Peace Corps is over, you will exit Fiji for life. You will not be issued a tourist visa during your lifetime."

I cried inside knowing that meant I would never see Patipati, the chief, or my pals again after December. I said, "I accept the deal, Ratu Levu, on behalf of the Valley Co-op, its member farmers and our great Paramount Chief Kavula. Goodbye, and may God bless you and the prime minster after independence."

I hung up the phone. I called Dr. Joe. It was five minutes until three o'clock. We had a fail-safe plan for him to hand the transcript and tape to his friend, who was a Fiji Times reporter. Dr. Joe was hiding with it at the friend's house. We feared they might try to arrest Dr. Joe if he was really at the paper's capital city office. Apparently, they tried. Police searched his friend's office only minutes before the call to me in Peggy Sue's office.

I hung up after calling Dr. Joe. Peggy Sue smiled. I picked up the abandoned Zippo lighter with my right hand from the hard, gray concrete floor. I flipped it open. I lit it. We both watched the flame freely burn in the dark, windowless, silent room. Today it had burned for the good of the village people. I blew the Zippo lighter flame out and flipped he lid closed.

CHAPTER TWENTY-ONE

THE POTATO CARTEL

I took a short nap in Peggy Sue's office until about five o'clock. It was interrupted by a surprise call from the ubiquitous Dr. Joe to Peggy Sue. I left to walk upstairs to visit the chief and his potato warriors. The call revealed a capital city liaison I hadn't detected in my previous trips to Suva between Dr. Joe and Peggy Sue.

It had long assumed the nerdy Dr. Joe was celibate. He spent most of his time running the kava co-op, the wine co-op, and doing "numbers" work for the rest of the PCVs who were liberal arts graduates and understood little about the applied science of accounting. I was not going to blow his cover.

Reality hit as a blast of 100° heat and humidity greeted me. I exited the Parliament building's side employee entrance. I walked around the building's corner toward the potato bag barricade to check on Patipati and the chief. I was a little sad since I knew I would only know them for three more months. Then, I would become persona non grata in the customs entry log at Nadi airport and Suva Harbor. I couldn't reveal the details of the meeting to the chief. It would anger him, and he might start trouble in the capital city streets. The potato war was almost won unless there was another surprise attack.

I arrived at the potato barricade as Chief Kavula was drinking kava with the prime minister's liaison who had delivered him the message that the legislation would be handled in the morning session of Parliament. The barricade was only partially manned since the temperature had driven 50-plus warriors to the nearby wharf bars for refreshment. This was trouble.

Fijians never had just one beer. It was a communal society. If a Fijian ordered a beer at a bar, he had to buy all his friends one. That meant half of the potato warriors were already four or five beers deep at the bar. They were lost for the night.

I found Patipati at the rear of the Land Rover, talking to Katie. She was wearing a Hong Kong-style slit skirt and an almost see-through, sheer white cotton blouse with no bra. Patipati was lost for the night.

Patipati said, "I cut a deal with the chief that half the men could take the night shift off. The other half would man the barricade and drink kava. You stay with the chief. Tell him stories about the USA to entertain him. A tropical cotton sleeping bag's in the Land Rover. There's more OFF in the glove compartment, but we didn't bring any mosquito netting.

"The prime minister's nephew says the legislation will pass at 10:00 AM, banning the bloody Aussie potatoes. I'm going to dinner with Katie and Peggy Sue at their house in Laulau Heights, so I'll see you tomorrow."

I answered, "What a deal! I get to yarn with the chief and the boys all night in mosquito alley while you dine with Katie and Peggy Sue. Here's my Zippo lighter, you may need it for candlelight tonight. The American girls like firelight."

Katie grabbed Patipati's hand. She led him from the group, with Peggy Sue trailing. Peggy Sue glanced over her shoulder at me and smiled silently. She puffed on a Fiji-made filter-tipped Marlboro cigarette and blew a perfect smoke-ring as a farewell boding.

The girls were gone in an instant. They ran to catch a bus with Patipati to their Laulau Heights house. It overlooked the harbor's east side. Its sunrises were from heaven. Patipati disappeared. The hand-operated bus door closed. The bus spewed black, choking diesel exhaust fumes as it accelerated away.

I had to stay with the chief and the boys or they would defect to the wharf bars and V.J. Singh and his spies might remove the barricade. This could still take the pressure off the prime minister if the Suva press lost its symbol of white colonial defiance. It was better to hear the chief's tired stories for the tenth time and tell him mine for the tenth time than risk losing the potato barricade until the embargo was decreed.

I lit a Fiji unfiltered Pall Mall cigarette and walked over to the chief. I began the story of the 1968 Democratic convention in Chicago where I fought the Chicago police hand to hand. I had stomped one's face into the green grass of a downtown city park in the wee hours of the morning.

The chief always loved this story. I told him it was like fighting the Japs at Iwo Jima in their tunnels, face to face and hand to hand, until one man died, and one man lived. The chief always loved a good war story. Tonight, we were at war.

CHAPTER TWENTY-TWO
CAPITAL CITY BAKED POTATOES

awn came early. I woke up in the back of the Land Rover parked in
front of the cold, gray, quarried-stone Parliament building. My back
and neck ached from a cramped night's sleep. The cotton sleeping bag
was the only padding between my body and the riveted aluminum floor
of the Land Rover's cargo area. I was covered with dime-size welts from
the capital city fly-size mosquitoes. They had penetrated the OFF spray
repellent (it evaporated because of the 85° heat). Hot nights were standard
for the leeward side of the island. It was heavily rain-forested and received
400-plus inches of rain a year.

I climbed out and stretched my aching muscles. I realized I was dirty. I
missed breakfast at home. I finished surveying the damage to my body by
the mosquito attack. A capital city massage girl approached me on her way
home from an all-night party. It appeared from her diminutive dark Asian
appearance that she was half Indian and half Chinese. She had a beautiful
bottom and flat round cupcake-size breasts under a panty-less minidress.
It barely reached mid-thigh.

She asked me the usual question: "Mister, you want massage and
bath...maybe?"

I answered, "Yes, massage only, I have two dollars Fijian."

That was under the regular rate of $5—$10.00 Fijian these girls charged sailors and tourists. To my surprise, she said, "OK, mister, go with me now."

She walked around and climbed into the Land Rover's passenger side. She narrowly missed being hit by an early bus. I climbed into the driver's side. I fired up the gray beast's cold engine. I pulled into a now empty street.

She said, "Go Mikiki Street 44."

This was in a cheap hotel district three minutes away. The foreign sailors stayed there on shore leave in the Port of Suva. Her minidress had now managed to slide up to the top of her thin thighs. She didn't seem to care that her light triangle of silken, straight, fine black hair was exposed. It was the badge of oriental working girls in this part of the world. I shifted into third gear. Suddenly, she grabbed my left hand. She pulled my fingers down against her triangle. She pressed my forefinger slowly in a circular motion. She giggled as it pushed into an opening no rounder than a quarter.

She was trying to make an add-on sale with this free sample. It would cost the full five dollars for a bath, massage and "suck and fuck", as the sailors called it. She tightened the quarter-size opening around my finger.

She giggled, "You Peace Corps boy have all me $3.00 Fijian. I like Peace Corps boys—they clean."

She cinched the deal. I pulled my hand away. I shifted into second gear. We arrived at the hotel. She pulled her skirt down to mid-thigh.

She rented a room with a wooden shower tub in a rotting colonial hotel. It was named the South China Seas Dragon. Locally made cheap bamboo furniture was scattered in the lobby helter-skelter from a late-night party. The hotel was silent at sunrise. I followed her through the lobby, then down a narrow musty first-floor hallway to her room, number A-7. She unlocked it with a 20-year-old cast iron key. We entered together.

The wooden shower tub was in the far corner next to an open toilet. She had a six-inch pile of village handwoven reed mats in the center of the room. They served as her bed as well as massage table. Three or four colorful minidresses hung in a doorless closet over a pile of cheap sandals with straps. They were capital city disco evening wear.

She crossed the room. She expertly pulled her dress over her head on the move and tossed it toward the open closet. It was a time-honored tradition that these girls worked nude. Then, she peed and showered. She was probably 17 or 18 but it was always hard to guess since these tiny smooth-skinned women of mixed race never seemed to age.

I watched her shower. She scrubbed down with a virgin Fiji natural sponge from a nearby reef. Her lithe body glistened in the water. Low rising sunlight backlit her from a window above the tub. Everything about her was perfectly miniature and perfectly etched walnut brown. She had long straight black hair and paper moon-size eyes.

She stepped from the hardwood shower tub still wet. She beckoned me to inspect her for sores or VD, as was the custom. I approached her as she squatted to open her vagina with her small fingers. She had no sores. I knew the Peace Corps doctor had plenty of penicillin. I signaled the capital city OK sign by hand. She rose and led me to the shower tub. I stripped off my shirt, dirty tropical khaki shorts, and stepped into the cold stream of capital city water.

She entered the shower. She faced me and began to softly sponge me in broad strokes. This soothed the swollen mosquito bites. She rubbed each mosquito bite with a piece of blue coral. Then she lightly sucked the welt for a second. The pain amazingly disappeared.

Her body's proximity aroused me. When she finished the mosquito bites, she dropped to her knees and sucked me in languid strokes. My early morning erection pulsated in her soft mouth. I released in a cascade of joy. Then she motioned me to follow her. We both stepped into the room. She toweled off first. Then she toweled me dry and led me to the mats. I lay down, stomach against them. She mounted me over the back of my thighs. She began to massage my neck, back, bottom, and finally my legs. Another level of pain disappeared after sleeping in the Land Rover for two straight nights. She rose on her knees. She signaled me to turn over on my back. She began a deep finger massage of my face, neck, chest, thighs, ending with my penis, which she brought back to life with soft strokes of coconut oiled hands.

Then, without warning or hesitation, she mounted me. She trapped my penis in a room half its size with rubber bands for walls. She raised and lowered herself in some ancient Asian rhythm unknown to western women. She fondled my nipples. I came minutes later in a magic white light burst. It made her giggle, but she did not orgasm. She continued her thrusts rhythmically, pulling from me slowly. Then, she sponged me off.

It was time to pay. She would sleep the rest of the morning until the $2.00 Fijian daily rent for her room was due. Then she would start another 24-hour cycle in this backwater port. I gave her $3.00 as promised. I left to eat breakfast with the capital city volunteers at the Banana Cafe before returning to the potato barricade for Parliament's impending vote.

At the Banana Cafe, the usual suspects were having breakfast, including Dr. Joe. He wasn't talking and I didn't ask if he had been with Peggy Sue, Katie and Patipati last night. I did share with Dr. Joe the first-hand details of the meeting with the Prime Minister's Secretary, Ratu Levu, and Minister of Co-ops, Ratu Sili. I detailed the look on the co-op minister's face when I pulled out the transcribed notes of the secret meeting between him and V.J. Singh. Dr. Joe said he felt the impact. He was now barred from the top floor of the co-op headquarters building and, as he left, he saw a telephone repair team on their way into the co-op building to fix the intercom system.

Tab made a special guest appearance with the prime minister's niece in tow. The ever present plainclothes interior ministry shadow sat in an unmarked Land Rover across the street, reading the morning edition of the Fiji Times. It had a big front-page picture of the chief and his boys. Tab had a month left and he was off the rock forever. The niece would be heartbroken as planned by the prime minister and her royal parents. They probably had a political royal wedding planned for her. After Tab exited, she would get the news.

Independence meant the country's first free elections. The prime minister would press all of his eligible unmarried female relatives, including his last unmarried daughter into alliance marriages. This would tie key chiefly families in other provinces to his powerful royal family from the Fijian Lau group. It ruled the capital city and therefore, the country. The niece was enjoying her last days of capital city parties before she was paired with a backcountry provincial chief to secure a key block of votes.

She and Tab knew this, but they never discussed it. It was sad to watch the end of this beautiful cross-cultural tango from a distance. In a more perfect, idealized world, she and Tab would have married. They would have produced a stunning bevy of chocolate-colored babies in a house by a pristine white sand beach facing west to catch the greatest sunsets in the universe. But the Peace Corps was rapidly teaching me that we were on real time here. Life didn't deal anyone, even in these still, secluded, fabled islands, many favors. People who lived happily ever after mainly lived in my long-ago abandoned childhood storybooks. The rest of us took it one day at a time, even in paradise.

I finished my cup of double strong Fiji coffee. It was always too sweet from raw brown Fiji-milled sugar. It was the country's main crop which was controlled by the British. After independence, the Fijian government would run the aging obsolete mills. I said my goodbyes to Dr. Joe as I left to meet the chief and his warriors for the big Parliament vote at 10:30 AM.

I felt healthy from the full body massage, bath, pastries, coffee, and passionfruit juice. It was going to be a special day. I climbed into the Land Rover. I started it and pulled it into the already busy capital city morning traffic behind one of V.J. Singh's light delivery trucks coming downhill from the east. An omen of sorts, I thought silently. I accelerated into the early morning traffic toward the Parliament building.

When I arrived at the Parliament building, the chief and the potato warriors, who had three-day beards, were sitting on their handwoven mats, drinking hot tea with milk and sugar. The debate on the potato embargo was going to begin in about five minutes. The chief was dressed in a hand tailored light wool sulu with matching suit jacket, white shirt and tie. He looked like the American Indian chiefs in old photos in the treaty room of the White House's executive office building.

The chief wanted to enter the Parliament building, listen to the debate and monitor the voting for the emergency legislation. His presence, he felt, would stop any last-minute problems. I assured him that was a prudent plan. I watched him walk through the large carved wooden doors to the VIP visitors' gallery of the Parliament building.

Patipati had still not returned to the potato barricade. I chuckled silently thinking about his late night with Katie and Peggy Sue. I assumed he was sleeping late. There was no work until Parliament voted. Then we would load the barricade's potatoes onto the truck and ship them to the co-op shed. We would start taking orders at the co-op shed as the capital city potato stock dwindled. No new foreign potatoes were on the horizon for three months. I loved free enterprise, especially when the government protected it with monopoly legislation.

The massage and bath were wearing off by 10:30 AM. The temperature reached 95°, and clouds threatened from the west. I tired of sitting on a straw mat on the hard concrete steps and wandered down to Peggy Sue's office in search of a chair until Parliament voted.

I wasn't completely surprised to find her office empty since Patipati hadn't appeared and she really didn't have a job. I sprawled on her desk chair and dozed until 10:45.1 woke refreshed in the cool concrete archival hideaway.

I returned to the potato warriors just as the chief emerged from the Parliament building. He gave the World War II GI victory sign. The co-op's legislation had passed. We were potato kings for 90 days. A few minutes later we received a mimeograph of the Act of Parliament. It verified our victory. It provided a last photo opportunity for the chief and his warriors to demonstrate how democracy worked in the island kingdom about to be free.

Patipati still had not returned. I needed him to wrangle the chief and his boys while the trucks, which were due at 11:00, were loaded. If Patipati didn't show, the unsupervised chief and gang might drift to the wharf bars to celebrate, leaving thousands of pounds of co-op potatoes unguarded in an always hungry capital city. I went back to Peggy Sue's office to call Katie at the Peace Corps office. I assumed Patipati must be there. They couldn't afford a home phone on Peace Corps salaries.

Peggy Sue was still absent when I entered her office. I called the Peace Corps main number. The new nurse answered the switchboard phones. She said in a pissed-off voice that Katie was AWOL.

I returned to the Parliament steps as the first truck arrived. I assigned one of the chief's older sons to supervise loading it while I went to retrieve Patipati at Peggy Sue's house. I assumed he was still sleeping. It was a five-minute drive east to Laulau Heights with light traffic at 11:00 AM in the morning. I figured a 10-minute round trip to get Patipati back in action. Then, I could go to the co-op shed and supervise the pricing of our current potato stocks. We were now a monopoly. I passed the empty Banana Cafe a minute later on the turn to Laulau Heights.

Five minutes later, I parked in front of the small, white stuccoed concrete block house Katie and Peggy Sue shared. It was quiet. The shades were down. I honked a warning. I exited the Land Rover and headed to the door. I knocked loudly, but no one answered. On the fourth or fifth knock, the unlocked door jarred open. I walked into the house to wake everyone.

I stepped into the sparsely furnished living room. I was shocked beyond belief at what I saw. Three nude figures lay sprawled feet to feet in a star configuration. Their pubic hair had been burned ash gray. They were not breathing or moving. All three were blindfolded with their hands tied behind them. They all had bruise marks on their necks. An open Zippo lighter lay on the floor next to them. Patipati, Katie, and Peggy Sue were all dead. Tears welled in my eyes for my dead best friend and the two women. They were all too young, too energetic, with too much future too die. Then, the crime scene made me vomit and I gagged violently.

Something had gone drastically wrong during the night. I needed expert police help fast. Was this a failed capital city sex cult ritual gone madly astray? Had my friends been murdered? I choked back tears. I blocked an impulse to touch Patipati and the women to comfort them in death. I knew from mystery novels I shouldn't disturb this hideous crime scene before the police investigators arrived. I was frozen in the door. I continued to sob. I looked at my dead friend who had traveled at my side for two and a half years through the wilds of Fiji. I couldn't believe what I saw. Peggy Sue had celebrated the potato victory with me only yesterday. Patipati was dead on the day of our province's biggest victory—the day we won the potato war with Chief Kavula, the valley's villagers, and the co-op.

There was no phone in the small house. I closed the door and ran to the Land Rover. Tears streaming, I fought for control. I started the Land Rover. I drove fast toward the Peace Corps office. I thought it better as a Peace Corps volunteer and a foreign national to make this call with the country director to the still English head of the colonial-run national police force in the capital city.

This call had huge potential international ramifications because of the deaths of a female Peace Corps volunteer and a Peace Corps staffer who was a genuine U.S. Government employee. Under the circumstances, there was no time to warn Dr. Joe. I had heard him talk to Peggy Sue yesterday. If he had been there last night, he had luckily missed death. I prayed Dr. Joe had not been there because he could become a suspect in the case. The Minister of Co-ops, Ratu Sili wanted his ass for the transcripts that had helped win the potato war.

A minute later, I pulled into the deputy director's vacant parking space at Peace Corps headquarters. I turned off the engine and collected my thoughts. I remembered the prime minister's secretary and co-op minister knew I was in Peggy Sue's office yesterday. They called me there. That wasn't unusual since all the Peace Corps volunteers with business at the Parliament building used Peggy Sue's office as a hangout. She was the only PCV that worked in the building. She had an office phone which was a rare commodity for PCVs in Fiji.

No one knew about the Dr. Joe link but me. I decided to tell the country director that I had gone to pick up Patipati at Katie's at 11:30 AM and that the pick-up had been pre-arranged the night before. I had stumbled into the most bizarre numbing scene of my short life. In two minutes, the country director was going to be in the depths of a crisis and riding a hurricane. He had to call the national police commander's office, then Washington D.C., and the U.S. Embassy. Yesterday's potato headlines were like a campfire. This Dresden-like firestorm was about to engulf the capital city and the American Peace Corps.

CHAPTER TWENTY-THREE

DEATH IN PARADISE

I drove on the mid-section of the coastal mountain road back to the Sigatoka co-op headquarters. I replayed the events of the past week in my mind. Like an old cow horse on its way to the barn, the Land Rover lurched left and right on the always muddy, twisting, narrow graded gravel road through the last of central Viti Levu's rainforest. Finally, I crossed to the more arid windward side of the island.

The Police inspector general had personally come to the Peace Corps headquarters. He drove me and the visibly shaken country director back to the death scene. The deputy director stayed behind to calm Katie's now hysterical co-workers, including the early arrived new nurse.

When we arrived back at the Laulau Heights apartment, ten or so Fijian policemen in uniform plus three dress blue-sulked detectives were at the very chaotic crime scene. A hundred plus neighbors and capital city drifters had gathered. The same half-dozen capital city photographers who had been at the potato press conference the afternoon before were there. They vied for position behind the police barricade. Ropes had already been strung to keep the restless mixed-race crowd away from the small house.

I retraced my earlier trip from the Land Rover to the front door. The inspector general, a former Scottish detective general from Edinburgh, listened carefully while a Fijian detective took notes. When we reached the now open door, I looked into the living room again where the still nude dead bodies lay. I watched the police pathologist and the chief coroner direct a crime scene photo session.

Common law was common law, whether it was Fiji, London, or New York City. It was like watching an all-black cast do a Dragnet episode, except one of the dead bodies was your best friend. It was eerie and surrealistic as I stared at the motionless nude bodies on the bare polished wooden floor.

All the bodies had the same gray ashen pubic hair. That made them appear surrealistically old from the waist down, except Katie—she had apparently shaved her pubic hair to wear her infamous Aussie mini-bikinis on Suva Yacht Club trips. Her pubic hair stubble produced a Seurat-like field of gray-ash dots. She faced the open door in her grotesque death pose.

I gathered from the police chatter that all three had sex together. Shortly after, they had been strangled. Then their genitals were torched with the Zippo. It was aided by lighter fluid. The Zippo had one smeared oily fingerprint on it. It was on the way to the national police lab.

The group had died around five o'clock in the morning. There had been a fourth person present. All three had been bound and gagged the same way. The police were already speculating on the mysterious rumored capital city sex cult, the same one that had extracted the Super Boss' testicle. So far, their investigation had produced no leads beyond Nurse Williams. She had simply disappeared without a trace.

It was a perplexing and deeply disturbing scene. I stood in the doorway and scanned the dead bodies for clues to their tragic end. Only Dr. Joe knew about the gathering and he was not capable of swatting a fly. At breakfast, he had clearly given no sign of being here at 5:00 in the morning.

All the bodies were completely nude. None of their clothes were in the living room. I surmised they must have made love in the girls' shared single bedroom. Therefore, it followed logically they were forced into the living room later and murdered. Every PCV in Suva I knew slept in the nude. Patipati, like all Fijians, slept in a sulu. There was no sulu in the living room. The burnt pubic hair was senseless and sickening. I wondered if it was a warning, revenge, or a just a sick act by the capital city sex cult, if a cult existed. Was the missing fourth person an untested cult member or recruited stranger who was psychotic?

The murders were terrifying, but I still couldn't tell the Fijian police the Nurse Williams/Super Boss secret. I silently hoped they didn't connect the Polaroid of Nurse Williams to me. Fortunately, Peggy Sue had burned it. But why had she? A connection could narrow the sex cult theory investigation prematurely. I had learned time after time, Fiji was a very small place. It was possible someone in Laulau Heights had seen or heard the fourth person come or go from the crime scene. Hopefully, information would surface quickly.

Dr. Joe had arrived at the edge of the police barricade. I took a last look at the dead trio. I walked back to the barricade to talk with him. I told him we needed a private talk. We walked to the rear edge of the crowd. I saw the Peace Corps country director give the Police inspector general my passport.

Dr. Joe was stunned and in tears. He listened as I told him I had overheard his call to Peggy Sue.

He said, sobbing quietly, "Yes, I've been seeing Peggy Sue for a year at least. As you know, I've never dated anyone here. I'm too busy with my co-op's work and helping all of you guys do your co-op books and annual reports. I don't like the capital city disco and party girl scene. I was going to stop here around eleven last night after I finished proofing Jim Thompson's annual report on the Lau Fish Co-op. It has gotten weird lately since Katie moved in with Peggy Sue.

"Katie is bi-sexual. Starting last month, they made me watch Peggy Sue give Katie head; then, Katie gave Peggy Sue head. Peggy Sue gave me head. It took an hour or more, but then to get Peggy Sue to orgasm after Katie gave her more head, Katie warmed up Peggy Sue's Zippo lighter. She pressed it against Peggy Sue's clit. This excited Katie. She pressed it against her clit. I was getting no sleep until 2:30 or 3:00 AM after I got back to my apartment in western Suva near the co-op's potato shed. So, I blew off the eleven o'clock meeting you heard about on the phone so I could get a full night's sleep. I had a nine o'clock meeting at the wharf with the deputy customs inspector on new procedures to clear Pacific Island Kava shipments."

Dr. Joe paused for a moment, then continued, "I also figured Patipati would be here since Katie started laying him. I knew you guys were still in town. He's the only guy on the island who's touched Katie, according to the capital city gossip. Katie did Peggy Sue, and she did Nurse Williams until she left, but no guys until Patipati. I didn't want to be part of a foursome last night. I'm beginning to wonder if that's why I'm still alive."

Dr. Joe paused again, sobbing, shocked, and stared at his flip-flop clad feet. He continued, "I'm going to tell the police I dated Peggy Sue because the neighbors saw me come and go. The police will find out sooner or later, so better now. By the way, Katie's got a past. She gave milk when she first arrived. Peggy Sue sucked her regularly. She either had a baby in D.C. or a miscarriage before her arrival in Fiji. She offered her milk to me. I declined."

This little bombshell dovetailed with a bit of information Tab had recently received from a friend back at PC HQ in Washington, D.C. He told me to be cautious around Katie because she was a long-time main squeeze of our single country director. The relationship had started during his staff days in Washington headquarters when she worked as a high school intern. The warning to Tab was to let us know anything we said around her was presumed to be pillow talk to the director. According to Dr. Joe, she wasn't doing the director in Fiji, only women, until Patipati arrived. Now I knew why the country director was so shaken.

I wondered if she and the director had aborted a baby before her sudden appearance as our new Suva HQ secretary. Also, Dr. Joe had not mentioned a sex cult of any kind. Clearly, his interaction with Peggy Sue had been needy and straightforward until Katie had arrived. Then, the girl-on-girl-on-boy sessions capped by the bizarre use of the Zippo lighter began. I didn't know that Nurse Williams and Katie played together until today.

Dr. Joe looked at me totally distraught. Here was a problem he couldn't solve for me or the Peace Corps with a calculator. He said, "I'm really going to miss Peggy Sue because she loved me like my junior high math teacher, Mrs. Accorn."

With that, he left to find the country director and the inspector general to tell them about his sexual link to Peggy Sue. She had replaced Mrs. Accorn, his clearly influential junior high math teacher. As Dr. Joe walked toward the capital city police barricade, I wondered if he had ever really gotten laid. I knew Dr. Joe was a dead end for the police in this case.

I made a mental note to give him the name and hotel room number of my morning's surprise masseuse. She was sweet, liked PCVs, and Dr.

Joe would still need some secret sex until he got off the rock after Fiji Independence Day.

A week later, I was thinking as I down-shifted into second for an uphill 100° turn in the co-op Land Rover that it now always seemed empty without Patipati in the passenger seat. His ghost, though, traveled with me. I could sense its cold presence next to me on the drive. His ghost had stayed with me to help me solve his murder.

The murders perplexed me. The police had developed no leads. Someone was being paid to keep quiet. I knew in the crowded, hot Laulau Heights, with its open windows, someone knew who had visited the three victims that fateful tropical full moon and high tide night. It had been almost daylight that night in the fresh clear tropical air. Three clues circulated through my brain.

One clue was that the prime minister's secretary, Ratu Levu, and the co-op minister, Ratu Sili, who was allied with V.J. Singh, called me in Peggy Sue's office. Bored PCVs regularly camped there. Had her lines been tapped because PC volunteers made calls from her office while in the capital city? Was V.J. Singh aware of this? Secondly, the autopsy revealed two razor-like cuts. One was on Peggy Sue's breast and one on Katie's neck. They could have been made by razor knives or switchblades which the Indian thugs carried in the capital city. The Fijians always carried machetes. Also, apparently, Katie used an electric razor to shave her pubic hair. The police found no razor blades in the women's apartment. Peggy Sue, like most PCVs and Fijian women, didn't shave her legs or underarms.

Also, I remembered, in my encounters with Nurse Williams, and in Dr. Joe's rambling discussion of his sex with the women, no knife had surfaced except the surgical one Nurse Williams used to partially castrate the Super Boss.

The razor blade cuts had to be linked to the murders. The razor knife or the razor-sharp knife had to have been brought to the murder scene. The girls must have sustained these cuts as they were forced at knife point from their bedroom to the living room to join Patipati. It now seemed he was killed in his sleep in the living room where he had apparently passed out. His blood alcohol level was .26, or two times the U.S. standard for drunk driving. He had also been smoking pot after two sleepless nights. That explained why his body showed no signs of struggle. He was suffocated in his drunk, drugged sleep by the intruder.

He was taken by complete surprise or there would have been a fierce fight. He had no tolerance for pot or alcohol, only kava. The girls had not realized this. They had carelessly destroyed their only defense.

The women had no alcohol in their blood, but lots of pot. They had slept in Katie's single bed together. It was unmade and semen spotted the sheets, according to the lab report. It had been determined by Fiji's chief pathologist that Katie's vagina contained semen from a Fijian male. Horribly, her pubic hair had been sprayed with lighter fluid. It was set on fire while she was alive and gagged. She had bitten her tongue almost in half from the pain.

It had turned out there was no semen in Peggy Sue. She had been sprayed with lighter fluid, also. She had been set on fire while still alive. She had bitten her lower lip severely before she was suffocated. She had also probably listened to Katie die first. Her death was one half hour later.

Patipati never had a chance, according to the police report. He was already dead when the girls were forced from bed at knife point into the living room to be killed and placed in the circle.

The police were more convinced than ever there was a capital city sex cult. They hypothesized that the girls, having failed to attract Dr. Joe to the party, dangerously erred and invited a deviant islander who psychotically turned on the group.

Another theory ran through my mind. I sensed the urgency in Patipati's silent ghost who still guarded me after his death. I had decided I would make a trip to the island of the fabled Fijian firewalkers. There, I would purify myself while I surfed. I would firewalk and cleanse my mind to seek the answer to these murders. I would strike at the perpetrator. First, though, it was a few weeks of peddling potatoes at the highest price possible to get the co-op out of debt and make a few dollars profit for its loyal members. I owed this to Patipati. He had worked so hard to convince the Valley Co-op farmers to grow this first ever potato crop.

I also had unfinished business at home. Dianne only had a month left on the rock. She was leaving for medical school. Also, the co-op minister had made it clear after the murders he wanted me out of Suva until I boarded a Pan Am flight and left Fiji forever. No more potato warriors were going to be tolerated with the Union Jack coming down. The capital city Lau Island-bred, Oxford educated royal chiefs were taking control from the British. The provincial chiefs were left out in the cold again. To ensure the provincial chiefs stayed docile, their Peace Corps co-op advisers were not being replaced when their tours of duty ended.

I drove back with one more trick up my sleeve. Then I was going surfing and maybe firewalking. I had one more score to help the co-op farmers settle. It was tobacco planting season and my farmers had been ripped off annually by an Anglo-American tobacco company. The company-controlled cigarette production and distribution in Fiji. Patipati and I had planned for a year to have the co-op farmers strike this planting season for higher contract prices. This would cripple the worldwide company's Fiji production.

I owed it to Patipati to start this one last war. I wanted to fuck the corrupt capital city politicians and business interests one last time. Four weeks was the exact amount of time I needed to do it.

The Land Rover whined, and loose gravel sprayed in a steady stream from the off-road tires as I shifted into fourth gear overdrive for the first time since I left Suva. I drove the flat western side, dry, dusty road at 50 mph, leaving a quarter-mile dust cloud behind the gray, mud-splattered Land Rover. I rocketed toward home. The ghost of Patipati rode shotgun.

CHAPTER TWENTY-FOUR
EQUILIBRIUM

It was great to be back in my home province. Life was always slow, basic, and uncomplicated, until capital city politics intervened. I stood by the potato sorting machine with its trays, belts and electric motors and watched the last of the valley potatoes roll through to the dwindling supply of reused burlap bags. We now owned 90% of the colony's burlap bags. They had housed the largest potato crop by the power of a thousand ever produced on a South Pacific tropical island. We had bought some of these burlap bags back six times from the retailer shopkeepers who sold the potatoes to the consumers of Fiji.

The island recycled everything constantly, from burlap bags to glass jars. Fiji produced little for itself in the way of manufactured goods. The system worked since the tropical weather eventually reduced everything to dust, rust, or sand. It taught me how wasteful the U.S. economy had been during the '50s and '60s in a world sense. The throwaway, oil-driven economy of the U.S. was out of balance. The great stopwatch in the sky was already running.

Potato profits were spectacular with the price rising to 12 cents a pound. The co-op farmers had paid off their loans to the Fiji Development Bank and made a nice profit. The last truck of harvested potatoes was unloaded from a co-op member's valley field. I watched the slow, bumping, moving lines of potatoes on the sorting machine. They reminded me of the faces of the PCVs that had helped this great marvel of Fijian agricultural progress.

A lumpy potato reminded me of Nurse Williams as it rolled down the undulating belt. I walked over to the last burlap bag. I painted a red "N.W." on it with a bag marker before it was slipped onto the machine to be filled. The ghost of Patipati was always in the potato sorting shed. The police had still not come up with any clues that led to the murderer or murderers of Patipati and the PCVs. They still believed the capital city sex cult theory. I heard they were even sending a detective to find Nurse Williams. The Peace Corps still could not find her in the U.S.

I knew information that Peace Corps Headquarters, Washington, never turned up in their FBI Peace Corps background check. Nurse Williams was a member of an elite 5-person cell of an underground SDS faction. It was known by the code name EQUAL. It planned to blow up President Nixon if he was re-elected in 1972. She had joined the Peace Corps after an FBI informant had infiltrated her cell. He was dead. I discovered Nurse Williams' little secret by accident that last night we spent together.

In the glimmer of the room's bedside electric light, I saw an indigo ink tattoo with the letters EQ on her inner thigh. I popped the question and she answered. She gave me a brief description of the group, without telling me its members' names or its location. She told me the story of discovering the FBI informant a month before Nixon's first inauguration—a day before she was planning to propose to the cell that it bomb the inauguration to set off a civil war in the U.S. I knew then I had chosen the right warrior to demolish the Super Boss.

When I heard a detective from Suva was searching for Nurse Williams in the U.S. to interview about the capital city sex cult, I silently laughed. It was September of 1971. Nurse Williams had returned to prepare for the revolution. The Fiji police had no chance of finding her in the USA as the Vietnam War continued and Nixon prepared to run for re-election. Somewhere in the U.S., Nurse Williams was re-forming the EQ cell.

I wondered whether Katie had been an FBI or CIA informant, sent to Fiji to look for Nurse Williams or radicals in general. The Nixon thugs believed many radicals were hiding in the Peace Corps and the domestic Vista operations. Had a plan to murder Nurse Williams accidentally swept up Peggy Sue, Patipati and Katie? Had Nurse Williams discovered betrayal by Katie before her departure and ordered her killed by an agent left in place in Suva? Had Patipati and Peggy Sue been haplessly present with Katie when the agent intruder, acting under Nurse Williams' orders, terminated Katie? Was Katie just the country director's ex-girlfriend on a South Pacific vacation after an unwanted pregnancy? It was a theory, but not a solid one, I thought.

The ghost of Patipati lingered near the last bag of potatoes I would see loaded in Fiji. I was sure Nurse Williams had told only me of the EQ cell after my accidental discovery. We were bonded by sex, capital city intrigue, and mission. A co-op worker sewed the mouth of the last burlap bag of co-op potatoes. I paused as the Nurse Williams memorial red N.W.-marked potato bag was loaded onto the last co-op transport truck. She was headed for an OK Corral of historic proportions if the railroad-hired posse didn't find her first. My own next gunfight was here. Then I had to solve Patipati's murder.

My thoughts were interrupted by the ringing of the potato shed's ancient British black, hard, brittle plastic phone. It finally arrived a week before the season ended. They still couldn't mold a decent plastic telephone 70 years after Bell or install it on time. This puzzled me still as I walked over to take a call from the Fiji manager of the Anglo-Aussie Tobacco Company.

I heard the yellow Toyota semitruck loaded with potatoes shift into third gear. It accelerated toward Suva, past old Chief Kavula with the cheering potato warriors. They had come to see the last truck depart and meet on the co-op tobacco strike. Then they planned to drink a few Fiji beers with their profits at the local men's only hotel pub. I was going to get drunk with them. That meant no sleep for 24 hours, but it would be a whole lot of fun. Potato season was over. The home team had won the championship.

CHAPTER TWENTY-FIVE
WHERE THERE'S SMOKE THERE'S FIRE

My head pounded in the hot noon tropical sun as I walked through a plowed, ready to be planted tobacco field with Chief Kavula and a couple of famous potato warriors. I drank beer and rum last night until the mandatory midnight closing of the town hotel pub. The pub was divided into two sections. One side was for the village Fijians who stood and drank until they dropped. One side was for the Aussies, New Zealanders, Brits, and stray Americans. The Aussies sat and drank until they dropped. Also, separation was now by custom, not by law. Independence was near.

Women couldn't drink in either section. They could get a cocktail in the dining room, or hotel lobby lounge. They were served on a silver tray just like teatime. In this remnant of the British Empire, ladies didn't drink in pubs whether white, black or red. However, feminist Peace Corps volunteers crashed the sit-down pub on Saturday afternoons after marketplace shopping. They ordered draft beers at the "Peace Corps table". They defied anyone to stop them from becoming serious tropical alcoholics, like the males on the island.

I had tossed a few in the sit-down pub with the local Brit banker. He was still amazed the co-op had paid back its Fiji Development Bank guaranteed loan to him. Then I drank with the chief and his potato warriors in a rolling brawl until closing time in the stand-up pub. My brain paid the price. Fiji beer was double the strength of the U.S. species. I also washed down 150 proof shooters of Fiji dark rum. This cheap, convenient by-product was from milling sugarcane. Sugarcane was the island's main crop and key to Fiji's export economy.

Sugar was still the king. There wasn't a Peace Corps volunteer within 100 yards of that bastion yet. The big time colonial white boys still controlled the mills until independence. After independence, they would be forced to sell them to the Fiji government at book value plus 10%. Until then, no help was needed. The 100 year-plus exploitation of cheap Fiji land, labor, and sunshine produced an unending supply of cheap sugar for the world market. Its by-product, rum, was for local consumption.

Nothing had changed in the 100-year-old British milling operation, except that they didn't trade the rum for black slaves in Africa anymore to sell to other British colonies. The current fire water was sold at rock bottom prices to the natives to keep them complacent. The tourists paid top prices for it in their fresh fruit punch drinks at the pricey beach tourist resorts. Some of the male tourists were apparently rendered impotent by Fiji rum during their holiday stays. Even Chief Kavula and his warriors trolled for women tourists on their occasional fishing trips to the beaches near the resort hotels. I had to get them real drunk to tell me their stories. The Fiji warriors were the secret favorites of some wannabe-liberated women from down under who endured working alcoholic husbands most of their lives.

Sport fucking was a good way to pass the time around the island's resorts with partners changing every three or seven days, depending on their package travel plan. Abortion was legal in Australia and New Zealand, so no one worried about the consequences. It was presumed the renegade American girls who participated were on the pill. It was America's first attempt at birth control in its 200-year history of manifest destiny.

Kavula, who was tromping through the freshly plowed field toward the shade of a palm tree at the river's edge, was mentally and physically remarkable. The chief was 71 years old, but was a testimony to natural foods, fresh air, and outdoor living. The chief reached the grove of palm trees by the sandy beach. We all sat. We talked over the nearby rushing river water that irrigated the tobacco fields. I explained to the chief the meeting with Mr. Biggs had gone badly at Anglo-American Tobacco. He refused any changes in the new 5-year contract. He argued world tobacco prices were falling and inflation was rising in Fiji as independence approached. Inflation meant living wages for the island's farmers and labor. It was not real inflation in an economic sense. One man's inflation was another man's full plate at mealtime. He argued the Fiji-grown tobacco was used only for locally made cigarettes. They were very cheap by world standards.

This fact had prompted a secret investigation, by one of Patipati's former schoolmates at co-op headquarters, of Fiji tobacco distribution. It was technically outside the co-op department's purview. However, the co-op's member farmers grew tobacco for additional cash income and personal consumption. Nobody here had thought about lung cancer.

The investigation, with the usual bailout from Dr. Joe, showed huge secret shipments of valley grown premium tobacco passed through the Fiji Royal Customs shed in Suva to Australia. It was "bartered" pound for pound for incoming shipments of poor quality, reject Aussie tobacco. Poorer quality Fiji tobacco stayed at home. It was blended with poor quality Aussie tobacco for local cigarette sales. The prime Fiji tobacco bought by the company at 2 1/2 cents a pound was shipped to the world market. It was sold for 80 or 90 cents a pound. These guys were making a double killing. They also had a monopoly colonial government license to manufacture cigarettes in the islands.

I showed Chief Kavula the pilfered customs documents. Dr. Joe had no access to a Xerox machine at his wharf office. I explained the scam to the chief. He was pissed. Flush from the potato victory, he promised to call a tobacco strike at the general co-op annual meeting the next week. The Fijian farmers would get a new price of 10 cents a pound. Otherwise, they would refuse to plant this year.

He would send word to the province's Fijian village farmers by bamboo wireless tonight. He would also tell the neighboring independent Indian farmers to stop planting. No one was to sign the new contract. If any farmer broke ranks before the vote at the co-op's general annual meeting, he would call the potato warriors to action. They were bored after their last insurrection and subsequent return to village life. They planned to machete the tobacco seedlings if they were transplanted from the companies' white cotton gauze covered seedling beds to plowed fields. A new and fair tobacco contract had to be won.

I saw a black cloud heading toward me again. I hoped no farmer planted a tobacco seedling. Five hundred plus co-op members grew for the
company along the 30-mile stretch of the fertile river valley. I had four
weeks left in the province. Dianne was training her medical center replacement. Then she finished her Peace Corps assignment. I wanted to spend
time in the province saying goodbye to friends and preparing the co-op for
life without me and Patipati after the independence celebrations. Then I
needed a month to visit the Island of Fire.

A tobacco war could get out of hand quickly in the multi-racial valley.
Tensions were already mounting as independence approached. Both sides
realized the 100 years of English refereeing, good, bad, or indifferent, was
over. The Fijians were getting edgy. They realized they had the Indians at
their mercy. They wanted all their land back. Much of it had been leased
at pennies an acre in the 1880s and '90s for 99 years. Most Indian farmers
were ten assignable sub-leases away from the original leases. They had
rented their farms for decades. They were panicked by real Fijian control
of Parliament, the army, the courts, plus the Native Land Trust Board. The
Board administered the leasing of native communal land. Almost all of Fiji's land was leasehold, not freehold under common law broad form deeds.

Fiji was like a giant U.S. Indian reservation with a lot of 99-year land
leases. The leases were about to terminate. The "Reservation Indians" or
Fijians were getting their freedom in three months and retaking control
of the reservation. The reservation would start being a real country again.
There were a lot of old scores to settle when the bell finally tolled. The tobacco contract could be dicey. The chief was strengthened by his victory in
the potato war. The Fijian farmers had money in their khaki shorts' pockets. He could use the tobacco contract to exert control over the retreat-
ing white colonists. He could leverage the valley's Indian farmers. They
farmed leased provincial Fijian owned farmland. His warriors could work
off a little restlessness with a machete attack on a tobacco field or two. I
was in the point position—expendable as always—since I was departing
before independence.

The chief liked this game. I would negotiate. He would lead. His boys
would threaten. The valley would be tense until a favorable tobacco contract was signed. It was this game or hang out at his village or the nearby beach resort hotel. The chief was getting old. He didn't have many
winters to live, which was the season ancient Fijians died in their bures

from pneumonia with their extended families present. Great-grandchildren kissed them goodbye as they shed the physical world for the spirit world of the village forests.

This year the chief and his warriors would pass up the beach blanket bingo game to settle an old score and prepare for a new order. There would be a more equitable tobacco contract. They would shut down Anglo-American tobacco. I feared they might burn its gas-fired curing barns to the ground, if necessary. Five years from now they could simply nationalize it. Now a better contract was the dangerous game.

We passed a cigarette pack around. We all smoked one of Anglo-American's premium cigarettes made in Australia. We now knew it was made partially with contraband Fiji tobacco. After the customary "Bula Talle" ("hello again"), I walked across a freshly plowed tobacco field to my Land Rover. The chief stepped onto a bamboo river raft. Four of his warriors poled him upriver for a night in one of the villages he ruled.

The sun was setting in both my side and rearview mirrors in brilliant hues of navy, red, blue, black, and purple. I cruised down the freshly graveled valley road at 45 mph toward home. I whistled an old cowboy song, "*Git Along Little Doggie*," as I contemplated life.

I had become, in the islands, a disciple of the sexual revolution. I realized the twists and turns of my 25-year-old life were too vicious to share. Fiji had unleashed a hidden energy in my soul. I knew I would be best solo on the trail ahead. Like a guerrilla on the Ho Chi Minh trail, I wanted to be able to travel fast, strike quickly, then fade into the bush—shadow dancing in the steps of the main force units of a growingly arrogant western capitalism and Soviet communism. Their feet of clay were going to be tested violently and often in the final three decades of the twentieth century.

The sun sank over a mountain, etching the river valley's winter brown hues into my memory. The Land Rover screamed in fourth gear toward many more important meetings with destiny.

CHAPTER TWENTY-SIX

GOODBYE GOLDEN TRIANGLE

Life at home after the potato wars in the capital city was strange and definitely temporary. The first week back was a trip into the Land of Oz. I had slept either in the Land Rover or at the co-op's potato shed in its military barracks style wing which served as a boarding school for the National Co-op Extension courses. A comfortable bed in a house with Dianne's famous Peace Corps' "just like home" meals was very appealing.

I mentally debated when to break the news. I thought our relationship should terminate with the completion of her PCV Fiji assignment. Better to say goodbye tearfully at the Nadi International Airport than to return home and breakup slowly. However, I wasn't prepared for the surprise attack which started seconds after I parked the mud-caked gray Land Rover in the front yard of the clapboard house after meeting with the chief.

Sitting in a newly arrived giant hanging Chinese-style chair basket, Dianne was nude from mid-stomach down, wearing only a sheer cotton halter top. It show-cased her golden-brown nipples. She was sipping a very dry martini in a real martini glass. Things had apparently changed while I was in the capital city.

She huskily bellowed a hello across the small room. She beckoned me to sit on a mat facing her at her feet. She had freshly painted, shockingly bright red toenails. I sat cross-legged, Fiji style, eye level with her knees.

They touched, closing her thighs tightly. This blocked my view of all but the top of her golden-triangle mane.

She said, "I know this part of our life and our relationship is over. Let's go out in style. I want to attend biology graduate school and then medical school, Cooper. You're too much baggage for the trip. I received a letter of acceptance from Harvard for their advanced biology graduate research program a week ago. I have already arranged with Peace Corps Headquarters to leave two weeks early."

The loss of Katie and Nurse Williams had ended my quick access to Peace Corps Headquarters information. I had heard nothing about this while in Suva.

She continued, "Your Nurse affair in the capital is common knowledge. There is even a rumor among the Peace Corps volunteers that you are linked to a sex cult and that somehow you are involved secretly in the murder of Patipati, Katie, and Peggy Sue. More probably, you were the intended victim because of your involvement in the potato war and your association with Tab."

Out of the mouths of innocents sometimes comes a vital clue. I was stunned, both by the dismissal I had received and her murder theory. I had never deduced that someone was after me. They instead snuffed out Patipati and the women, either as a warning or while waiting for me. A chance encounter with the massage girl had probably deterred me from an early morning trip to the cursed apartment for a shower. I went cold for milliseconds. I realized again that the late-night story session with the chief and the early morning diversion to the massage girl's shabby hotel might have randomly saved my life. Immortality is the great feeling of youth. In seconds, it was stripped away from me. I sat cross-legged on the floor in total shock.

The computer in my head reeled as she continued, "So there's no reason to continue this relationship after we leave Fiji, but let's have fun while it lasts. We both love good sex, the beach, and pot. Let's go out in style, the way we started. I'm horny...I could masturbate, but I'm all out of green bananas." She laughed at her joke.

Then it hit me on some subconscious level. Was it the very evil, very greedy V.J. Singh who plotted the murders in an attempted revenge for the potato war, and perhaps our attack on the Super Boss? I felt faint, and I must have looked stark white.

She said, "You look tired and you need a drink. Try this Russian Vodka martini. Leilei, our house girl, got it for sleeping with a Russian trawler captain. She was in Nadi at her sister's. She traded it to me for my old Timex watch. It's great. With a little ganja, it's gangbusters, just like the Peace Corps training parties you got me drunk at Hawaii to get in my panties."

My mind raced. I sipped the martini with my eyeballs glued to her golden triangle top. I tried to remember a clue or signal which would implicate V.J. Singh. There were none. I felt the ghost of Patipati nearby. It lurked, waiting for me to revenge his killer who destroyed his warriorhood in his sleep in the safe haven of his woman's house. That was taboo by Fijian war rules. Clearly, a Fijian warrior did not kill Patipati. Maybe it had been someone acting under V.J. Singh's orders. I vowed again mentally to go to the island of firewalkers to walk the burning path. I would clear my mind and find a path to Patipati's murderer.

Suddenly, my eyes caught the movement of a long sun-browned thigh. It opened to reveal the entire golden triangle tip. It was pushed slightly open against the woven bamboo of the hanging basket which was suspended from a hook in a wood beam by an old island sailboat's coarse woven line. I noticed the weave of the basket opened near its bottom center. I couldn't see it entirely from my sitting position. Dianne swung the basket in gentle half-circle arches. She used the tips of her red-painted toes to rock it back and forth on its arch. Each rock of the basket opened her slightly exposed, silky golden-veiled lips a fraction. They seemed to glisten in the western sunset's low orange-hued light. She continued the rocking motion while The Rolling Stones played on the Japanese recorder.

I hadn't made love since the death scene. I felt no sexual desire. I had also worked around the clock to sell the potato crop to the capital city gang. Patipati and the dead girls started to fade from my brain. I sipped the cold Vodka as I watched the golden triangle make its rotation as the basket slowly arched from side to side. The beat of The Stones matched the pounding high tide surf on the reef.

She said softly, "An old Chinese woman from the general store in town gave me this basket with a diagram of stick figures. She heard you were in Suva again. I can't read Chinese characters, but the stick figures explain everything. She thinks the basket will keep you at home. It is a special basket. Run your left hand under the basket slowly while I swing and you will understand why, without seeing the stick figures."

She then reached over to the top of the bookcase. She picked up a fat Fiji joint. She lit it, inhaled a big-time hit ,and blew a perfect smoke ring in my direction from her rounded mouth which I pierced with my right index finger as my left hand, palm up, reached under the basket. I found a lateral opening where a missing weave exposed her opening. It was dead vertical with the mat-covered floor approximately a foot under the slowly swinging basket.

She said, as my fingertip began to rub her, "I know the basket won't keep you at home, or even in my life, but let's have fun with it. We'll call these the 'Chinese Basket Days'. I'll remember them when I'm an old lady."

She handed me the joint. I took a hit for the first time in weeks. No doubt one of the co-op members had grown the very good, strong local pot which the Hindus had brought from India. They still used it in their religious ceremonies, including firewalking.

As the basket swung, my finger moved deeper. I realized my mission without even seeing the stick figures. The basket gave her distance and sexual power. I touched the tip of her womb with my finger. I watched her nipples harden and strain at the cotton halter top. With a sudden motion of her hand, the halter top was gone. She began to caress her nipples, one in each hand.

I withdrew my finger from her. I stood and dropped my khaki shorts. I had run out of clean underwear a week ago. I was nude after I pulled off my Earth Day One tee-shirt. I then sat back down on the mat-covered hardwood floor. I slid under the basket on my back. She brought it to a stop. I giggled. I inserted my penis into her through the open basket bottom, not knowing what to expect. I loved the initial feel of the penetration. I welcomed love making back into my life. With it, immortality started to return.

Then, to my surprise, as she hummed to The Band, which now played, she began a crab-like motion with her feet. She turned the basket in circles, twisting her canal in 360° circles. That caused me to pull out a little more with each ascending circle until the rope started to knot. Only the tip of my penis was in Dianne. She paused the basket and took the joint from me.

She had a giant hit. She drank her martini in a delightful gulp. She looked at me wide-eyed and said, "Bonzai!"

She lifted both her feet from the floor. This caused the basket to start a sudden unraveling, descending circular motion. It arched her canal around my penis in ever faster, ever deeper 360° swings. I compressed her womb in the final four or five rapid, tight circles. Suddenly, her vagina contracted severely. It stopped the motion as it created a vacuum seal, which left my penis compressed in her. I orgasmed. I felt wild ecstasy.

We were perfectly still. We were locked together with the basket hanging over me. The sun dropped into the ocean while dark descended on the Fiji coast. The crashing of the waves subsided as the tide went out on its 12-hour, never-ending cycle. It provided the island with its only real clock.

We meditated in this position. We used a Hindu tantra yoga chant we had learned from a Hindu co-op member. Then we visualized the point where the head of my vacuum sealed penis met her womb. We felt their droplets merge as the walls of her canal contracted in slow spasm in natural rhythm. She lit a candle without moving the basket. She dropped her golden waist-length hair. It splashed over her taut breasts. It revealed her nipples as she smiled with her eyes closed in the candlelit, poverty-stricken room. The only real fixture was the Japanese reel-to-reel tape recorder. It sat on the end of a small, wooden, blue-painted full bookcase.

For minutes we were motionless and breathless as we listened to the drug enhanced music and lingered, locked together. Then, in an easy motion, she picked up a short, smooth, thick, handblown glass tube with open rounded ends. She handed it to me without moving the basket.

She said, "The old woman said this is a very important glass tube—the only way to unlock ourselves. I believe we have created a perfect biological vacuum which has sealed us together. Insert the tube very slowly and very carefully along your shaft until it meets the tip of my cervix. Be careful not to force it. It is part of the meditation.

I carefully took the smooth glass tube. I tested its strength with a tap on my taut stomach muscles. I maneuvered it under the basket against my right thigh. I slowly moved its rounded upper glass tip across the basket bottom. Finally, it met the point where my penis shaft touched the anal end of her lips. With a light push, I moved only milli-inches at a time. I started the hollow glass shaft up the passage. I felt her continued contractions each millisecond of movement.

It took ten minutes for the shaft to move three inches, leaving six inches of it still exposed as Dianne pulsed into orgasm after orgasm in intervals. Minutes later I felt it meet the tip of my penis. We were still locked together by the vacuum. Then the tube went slightly into her womb. It opened with a loud suck of air up the tube to her open womb. She orgasmed a last time. Her vagina muscles released me. Exhausted, I held the fragile glass tube very still.

Then she handed me the candle. She said, "I think the old Chinese lady said to burn the candle at the end of the glass tube before it is removed. The hot air will cleanse my womb. It will drive the evil spirits away, preparing me for childbirth. Apparently, the old lady thought I was barren. I was unable to produce a child for you, which drove you away. The basket method is a Chinese way to get pregnant. She didn't know that I take birth control pills."

She giggled as a blast of hot air hit her open womb. I held the candle under the glass tube. It was now burning my finger. I put the candle down. I very slowly pulled the warm glass tube from her canal, which contracted as it gripped it. The tip of the tube exited, and a droplet fell onto me.

She said, "Let's hope I remembered to take my pills everyday while you were gone or the Chinese basket method might prolong our journey, boy wonder."

She rose. She stepped over me and headed into the bedroom. I listened to her soft crying for a future life and a baby we would never have together. Then, sleep, like a temporary death mask, began to overtake my body and soul. Dianne's spirit flickered in the candlelight of my mind's third eye as the never-ending tides beat against the reef.

CHAPTER TWENTY-SEVEN

EYEBALL TO EYEBALL

I woke up at 7:00 AM the next morning with gray walls of water lashing the house. I suspected it was a typhoon day. The wind was howling from the leeward western coastline at 60-plus mph already. I couldn't see ten yards out the south window of the living room of the tiny wooden bungalow. The weather reports had worsened all week. The shortwave radios had predicted a major storm was headed toward Fiji.

Dianne had already departed to her medical post at the nearby Fijian staffed Mid-Valley Hospital. She was assigned there as a volunteer for emergencies. As a trained paramedic, she would help the medical staff. If the wind reached 100 mph, it would blow down entire Fijian villages and Indian farmhouses.

I lay on my back against a Fijian reed sleeping mat on the hardwood floor. The dark brown Chinese basket hung silently. Dianne had covered me with a cotton blanket during the night when the heavy rain began to chill the tropical air. Sleep had been refreshing. I felt limber after a night on the finely hand-woven reed mats. Our Sikh yoga teacher believed soft mattresses damaged the spine as well as internal organ alignment. The Fijians had straight, strong backs. They slept on mats in their bures on swept, hard bare earth floors.

The only message Dianne left was a Polaroid. It was sitting on my chest photo side down. I flipped it over with my left hand. I was pleasantly surprised to see a kerosene oven baked Polaroid close-up of her golden triangle. It seemed every female I knew in the Peace Corps was snapping Polaroids of their private parts. I wondered if Polaroid received them in the mail, too.

I chuckled as the Polaroid caused the desired effect under the blanket. It would be my new lucky Polaroid. I would tape it under the Land Rover dashboard for good luck. I wondered if the ultimate toy of sexual revolution would be the Polaroid Instamatic Camera. It avoided photo labs. Everyone in the world could have a sexy travel photo of their mate. Modern technology was changing the world. I wondered if Mr. Land, who invented the magic camera, experimented with it on his private parts during research and development. I wondered if he would confess to Walter Cronkrite. Archivists examining this period of history would have some great beaver shots if these hi-tech photos didn't fade away like almost everything else made in post-war America.

I stared at the baked Polaroid. I knew my transition was underway. The wind howled through the big palm trees in the front yard. It tore the green, unripe coconuts off. It hurled them like baby bombs at the tin-sheeted bungalow roof. They were landing like a heavyweight fighter's left-hand jabs. Some knockout punches were coming soon.

I scrambled to my feet. I secured my new Polaroid in my canvas briefcase. I looked out the window west toward the ocean. I couldn't see the surf line a hundred yards from the bungalow, only a gray wall of wind, rain, and water. I heard the stories from Chief Kavula and his warriors about Fiji's legendary typhoons. They are called typhoons or cyclones in the southern latitudes, not hurricanes. The chief's stories were hair-raising. Winds had blown 200-plus mph over the lower leeward side of the island. They flattened everything in their path, organic or inorganic.

Fiji, culturally and biologically, was evolved to blow down. Palm trees stood high. To survive, their fronds evolved to let the wind rip through them at high speeds. Even their seeds, the coconuts, were waterproof. They traveled by river or ocean. The houses or bures of the Fijians were built with thatched roofs. The thatching could be regathered, rebound, or replaced quickly and cheaply by the communal village labor pool.

Their modern woven bamboo walls blew off in easily collectible bamboo sheets. The four rainforest hardwood log corner posts stood ready for rebuilding. In the cannibal days, Fijian villagers buried a captured warrior alive under each corner post of a village chief's house. This kept evil spirits away.

Chief Kavula claimed there were no skeletons under his corner posts. One of the other villagers told me the chief's great-grandfather set the current corner posts of the chief's large main bure. He said there were captured warriors buried under the chief's posts. It had survived the great typhoon of the 1920's which blew 200 mph in some areas. It reportedly killed 8,000 Fijians throughout the 300-plus island chain. I was worried. This looked like a day from hell descending on the normally tranquil island of Viti Levu. I knew the co-op Land Rover would be needed for search and rescue.

I hoped Dianne had made it by early bus to her mid-valley river emergency medical post. I would not know until the storm was over unless I could reach her by radio telephone from the co-op's administrative headquarters in town. Mother Nature was alive and kicking. A score with Fiji was about to be settled. I hoped my karma was good today. My Fijian guardian, Patipati was dead.

I took a quick shower, and I drank some native coffee. I ate a couple of eggs over easy with fried banana chips. I put on my foul weather gear from college sailboat club racing days. I decided to brave the walls of wind-blown water. I also put on a pith helmet; my Aussie friend's wife had given it to me for my birthday as a joke. It also came with a book of Kipling poetry. Kipling promoted the "White Man's Burden". It was the way the Aussie and English still looked at the "Wogs", whom they called the Fijians behind their backs. I thought the pith helmet would at least keep my head dry. If I was hit by a coconut it might save my life.

I also found Dianne's heavy cotton gardening gloves to stick in the slicker pocket in case there were any downed power lines on the road to town. As a ranch kid from the southwest, I knew more people in snow or dust storms were killed by downed live power lines than the weather. Good insulation was the key to handling live wires if you handled them at all.

I pushed open the door to the small porch and I stepped out into the storm. I was amazed at the power of the wind. I fought it to reach the rain-blown-clean gray Land Rover. Palm branches blew past me like small rocket ships in the rain. It was dark gray outside. The Land Rover blended into the sky like brown western jackrabbits on a dry mesa in Colorado.

I tried to start the Land Rover. 1 wondered if there would be any paint left on the Land Rover's aluminum skin after the wind stopped. The engine roared to life. While it warmed up, I closed all the air vents. I fished Dianne's Polaroid out of my canvas bag. I taped it under the passenger side dash with some black electrical tape I kept in the glove box for electrical emergencies. It was my new good luck token. The Brit-made Land Rover's various lights incurred electrical shorts. Rover designed the machine to run four feet deep in water. They forgot about night driving. I presumed British gentlemen with an empire to manage, didn't drive at night. I spent hours taping taillight or headlight wires and leads back together. Night driving was an American passion clearly.

After the Polaroid was securely taped, I backed out of the soggy, reef-rock, sandy driveway onto the coast road. It was already a foot deep in running rainwater. I heard a coconut clink against the aluminum-skinned top of the Land Rover. The entire island including every person, animal, and machine, was under assault. I clicked the co-op's battery-powered shortwave radio to the national radio channel. I heard static. Our province's transmitter must have blown down already. Without radio information things would get crazy fast. The phones were probably dead, too.

I drove toward the co-op's concrete block headquarters building in the small river town of Sigatoka. I drove on a completely deserted national coast highway. It should have been bustling with weekday morning traffic. Visibility was 20 yards. The worn-out Land Rover windshield wipers swept back and forth at their highest speed. A wall of windblown water smashed into the vehicle from its left side.

I passed the traditional bure-style Fijian village on the outskirts of Sigatoka. I could see its houses clustered near the road. They were being damaged as bundles of their thatched roofs tore away randomly. The wind gusted to 80 miles an hour. The storm was only a few hours old. A police vehicle passed me leaving town. It was followed by a tow truck. Someone was probably in trouble on the mountain part of the province's coast road. I hoped it wasn't the early Suva bus. I needed to make sure our co-op trucks were secure as quickly as possible.

I reached the quarter-mile-long, single lane concrete bridge over the river into town. I was shocked by the roaring waters which were only 20 feet under the bridge instead of their normal 50 feet. A policeman stopped me on the approach. He advised me to proceed at my own risk across the bridge into town. The river was rising three feet an hour. The bridge would have to be closed if it rose another ten feet. He also said the national weather center in the capital city had advised the regional police command that the wind could reach 200 mph on the western coast of the island by 6:00 PM today.

The typhoon could be the worst in the country's recorded written history. It was tracking straight at western Viti Levu, Fiji's main island. Sigatoka was on the southwestern coast so conditions would be deadly.

I was scared for the first time. I rolled up the window and waited to cross the bridge when the signal light turned green. The coast highway traffic was alternately one way into and out of Sigatoka. I exited the bridge and turned right onto the town's main street. I saw people boarding up their storefronts, offices, and homes. They were sandbagging their doorways. They clearly expected high winds and flooding.

I had locked our house's solid wood storm shutters tightly from the inside before I left. I had never closed them in my two years there. I had wondered why the house had them. Even when propped open they still blocked light and air. I was learning first-hand that when a typhoon roared across the wide open Southern Pacific straight at Fiji, it picked up enormous moisture, speed and power. The leeward side of the island was flat. It would clobber us if its center hit western Viti Levu directly.

I turned right at King George's Street. I parked the Land Rover in front of the co-op's main office. I rolled its windows tight. I opened the door. I dashed through the heavy cool rain into the front office. Raja, the head town staffer was there. His report in broken Hindi-English was precise as usual. The national telephones were out completely. We had no contacts upriver to our two field offices except by radio phone and no one was answering. We had no municipal power. Our backup, newly acquired Honda generator was powering the office lights. There was plenty of fuel for it.

The three co-op semitrucks were still in the capital city delivering the last of the co-op's potatoes. He presumed they would take shelter in Suva. The winds would be lower since the windward eastern side of the island had the central 4,000-foot mountains to break the storm's force. No other co-op workers had reported. He presumed they were struggling to secure their homes, bures, families, and possessions. Raja had no family. He had come from his uncle's apartment where he boarded in town to secure the co-op office. He advised me not to drive upriver. The low concrete causeway-type bridges would flood quickly in the lower valley. Trees would also fall and block the narrow gravel road. The valley would be cut off from Sigatoka.

Dianne had left a message under the door. He gave it to me. It said: "My morning bus didn't go upriver. I am in town at the provincial hospital. I am assigned triage patients if the storm gets worse. We already have a few. They have been wounded by flying objects. Be careful. There is also a report of a bus accident on the mountain part of the coast road east of town. We do not know the extent of it. The police have left with a doctor and nurse. All businesses are closed. We have radio phone contact intermittently with Suva.

"The forecasts are 200 mph winds by 6:00 PM. Injuries and death expected to be heavy. The police and army are evacuating all coastal villages on the western side. The hospital needs you as a driver with the co-op Land Rover, once you secure your operations. Good Luck. God Speed."

The note was sobering. It ended any illusions about the storm. In eight hours, it would become a killer. This was a real third world island paradise. There were no backup communications or highway patrol guys to make everything OK. We were cut off from the world on a small island in the middle of the South Pacific. Who knew if we would see tomorrow or care about it. Nature had reduced life to the pure survival plan with no frills.

Raja and I worked out a plan. We began to secure the co-op headquarters. All key files were packed and moved to a second-floor interior room. We also moved our two typewriters and adding machine. Our safe was too heavy to move upstairs, so we made sure it was locked tight. We closed our vented metal storm shutters over the exposed windows, sealing the building. Next, we found 20 leftover burlap potato bags. We put on our rain gear. We went outside into the sandy parking lot. We filled them half full and folded the tops. We sandbagged the entrance and rear exit to the building to keep water from flooding the doorways.

Then Raja brewed a pot of tea as we dried out in front of an electric portable heater the co-op secretary used on cool, rainy days in the winter season. In Fiji, we had morning tea, even with a typhoon approaching. Raja had worked for the British local bank before joining the co-op staff.

The hot cha, a tea with milk, warmed me and provided a momentary feeling of security which vanished as the wind began to howl loudly after the tea break. Raja agreed to stay at the headquarters until 4:00 PM since his uncle had six sons to help him. The co-op building was stuccoed concrete block and very strong by Fiji standards. Even if the river flooded, he could take refuge on the second floor. He agreed to sandbag the generator room in case the first floor flooded. We could use the building as a refugee center if needed.

After a final brief visual check to make sure all the key records were safe, I said my goodbyes. I had a proper stiff upper lip which Raja expected. I clambered into my rain gear and rubber field boots. I put on my pith helmet. I exited the front door with a leap over the sandbags. I climbed into the Land Rover for a quick trip to the regional government headquarters for assignment.

I pulled into the regional government headquarters compound two blocks away. I dodged a police Land Rover exiting with two grim-faced officers clad in green battle fatigues and helmets, instead of their usual blue and white uniforms. The Fiji military arrived in a small convoy of two light canvas top trucks led by a Land Rover.

I parked. I dashed to the regional officer's waiting room. I found organized chaos. The regional officer hand held a military field radio shouting instructions in Fijian, English and Hindi. The coastal villages were being evacuated. There were deaths already on the outer small islands to the extreme west. Some atolls were now partially under water. There were Peace Corps volunteers stationed on the outer western islands. I wondered if they were still alive.

He was also securing the island's southern tourist hotels. They were all on the coastline, but thankfully, half-empty since it was off season. Dead visitors were not good for public relations in a developing tourist economy. The military had been mobilized. Many of the Fijian villagers who filled the Island's two regiments were cut off from communication and transportation already. The ranks were thin.

All available four-wheel drive vehicles were being commandeered, so I had reported to the correct place. The Fijian regional government officer knew me well. When the radio lulled, he gave me a short Fijian salutation. He assigned me to emergency medical evacuation duty with the co-op Land Rover under the provincial police dispatch at the provincial hospital.

I was out the door in a splash. I ran through the rain to the Land Rover. Two more military trucks appeared. Their canvas tops were damaged by the wind. They were filled with Fijian women and children from a coastal village. Everyone was drenched but happy to be safely in town.

Back inside the Land Rover, I patted the Polaroid for good luck. It started with a roar. I was off to the hospital a block away. I passed four more army trucks loaded with villagers heading toward town. The hospital parking lot was chaotic. I drove down its palm tree lined driveway. Two police Land Rovers were unloading stretchers. A military Land Rover waited in line. Rain-soaked nurses and orderlies ran from the building to an ambulance next to the Land Rovers. Cars and taxis were strewn everywhere. Some had drivers, others didn't.

I imagined a "Gone with the Wind" Atlanta scene inside. I parked well down the concrete drive to be ready for a quick exit when assigned. I turned off the engine and checked my gasoline gauge. It read 3/4 full. I had four five-gallon cans inboard and outboard on their locked carriers for emergency use. My spare tire was full and mounted on the hood. This freed up the cargo compartment with its fold-down seats for human transport.

I ran through the wet chaos of the parking lot into the receiving lobby. I found Dianne near the reception desk, handing out numbers. She assigned patients by priority to the head emergency receiving nurse. I was happy to see her alive in person. We hugged each other simultaneously. Involuntarily, our young bodies pressed against each other for security. After a long moment, she pulled away. The typhoon was not going away any time soon.

Professionally, she said, "Hello, Cooper, I'm glad you're here. We need help. The local count is already 75 injured, two dead on arrival—one killed from a falling tree, the other drowned in the river. See the police sergeant by the pay phone booth. He will assign you. Be very careful."

"It's already hell in the extreme western outer islands. Winds are 150 mph, according to a report the police received by radio phone minutes ago.

The Nadi international airport is closed. A freighter is floundering in the port at Lautoka. It may sink in the harbor. Western Fiji is cut off from the world. The winds may hit 200 mph at peak like in 1922 and no one wants to talk about the consequences. God Speed! See you in the next lifetime if your karma runs out here."

She disappeared to help with incoming injured. A stretcher with a six-year-old boy was carried in through the open door. His Fijian village mother wailed in grief.

A police sergeant dressed in green fatigues who I knew from the local pub had set up shop with a military radio phone in the hospital's British-style living room-size phone booth. It took Fijian coins, but never worked. It was a perfect mini-office out of the din of the main waiting room.

After the proper salutation, I said I was assigned to him. He deputized me. I didn't have to raise my hand like old TV westerns. I just signed a form which he had on a clipboard. He also commandeered the co-op's Land Rover. Since the government owned it anyway, I signed.

I was quickly made a driver in the Fiji police battalion six, region five. It was a fitting place to end my life if Karma called. At least there would be a western-style paper trail, since the English were still in charge. My Peace Corps benefits would be paid to Dianne. My mother's attorney would not be able to sue anyone. She owned a big ranch in western Colorado. My dad was dead.

I waited for an assignment. I sipped another cup of hot tea. It was brought to me by an Aussie woman in a clinging damp minidress. The dress revealed the faint outline of not only her underwear-less black triangle, but two prominent nipples through a thin sheer, lace, white bra. I wondered if Aussie women ever managed to put on all their clothes, even in a national disaster.

She smiled and said, "Hello, mate!" as she handed me the cup of tea. She caught my quick glance to her crotch. She winked and was off, bottom wagging. She went to serve more tea. I vaguely knew her as the very young wife of a resort hotel owner on the coast road about 18 miles east of town. Her name was Anne. She was 20 or so. Her husband, Roger, was 60 plus with silver-gray hair and long sideburns. He ran a small, expensive, but popular 20-room resort hotel for the smart, Aussie, bored rich set mainly from Sydney. She disappeared around the corner toward the hospital's kitchen. I had barely had a sip of tea when the sergeant received a radio call.

It was from Anne's husband's hotel. In Fijian over the hotel's radio phone, I heard a village chief say that a Fijian-crewed inter-island freighter was breaking up on the outer reef near a village called Bauio. It was a mile west of the hotel. There were injured passengers and crewmen who needed to be evacuated from the village to the hospital. The hotel Land Rover had sunk suddenly in quicksand-like mud on its way to the village along a beach road. However, we could reach the village on a drier gravel road through an old rubber plantation from the west off the coast highway.

The sergeant looked at me. He said it was my assignment and to take Anne, the Aussie woman. She knew the west road into the village because most of her husband's hotel workers lived there.

He said, "Bring only the very badly-injured back here and give the village midwife a first-aid kit. You can get one on the verandah from the nurse in charge."

My heart raced. It meant crossing the Sigatoka river bridge. I could be permanently cut off from town if the river continued to rise with a 20-year-old brat fresh from Sydney. I needed Patipati. I almost cried, but it was stiff upper lip time as I saluted. I ran off toward the kitchen to find Anne. She promptly volunteered to help. She said she hated serving tea. I figured she really needed a ride home. I would probably make the return trip alone. Dianne had disappeared into the emergency room. I left with Anne trailing me to find a first-aid kit for the village midwife.

CHAPTER TWENTY-EIGHT

DRIVE FOR LIFE

Anne closed the passenger side door of the Land Rover. I secured the military issue first-aid kit decaled "U.S. Army surplus" behind the driver's seat. The wind and torrential rain gusted against the aluminum skin of our vital shelter. I swung my left shoulder around after securing the first-aid kit. The back of my hand accidentally brushed Anne's rain-slickered chest. She had turned to help me secure the kit. Her rubber slicker top road up to mid-thigh. She hadn't bothered with the men's green military slicker pants, since she was about five feet tall and 100 pounds soaking wet.

She smiled as she turned away. She blushed as my eye scanned across her exposed, tanned, dark brown thighs. Her wet mini-skirt had bunched when she scooted into the high-seated Land Rover. She didn't seem to mind her mini-skirt's sexy reveal. I wiped the fogged windshield and started the gray beast for another Fiji adventure. I turned on the heater to dry out Anne. I drove off in a spray of water. The wiper blades cleared the new safety glass windshield enough to drive at 15 mph. The wind was gusting 60-80 mph with steady rain. It was hard to handle the top-heavy machine. It wanted to steer sideways instead of straight. It was one o'clock. The 18-mile drive would take an hour each way at this speed. The river would continue to rise.

Anne said, as I swung onto the town's main street, "Go about 18 miles past the bridge to a cluster of three palm trees, if they are standing. Turn right. The village is a mile down a crushed shell and sand road. Then we cross a small concrete causeway on the edge of the reef. It's like a very small island."

I had never been to this village. It was a fishing village with no farmers and no surf because of its reef. I was glad to have a guide in this weather. Village roads in Fiji had no markers. You could drive forever hunting for one in blinding rain.

The trip across the swollen river was easier than anticipated. The river had stabilized at 20 feet below the bridge. Apparently, the rain had lightened in the interior valley. Still, it was "cross at your own risk", and "you may not get back".

Anne chattered about her husband's Fiji resort hotel and Sydney. We drove down the coast road at barely 15 mph with poor visibility while dodging objects in the road. A work crew ahead of us had cleared fallen palm trees, like a snow-plow crew in the Rockies. My storm-shuttered house was standing as I passed it. I started to drive faster away from town.

The hour passed quickly. Anne's minidress remained high on her thighs as we drove. She was too excited to care. She had also pulled off her slicker top. It was hot in the Land Rover. Its air vents, except for the defogger, which barely worked, were all closed to avoid flooding.

Suddenly, she yelled, "Slow down!"

I saw the village turnoff road too late. One of the marker entrance palm trees had fallen. She had almost missed the turn since visibility was down to ten yards. The crushed shell and sand road was dangerously slick, but still solid. It sloped slightly downhill to the coast's edge a mile away. It ran through an ancient rubber tree plantation gone wild after World War II when Fiji's marginal rubber production was abandoned. It was put out of business by synthetic rubber developed by Dupont in the U.S.

The rubber trees had rotten shallow roots, so I was worried about them falling on us as we cruised at 5 mph toward the coast. Anne found the turns on the road from memory since she drove it often. About a half-mile down the road, I hit the brakes. A rogue palm tree had fallen across the road. I mapped a route around it that kept my wheels on solid ground. I executed the maneuver. The knobby tires spun wildly a couple of times, exciting Anne. She clutched at the passenger side handrail once. She clutched my left arm the second time. I accidentally brushed one of her firm breasts as I upshifted around a rubber tree back onto the slick road. It was covered by the damp cotton dress and a cotton bra.

She giggled and released my shoulder and said, "Good going, mate. We're only half a kilometer from the short causeway to the village and we're there."

Minutes later, I exited the last of the perfectly rowed abandoned rubber trees. I saw the edge of the causeway and stopped. Disaster had struck again. It was almost high tide and the wind driven water covered the causeway to the village by 5-6 feet. It was well above the maximum of four feet the Land Rover could survive. The village located across the causeway was now invisible from wind and rain. The villagers couldn't see or hear us.

Mentally, I calculated by three o'clock, the water would drop to four feet as the tide receded. Then we could risk crossing. We had made it in an hour, so we had another hour before attempting a crossing. It was too dangerous to attempt to swim the 400 feet in the strong, wind-driven tidal current. Even roped to the Land Rover bumper, I could be pulled under and drown without village men to reel me back. The Land Rover didn't have a winch. The co-op department was too poor to provide one.

I explained the situation to Anne. I talked facing her as I laid my plan. If I crossed at low tide, I gave her options. She could stay behind and rope herself to a rubber tree, because the Land Rover could be swept off the causeway. Or she could go with me rather than risk the typhoon exposed to the high winds and coconut bombs. She elected to go with me.

She said, "Well, Cooper, let's kill the hour with some Aussie-girl out-back fun until we rescue the "wog" sailors or die trying, if that's our plan."

Anne was personally willing to die in the rescue effort. She was a surprising, enchanting, brave woman. I was glad to have this girl-woman with me in the storm.

I flipped open the glove box. I turned on my battery-powered Sony mini-cassette tape player which played the Beatles. She placed her right hand on my khaki shorts zipper. It was down in a single motion. In two or three well-rehearsed strokes, I had a hard-on sticking through my fly under my rain poncho. The rest was truly wild and wonderful, as the typhoon's wind howled, and the heavy rain pounded the Land Rover.

Anne apparently had made love in a Land Rover before. She stripped off her damp minidress and bra revealing beautifully matched 34-C breasts with small black nipples hard like diamonds. She flipped over onto her knees. She pulled off my sailing rain-gear bottoms. Next, she pulled my shorts off. Then she sucked me for a couple of minutes. I stimulated her to the beat of Ringo Starr and the storm.

With a hop, she was over the gear shift. Her small body wedged in between me and the steering wheel. Her breasts jammed against my chest. Her knees were against the seat back. She deftly rose and fell on my rock-hard penis. Her hot tongue found mine. She pushed the building wind and rainstorm sounds to the outer reaches of my mind. She drove her body up and down to the beat of the Beatles, which played full blast. She began to howl eerily with each down thrust. Her thrusts went up a tempo and her ear-piercing outback aboriginal howl fought with the raging storm's noise. We climaxed minutes later together in the fogged, warm cocoon of the co-op Land Rover cab.

She finally sagged against the steering wheel. I lapsed into momentary fatigue. It was an unforgettable sensual experience. The building typhoon tore at the ocean, the aging rubber trees, and the Land Rover. It searched for our young lives to destroy them. Fijian sailors were probably dying on the other side of the low concrete causeway.

I was still surrounded, physically and emotionally, by the mysterious dark woman's passion in a fragile life raft of a Land Rover as the jaws of the storm's sheer hell crept closer. I wondered if this was how my ROTC frat brothers, who were now Army Airborne first lieutenants in Vietnam, felt in Saigon whorehouses the night before battle with their china-skinned Asian teenage dolls. Was this how all men and women felt if they were lucky enough to make love before they faced death—whether death from a well-aimed bullet in war or a powerful avalanche on a high mountain snow field. Sex had never seemed this sharp, this sure, or this focused. Anne started to cry softly as the wind started to blow harder.

She cried and said, "I don't want to die on this island, 2,000 miles from my mates in Australia. But if I am to die in this typhoon, I want it to be helping the Fijians, not sitting at the hotel bar drunk with the guests if the wind blows the building down."

Then she raised slowly up onto her knees. I could see the junction of our bodies for a moment. The wind howled. She scrambled into the passenger seat. Our lives had touched briefly, possibly, maybe even irrevocably. Today, the Fijian sea and wind gods held the cards.

I glanced at my cheap, duty-free Swiss diving watch. It had slid up my wrist. It was 2:45 PM, about five minutes before the estimated time for a low tide crossing. The wind kept building. Anne sat frozen in time and space. She barely breathed and seemed to meditate.

Suddenly, Anne said, "Be still, Cooper, listen to the wind and grip my hand firmly. If you lose your concentration, you will lose me and maybe your life. If you hold your concentration, you hold me. Just use your mind, my naive, brave American boy. I am part Aborigine, one-fourth, that's why I tan so brown. I will call up a spirit to enter my body now. It will enter you through me. It is an Aboriginal custom used only by sexually joined men and women in the high open desert. We use it when a funnel cloud or tornado, as you call them, approaches. If the spirit is powerful and good, not evil, it will save us. In Fiji, like the open desert, we have no place to hide from this monster wind. My grandmother told me about this custom of how a man and a woman can save themselves from the wind when surprised in the open desert. Now concentrate, while I bring us hope."

The third world always surprised me. This was another one of those special moments. I felt her whole body start to quiver, first her head, then her neck, her breasts, her back, and then her thighs in a pulsing rhythm. It took my thoughts into her soul. She chanted in a language I did not know and had never heard. Her hand strained against my hand as she shook from head to toe.

I felt a new power enter our space. I realized what had happened. She had absorbed Patipati's ghost. She sensed it in my presence. His power had entered her body. She had channeled half of his spirit to me. We were ready now to face nature with the ghost's senses in our bodies. It would alert us to the dangers ahead during and beyond the typhoon.

I watched her dress. From the slicker pocket, she produced a pair of dry white mini-panties. She had apparently stored them for safekeeping.

Finally, she pulled on her rain slicker top as I pulled on my shorts and rain pants.

It was two minutes till three o'clock. It was time for action. I fired up the Land Rover. I pulled the defrost toggle switch so I could view the lagoon. She wiped the inside surface of the windshield with the towel. I gunned the engine in neutral to ensure we had full power. We did. The countdown started. The causeway loomed into view.

I glanced silently at the brown witch girl once more. I knew her se-cret. She was part Aborigine, probably from a station or ranch in the Aussie outback. She was a kindred spirit and relative of the native Fiji-ans. That's why she had been at the hospital volunteering to help. That's why she was in my Land Rover. She could have been at the hotel bar a mile down the road, riding out the storm with her husband and his guests. That's why her breasts were firm and heavy while her body was lithe and light. She was a part-European, part-desert-child-woman, born by nature to survive in the outback's desolation. Granddaughter of a witch, a wom-an of the wind and sky.

Today, the Great Spirit of the Fijians, who had guided them in their long boats from the coast of Africa to Fiji in the old days, had chosen her to guide me. I felt strong. If I ever mated, it was a woman like Anne I want-ed. I knew she was rare. She was almost non-existent in the vanquished naturalism of an emerging high-tech world.

I saw the causeway center marker pole. The water level was on the four-foot line, surging to six feet as waves hit it. I could have surfed the reef-protected lagoon, but I didn't have my surfboard today.

I set my diving watch ring. I timed the waves at one-minute intervals in sets of three. We had one minute to cross the causeway's 400-foot solid concrete ramp. It was exactly four feet underwater at its center. If the Land Rover was hit by a three-foot wave, we were doomed. The Land Rover would stall. It would be swept off the causeway into the fast-moving cur-rent. I rolled down my window. I ordered Anne to do the same so we could swim free if we were swept off the causeway.

I timed the last set of waves after they broke, and then gunned the en-gine. I shifted into low four-wheel drive and first gear. The Land Rover rolled onto the causeway at 5 mph. It started taking water. First, a foot, then two feet, then three feet. I had to steer it to the left to avoid being swept off the right side of the causeway by the current. I steered to a mark-er on the exit ramp 300 feet ahead. I couldn't see the roadbed, but only feel it under the water.

At four feet of depth, water rushed through the floor of the passenger compartment. Anne raised her bare feet. She rucked them under her on the seat. The Land Rover was difficult to control, even with low four-wheel drive, but I kept a slippery traction with a delicate touch of the gas pedal. I didn't want to spin the rear wheels. I kept over-steering to the left as we endlessly crept across the causeway. The Land Rover was hit with gusts of 100 mph wind frontally. I drove due west into the wind.

Only 50 feet of the four-foot deep water was left to cross in the low center section of the causeway. I needed 30 seconds to make landfall. I saw a rogue six-foot wall of water round the village edge of the lagoon. It headed toward the Land Rover. It was driven by the wind's fury. Our only chance to live was to gun the engine at the last possible moment. I had to crash through the water wall with enough momentum to accelerate along the final, slightly uphill 100 feet of the causeway. If years of surfing had a payoff, this was the perfect moment. The witch girl-woman started her chant. The wave rolled toward us. With only 20 feet of four-foot deep water left to cross, I hit the accelerator.

The Land Rover shot through a six-foot wall of ocean wave. Its wheels churned as the causeway started to rise toward shore. Suddenly, I felt the rear wheel lose its grip. It spun off the side of the causeway. I drifted right to stop the over-steer which would have spun the Land Rover. I prayed the front wheels, and the left rear wheel would hold traction. I accelerated again. The right rear wheel hit the causeway side. Then it clunked up and over it as the front wheel drive power pulled the Land Rover back onto the causeway. We humbly drove off the causeway into the village.

Anne was still chanting. I felt Patipati in my heart. It was better than that long ago day at Mikimiki when we roared out of the river into the village for fun and glory. Anne stopped chanting. She threw her arms around me. She kissed me like a proper Sydney girl on New Year's Eve. This new friend was special. Physically, emotionally, and sensually, she lingered in the recess of my mind. Then, without warning, I four-wheeled into a scene from war in the middle of the village common area.

Dead, wave-driven, reef-beaten, bloody naked bodies were lined up in rows. Not many of the inter-island freighter's Fijian crew or passengers, it appeared, had survived. A villager yelled it had wrecked on the village's outer reef opening about a half-mile out to sea. The freighter had missed the reef's opening to the village's lagoon and small harbor in the storm. It had floundered on the barren reef in the 20-foot seas. The scene was horrible. We four-wheeled through the village to the chief's bure. I told Anne to stay dry while I talked to the village's chief. I jumped out of the Land Rover. I dashed into his bure's side door without asking permission.

I quickly dropped to one knee. I gave the chief a brief salutation. It was necessary even in a disaster. The village's chief knew of me through Ratu Kavula who had led the potato warriors to Suva. Fiji was one big family. This made it easy to get things done. The Paramount Provincial Chief's high regard of me ensured this coastal chief would co-operate.

He said, "We have two children who were swept ashore, a boy and a girl from the ship. They are still breathing, but bleeding badly. Everyone else who we have recovered is dead, uninjured or the witch doctor and midwife are treating. You take the two children in the Land Rover to the hospital. They are young, strong, and may live to help our country after independence. I will send an elderly village woman who is a trained midwife to help with the children while you drive."

I thanked him, but politely declined the village woman. I had a female helper with me. I said she was the granddaughter of a witch doctor from the great continent to the west and that the spirit of Patipati was guiding us through the storm. The old chief understood. He urged me to hurry because the storm would worsen quickly. He ordered me to leave before the causeway flooded with 10-foot waves. He pointed to the bure ceiling. His father had seen them that high in the 1922 storm.

Fiji rarely had 10-foot waves on an inner reef, and never in a lagoon protected by three rings of reefs. Hell was an hour-plus away. I wanted to be in town when the devil storm arrived.

I ran back to the Land Rover. I drove behind the chief. He ran in khaki shorts in the rain and wind. He led us barefooted to the village school a hundred yards away. The midwife carried the tiny, injured children out one by one. She placed them on small, wet, child's woven sleeping mats in the back of the Land Rover. They wore reef-torn clothes. Their soft skin was cut and bleeding. The villager midwife had bandaged them in torn cotton Tee-shirt strips.

Anne leaped over the passenger seat. She opened the first-aid kit and went to work as the two children cried intermittently. The little boy was barely conscious. The older girl's eyes were open. They were light-skinned and looked to be Lau, maybe even part Tongan children. They probably were about five and seven years old. I choked back tears as I looked at them. I heard their cries in Fijian for their parents—apparently now dead in the lagoon or on the village green. I prayed silently to the Great Spirit to spare their small lives. I offered him mine to save these beautiful, defenseless young humans.

Anne started a low, soothing chant. I comforted the children. She cut gauze and tape to stop their bleeding. They had probably survived because they were small and light in adult life jackets. They had probably been swept up and over the barrier reef by the monster waves like coconuts.

I gunned the Land Rover engine. I followed the chief, who ran in front of it to guide us back to the causeway. It was 3:30 PM. The tide was a little lower, so I decided to gun the Land Rover all the way across the causeway this time and not chance a rogue wave. The last set of 5-foot waves cleared the causeway. It now had three feet of water at its center marker. The visibility was worse. I gunned the Land Rover engine again. We drove in a 10 mph splash all the way across the causeway.

I used the causeway's center water level pole for my first marker. I used the exit ramp up onto the road at the edge of the rubber trees to guide us onto solid ground.

As I raced through the rubber plantation, Anne said, "Take whatever chances are reasonable; the boy is dying. He is very cold. We must get him to a hospital and a blood supply quickly." She continued to sing to the children some half-remembered Aboriginal song. Patipati's warrior spirit filled me with the strength to drive on the edge of my vision and yards beyond.

If I drove too fast, up the center of the village road, I risked hitting a downed tree or some wind-blown obstacle. This could damage or flip the Land Rover. If I drove too slow the boy could die or worse, the bridge at the edge of town would be closed. We would be cut off from the hospital. It was raining wind-driven walls of water as the last stage of the typhoon moved on shore. It had come to ravage the island and its people. I gambled and kept driving too fast. I hoped to save the tiny lives in the back compartment.

I glanced in the rearview mirror. I was shocked to see an almost nude Anne squatting against the Land Rover's back door for support. The first-aid kit was empty. She was ripping up her mini-dress and underwear for bandages to stop the boy's bleeding. Her elastic bra was now a tourniquet around his right arm to stop a puncture wound from bleeding. She worked feverishly in the gray light of the dark, stormy afternoon. Her brown skin was smeared with blood. Her black hair wet and windblown from an open Land Rover vent. She continued to rebandage the boy and sing.

I turned sharply left onto the coast road. I raced the 18 miles back to town at double the 15-mph speed we drove on the way to the village. We were lucky as I harmlessly crashed over palm branches, and dodged a dozen fallen palm trees. I prayed silently as Anne continued to sing.

I tossed her slicker top to her. She pulled it over her head. It covered her squatting body like a camp tent. She smiled while she held the hand of each child. She balanced on her wide feet against the rear door of the Land Rover which hurtled along at a dangerous 30 mph. One hundred-plus mph gusts hit the Land Rover's hood. My lights searched the almost-darkness at four in the afternoon.

Trouble loomed as we neared town. A power line was half down across the road. It swung wildly four feet above the road. It sparked. I slowed the Land Rover. The Land Rover had rubber tires and an aluminum body which didn't conduct electricity efficiently, but it was wet. I edged under the line until it reached the windshield. Then, with my gloves on, I lifted it up and over the Land Rover's roof. I drove under the hot line. The rubber tires kept us from grounding. My high school physics was correct, and the maneuver worked. The power line finally slipped over the rear of the Land Rover. I sped toward the bridge which was 10 minutes away. I prayed it would be open and still standing. I desperately wanted the children to live. The wind turned up another notch. I pressed the Land Rover's narrow accelerator pedal harder to maintain speed. We drove almost due west into the typhoon.

The fate of my tiny passengers' lives depended on the single lane concrete bridge ahead. Anne was sobbing between verses. The small brown boy was fading fast. I pressed the accelerator a little harder.

CHAPTERTWENTY-NINE

THE BRIDGE

Visibility remained a dangerous 20-30 yards. We raced the final mile through the howling winds at 30 mph toward the Sigatoka bridge. Suddenly, through the wall of rain, I saw the bridge. The crossing gate was down with an armed Fijian soldier on duty. I climbed out of the Land Rover. I glanced back at our tiny human cargo as I approached the soldier. We were both being blasted by 100 mph gusts of wind two miles inland from the ocean. Some of the world's largest white sand dunes at the mouth of the Sigatoka river delta usually helped protect the bridge and town from extreme winds.

I looked down at the raging muddy river. It was only 10 feet under the bridge. Tons of upriver debris were being washed against the bridge's concrete pillars at a high velocity. Tin roofs, palm tree trunks, banana plants, bamboo bure siding, and even clothing were being washed downriver to the sea by the muddy raging water. The river had risen 40 feet since the storm started. The single-span concrete bridge was swaying under the strain, but it was still standing.

I approached the steel helmeted soldier, but he signaled me to return to the Land Rover. He said in Fijian, "The bridge is closed; it may fall soon.

Stay dry. Get out of the wind before you are hit by flying coconuts."

He smiled and waved goodbye. Fijians always seemed to have a smile, even in a typhoon. I shouted over the wind in Fijian that my tiny child passengers from the shipwreck were dying in the rear of the Land Rover.

I said, "They must reach the provincial hospital quickly. Otherwise, there is no hope for them."

He replied, "You are a fool to drive across the bridge. It could be washed away at any second. The vibration caused by the Land Rover on the steel mesh roadbed could knock it down. I am under orders to let no vehicles cross to protect lives and the bridge. It is the island's only southern coastal link east and west across the Sigatoka river. It will be needed after the typhoon to supply and rebuild the western province which has the tourist hotels."

I knew the hotels were vital to Fiji's economy. I pleaded, "I will take the chance."

He refused firmly, rifle in hand.

I then said, "View the children through the Land Rover's side window."

I hoped their condition would appeal to his village conditioned emotions. He walked downwind toward the Land Rover. We were both knocked off balance by a wind gust and bounced against its hard slick side.

I remembered too late; Anne was wearing only a slicker top last time I looked into the rearview mirror. I had no time to explain that she had sacrificed her clothes to bandage the children. I hoped for a miracle as he peered through the window.

Anne had found her rain gear pants. She looked like a tent holding the small boy. He was gasping for breath. The young village soldier had tears in his eyes. He turned and motioned me to follow him to the gatehouse at the edge of the bridge. Fijians loved children. Inside, he picked up an army field radio. He called an army captain in town on the opposite bank at the provincial government headquarters.

I translated his Fijian village dialect in my mind. He was from the eastern province. He spoke in its dialect. He assumed that Peace Corps volunteers only spoke the national dialect taught in school. He clearly didn't want me to monitor his conversation with the captain, who was probably a relative.

They had been placed in charge of a major national asset. The loss of this vital bridge would damage the rebuilding of the island after the typhoon. It cut off cargo and tourists traveling to the capital city by road from the international airport at Nadi. It was the only bridge that crossed the mighty Sigatoka River on the south-central coastal road. My limited interpretation of the radioed conversation was that the captain's answer was "no". They had orders from Suva to secure and save the bridge.

I heard a loud explosion near the bridge's concrete base. It was anchored by a huge mass of concrete into the riverbank. I realized the army was dynamiting debris with grenades to protect the bridge's base. I needed a quick winning strategy. I spoke in national Fijian dialect. I did not tip my hand that I had interpreted parts of his conversation with the captain. I asked to be permitted to carry the children across the bridge on foot. I requested an ambulance meet us on the town end.

He looked in amazement. He didn't believe I would risk my life to save two Fijian village children. He proposed the solution to the captain. The radio went silent for two long minutes. The silence from the other end of the bridge continued as the rain and wind gusts raked the gate house.

Then the voice of the chief provincial police officer squawked over the field radio. In Oxford English, he said, "Cooper may proceed with the children by footpath across the bridge at his own risk. God speed, Yank. There will be an ambulance stationed on my side."

The radio went dead. I pushed the gatehouse door open. I ran through the savage wind to the Land Rover. I jumped into the passenger side. I explained the plan to Anne. I told her I would make the first trip with the dying boy and then come back for the girl.

She said, "No, Yank, we go together. It's that kind of day."

There was no pause for argument. There was no fear or hesitation in her voice. This Aussie outback girl-woman was going to run the 100-yard dash across the bridge with me. She would carry the small boy in her arms in 100 mph-plus wind in driving rain on a bridge that had been given a death sentence. The typhoon was nearing its maximum fury. My love for her was pure, clear, and instant. I hopped out of the passenger side of the Land Rover. I started to go around the Land Rover to open its rear door.

The wind pressed me against the Land Rover's side. I inched around it. I opened the rear door. It was immediately almost torn from its hinges by the wind. It ended up pinned grotesquely to the Rover's side. Anne jumped out, shrouded in the military-issue slicker top. She was barefoot for the slippery run carrying the small boy in her arms.

I reached into the Land Rover. I cradled the older girl who weighed about 60 pounds. I lifted her and turned to follow the already running green slicker as the guard raised the gate. In a second we were on the bridge. I felt my wet sandals hit the steel-grated roadbed. Anne was running bare-legged, bare-footed, and bare-headed into the storm. She ran ahead of me like an Olympic distance runner with long, slow, controlled strides, anchored by desert and reef hardened bare feet.

The bridge rolled at every surge of the river's torrential current and with each blast of the wind. Its creaks were awesome. They produced sharp pangs of fear. The tiny human cargo in my arms cried. Every hour of high school track practice went into my strides. I accelerated past Anne with the now dying little girl in my arms. She had seemed to stop breathing as her cries ceased. She was in shock. The sudden exposure to the storm had caused her mind and body to reel in terror.

"God speed, Yank," echoed through my mind. I loped across the rain-slicked bridge at 100-meter Olympic speed, starting to gasp for air. I could no longer hear Anne's steps. The bridge suddenly lurched a foot or more downstream. It rebounded in a sharp, loud snap.

The bridge's snap caused me to skid. I lunged to the right, off balance, with the dying girl in my arms. I thought I was going to be tossed over the bridge's low concrete side railing if I hit it off-balance. With both arms around the child, I had no way to break my fall. I veered toward a crash into the one-lane bridge's 3-foot-high concrete side wall.

I could see the water 10 feet below. It carried whole palm tree trunks downstream in its torrent. An 80-plus mph wind gust hit me in the face like an anvil. It tore my pith helmet off with a snap of its leather neck strap. It accelerated my uncontrollable lunge toward the railing. In one second, I would hit the railing and pitch into the river. I had to drop the girl and grab the low concrete railing to break my fall.

At the last possible moment, I felt a small, unexpected strong hand from behind. It pushed my right shoulder hard to the left. The shove took the weight off my buckling right knee. It allowed me to catch my balance. It stopped the disastrous skidding fall on the wet iron bridge's grated bottom. Anne had caught me from behind. She had managed to hold the boy with one hand. She used her free hand while in full stride to shove me back from the beckoning danger of the low railing.

Anne was amazing. I owed her a life. One of my seven had been lost on the bridge. I hoped it was in exchange for my tiny human cargo. I regained my balance. I resumed a slower, safer stride. The wind continued to howl from the west. The storm summoned its full fury for a final deadly assault on the islands of paradise and their inhabitants.

I saw the end of the bridge's roadbed. The ambulance's flashing lights appeared as we approached the raised town bridge gate. I could hear Anne's bare footsteps behind me as we loped the final 100 feet on the town side of the bridge. The little girl was not breathing audibly. I prayed for her as I ran. The bridge's structure snapped and lurched again. This time, I was prepared. I took the resulting vibration in stride. The bridge was failing. I hoped it would hold together a few more seconds until we reached the waiting ambulance.

After a long tired final stride, I was off the bridge. Anne strode up beside me. She was gasping for air. A Fijian doctor took the little girl gently from me as a nurse took the smaller boy from Anne. They disappeared into the back of a green military ambulance with a red cross. The ambulance accelerated away in the dark gray storm spraying us with a sheet of water.

Anne fell into my arms. She gasped for air as she cleared her eyes. I gradually caught my breath. I felt the Aussie girl-woman's body press against me through her slicker. We had survived an ordeal few people would encounter in a lifetime. We had bonded in a special way. I felt her hard breathing under the wet, military slicker top.

A sharp crack like a dynamite blast knocked us to our knees. The bridge had surrendered. We watched the center span plunge toward the Sigatoka River. We stared at the falling section over which we had run. The shattering, thundering crack was followed by a giant splash as the center span disappeared into the raging brown river. Only the end spans rested on their concrete pillars on each riverbank.

Sigatoka and its inhabitants were cut off from the capital city side of the main coast road. The wind howled. I grabbed Anne's arm. We fought through the wind down the block to the co-op administrative headquarters. We pounded on the door and Raja finally heard us. He had remained on watch at the office. He had a British candle lantern burning for light to conserve the generator's fuel.

I ordered him to go to his uncle's house to help his own family. I planned to stay at the co-op office. Without the Land Rover, I had no reason to return to the hospital. Driving conditions were almost impossible anyway.

He warned me the four hours after 6:00 PM would be the worst. It was already past 5:00 PM, so the typhoon's center was advancing. The wind was predicted to hit 180-200 mph based on reports being carried by the emergency short-wave channel. He said four freighters had already sunk off the coast in heavy seas. All hands were presumed lost. It was rapidly becoming the worst recorded storm in modern written Fijian history.

After Raja left for home, Anne and I both climbed the steps to my second-floor office. She sat down exhausted on an old Fiji army-issue cot. I slept on it occasionally after too much alcohol or grog with the boys in town at night. I got a dry beach towel from a storage cabinet. She pulled off her wet slicker. She tossed it on the floor with mine and began to dry her face, then her body. She was exhausted from the drive and run.

The wind howled at death speed. The rain blasted the double-walled, European style cinder block building in waves. Its closed metal storm shutters tore at their hinges. In the candle lantern light, we consummated a day that would thread our lives in ways that only the gods would reveal to us as they changed the corners of our destiny. Anne had been sent by the Storm God to collect my soul in the island of paradise.

CHAPTER THIRTY
THE STORM

Anne clung to me in deep sleep. The storm battered the Fijian provincial town on a remote island at the edge of the world. There was an even chance we were going to die together. At six o'clock, daylight was fading fast as the storm started to reach its peak. It hit with 200 mph gusts causing the concrete block stucco building to shake. Fortunately, it had one of Fiji's few modern tar and gravel roofs. I wondered if the building could withstand the powerful wind blasts much longer. I could hear large pieces of debris strike the building and impale its painted, stuccoed, cinder block sides or smash against its modern light steel typhoon shutters.

It was almost dark in the second floor co-op office. I had a torch (or flashlight) at cot side for emergencies. The candle lantern had been extinguished by the room's breeze. The louvered storm shutters leaked blasts of air through broken window panes. I hoped Dianne was safe at the old stone hospital on its higher grounds. It also had an emergency basement and emergency generators. I now wished Anne and I were there, but fate had brought us to meet our destinies at the co-op office after the rescue effort. I knew an attempt to leave the co-op building would be suicidal. A move from the cot seemed a waste of energy. We were both warm under an old green GI army blanket my mom had sent me after I arrived in Sigatoka. It was for cold nights in the tropics. I had finally unpacked the blanket from its cardboard shipping box when the full chill of the typhoon hit.

The last hour had passed slowly. The storm had become progressively worse. Fiji was taking a head-on direct western hit. A lot of life was at risk. Nature always had interesting ways of reducing the population. This was one of its most awesome balancers. Anne stirred again from her deep sleep. All I wanted was her when she woke up—if we were still alive. Finally, with some time to think, I recollected local rumors about Anne and her husband. The rumors were that she had met the aging Aussie Fiji hotel owner on New Year's holiday in Sydney. She hopped across the Southern Pacific to a new life in Fiji on its Gold Coast. The spoiled urban New Zealand and Aussie rich hung out at her husband's hotel. She was his mate for long days and nights of drinking. Local Fiji village gossip also included stories of wife-swapping with guests. The Fijian village Methodist women who worked as maids at the hotel did not approve of these semi-orgies, according to Dianne.

Another half-hour passed. Suddenly, a giant explosion shook the co-op building. A set of storm shutters imploded into the room on their hinges, breaking window glass. Anne woke and screamed in shock. I leapt from the cot instantly. Wind blown glass and rain showered into the room. I saw that the old colonial hotel on the opposite corner to the co-op building was on fire. It was burning in the rear where the kitchen was located. No one was fighting it. The wind was too fierce for vehicles or men to move. I hoped the hard rain and their inside fire hoses could save the classic colonial wood framed hotel.

I struggled against the blasting wind and finally forced the damaged storm shutters back into place. Then Anne helped me push a tall steel storage cabinet against the broken window, blocking it completely. Next, we pushed my desk against the storage cabinet to complete the barricade.

Anne held the flashlight in one hand as she worked. From time to time, it highlighted a portion of her blanket-draped, lithe, nude body as we anchored the cabinet and desk. Finally, with a side-by-side shove, we pushed the old teakwood desk firmly behind the cabinet. We were both standing in glass with small cuts on our feet.

Anne said, "Let's play 'I Spy'," as she perched, legs dangling from the desk. She pointed the flashlight into my eyes, so I was completely blinded.

"What's 'I Spy'?" I asked vaguely remembering a childhood game.

"You'll see," she said. "It's very easy to learn and very exciting. We play it at the hotel on very boring nights. We use a dark room like this. You take the flashlight while I move about. When I pause, you point your flashlight beam. Try to hit my 'black triangle', as you Yanks call it, with the beam of light. You get five chances, Yank, to spy the black triangle. If you do, you can do anything you want to the black triangle. If you miss, Yank, I get the flashlight and you move about the room. I try to spy your 'wonk', Yank. If I do, I get to do it any way I want. So let's get on with the game until this hellish storm ends and we have to start the cleanup."

We played 'I Spy'. The flashlight beam zapped into a wall, then a breast, then a head, then a thigh, but never her black triangle. It was a great way to ignore the storm. An hour later, the beam fortunately zapped my wonk as the flashlight batteries were waning. I heard the wind drop for the first time in an hour. I thought I heard a police vehicle siren. Maybe we were going to live and play 'I Spy' again.

The wind was finally receding. Anne would have to collect later. It was time to check the storm damage. I dressed by the dim flashlight. We both put on rain gear. I told her to stay inside downstairs. I was going out to check the building—maybe the town.

She said, "OK, Yank." She turned to wave goodbye as she struggled to roll up her too-long slicker pants.

I crept down the dark steps one at a time. By memory, I crossed the dark first floor office to the front door of the building. I bumped the corner of a wooden desk only once. Fijian co-op offices were always sparsely furnished. Everyone sat on mats for all important occasions, including co-op meetings. I removed the door's inner iron crossbar. I opened it.

The eye of the typhoon was passing overhead now. It was eerily quiet. Debris blanketed the street. The almost-full moon peeked through the clouds to illuminate the town. The river was over its banks. A foot of water rushed against the sandbags in front of the co-op building. Both buildings across the street were damaged. Their pitched tin roofs were blown off completely. Pieces of roof tin were imbedded in the stucco-covered cement block walls of the co-op building like flat spears. Palm trees were blown down and twisted in grotesque shapes. Shattered green coconuts littered the town and bobbed in the flood water. The main part of the hotel had miraculously survived the fire.

A few people were out wading in the flood water. It was up to their knees by the hotel. Everyone seemed dazed and lifeless as they surveyed the damage to the town in the moonlight. No vehicles moved in our sector. The water and debris were still too deep in the street.

I closed the co-op building storm doors behind me. I stepped over the low wall of sandbags in front of the building. I waded into the slow-moving current of water. A coconut banged into my leg. A dead mongoose floated by. The mongoose had been brought to Fiji from India by the British to kill the rats in the sugarcane fields which had migrated to Fiji by sailing ship. Now the mongoose threatened to overrun the islands. They had no effective natural predators except India's cobra. This one had tanked in during the storm. It was on its way out to sea.

I crossed the street in knee-deep water and waded toward the bridge. I couldn't believe the devastation. All three single concrete spans had disappeared. The support columns were completely underwater. Jammed against them in the river, lying on its side, was a 180-foot-long inter-island freighter. No ship had been up the Sigatoka River since clipper ship days when the town had a port. Agricultural run-off from the valley's lush sugar cane fields had silted up the mouth of the river. The channel hadn't been dredged in 30 years since it was used by U.S. Navy PT-Boats to protect the southern side of the island from a feared Japanese attack; although, the Japanese never did attack Fiji.

Apparently, the stricken freighter had attempted to run the mouth of the river and seek safety during the storm. It had crashed into the wounded bridge. It had knocked the remaining two spans down. That was the sonic level explosion Anne and I had heard when the shutters blew open, not the hotel fire.

There was no sign of life on the inter-island freighter. It listed eerily on its right side and blocked the river almost bank to bank. I wondered if all hands had been lost in the storm.

Stunned, I watched the ship slowly pitch in the tidal river. A fatigue clad Fijian soldier approached me. He said in Fijian that only five of the crewmen had survived of the 40 sailors and passengers on the Tongan freighter. It was carrying gasoline filled drums to Fiji from New Zealand. The steel gasoline drums had begun to leak posing an ecological danger to the reefs downriver and fire danger to the town. The five crewmen were at the hospital. One was badly-injured and not expected to live.

I asked him if he knew the fate of the little boy and girl we had rescued. He didn't. He had been upriver moving villagers to more protected higher sub-valleys before the peak of the storm. Twenty villages along the river had been evacuated. The typhoon had leveled them. They were also flooded. Over a hundred lives had been lost already upriver. The body count included soldiers and three policemen killed during village evacuations. The annual sugarcane crop had been ruined in the lower valley.

The soldier also had heard that an American Peace Corps teacher was dead up at Mid-Valley School. He had been killed when the school's roof collapsed. The main valley road was closed and washed out by the river in many places. The valley's alluvial river plain flats were underwater. Nature was re-silting some of the world's richest farmland. Nature was depositing new topsoil and decreasing the island's exploding population. Larry, a PCV friend who taught sixth grade, was now in heaven. I was in semi-shock.

I asked him if the hospital was OK. He said, yes, there was no major damage. It was severely overcrowded as more injured people arrived in town. He responded to an Indian merchant who yelled for help from an apartment above the duty-free shop. Apparently, he had lost the roof on his two-story building.

It seemed from the report, most of the Fijian villagers had survived in the partially sheltered high interior valleys upriver. According to the village stories passed down through the generations, the interior valley villages had survived the storms throughout Fiji's 1000-year history. The news, I feared, from the coastal villages would be worse.

I turned and walked past the co-op building. I walked toward the hospital and slowly sloshed through the murky water. I walked up the long driveway. It was littered with government Land Rovers. I raced up the steps of the majestic concrete and stone white colonial building. I wanted to see Dianne.

Inside, it was bedlam. Nurses, doctors, and patients darted everywhere. Dianne was in the center of the lobby. She directed traffic in three languages. Her long auburn golden hair pulled back in a bun a la Florence Nightingale. She saw me. She quickly walked over to me. The sad tension in her eyes revealed all I needed to know. She collapsed exhausted into my arms for a couple of minutes fighting back sobs.

Finally, in a whisper, she said, "The little girl fought for her life. She died an hour ago. The boy is in intensive care, but he is expected to live."

I cried in anguish for a long moment. I remembered the warmth of the tiny fragile human child in my arms when I raced across the bridge. I vowed to remember that tiny, beautiful face always. I silently prayed to all gods, including Fiji's, to grant her small soul peace forever. After I recovered, I told her Anne and I had stayed at the co-op building, because it had been too dangerous to return to the hospital after the co-op Land Rover was trapped on the east side of the collapsed bridge. Dianne gave me a short quizzical apprehensive look that held back a terrible thought.

I broke the silence and asked her if she had news from the capital city of the provincial police headquarters.

She answered, yes. It was very bad in western Fiji and our province had taken a direct hit. Also, 300 Fijian villagers and Indian farmers were estimated to be dead along the southwestern coast. Forty to fifty-foot wind-driven waves had crashed over the barrier reefs, propelled by 200 mph wind gusts. At least a hundred tourists were also dead at western outer island hotels. These islands had only sporadic radio contact. Six ships were known lost and abandoned. That included the Tongan freighter which ran upriver on the high storm tide and hit the bridge.

Dozens of small crafts were missing along the coast. A Pan Am jumbo jet had been destroyed at the international airport. It flipped upside-down in the wind. Upriver was better with only 100 or so deaths. She confirmed our friend Larry, a Peace Corps teacher, was crushed by a school building roof beam. He had died in the mid-valley satellite hospital two hours ago. A Fijian policeman had carried him there on foot, at great risk to his own life.

"Finally," she said sadly and looked directly into my eyes as she searched for my reaction, "Anne's husband is dead. Their hotel is badly damaged. He refused to evacuate with several of his drunken Aussie guests. The police radioed a half-hour ago. Thirty-foot waves washed the stricken freighter off the reef into the hotel at the typhoon's peak. The freighter destroyed the hotel bar and restaurant when the waves battered it against the hotel main building."

Without emotion, she said, "When you return to the co-op building, you need to tell Anne or she will hear it on the street. But, if she can work, we still need her here. Our nurses are starting to drop from exhaustion. There are 500 injured patients here. Fifty more an hour are arriving for emergency treatment. We can use you to drive as soon as the river recedes. Some of the drivers have been on duty 18 hours now."

I said, "OK."

A nurse yelled and Dianne dashed off to help solve another crisis. A stretcher was rushed through the front door. I turned and strolled quickly down the slick concrete steps back toward the co-op building my heart empty and my stomach hollow. Nature was often fatal, I thought. A Peace Corps teacher friend had been killed in the shelter of his school room. He helped build it with money he raised from the small Ohio town where he was born. His dad published the local newspaper. I was young, so these sad facts only circled like airplanes. They had no place to land. There were no judgments or conclusions to be made today. I was amazed at it all.

I sloshed back into the receding river water as the wind began to blow hard again. The eye of the typhoon was about to pass. It was getting dark again. The moon disappeared under a bank of clouds. I walked the block to the co-op building with a death message ready to deliver. I wondered how to deliver it. I wondered how Anne would react. I had never delivered a death message before.

It was almost pitch black. I opened the storm-shuttered doors of the co-op building. I met Anne face to face as she happily threw her arms around me. She kissed me with pure joy. Her body pressed against mine. I froze in the door frame as the wet chilly west wind rushed to fill the candle lantern lit room. My lips started to move in slow motion, one word at a time as I told her the tragic news.

CHAPTER THIRTY-ONE
AFTER THE STORM

Anne took the first motorboat across the receding river. She had the spare set of co-op Land Rover keys in hand. She left to survey the ruins of her late husband's almost completely destroyed beach resort hotel. She owned it after her husband's untimely death during the typhoon. I watched the motorboat cross the river. It had dropped 20 feet but was still above flood stage. The river current rocked the still aground inter-island freighter as it flowed through the gray concrete ruins of Fiji's second longest and highest bridge. The wind had almost completely ceased. The tropical sky was blue accented with white, blustery clouds that passed through like bands of Plains Indians chasing a buffalo herd that had thundered through the day before, trampling the high plains wheat grass.

Anne's motorboat reached the safety of a temporary army pontoon mooring on the river's eastern bank. She turned, waved, and then scrambled barefooted up the muddy riverbank with the aid of a rope ladder. It dangled from the ruined bridge's gatehouse. Memories of Anne and the storm merged in the recesses of my mind. This girl-woman widow was a major new drug. I had sampled it at nature's biggest party. My life's course had been irrevocably changed. Her courage had been stunning.

I watched the Land Rover turn and drive away from the muddy river. My heart raced and my stomach muscles tightened as she disappeared.

I walked back to the co-op office building along the muddy streets of the provincial capital. Its citizens scurried everywhere. They unboarded windows. They removed sandbags. They surveyed the damage to houses, buildings, vehicles, and nature itself. Almost everyone was in a good mood, island-style. Everyone was happy to be alive. Fiji always amazed the western mind. With no bridges, no insurance, no electricity, no water supply, few vehicles functioning, huge property damage and death, everyone had a "Bula" wherever I walked. Life always came first in these magical islands. Even grief for the dead was subjected to respect for nature. The will of the gods—Christian, Animist or Hindu, had blown through. They would strike again on some other day in some other form like a tidal wave.

Nature held the dominant hand in the balance between man and God in Fiji. All the planning, manipulation, money, insurance and whining never altered the equation for long. These island people knew this instinctively from birth. The storm had forever imprinted this philosophy on my brain. The storm had rubber-stamped my inherent western ranch-bred belief in the fatalism of nature versus the false ideologies of mankind. Nature held all the power over capitalism, communism, materialism, socialism, or fundamentalism.

The town of Sigatoka was about 50% missing. I returned to the co-op office building. It remained without local electricity, phones, or water. It was still storm shuttered and sandbagged. No one except Raja had reported to work. The town and its surrounding villages had started vital repairs to houses, vehicles, bridges, and roads. It was a grand communal effort without the aid of State Farm or the supervision of big government.

I walked into the dark co-op main office. I froze as a pale white ghost appeared. It was Patipati. He spoke with a soft voice.

He said, "The windstorm had blown my spirit back from the sea before it completed its journey to the entrance of the Spirit World on the Island of the Dead in the Sea of Souls west of Fiji. In another day, I would have entered the Cave of Waiting joining the netherworld of murdered souls. Only the Great Sea Wind can move a newly dead spirit back to the island village of its life before it transcends the Earth World to the Spirit World for rebirth to return to the forests to protect my village.

"You must avenge my murder. You will go to the island of the Firewalkers, you will abstain from kava and sex with any woman while you surf in the Mother Ocean. Purify your soul and prepare to walk the fire at the second full moon after the storm.

"This purification on the Island of Fire will cleanse your thoughts so you can identify the murderer who killed me in my sleep and who is unknown to my spirit. I cannot leave the Cave of Waiting and enter the Spirit World for rebirth until a warrior can identify the murderer of my earth body and avenge my death. Now only you can help me with this task, or my spirit will remain in the Cave of Waiting for eternity. When you know the name of my killer, you must avenge my murder. I must enter the Spirit World and be reborn and complete a full life in my village. Then I can live peacefully in the forest after death in the Spirit World as a guardian of my clan and its village forever.

"After you walk the fire, go to a bure named Kennedy, in honor of your dead president. The chief of the Firewalkers is a very wise man who will be your guide for the journey. He will call his witch doctor, the Master of Fire. He will send you to the Land of the Dead Chiefs who rule the Spirit World and the Land of Rebirth. Be brave. Carefully follow the chief's instructions. This is magic which does not exist in your world's realm.

"When you enter the Land of the Dead Chiefs, the great-grandfather of my mother, a gatekeeper, will guide you, and you will tell him the name of my murderer. If he does not reply, the name is correct. When revenge of my murder is completed, the Gatekeeper will let my spirit enter the Spirit World for rebirth.

"I must go now. While the winds still flow in a circle to the Island of the Dead, I can re-enter the underwater Cave of Waiting on the next low tide.

"Have courage always, Cooper. I will guide the tiny child spirit, whose earth life you tried to save upon my return. She will be safe on her path across the vast ocean to the Spirit World's Land of Rebirth. I was on the bridge and helped save you from the fall through Anne's hand in the great wind. Someday you and Anne, if you choose, may leave your realm. You may join the Fijian spirits. Survive the Island of Fire. Goodbye, 'Bula telle'."

The voice lingered a millisecond longer than the ghost and Patipati was gone... My course of action was set. After I helped with the storm's cleanup and sent Dianne home to the States, I would go alone to the Island of the Firewalkers. I would purify my soul, surfing in the last giant winter storm waves. I would walk the fire at full moon. I would identify Patipati's killer or die trying. If I succeeded with these two tasks, I would enter the Land of the Dead Chiefs. My future was set.

I had heard around the village kava bowl, his great-great-grandfather was a powerful war chief. He was a keeper of the sacred burial caves up-river. They must be an earthly entry to the Land of the Dead Chiefs. Anne would have to wait, maybe forever.

If I failed Patipati, then I died also. I had to trust him completely one final time as I journeyed from my realm to his realm in search of a silent murderer. The murderer must have revealed himself to me. From the recesses of my mind, I had to unscramble the puzzle.

I stood staring at the floor into a shaft of light. It beckoned me to hurry my co-op's work and to start my journey into the heartbeat of Fiji. A journey deep into a spirit world taboo to all non-Fijians.

CHAPTER THIRTY-TWO
THE RIVER VALLEY

Thoughts of Anne danced in my head as the Land Rover skidded through the wet, silt covered valley river road. I traveled to check the co-op's remote upper valley outpost. Anne had returned the Land Rover to the town three days after the typhoon. The Fijian army engineers had built a U.S. AID loaned military style pontoon bridge across the river.

Anne had showed up at dusk. She found me in the co-op's Honda generator room. I was adjusting the generator's amperage output. I didn't hear her enter the small room because of the roar of the generator. It still was the building's only source of electricity. I finished tweaking the output level which stabilized the electric lights on the building's first floor. I turned around startled to see the Aussie girl-woman clad in a cotton print muumuu. Her hair was in a bun. I was happy to see Anne.

We went out the back door of the co-op building and crossed to the town's old colonial style hotel for dinner and drinks. She told me her husband's body had been recovered in his collapsed beachfront hotel bar. He died with four of his Sydney friends. They had all died when the wave-driven freighter crashed on shore. It collapsed the bar's fragile thatched roof hewn log-beam supported ceiling. It was built over the lagoon's inner reef.

They were, in essence, trapped unconscious in a circus tent and drowned in the high tide and wind driven water.

She said it was macabre watching their water-logged decomposed corpses being pulled from the collapsed hotel building. She sobbed quietly that she had nearly been forced to have sex with one of the men during her husband's drunken, degenerate parties that took place in their quarters near the hotel. She added, shaking, that she avoided sex with one of the dead men only by convincing him, while drunk, to stick his dick in a wine bottle. He couldn't free it. He passed out trying to get it out of the wine bottle. He was furious the next day. She had fled to town the day before the storm to hide from her husband.

According to her Fiji lawyer, she would inherit the hotel. Her husband had only one son with an ex-wife who had committed suicide. The son had been killed at 18 in Vietnam. He was a volunteer in the Aussie Special Forces. They were aiding the U.S. in the war. The lawyer was now attempting to collect the hotel's insurance from Lloyds of London. She wanted to rebuild and reopen. She said her dead husband had invested the last of his trust inheritance in the hotel over the past five years. He had believed in the world's growing tourist interest in Fiji.

Anne said she had nothing to return to in Australia. I didn't tell her I had to exit Fiji in December forever. My heart skipped a beat as my mind saddened.

As I ate a bowl of ice cream with British biscuits from a French hand painted tin, I felt a finger tug on my khaki shorts zipper. The small round hotel dining table for two was covered by a proper British white linen tablecloth; it dropped to our laps. While Anne teased me, I quickly paid the check. The girl-woman was a bold free spirit, untamed, and unequaled. She was definitely becoming part of my life.

The Land Rover slid suddenly to the left. I steered right to get back in the muddy deep track created by the valley buses. They ran the valley road twice a day. My trip upriver had been visually devastating and shocking. The co-op sheds and building structures had mostly survived intact but lost their tin sheet roofs. The riverside crops were buried under a half-foot of silt. There would be no tobacco strike this year. The seedling beds were 90% washed out and their riverside fields were still partially flooded.

A stop at the mid-valley, Aussie-managed, Anglo-American Tobacco Company brought a quick unexpected surrender from its expatriate manager. The company agreed to raise the price of high-grade tobacco immediately to eight cents a pound. They hoped the immediate price increase would be enough incentive for the farmers to grow a small crop this year. They were pragmatic. They knew they were out of business if they stayed at the old price.

The typhoon had won the tobacco strike. The chief and his warriors would not fight again before independence, which would be after I left Fiji. They had to rebuild their villages. They had to quickly get their communal cash crops, like bananas, broom corn and passionfruit, back into production.

Everywhere in the wide, flat alluvial river valley, the storm had wreaked equal havoc. Nearly every wooden house and village bure had damaged roofs and sides. Half were blown down completely with only their corner posts standing. It looked like the valley's entire population had moved on sound stage flats in Hollywood. I looked into the houses' rooms as I drove. Fences, passionfruit trellises, and uprooted trees were blown down everywhere. Palm fronds, tree branches, tin roof sections, and bamboo poles were scattered for miles. Every field the river had flooded had six inches of rich new black silt.

The Fijian villages were mostly built on bluffs above the river or in interior sub-valleys along the river. They were well spaced, showing good planning by the Fijians. They had survived these typhoons for a thousand years. The Indian farmers, however, who leased the river flats for sugarcane or other agricultural production from the Native Land Trust Board, had lost everything as the river rose. The river submerged their houses, tractors, cars, and crops. In some tragic cases, whole families drowned when they didn't evacuate to high ground.

The river rose rapidly. It flash-flooded. It absorbed the runoff from the typhoon's four inches of rain per hour. An estimated 50 people drowned in the valley, plus another 1,000 cows, horses, and oxen. Another 100 or so people were killed by the wind or flying objects. Fiji's death toll had risen to almost 1,100 people. Most had been killed on the southern and western coasts of Viti Levu, Fiji's main island and its remote western islands.

It was the worst modern recorded storm, but probably not the worst in history. Fiji legend recounted a storm some 500 years before that killed almost every living animal and man in the island chain. According to the legend, the gods had been angry at a great chief who burned Viti Levu's rain forest in an attempt to end a ten-year drought. It was during the time of the Pacific's great volcanoes that filled the sky with ash for years on end. It was because of the legendary disaster that Fiji's island culture had adapted to survive total blowdown.

The more sheltered upper valley Fijian villagers had already collected the pieces of their tear-away bures. Many had been partially rebuilt within a day or two of the storm. Nature readily provided new building materials; some blew in with the wind to replace the old building materials that blew out with the wind. The other residents of Fiji from eastern and western cultures lived in wooden or cinder block buildings with tin roofs which would take months to rebuild.

The Valley Fijian villagers, however, were amazing. Four days after the storm, they had repaired fifty percent of their essential housing. They were already working on their large village ceremonial bures to temporarily house the village schools. It would take months to rebuild their European-style wood and tin roofed government school buildings. The kids would miss some school until the long, large, ceremonial bures would be ready for daytime classes. By night, the bures would be used as kava centers by the tired village men. The kids who studied by day, at night would fall asleep in their father's secure laps while the village elders dispensed wisdom, history, religion, and legend through story. Fiji was still a verbal society. It had written words for only 80 years provided by the white Methodist missionaries from the colonial mother country.

B.J. was the co-op's top Hindu valley staffer. He met me at the missing gate to the upriver co-op office and grain storage depot. The depot roof was gone. Only four corner poles and bare rafters remained. The bamboo woven-sided office had survived intact somehow. The wind had only reached 100 mph in the upper part of the valley. This stop completed my tour. I mentally estimated it would take six months for the co-op to rebuild. I was to be discharged in two months and Dianne left in two weeks.

I told B.J. since Patipati was dead, he was in charge of the rebuilding effort. I would organize the funds for him before I left for Nadi Airport with Dianne. I would also call a final meeting to turn the co-op over to Chief Kavula. The chief's younger nephew, Aliali, would run day to day operations. B.J. would run the books. The Chief and Aliali would run the politics. The Co-op Department, hopefully, would also send a trained Fijian manager from Suva to replace Patipati and me.

The loss of Patipati, I explained, was a major setback. He had studied at the National Co-op School for a year. He had worked for me for two and one-half years. He could not be replaced easily. The chief's nephew was a compromise at best. He had attended agricultural college at the University of Hawaii. From his stories, though, he had apparently mostly majored in rock and roll and California beach girls. However, he had married one of the prime minister's nieces recently, so, maybe he would settle down.

I explained, I could not stay another year. I had been in Fiji almost three years already. I didn't explain I was exiled forever because of the potato war. The chief still couldn't and didn't know this information. No one knew the terms of the deal, not even Dianne.

A half-hour meeting with B.J. covered every detail of the co-op rebuilding plan. I budgeted the amount of funds which the co-op needed. We adjourned from the damp, cold, lantern-lit co-op office to his quarters. It was also located on the co-op compound. He lived with his wife and four kids in a two-room bure. It was different from the village variety because it had a tin western-style roof to catch rainwater in the co-op's concrete cistern. The cistern provided water for the compound, which was a quarter-mile walk to the river on a high plateau. His Hindu sari-clad wife, who was dark, mysterious, and sexy, met us at the door. We removed our sandals. It was the custom in Fiji. We entered the rain-damaged, mat-covered floor of the bure's main room.

The smell of homemade curry permeated the room. I surveyed a feast of curried river prawns, potatoes, eggplant, and homemade chutneys with Indian home-baked breads. An open bottle of Red Label Scotch accompanied the meal. It was spread out on a cotton print tablecloth on the mat-covered floor of the bure. B.J. and I ate alone. It was the custom since this was a business visit and not a social occasion.

His wife had eaten with their four children. She would put them to bed after they greeted me. They had been well-scrubbed for the occasion. After a handshake, they disappeared through the string bead doorway into the bure's sleeping quarters. Their mother was a step behind. Her bare brown feet slapping against the still rain-damp mats of their house. It still had a small part of its roof missing above the center of the front room. The missing tin section had been covered with a canvas tarp borrowed from one of the co-op trucks that was usually headquartered at the upriver depot to transport bananas. The bustling sensual sari disappeared through the bead curtain as my mind wandered momentarily to Anne. My thoughts were broken as I listened to a muffled bedtime story in Hindi punctuated with whispers and giggles.

B.J. and I drank quarter-glasses of straight warm Scotch with no ice or water. We sipped the Scotch in between handfuls of rice and curry dipped in homemade mango chutney. We ate Hindu-style with our right hands only. Hindu's used their left hand for bodily functions, therefore it was not available for eating. We sat cross-legged facing each other over the feast on the bure floor. We talked about the storm as we ate. We used English as a common language. I spoke good Fijian, but little Hindi. He spoke a little Fijian, but high school level English.

The curry was permeated with homegrown chilies and was very hot. After two and a half years in Fiji, I ate a couple of platefuls. I used the Scotch to wash it down. I was convinced Hindu curry was slowly eating a hole in my stomach. B.J. and his friends all had stomach ulcers in their mid-thirties. I watched my Scotch intake carefully since I had to drive back down valley with a half moon and headlights on a muddy, storm-damaged road. My final dinner with B.J. passed in a routine manner.

I had a slow two-hour drive down the dark muddy valley road to Anne's beach hotel. The curry would keep me awake. I planned to make a surprise and secret late-night visit before returning to town the next morning. B.J. chatted casually as we feasted. I heard B.J.'s wife read in Hindi to their children. I wondered if the mysterious, sexy Anne would be the woman to bring a home and children to my life someday.

CHAPTER THIRTY-THREE

THE BEACH HOTEL

The drive down the partially moonlit, deserted valley road was eerie. The headlights of the Land Rover ate the on-rushing wall of dark 25 yards ahead. It was a slow trip on the muddy gravel road which still was scattered with light debris, and only one lane wide. The upper valley bridges which were low concrete ramps with culverts were still flooded. My brakes were constantly wet after each ford in a foot or two of muddy water.

I drove past the sleeping villages. Only one or two Coleman kerosene lights flickered from open bure doors. People were working hard all day from sunup to sundown to rebuild. They turned in early to rest for the next day's tasks.

I drove the forty-plus mile stretch of road in two and a half hours. I never passed another moving vehicle, only a couple of parked semitrucks. They were delivering building materials to the school where the PCV teacher was killed during the storm. I had heard his parents donated all the money for its rebuilding. Americans always pleasantly surprised you with their generosity, even in time of great personal tragedy. The village, I knew, by Fijian custom would name the headmaster's doorway of the school for him, and therefore the school. It would be a memorial for their fallen friend from America.

I drove through the silent, dark, rain-saturated, and wind-damaged breadbasket of Fiji. The communal villagers were reweaving the fabric of their existence. There was a real sense of security in this approach. In Fiji, there were no tallies of the storm's winners or losers by the media. Fiji's urgency was to rebuild. There were no ruined, uninsured farms or businesses for greedy speculators to snap up at bargain prices. The villages communally owned everything, including house sites. The community endured the tragedy together and it rebuilt together. After the last of the dead had been buried or cremated, the hammers, axes and saws would sing in the late winter trade winds. Schools, medical centers, bures, houses, and farms would be repaired. The summer crops of the island's year-round tropical growing season would be planted.

The summer fields would be extra fertile from the silt that would be plowed into them to replenish the soil depleted by the constant tropical farming cycle with no fertilizers. Nature knew its job and it had done it well four days ago. The valley farms were rich in soil nutrients for another decade. The Fijian farmers avoided the use of fertilizers which washed out to sea and killed the vital reefs that provided the island with fish. The reefs protected the island's land from the eroding power of the waves. The waves had pounded the islands for millions and millions of years.

After another hour had passed in darkness, I saw the temporary entrance lights of Anne's closed beach hotel. The hotel had its emergency diesel generator running. It normally received its electricity from the town's oil-fired plant beside the river. The plant was still out of commission. I guessed where Anne's bungalow was located. I drove slowly toward it. I bypassed the badly damaged hotel compound which was dark.

I pulled up to her bungalow. I cut the headlamps of the Land Rover and its engine. I coasted silently up to Anne's colonial style, broad, partially missing front porch. It faced the ocean to the west. It was pitch black dark. The clouds blocked the moon, and I could hear the pounding surf on the reef-lined shore twenty yards away.

The roar of the still violent ocean drowned out my entry. Anne's front door was not open, so, I stared through the open front sliding screens. I saw a Coleman gas lantern-backlit nude figure. She stretched toward me on an Isfahan oriental carpet facing the open porch screen. Her eyes were closed, in a Yoga meditation. Her fingers were in lotus position. Her neck and head angulated properly with her ankles together.

Anne practiced a form of Hindu Yoga called Kundalini. She had learned it from her yard boy. He was the son of a valley Hindu priest. She practiced it while her late husband was on his month-long business and tourist promotion trips in Sydney. She had mentioned this passion to me during our dinner. She had indicated she was now experimenting with the Yoga and its meditation sexually. This practice was called Tantra Yoga. I watched her perfectly still body. In the low light, it seemed almost to be surrounded with an aura of yellow-gold light.

I didn't move and barely breathed. I watched Anne's secret world a dozen yards away behind the windscreen of the Land Rover. I quietly swiveled it down to enhance my view of her stunning, nude body. My eyes focused on her body which faced me at 12 o'clock high. The roar of the surf and the hum of the generator secreted my presence.

Suddenly, she rose slowly. She released her free finger and thumb from lotus position. She left her legs extended touching at the ankles, eyes closed, not sensing my presence. Her hand moved to her left breast. She massaged it slowly. She called this her heart center. I watched her left nipple harden. It protruded as she caressed her breasts softly with only her fingertips. Her motion was simple, erotic, and beautiful to watch. She chanted. I saw the rhythmic motion of her lips, but I could not hear her chant because of the pounding of the ocean on the nearby reef.

I watched the girl-woman for many minutes. Her finger constantly circled her left nipple. Then she moved her left forefinger to her nose. She moved it from nostril to nostril to control her breathing. The chant stopped. She simultaneously opened her legs to an extreme but comfortable vee. With her right finger she began to massage her clitoris in a circular slow motion. Her lips glistened in the low lantern light of the room. Her face muscles relaxed; her breathing was in a slow rhythm. Her thigh muscles tightened in their stretched-out flat position against the antique oriental carpet.

Her discipline was incredible. She did not move her body for ten minutes—only her forefingers. One moved from nostril to nostril to control her breathing and meditation. The other forefinger still circled her clitoris. Then she moved toward a physical climax as her toes curled. Her muscles rippled along her thighs and across her taut pelvis. Her right forefinger plunged deeper into her opening. Her diaphragm heaved to the rhythm of her meditative breathing.

I tried to time her orgasm with the rhythm of her breathing and the motion of her forefinger as it stimulated her whole spiritual being. I reached for the headlamp switch. I wanted to pull it at her peak. Seconds later, she plunged her right forefinger deep into her yani. I switched on the low beam of the Land Rover lights. She rose and folded into cat cow position to rest with her arms stretched toward the light, forehead against the carpet, knees tucked under her stomach and ankles together.

Later she told me the blast of white light was like the eastern sun rising. It enhanced the golden light energy she moved from her sexual organs or sexual chakra at the base of the spine to her heart center then out through the opening in the top of her skull. It formed her aura. She had often done this meditation at sunrise. The flash of the headlamps provided a timely substitute. She knew they were mine. She said she hadn't expected me to arrive until later because of the valley road conditions. She knew I would come tonight even though I had not sent a message that I was coming. She had passed the evening centering her spirit and mind. At noon, she had shipped her husband's body back to Australia for burial. A cousin had refused to allow his burial in Fiji. She didn't know I had watched her meditation. She assumed I had arrived when the headlamp beam burst into the room. I never told her my arrival had been earlier.

I walked into her living room and cast a dim shadow over her body.

She said, without raising her forehead to look up at me, "My orgasm was so intense, I cannot move my body. I am very wet from the experience and I want you sexually. Drop your shorts and enter with your eyes closed from behind in a kneeling position. Do not touch me except with your sexual organ. Quickly, Cooper, while I am still contracting from the orgasm."

I kneeled behind her. I saw her opening. Her bottom tilted up toward the ceiling. Her back arched over her thighs. Her knees were tightly folded under her breasts. My entry was swift and satisfying. I was already aroused from watching her meditation. She spontaneously contracted in rhythmic circular motions. She could not control them. We made love to the beat of the surf. I closed my eyes as the lantern light pierced my thin eyelids, filling my brain with yellow and white light. My orgasm was quick, emotional, spiritual, and deep. She neither moved her body nor made a sound. She signaled her pleasure with a final wave of warm fluid. She relaxed and expelled me into the warm, tropical Pacific Ocean air to face my own devils and destinies. She stretched out nude on her stomach with her small hands in a yoga position at her side and she fell asleep on the ancient, handwoven oriental carpet.

CHAPTER THIRTY-FOUR

FLY AWAY ANGEL

I watched the Pan Am jet lift off the tarmac at the Nadi International Airport. I rubbed the small antique silver ring between my thumb and forefinger. Dianne flew off like a bird forever. The giant silver plane lifted off for a Honolulu stopover, then Los Angeles. Tears flooded my eyes while memories raced through my mind like bumper cars at a county fair. Our relationship had burned brightly for a year. It slowly died during her last year in Fiji, held together only because of mutual daily survival needs. Fiji was a strange tropical time-scape of adventure, intrigue, beauty, sickness and boredom. Our relationship was lost forever in the sands of time. It was a small, faceted grain of human relationship left to drift forever in the currents of the universe.

The ring I rubbed softly between my fingers had been my great-great-great-grandmother's. She had been wounded by a Cherokee arrow, crossing the Cumberland Gap in the late 1700's to settle east Tennessee. It was special. It remained as an icon to protect me in my final quest for the killer of Patipati. It was time for a resolution of my affairs in the islands of paradise lost.

Maybe Anne would wear it on her right-hand ring finger someday in the style of the Aussie women. Maybe Anne was my great-great-great-grandmother reincarnated to protect me on this final mission across the gap of western civilization into the dark mysteries and voids of the nether-world of Fiji's dark spirits and black magic. This was not the trick illusions of touring magicians. It was the spirit world of live witch doctors. Their magic powers traveled with them on their voyage from the ancient dark continent to the islands of Fiji in long dugout canoes.

The airliner pivoted on its right wing. It jetted away from the setting sun. It turned northeast toward Hawaii six hours away across the equator, above the vast expanse of the endless blue Pacific Ocean. It became a tiny silver dot. Then it was lost forever from sight, mind and sound as the shadows of the evening sky lengthened. Twilight neared. I stood frozen and alone. I was not able to breathe standing behind the waist-high wooden fence beside the departure runway of Nadi International Airport. I realized I would never see Dianne again. Nothing moved except an armored army truck which had delivered a load of gold bars to the plane's cargo hold. They would be sold to purchase U.S. dollars in Honolulu for the Fiji Central Bank's reserve fund.

The U.S. dollar was at its zenith in world trade, like ancient Rome's gold coins. Countries like Fiji sent the labor of its sweaty black miners, who were paid 20 cents an hour to descend into hell, to Honolulu for deposit at the Federal Reserve Bank of San Francisco, California. Fiji paid its international dollar debt like tribute to Caesar's army, collected for return to Rome. Hippies naively thought they could bring down this giant world-wide cash register.

A small army guard truck rumbled by. Its Fijian Army guards relaxed their fingers on their machine gun triggers. A trip to the beer bars of Nadi was only two miles away, after they checked their weapons at their barracks. They had a night of R&R before returning to the mines at Vatukoula to guard another load of gold bars bound for London or San Francisco. Fiji had started buying back its obsolete sugar mills before the Union Jack was hauled down at Independence. Without a key currency, the Brits were already getting poorer.

I slipped the magic ring on my left index finger. It fit snugly. I planned to wear it for protection during the adventures ahead. If I died, I wanted it with me as the last link to the spirit of my renegade great-great-great-grandmother.

Anne was five hours away at her hotel. I was too emotionally drained to make the drive back across the southern coast of Viti Levu in the dark. Also, a period of mourning for Dianne was in order. Then, I planned to travel up to the boat landing for the Island of the Firewalkers to catch the Island's sail powered freighter in two days. I drove toward the Nadi Sky Lodge Hotel. I knew any available off-duty Peace Corps single male friends would gather there to hustle the incoming Pan Am stewardesses. I had seen the stewardesses disembark. They climbed into a well-marked Mercedes van, with two pilots and a flight engineer. They stayed in Fiji until Saturday when the next flight rotated through to Hawaii.

I knew one friend near the end of his Peace Corps tour who had practically moved into the Sky Lodge Hotel. He was burned out on island party girls. A Pan Am married stewardess he had seduced, offered him free airline tickets to Fiji, or anyplace in the world.

The paved road from the airport raced smoothly beneath the large, knobby off-road Dunlop tires of the tired co-op Land Rover. I had still not washed it since the typhoon. The tired four-cylinder engine whined in fourth gear on one of the island's only two-lane paved highways. It ran from the harbor to the island's international airport. It had been built with U.S. AID dollars. If the USA ever needed to land troops in Fiji, their armored personnel carriers could race through Nadi to the Sugar Port of Lautoka (Fiji's other main port) to secure it. This info was from the U.S. Consul's military attaché, revealed during a drunken bout with one of my PCV friends in the capital city. He asserted once the Pentagon secured the airport with its 12,000-foot runway and then the deep-water sugar export dock at the Port of Lautoka, that the U.S. could secure all of the main island of Viti Levu in two days. I had wondered, from whom was the island going to be secured?

The Sky Lodge loomed in the near distance in my low beams. I turned too fast into its parking lot. I had cut across a lane of traffic, still in third gear. I hurdled toward the Pan Am Mercedes mini-shuttle bus. Its side door was open. Pleated-skirt stewardesses ran for safety. I pumped the worn-out brakes but they failed. It was too late. The gray Land Rover tore the door off the Mercedes van with its low steel bumper. It hit the stack of Pan Am flight crew's luggage with a bang.

Aluminum suitcases exploded open in all directions. There was a storm of bras, panties, bikinis, dresses, and shorts. They covered the Sky Lodge's open reception area like snow in Aspen at Christmas. The girls were going to be pissed. I hoped one of them was dating my PCV friend. She might help me out of this disastrous situation if the Land Rover ever stopped.

Finally, it stopped six inches from the polished native hardwood reception desk. I was blinded by the various clothing items on my windshield. I was laughing too hard to exit the Land Rover. The right door opened with a thunk. I was face to face with a drunk U.S. airman who worked at the NASA satellite tracking station near Nadi. They all lived at the hotel in an annex building. These Air Force enlisted guys all hated Fiji's Peace Corps volunteers. The PCVs hated them with an equal passion. They called all PCVs draft dodgers. I didn't wait for him to get the advantage.

I had grown up in Colorado. I knew the first quick draw won a gunfight in the open street. I slammed my right elbow into his open mouth. I felt his front teeth break. I pivoted to exit. I raised my right knee into his balls. He doubled up in pain. I hit him in the stomach with a hard left-hand punch. I karate-chopped the back of his head as he crumpled to the polished wooden floor semi-conscious. This uncalled-for act was to settle three years of bullshit from these guys. I wouldn't be back in Nadi again except to exit Fiji forever. I turned to apologize for the brake failure to the Pan Am crew.

I heard my PCV friend, Jeff, yell, "Look out, Cooper! Hit the ground!"

I heard a pop-bang. I dove. An Air Force sergeant fired at me with a small service automatic pistol which was illegal in Fiji. He turned out to be on illegal R&R from Vietnam. No one, not even the American military was allowed to carry a loaded weapon in the islands. The police weren't even armed in Fiji. He had it concealed in his bloused pants at boot top.

The bullet went through the Land Rover's open door. It ricocheted off the roll bar into the polished monkey wood reception desk. The hotel's perfectly pressed Indian desk clerk dove for cover. The sergeant had made a huge mistake. He would probably spend a year in a Fiji jail if he didn't dash for the U.S. Air Force NASA compound a mile down the road. But he was too drunk. He aimed at me at point blank range.

I dropped and rolled left under the high Land Rover for protection. The second shot shattered a floor plank inches away. Pan Am stewardesses screamed at the top of their lungs for help. He never fired the third shot. Baba, the 6'6" Fijian bellman-greeter and legendary All Fiji Rugby player loved the American PCVs. He hit him from behind with a block that broke his back with a sickening snap. The block felled the drunken air force gunman like a tree. He never moved again.

Stewardesses cried. The two Pan Am pilots rushed to restrain Baba. He turned toward two other Air Force corporals who had started toward the Land Rover. They stopped in front of the sickening sight of their fallen comrade. Jeff was the Peace Corps' most famous rugby player in Fiji. He was a former All-Pac Ten fullback at USC. He moved in between the Land Rover, which I was still under, and the other two more drunken American airmen. He talked to his rugby teammate, Baba, in quick Fijian sentences. He urged him not to attack the other two airmen. They were unarmed. Baba stopped a foot from them with pilots hanging onto his giant forearms. They had been unable to stop his progress.

I still lay stunned silently under the Land Rover. I had just lost Dianne. Then, my brakes, which were worn out from wet typhoon duty and unreplaceable due to the lack of spare parts after the storm, caused this mess. Now, instead of a fist fight victim, there was a seriously injured, if not dead, American airman. Baba had saved my life. I knew no charges would be filed. All handguns were illegal in Fiji. I knew Baba would walk after a brief hearing by a Fijian magistrate. The drunk airman who pulled the illegal gun, might never walk, or see home again.

The blue-sulued Fijian police arrived seconds later. The policemen practically saluted Baba. He was a national hero. He had led the Fiji team to successive upset victories over the British Lions and New Zealand's hated 'All Blacks' team. I emerged, scraped and bleeding slightly, from under the Land Rover.

Jeff and Baba explained all to the local police in Fijian. They said I had been attacked by the two unconscious airmen after my brakes failed—one had shot at me with the gun the police were now holding. Baba had intervened only to save my life. The policeman gave the downed gunmen a disgusted look. They talked to Baba another minute before they called an ambulance on the radio phone in their Land Rover. The Fiji police didn't even bother to take the names of the stewardesses and pilots as witnesses.

The investigating Fijian officers were closing the case on the scene. They were also apparently tired of breaking up fights between U.S. airmen and local Fijians over the stewardesses. They weren't going to waste Fiji government time on the downed gunmen in a country which seized all guns at its customs entry points. U.S. military issue was included. There were no exceptions to this law.

CHAPTER THIRTY-FIVE
THE LAYOVER

The next afternoon the escape from Nadi was easier than the arrival. A Fiji police lieutenant called the prime minister's office. He told me to get out of town. He added not to come back until I was ready to catch a plane home. The American airmen were charged with drunk and disorderly conduct in public, plus carrying a loaded firearm in public. The individuals involved were ordered out of the country, including the injured and non-injured. The police report would note the Pan Am van driver had stacked the crew's luggage in a check-in parking place which had made the collision unavoidable at dusk.

The report also noted an unidentified, unregistered Peace Corps volunteer was assaulted by an airman. He had left the scene after being assaulted by a second illegally armed and publicly drunk visiting visa-less American airman from Vietnam. It noted Baba, a national rugby star and employee of the hotel, broke up the brawl heroically. The facts were Fiji facts, and I was on the road again. It was absolutely clear the Fiji government valued the service of 412 Peace Corps volunteers more than a dozen U.S. satellite-tracking racist U.S. airmen who mostly hated their duty tours in a Melanesian/Hindu country. The Pan Am crew wanted to avoid an international incident. It was bad publicity for the airline. Pan Am was a major charter contractor for both the Peace Corps and the U.S. military. The Pan Am Washington lobbyist would cover the airline's flanks.

I had boarded the Peace Corps Pan Am charter three years ago at 1:00 in the morning at Honolulu International Airport bound for Fiji. I had walked bula-shirted, flip-flop clad past gate after gate of battle-dressed crew-cut GIs boarding 747 Pan Am clippers for Da Nang Air Force Base in Vietnam. The contrast was horrific. The long-haired, mustached, casually dressed PCVs joked and laughed with their Fijian language instructors. We had anticipated two years of hard work and fun in the islands of paradise.

The grim-faced draftees were surrounded by crying wives, relatives, kids and friends. They were dressed in green battle fatigues with full field packs and Ml4 automatic weapons. Death was mirrored in their young faces. They stared suspiciously at the long line of PCVs boarding the Pan Am charter to Fiji. The PCVs had hope and love in their hearts for the nation and people they were about to meet. The PCVs wanted to help them achieve a peaceful and fulfilling independence.

The departure in Honolulu was the essence of Sparta, or America after World War II. Young warriors were sent to die in a massive military-industrial-central-government directed war in an obscure, former Chinese vassal state. It had already been abandoned as a colony of France, as the Southeast Asian base of the pre-World War II great decadent colonial power. If the French army couldn't hold a country, nothing could. The Foreign Legion assassins and the elite French airborne commandos surrendered Vietnam. A poorly trained U.S. draftee army was getting its butt kicked. It would have to use nuclear weapons to obliterate the enemy in the Vietnamese civil war.

I knew Sparta wasn't desperate enough yet to use its tactical nuclear weapons. The soldiers standing in line to fly to Da Nang were going to be chewed up fast. They knew it instinctively as they sullenly stared at the chattering equally young PCVs.

Only Pan Am was a big winner that night. It hauled both Sparta's warriors and its Dr. Livingstones to the edges of the Pacific Rim. One group faced violent death and dehumanization. The other group would find the islands of paradise about to be lost. The PCVs were the tripwire of the decline of the American empire and its impact on the world's ecosystem.

Fiji's recently pesticide poisoned reefs and its rental fleets of compact Japanese cars signaled the decline. Bulldozed pristine beaches prepared for tourist hotel resort development signaled the beginning of the end of paradise. Fiji was one of the last remote tripwires nature had left in place. The total assault on its fragile environment was overwhelming.

Vietnam was a needless riot gone haywire after Sparta's World War II Super Bowl. It partially disfigured everyone's life it touched, from Ho Chi Minh to Jane Fonda to Lyndon B. Johnson. Vietnam was historically a Chinese prisoner of war. U.S. intervention in its civil war was a sheer act of madness in its sea of history as a Chinese rice bowl, but America never studies history. America has a history it does not want to remember. America is a country that revolted against its English founders and killed them. Then it killed most of its native inhabitants. It imprisoned the remainder on reservations. Next, it killed any country or empire that tried to fuck with it.

Now, America just killed on reflex—like an old gunfighter—just to make sure the world knew it was a killer. It was even killing its land, animals, fish, and birds. Next, it would start killing its children. American manifest destiny had triumphed. I wondered if maybe the soldiers in the other Pan Am line had been lucky. America chewed them up quickly, while the PCVs had to return and contribute their knowledge to the killers—unless they could change America's destiny. That was the genius of the idea of the Peace Corps.

The Nadi paved highway ended as I drove north toward the Island of Fire's boat landing. I passed the entrance to Fiji gold mines where black-faced miners descended into hell for 20 dollars American a week on 12-hour shifts, six days a week. The dried blood of the airman I boxed still stained my clothes, so I stopped at a small lagoon to bathe and soak my clothes and sleep. The next day, I planned to drive to the Island of Fire's boat landing.

Chattering Fijian village kids woke me at midmorning on Saturday. They walked toward the lagoon to play in the warm water and to dive for reef fish for their lunch. I scrambled awake in a pair of khaki shorts. I dove into the incoming tide of the lagoon to bathe again in the warm South Pacific salt water. I scrubbed with a floating piece of natural sponge. It had been caught in the lagoon's eddy.

The children were surprised to see the Land Rover. They surrounded it

before I stood up, soaking wet, and waded toward the group. They ranged
in age from four to twelve, both male and female. The younger kids were
completely nude. It was the custom in the village in hot weather. The older
boys and girls wore only shorts or sulus.

They giggled and shouted "bula" or hello. I waded onto the beach. I
walked to the rear door of the Land Rover and opened it. I took out an aluminum U.S. Army surplus ammunition box. It was my suitcase. I stored a
secret supply of bubble gum for this kind of occasion. I tossed bubble gum
to the crowd, which numbered 20 or so. Everyone caught a piece. Fijian
kids loved to blow bubbles. Soon a sea of bronze-brown faces were covered with large pink balloons of Bazooka Bubble Gum. The kids popped
the bubbles randomly like small firecrackers to the soft slapping of the
lagoon's tidal pool surges.

The kids asked me to show them how to surf when they saw my surfboard strapped to the top of the gray co-op Land Rover. I said I needed big
waves not lagoon shore-break. I told them I had to reach the Island of Fire
by nightfall, so I had to leave for the boat.

I reached into the ammo box. I pulled out the co-op's new Polaroid
camera and snapped a couple of shots. This was always a crowd pleaser.
After they developed on the tailgate, I passed them around to approving
looks. I said my goodbyes as I pulled on my dry shirt and flip-flops. I buttoned up the ammo box. I closed the rear door of the Land Rover. I walked
around to the right-side door which was still open from the night before.

I started to climb into the Land Rover. I remembered a red coral stick
I had found in the lagoon. I picked it up. I put it in the glove box for
good luck. I climbed in and turned the key with my left hand. The engine
whined into life. I honked to clear a path through the kids. I started to back
out to the main road. It was 200 yards beyond the thick rim of coconut
palms that guarded the lagoon.

The waving kids scattered, shouting, "Goodbye, Mister!" The salutation
was left over from World War II when the GIs were based at Nadi to guard
the airport. It had sent squadrons of B-25 bombers north to slaughter the
Japanese at Guadalcanal and at Iwo Jima. Many of the Fijian lead scouts
for the U.S. Marines were killed by these bombs. The bombs fell blindly
from 20,000 feet onto the Japanese jungle positions on the islands below.

One of these kids' grandfathers probably died helping the USA whip
the 'Japs' in South Pacific jungles.

I had to see this Patipati thing through. It was time to get my feet on the Island of Fire so I could cleanse my mind and hopefully identify the killer of Patipati before I left Fiji forever. I drove at full speed. The interlude at the lagoon dimmed into a dream like so many experiences in Fiji. I had an hour of washboard gravel roads until I reached the boat landing for the Island of Fire. I hoped to meet the Saturday afternoon sailboat. It carried villagers back from their weekly trip to the Nadi market and to visit the gold mines. Many of the village's men worked in the gold mines. I had heard from PCVs that mid-Saturday afternoon the largest village sailboat always returned to the island. Sunday was a day of total rest in Fiji. The one thing the Fijians liked about Methodist colonialism was the Lord's day of rest. Every Fijian slept in on Sundays. Nothing moved nationwide, except an occasional bus, truck or taxi driven by an Indian. Double wages would not bring a Fijian to work from his or her village on a Sunday. It was one great nationwide slumber party. All the bars were closed. There were no kava ceremonies, only a trip to the village church occurred.

I needed to catch the last daylight boat on Saturday or wait a week. I pushed the accelerator a little harder. I neared the north coast boat landing near the coastal village of Bakaka. It had been a PT-Boat station during World War II.

All of Fiji's modern docks were recycled U.S. Navy World War II facilities. They had started to crumble from lack of maintenance. The young navy Seabees had built them well to withstand the Japanese bombing attacks, which never occurred. I was 25 minutes from the landing turnoff. I planned to hide the co-op Land Rover in the bush. I didn't want it found during my month or more on the Island of Fire.

I was officially on two weeks of accumulated Peace Corps annual leave plus one week accumulated sick leave. It would be a month before the co-op department or the Peace Corps headquarters staff missed me. The seasonal potatoes, watermelon, broom corn and corn crops had been harvested. B.J. could handle the surviving typhoon damaged banana and passionfruit crops. They were the co-op's routine weekly exports.

I had sworn him to secrecy about my month-long disappearance. I told him that I was going fishing and surfing with another PCV on the north island of Vaneu Levu. I trusted no one. I knew there were no phones or roads on the north coast of Vaneu Levu, so no one could check the story or find me easily.

I had also written my mother at the ranch. I told her of my planned surfing disappearance. I wrote that she would have to attend any funerals for me. No one could contact me. I left out the firewalking because I didn't want the government or the Peace Corps to know I was on the Island of Fire. I planned to walk the bed of flaming coals. My life was about to be condensed into a month—maybe less. I had survived the typhoon with Patipati's spirit and Anne at my side.

Tomorrow, I would start training for the walk on fire. I planned to ride the last month of legendary giant winter surf that struck the Island of Fire's south coast in walls of water sometimes 30 feet high. The giant waves passed over open, exposed blue coral beds with razor sharp edges. Then, if I walked the fire pit, I could enter the Land of the Dead Chiefs. I wanted to save Patipati's spirit from eternal waiting at the entrance to the Spirit World.

This adventure was different than final exams at university or Peace Corps training camp in Hawaii, or state finals of basketball in high school. I had no team, no frat brothers, no paid Fijian instructors. I would be alone on the Island of Fire—vulnerable mentally, emotionally, and physically in a world of shadows, evil, and magical forces. I did not fully understand or comprehend this world yet. One miscue, one misstep on the Island of Fire meant vaporized death in obscurity at the edge of the world in paradise found and lost. There probably wouldn't be enough left of me to send home in a Ziplock bag folded in the crease of an American flag.

I liked the clarity, win, or lose here, no compromises and no quarter. I was about ten minutes from the turn to the boat landing, according to the directions. Ten more minutes to enjoy my old life. The lush, tropical, brightly-flowered scenery swished by at 10 miles an hour on the typhoon damaged gravel road. Then it was time to hide my gray horse and start my assault on paradise's version of heaven and hell.

A small wooden sign marked the entrance to Bakaka. It was two miles down a dirt road by the old PT-Boat docks. They were in a dredged lagoon with an opening due north in the reef. The Island of Fire was a four-hour sail to the northwest from the docks in the trade winds. It was about 24 nautical miles off the coast.

I had decided to drive the Land Rover a mile down the landing road. I wanted to stash it in the underbrush a hundred yards off the road. I planned to cover it with palm fronds and banana leaves. Hopefully, none of the local kids or villagers would find it. Normally, I paid a villager to look after it, but this time a local government official could find out I was on the Island of Fire. Villagers talked to other villagers. Then the co-op department or prime minister's office could order me off the island by short-wave radio. Fiji was a large- small place. Everyone gossiped constantly. A trip by a PCV from the southern province to the Island of Fire would attract attention. The co-op's Land Rover would be tangible evidence of the trip.

Only Anne knew where and why I was going for the month. She had promised to come and find me if I didn't return to the hotel in five weeks. There was no other lifeline. No one else knew where I was going, except Patipati. He was a ghost.

I motored slowly down the rough, rutted landing road. It had not been graded in a year. It still had large mud holes in spots from the typhoon, and the recent rains. They marked the end of winter and the beginning of the summer season in the Southern Hemisphere near the International Dateline. Fiji was always a day ahead or behind. I could never figure it out without Dr. Joe or a globe.

I drove along at 5 mph. I saw an old, unused track into the bush. It was barely visible to the naked eye. It was really just a notch in the thick brush and palm trees of an abandoned copra plantation. At a mile an hour, I was careful to push the brush slowly under the Land Rover's bumper. It would pop back up, leaving very little trace of the journey. Once it rained even the tread marks in the soft red clay soil of the north coast would disappear.

A hundred yards into the thick grove, I nosed into a double-trunked palm tree. I cut the engine. I hid the key under Dianne's good luck Polaroid. It was now taped under the driver side seat. I climbed out of the Land Rover. I walked to its front hood. I popped it open with a small wrench I kept duct-taped to the inside of the hood. I loosened the battery terminals. I then lifted out the heavy British lead battery. I walked several palm trees away.

I hid the battery under a piece of plastic I kept for this purpose. Now no one could hot wire the Land Rover. They also could not steal the battery. It was a year's cash income for a villager on the black-market.

I walked back to the Land Rover. I closed the hood and went around to the rear door. I opened it and pulled out the aluminum ammo box. In the ammo box, I had one change of clothes, the new co-op Polaroid camera, a sulu, a toothbrush, a Swiss army knife, a PCV first-aid kit, bubble gum, a surfboard repair kit, my international driver's license, my draft card, my PCV ID card, three Trojan lubricated rubbers, a letter from my mom, a plastic flashlight with fresh dry cell batteries, a red bandana, a movie poster of The Endless Summer, and other miscellaneous items. I had found the poster at a shuttered movie house after the typhoon.

The box weighed about 10 pounds. I carried it with my left hand. It would counter-balance the 10-foot triple stringer Greg Knoll surfboard I carried under my right arm after I removed it from the Land Rover's roof rack. My load was balanced perfectly. It would be easy to manage for the half-mile walk to the abandoned PT-Boat port.

I had everything I needed for life on the Island of Fire. I also had 50 Fiji dollars in small bills. I had saved them over the past year in a metal tin in my shorts pocket. I would bury it as soon as I reached the island. I would use the money for an emergency only. I had to pay a couple of dollars for the boat ride and ten dollars to the chief for a place to stay.

The last thing I took out of the Land Rover was a small whale's tooth which I put in my other pocket. This would be my key present to the chief and witch doctor. They would allow me to surf and hopefully to walk the pit of fire at full moon a month away.

The small sacred whale's tooth had been given to me by the prime minister a year ago for co-op work before the potato war. He had personally carved his initials in it. He was the highest chief in Fiji. This special sacred gift would hopefully be the pass for my firewalk. It would be assumed without question that the prime minister had sent me to walk the fire after I presented the whale's tooth. It was better than a bank letter of credit. It was a command to teach me, feed me, and take me on this journey. The prime minister knew any whale's tooth he presented was a blank check in the sacred currency and custom of Fiji ceremony. I hoped he didn't want this one back after I finished my passage, dead or alive.

After the small whale's tooth was secured in my deep khaki shorts pocket, I closed the Land Rover door. I pulled the long surfboard from its straps. I leaned it against a palm tree next to the ammo case. I picked up palm fronds blown down by the typhoon and covered the Land Rover so its glare would not alert any wandering villagers.

When that task was finished, I peed against a small orchid bush. I zipped up my khaki shorts. I picked up the ammo case first and then the surfboard. I walked slowly through some red hibiscus toward the road. I tried not to leave a path. I walked toe to heel, softly brushing the high grass and bush. The tropical thick brush closed like a curtain in layers. I walked toward the village road. In ten steps, the hidden gray co-op Land Rover vanished into its umbrella of palm trees. It disappeared like a magician's white rabbit in a black top hat.

I reached the village's boat landing road in a few yards. The new journey began. I fought back tears and a strong desire to turn back to the Land Rover. The Island of Fire loomed in my mind like Little Round Top must have for Lee when he ordered Picket's brave soldiers to charge. No one could help now, no words could explain the moment, no drums could cue the march. No books had told the story, no movies had shown the ending, and no god could intervene. At the end of this ordeal, I would either see the light or be the light forever and always.

CHAPTER THIRTY-SIX
THE SAILING TRIP

One hundred yards down the road, I heard the chattering of village kids in a strange dialect. I presumed it was the Island of Fire's. I understood only every fourth or fifth word, which was unusual after nearly three years in Fiji. I rounded a turn in the muddy dirt road. I saw the crumbling, barnacle covered gray concrete dock.

At the center dock, which was perpendicular to the coastline, a half sunken rusting inter-island freighter leaned crazily to its starboard side. It filled the entire slip. In the left slip, a 40-foot inter-island sailboat swung on its thick tattered bow and stern ropes. A Fijian crew dressed only in khaki shorts loaded it with steel drums of kerosene and burlap bags of flower. This was my vessel. Its billowing brown canvas multi-patched sail bore a faded stenciled flame.

The four-man crew worked effortlessly. They chanted a Fijian song while swinging 112-lb bags of flour into the 40-foot wooden schooner's hold. On the dock was a row of ten 44-gallon drums of kerosene for the village store, village lanterns, and the village medical center fridge and radio telephone generator. Miscellaneous cargo was scattered on the dock. It included a Fiji Postal Department mail bag, a government message pouch marked OFFICE OF THE PRIME MINISTER, and a stack of roofing tin, probably to repair the school's roof which I guessed had been damaged in the typhoon. The center of the typhoon went south of the Island of Fire, sparing it major damage.

Life was very simple on the small outer islands off Fiji's main island, Viti Levu. Every item on the dock had a specific purpose, which seldom varied from island to island. There were no general stores, so no unsold speculative merchandise was boarding the small-village, sail-powered freighter.

In an hour or so, the village men and women would arrive by local bus from the gold mine's or Nadi market. They had sold fresh fish, Pacific lobster, prawns, eggplant, kava, tapioca plant and coconuts at the market. Some would be miners' wives who had visited the men's barracks. Their husbands slept in bunks separated only by blankets hanging from makeshift lines. A few were also village amateur prostitutes, who for Fijian pound notes worth $1.00 U.S. currency, serviced the single miners; this was a tradition each Saturday after the shift miners emerged with dirt-streaked faces from the deep, hot, gold pits ending their six day work week.

It was rumored these girls, who protected themselves with a potion made by the island's witch doctor, made five Fiji pound notes on a Saturday afternoon. I had been warned to stay away from the island's single girls because they were in the regular pay of the miners. There was no doctor on the island of fire, so penicillin was impossible to obtain. Maybe death was nearer than I perceived, nothing interested me anymore except my big wave surfboard and walking the fire pit to avenge Patipati.

I found the sailboat's captain. He was an old villager with gray hair. I gave him two Fijian pound notes. I asked him to wake me to board the boat when it was ready to depart for the Island of Fire. He said it would be an hour or so. I knew it could be one hour, or Monday. It depended on whether his bus passengers arrived before dark, plus whether the late afternoon trade winds held for the fast reach to the island. These sailors hated to tack, and they would not leave if the winds shifted north. If the winds calmed, which would require them to run their two ancient British outboard docking engines the whole way, the trip was off. They could always party in nearby Bakaka Saturday night with relatives and attend the Methodist church there on Sunday.

Many of them had intermarried with families from the village of Baka-ka, so everyone had a place to bunk tonight but me. I walked over to a rotting co-op department wooden tin roofed shed on the empty right dock. I opened its screen door and found a rotting canvas cot.

One of my colleagues, a PCV diver from Kansas, had tried to revive the northern Viti Levu Fishery Co-op. This had been his home and office until he was eaten by a shark off the Island of Fire's main reef while inventorying the fish population. A picture of his girlfriend in a dusty tin frame was still on his steel green Co-op-issue desk. It was covered with dust and spider webs. I picked up the picture. I saw the smiling face of a well-scrubbed Air Force brat in a bikini halter with a grass skirt at some fake island style Honolulu military party. She was probably 18 or 19 when it was taken. I wondered what it felt like to have your fiancé eaten by a shark. I had heard all the Peace Corps found to send back to her were his dual air tanks. They had white shark teeth dents in them.

I put the picture back in its place of silent wake. I mused that maybe his spirit visited her here on this musty, rotting tropical dock on long, lonely nights. Maybe he made love to her on this cot. Maybe they both partied with ghosts of the young American PT-Boat crews who had died in the abandoned infirmary across from the dock after raids on Japanese shipping off the coast of Fiji during World War II.

This dock had squirrelly karma. I was glad to be leaving it soon. I opened the ammo box. I spread my ancient blue cotton sulu on the dirty canvas surplus army issue cot. I put my ammo box on the cot's end for a pillow. I covered it with my clean pair of khaki shorts. I dozed off waiting for the captain's wake up call. I thought about Nurse Williams. I wished she were here to accompany me on this journey...

I felt someone shaking me. I opened my eyes feeling like an American Ute Indian. The real world had become my dream world and my dream world had become the real world. Therefore, when I was awake, I was really in a dream world which did not exist in reality. If this is your basis for life, there is nothing much the white man can say or do to fuck with your spirit. I liked the switch and wondered if I would ever be able to reverse my state. There was a certain security in being beyond the reach of the white man as I knew him in the last half of the 20th century. I decided not to rush to reverse my state of mind.

The captain shook me again. I jumped into the dream world of the

Island of Fire's sailing boat. He said we were sailing now; the bus had arrived from the mine at Nadi and the east wind was strong. I hopped up and packed the ammo box. I picked up my surfboard and kicked the rotting screen door open with my right foot as I exited.

Sixty men, women and children were now climbing aboard the 40-foot sailboat. They carried everything from hobbled chickens to a hand-carved hardwood kava bowl. The boat rode only a foot or so above its water line. It was clearly 'sold out', but in Fiji, there was always room for one more, so I hopped aboard.

The first mate took my surfboard and ammo box. He loaded them in the top of the still open hold. He then closed it with the help of another seaman. I found a place to sit. My feet dangled over the side near the bow next to a boy of 16 or so and his ancient grandmother. After the proper salutations, I watched the first mate and the seaman cast off the bow and stern lines. We motored backward out of the slip to the putt-putt of the ancient British outboard docking engines. We backed a hundred feet or so into the lagoon. We scraped bottom several times since the tide was ebbing fast. Then with a burst of wind, the main sail exploded into position. It was followed by the foresail. We pivoted into the wind and sailed toward the due north opening of the lagoon's barrier reef.

As we neared the reef opening, two Fijian Bakaka village kids who had hitchhiked across the river-fed lagoon on the boat, dived from the main sail's beam. They splashed headfirst into the murky blue lagoon. It was still unsettled by the runoff from the recent typhoon. The boys swam for shore. I looked at a rapidly dropping western sun. It was probably four o'clock. It would be dark on arrival if the wind held, and the next day if it calmed.

Last night had been a full moon. Tonight, it would be bright. However, night sailing in open ocean with no lights or radio contact was not my idea of fun. The wind was strong. We clipped along as the boat's bow spray splashed my bare feet. They hung only inches from the water. The wind felt fresh as a very old Fijian grandmother began to chant some ancient crossing song. It was a version of the one they steered by on the long trip from the dark continent ten centuries ago.

Fijian captains and crews could sail with the best in the world. I settled back into what amounted to first class in Fiji. I began to meditate on the bursts of sea spray which were backlit by the low western sun. I hoped for an omen in the dream world which was now my daily reality in the islands of paradise.

Traveling inter-island in Fiji was always breathtakingly beautiful. It was also dangerous by western standards. The ocean was dark, clear blue, and was relatively smooth. I could see 20 feet-plus below the surface. The Fijians built and sailed shallow keeled wood boats. They could cruise over reefs ten feet below the surface, shortcutting to and from their inter-island destinations.

Sail power was their main mode of propulsion, although a couple of their docking outboard engines could push a boat along at four knots in a dead calm—if they ran properly. Running at all was always tricky for these old engines. They were usually held together with temporary welds and bailing wire. The village boats always sailed fully loaded. The deck and main cabin were crowded with villagers and provisions—the hold filled with supplies for the village. I had only enough space to sit, stand or stretch on deck. Below deck, in the cabin, travelers sat back-to-back, cross-legged, Fijian style. They played cards, sang, and drank kava.

The sailboats road low in the water. They wallowed because of their broad beams, shallow keels, and poor canvas sail trim. Seasickness was common among the rare tourists, PCVs or other westerners who traveled by these village inter-island sailboats. It struck hard, especially on long reaches and runs with the constant surging motion of the handmade, wooden, village-built boats with their peeling paint and unvarnished decks.

Whatever the Fijians lacked in boat technology, however, they made up in seamanship. These sailors were the ancestors of the chiefs and warriors who sailed in long dugout canoes to Fiji originally from the east coast of Africa. They navigated by the stars without sextants. They stored the inter-island routes, tides, currents, and reefs in their minds. Most of Fiji was still poorly charted. Sailboats and yachts from Australia, New Zealand and the U.S. regularly ran aground on uncharted reefs, rocks, and sand bars. Sometimes, they lost all hands in stormy weather at night.

Fijian crewed boats skirted hidden reefs and rocks like air-to-air missiles. They used the trade winds, tides, and currents to their maximum advantage. Physically, the crews were superb. They shimmied the wood mast to re-set sails barefooted. They repaired their ancient docking British outboard engines while under sail. When they were at sea, they were all business, in a Fijian way. It was unmatched on land—except in rugby, war games or a traditional dance ceremony.

I watched a ballet as the captain, his mate and a trio of sailors ran the 40-foot village built wooden sailing craft loaded with 50-plus passengers and two tons of cargo. These muscular, handsome, bare-footed, bare-chested, bronze-black sailors were clad only in khaki shorts with colorful blue and red bandana headbands. They exerted a native instinct and power over their craft and the sea. It came from a lifetime of experienced adventure in the South Pacific.

Our boat lumbered along at six knots in the trade wind. I meditated on the clear, dark blue water. It passed only inches under my dangling feet. I watched an occasional shallow coral reef pass beneath the boat. The captain shouted orders for sail trim from the tiller to his mate. I watched for South Pacific porpoises. They often swam with the sailboats. They played by jumping over the foresail bowsprit in barrel rolls like fighter planes in an air show.

The sun rapidly became a dying, large orange ball to the west. The afternoon trades also were dying fast. The sailboat slowed to three knots and the ocean started to become glassy. We had left the main island late. The trades had died an hour early. We were out of good wind with about 10 miles left to the Island of Fire's landing near its only village. We would definitely arrive by moonlight. I did not want to float all night long. I stood up and stepped over the villagers. I walked back to the captain at the tiller.

After a brief conversation, I gave him $10.00 Fijian to cover the cost of two hours' fuel. He agreed to fire up his main reserve outboard docking engines and motor sail to his home port, the Island of Fire. His announcement of my donation caused a loud cheer from the villagers. I had earned my first credit in these strangers' eyes. No one wanted to drift in fluky winds on Saturday night after a three-day trip to the mines and the Nadi market. At home, there were stories to be spun, kava to be drunk, and a Saturday night feast to be eaten before a restful Lord's Day on Sunday, with the ubiquitous Fijian Methodist church service.

The engines burst into life to assist the sails. The boat surged back to a 5-knot speed as the orange ball sank in a blink in a cloudless western sky. Our vessel lumbered toward the landing at the Island of Fire. An hour later, a lantern lighted dot on shore would hang to guide the captain and his crew. Kava magically appeared on the foredeck. I was served the first cup as a token of appreciation for my gift which ensured the boat's speedy passage.

Then, without warning, one engine sputtered, died. There was a collective moan from the passengers. A crewman dashed back from the bow-sprit. I feared the worst as he and the captain chatted in the village dialect. I couldn't translate it. Then everyone around me laughed. The boy next to me who was returning from secondary school in Nadi explained the crisis to me in the national Fijian dialect. A crewman had forgotten to hook-up one of the 5-gallon auxiliary tanks of fuel I had purchased for the outboard engine. It stopped when it exhausted the fuel in its smaller onboard tank. Once the auxiliary fuel tank was hooked-up, the boat would regain full speed again with both engines operating.

Fijians always amazed me. They could navigate to Africa by stars but could never remember to carry freshly charged walkie-talkie batteries or hook fuel tanks to engines as a routine procedure. This never seemed to bother them, while it often maddened unsuspecting westerners in their company or under their control. After almost three years in the Peace Corps, I had come to accept it as their way of life. Any inconvenience was more than compensated by their magical ability to turn a routine day into a romantic adventure in the cradle of one of nature's greatest playgrounds of the fabled South Seas. I was a privileged guest wandering through the twi-light of their isolation from the main stream of world commerce in 1970.

The jumbo jets and the Japanese/Australian, California/Hawaiian econ-omies prepared to demolish the islands of paradise with miracle drugs as their accomplice. Already, 80% of Fiji's population only 25 years after World War II was under 21 years of age. The unparalleled island historic baby boom explosion was ripping apart the underpinnings of the tradition-al village-oriented society. This unharnessed labor force was attracting a tourist service economy to exploit it. It was causing the inevitable, irre-versible end of Fiji's splendid, historical, self-sufficient isolation.

Even the island's firewalkers were performing for money in town at the island's tourist hotels timed to attract the cruise ship passengers on their shopping days in the ports of Suva or Lautoka, near Nadi. I felt the curtain closing on one of nature's greatest plays. It was shutting down to become television for the tourist masses to aimlessly wander through in their wonderful sunshades of meaningful boredom. They now consumed whole cultures in their endless search for the meaning of life away from their natureless industrial cultures and country clubs.

This all seemed a million miles away in my dream as the dull dot of lantern light at the village boat landing grew larger and larger. The craft now glided across the mirror smooth twilight sea closing in on my destiny 10,000 miles from home. I was finally out of touch with even the Peace Corps network which provided my daily safety net. Because of the fire-walking and its unspoken associated witchcraft, PCVs had been barred from teaching, working, or living on the island full-time. No volunteer had walked the fire pit, or the government and the Peace Corps staff would have put the island completely off limits.

Life was perfectly peaceful and perfectly centered as the now sail-less, peeling, white, wooden boat motored into the Island of Fire's dark, moon-less, lagoon protected harbor on a silent, motionless sea. My too long, dirty blond hair blew silently against the back of my neck as the soft, warm evening offshore breeze met the boat, carrying a wave of mosquitoes and fireflies with it.

The smell of new land permeated my nostrils. They had been cleared by the salt air during the journey. Smoke was in the air, so a feast was be-ing prepared for the arrival of the passengers with their mainland gossip and new provisions. Tonight, would be a celebration of my arrival on the island before I met the witch doctor to learn the art of firewalking by the next full moon's walk.

I would bide my days here waiting for the monster late winter surf which the Southern Pacific storms sent north to Fiji from the Antarctic Ocean. A fabled 30-footer would come, I hoped, on the island's due south facing beach. It opened through the reef directly all the way to the South Pole. These waves had formed the bluff below the island's only village. It overlooked the narrow beach where the big waves crashed. The novice firewalkers reputedly practiced their art on the sun-heated, sandy coral beach before they walked the pit of potential death the first time.

The boat landing loomed in another abandoned World War II PT-Boat pen. The captain cut his main docking outboard using only the smaller en-gine to steer slowly toward the village-built, rotting, hand-hewn wooden dock in a semi-reef protected area of the eastern lagoon's shelter. It was a two mile walk to the village. It was on the southwestern corner of the bluff on the five-mile-long and three-mile-wide island. It was a chip of continental shelf that had drifted away from Viti Levu's northern coast a million years ago in some tectonic plate shift. The same minerals of north Viti Levu were found on the Island of Fire, including, occasionally, gold nuggets in its streams. However, no source of these ancient gold nuggets had been located on the island itself. They were probably from the mine's veins on the mainland 24 miles across the ocean.

The soft gold nuggets were prized by the women of the island who pounded them into jewelry. They wore gold pierced through their ears, nostrils, nipples and, I heard, sometimes the outer folds of their vaginas. It was believed the ancient gold was very good for fertility. It also guarded against evil spirits entering the woman and devouring the unborn child.

The missionaries had tried to stop this practice—so had the Fijian postwar government trained public health nurses and doctors. Rumors persisted among the PCVs assigned to Nadi and Lautoka that a village party girl showed up recently with fiat, tiny rings of round, ornate gold medallions pierced into the outer folds of her vagina lips. Their rounded edges produced an electric deep penetrating prolonged male orgasm. This was the common sense of the village fertility theory. However, they also sometimes tore the soft vaginal tissue of the girl in vigorous intercourse. They caused bleeding and therefore the resulting tropical infections. This led to the public health officials' vigorous effort to stop this practice. It was still, I suspected, widely practiced on the Island of Fire.

This unique, still isolated South Pacific island, with its ancient gold nuggets, firewalking, and fabled killer waves made it mythical even to the magical Fijians. Few Fijians visited the island, although all of Fiji's villagers talked about it. Its witchcraft and black magic were secretly feared and considered too dangerous for outsiders to master. Its women had been historically isolated until motherhood. They perhaps were captives of the cult of the gold fertility god. They probably hid this practice effectively from the religious and governmental authorities.

Our boat approached shoreline. My heart thundered as my head conjured up the white light I would need to survive the ordeal. I heard the hollow wooden log drums on shore thunder a message from the boat landing to the village on the bluff that we had arrived. The boat was stirring as its village passengers prepared to disembark. I had learned little more than I already knew about the island on the trip to it. This was unusual for Fiji travel. Villagers usually talked openly to PCVs.

This was an iconoclastic clan. I would have to make my presentation to the high chief and then earn the respect of these strange, proud people. They were unhumbled still by colonialization, and untamed by industrialization, government, or western religion.

CHAPTER THIRTY-SEVEN
THE FIRST NIGHT

While the sailboat was being moored. 1 gathered my ammo box and surfboard. I waited my turn to jump into the rickety wooden dock. It was pitch-black dark. The moon was hidden behind the island's central, long dormant volcano cone which was silhouetted on the starlit horizon. The crew secured the sailboat bow-first to the dock and its passengers began to disembark. I jumped the short foot to the dock. I landed balanced, surfboard under my right arm and aluminum ammo box under my left arm. The villagers followed me, carrying their burlap bags of supplies from the Nadi market. They had new gossip from Nadi and the mine for their clan members who had prepared fireside meals in the village bures.

A line of chattering villagers had started up the steep, narrow path to the village. The village was on a bluff overlooking the pristine lagoon. The sailboat was docked until its next trip to the Nadi market on Wednesday or Thursday if weather permitted. The crew had already started to hoist cargo from the boat's hold to the wharf. They worked by lantern light. The wharf had a newly repaired, open sided, tin roofed storage shed which protected cargo from the sun but not rain. The dry winter season was about to end and soon it would rain part or all of every day in Fiji.

The line of returning villagers snaked along the path to the village without flashlights or flaming torches. The Fijian villagers knew this path by heart. They could walk it blindfolded. Their night vision was superior to westerners. They were not addicted to electric streetlights.

I fell in behind an older man who I asked to show me to the chief's bure once we arrived in the village. I had arrived unintroduced to this Fijian village. By custom, I could not talk to the younger women or men until I had been formally welcomed and invited to stay by the chief. A premature conversation with a younger female or hostile young male might end in a disaster. Punishment ranged from being asked to leave the village immediately, to physical violence at the hands of a jealous boyfriend. Ceremony ruled in Fiji.

Younger Fijian men sensed that the reins of colonialism had disappeared. They were starting to settle ancient scores with their white rulers. Talking to a girlfriend of one of them on his village turf was very dangerous. I was a hundred miles from my province which was like 1,000 miles Stateside. I walked silently, carrying my surfboard as I ascended the ancient path up to the bluff in almost total darkness. I put my bare feet in each ancient carved step vacated by the man ahead of me. I fought to keep my balance. I did not want to slow the march to the village a thousand feet above the lagoon on the slope of a dormant volcano.

I secured one foot at a time in the footholds on the trail. They had been worn over the last thousand years. Then, I moved the next step forward in a rhythmic ancient pace. It was hypnotic as I ascended the path to the village. Women balanced heavy loads on their heads. Men carried 112-pound burlap bags of flour or rice on their backs. The children carried chickens with bound beaks and claws, or small cooking pots and pans.

I carried my surfboard and ammo box. I swung them in an uphill rhythm, as I relaxed into the long climb from the ocean below. Twenty minutes later we were at the village edge.

We were greeted by barks from the village's mongrel dog pack. It met us as we neared the village. Fijian villages had skinny, hungry dog packs. They existed on scraps between wild boar hunts in the bush. These scarred, ugly creatures had exposed ribs. All of them were vegetarians, because fresh meat was scarce in these fishing and subsistence crop villages. Their scars were from the tusks of wild boars which they chased and cornered for the village hunters. The hunters rode on horseback with bamboo spears to kill the pigs, after the dog pack surrounded them.

Wild boar attacks in the bush added a daily element of danger to life in Fiji. I judged by the number of barking dogs this volcano-peaked island had plenty of wild boars. The boars were descended from the ancient African pigs who had made the trip a thousand years ago in long canoes across the Indian Ocean. They were, except for humans, the only source of protein in Fiji, until the whalers landed cattle, dogs, and horses in the early 1800s. Legend had it that Fijian nursing mothers in the longboats had suckled the piglets with their own newborn children. This kept them alive during the long migration from East Africa.

Legends were legends, but the wild boars were in Fiji when the first shipwrecked white sailors washed ashore during the South Pacific's whaling era. While I waited for the big surf and prepared to walk the fire pit, I planned to hunt wild boar on horseback to pass the long island days. Hunting contributed to the village food supply.

I had grown up riding polo ponies during my childhood on an isolated western Colorado ranch at the edge of the San Juan Mountains. I had quit playing polo after I had been shipped to the southeast for college. I hadn't ridden much in seven years, but the skills were still stored in my brain and muscles. Riding would be a return to something familiar while I studied the firewalkers to learn their craft.

The village horses I had observed throughout Fiji reminded me of the fast, smart, compact polo ponies of the southwest. They could turn on a dime or stop in three or four strides. Hunting wild boar with bamboo spear in the thick bush of the leeward side of the volcano would require the darting, rugged, fast style of riding like polo. It would quicken my reflexes for the big waves if they arrived. I knew riding and hunting would steady my nerves for the walk across the hot rocks and embers of the fire pit.

Suddenly, the trail widened and then leveled. The front of the human line entered the outskirts of the village. It appeared to be about a quarter of a mile wide. It was built in the traditional rectangular shape with the chief's house in the center. A quick rough count in my mind identified almost 75 lanterns from individual bures. Each one usually housed six to eight people, depending on how many children and elders each family had living with them. This was a big, traditional, well-maintained, tightly organized village. It had no daily contact with the western world or the Peace Corps.

I had to be very careful here because the power structure would include a very powerful witch doctor. I clicked my mind back almost three years to the strict Peace Corps training on the big island of Hawaii. Fijian customs had been drilled into my head by Aki. He was my language instructor and drinking buddy who was from the Nadi province. This island was in the Nadi province and governmental district by luck.

I could perform my introduction ceremony almost perfectly because Aki had taught me so well. I had also used my province's version of it almost weekly for three years whenever I entered villages for ceremonial, economic or diplomatic missions on behalf of the Valley Co-op. Patipati had always been there to assist me, though, if I stumbled. The small but very special sacred whale's tooth I carried in my khaki shorts pocket was my insurance in this village's very traditional structure.

After the welcoming ceremony, I would still be vulnerable to village politics, jealousy, pent-up hatred of the 'Vulagi' or white man, and maybe the evil black magic of the witch doctor. He might not want to share the power of the firewalk with me. The days after the ceremony would be brittle with chances to crack the seam of my existence in this village. Unknown furies might be unleashed. I might not be able to defend my life against them.

The physical part of life had always been straight forward. At this level of play, I either won or died. Either consequence would be admired by these Fijian islanders who sailed the Pacific, fished the reefs, and hunted wild boar on island ponies, surfed the 30-foot waves of the fabled blue reef, and walked the fire pit.

If I died in action, they would bury me a hero on the island or ship me to the Nadi airport with a Fijian flag in a village-made, wooden plank casket by sailboat. It would be transshipped through the international airport to western Colorado for burial on the family ranch under a lone pine. It was the mental game that was dangerous in Fiji or back home in the USA. Surfing the blue reef might cause jealousy to surface in one of the young village warriors. It could bring a challenge I could not win on his turf. Walking the fire might draw the ire of the witch doctor. His curse could be fatal. I had no allies and no escape route.

The mental stuff separated great pilots from aces, athletic quarterbacks from Hall of Famers, and dead Indy drivers from repeat champions. It was life essential on the Island of Fire to pay attention to the nuances of my intrusion into its physical and situational political relationships. I had to play the game *within* the game of life on the edge of Fiji.

One by one nature had stripped my teammates away for this showdown with destiny on the Island of Fire. Dianne had gone in the great Pan Am bird that disappeared toward Hawaii three days ago. Patipati was dead. His spirit had returned to the Cave of Waiting and his destiny was in my heart. Anne was 100 miles away at a remote beach hotel bungalow awaiting my return in 30 days. Chief Kavula was in his village, powerless to intervene on the Island of Fire, which was in another province that had warred with his villages over the centuries. Dr. Joe was unaware of my journey as he completed my annual books for the Valley Co-op. He awaited my final trip to the capital city in a month. Tab awaited departure in two weeks after the prime minister announced the marriage of his niece to a key political lieutenant from the northern island of Vaneu Levu. It was Fiji's other large population center. Nurse Williams was somewhere in the USA anti-war underground, preparing to assassinate Richard Nixon if he was reelected. No one could help me, not even the U.S. Marines.

My plan was simple, like all good plans. First, I would do my cere-monial introduction with the village chief an hour or so after he finished dinner. By custom, he would assign me a village family for my quarters. I would be expected to give them money to feed me. They provided a mat to sleep on during my nights on the island. No village guest could be reason-ably refused a bure to eat and sleep in by Fijian custom. I would scope out the village politics during nightly kava sessions with the men.

Maybe by the fourth or fifth night, I could broach the subject of walk-ing in the fire pit. I had to understand the power of the witch doctor first. My cover was my mission to surf the big waves while on a Peace Corps vacation. My motto was 'no Fijian chicks' until I knew the liaisons and politics of this village.

I knew the gods probably had a few surprises for me I hadn't anticipat-ed. That's life on this planet which must be a prison camp for rebellious spirits from more perfect worlds on the edge of the universe's more ad-vanced galaxies.

CHAPTER THIRTY-EIGHT

THE HUNT

The village horse I rode was sure-footed but dumb. The chief had given me his biggest horse. It was a gray stallion about 15 hands high and maybe six years old. Village horses lasted 8-10 years in Fiji's tropical heat with no vets. My mount was mature but on the down curve of his wild boar hunting days. I rode him on a burlap bag saddle. The chief had managed to find me a tattered leather bridle instead of a rope halter that was the standard village issue. My leather bridle had rotted from age and lack of saddle soap in the interminable tropical humidity. It was one hard rein away from disintegration, so my horse, who had no name, was running free rein basically. He followed the other horse-mounted pig hunters on a bush path up the windward side of the dormant volcano. He had known the path since he was gelded. He appeared to be part thoroughbred and part Australian quarter horse. The tropical crosses were usually opposites and created exotics in nature's long running Fijian show.

He reminded me of the half-Portuguese and half-Hawaiian exotic women who populated Honolulu's expensive bars on Waikiki Beach. The initial sight of these dark-skinned women in short skirts and high heels with sheer cotton halter tops assaulted me sensually and instantly.

My horse moved at a brisk clip with the stride of a thoroughbred and the footing of a high beam steel welder. I reflected on the night of my arrival while I galloped toward wild boar heaven with the six other horse mounted village hunters...

After I waited two hours at the great chief's formal ceremonial house, he arrived from the bure of his young wife. He had been eating there. Most island village chiefs could afford two wives. The original wife had raised their grown children and lived in the main bure. A younger wife who bore a smaller second family lived in a separate bure. The younger wife performed the hard day labor of routine village life while the old wife enjoyed her later years with her friends. The older wife traveled for visits to her home village and the Nadi market to gossip. This system seemed to work in the still isolated rural Fijian villages. It had defied the government's and missionaries' attempts to eradicate it, although everyone including the village practitioners denied it existed, including the chiefs' old wives.

Day to day village women's work was tough labor. It included carrying water, wood, and food long distances as well as cooking three meals a day. Also, the women reef fished at low tide in the village lagoon in the outer islands. The old wives were considered winners since their routine daily duties went to the young wives. Also, the old wives exercised the power of a queen.

The village paramount chief was in a relaxed but cautious mood when he arrived. He sat cross-legged before the great hand-carved, hardwood, ceremonial four-legged kava bowl with the village elders behind him. There was no immediately recognizable village witch doctor present, which was odd in an island village. The usual suspects were seated behind the chief. They consisted of nine 40- to 70-year-old men who ran the village council. No one below 40 had any power in a rural Fijian village. In a warrior culture, male mental childhood was prolonged, and power rationed carefully to an experienced elite group of the village's elder survivors.

My quick mental take was that most of these suspects had fought with the Marines in WW II, or with the British army in Malaysia against the communists. They were world class warriors, hunters, fishermen and sailors. Most were well off enough to have a young wife, too. Intellect, in a western sense, was a shared function. Their brains were trained to function communally to ensure the survival of the village for their constituents in a playground created by nature that was as generous in its gifts as it was equally harsh in its punishment.

The lagoon side of its wave battered reefs fed the village daily. Sharks patrolled the ocean side. These village elders had survived childhoods with no western medicine, jungle warfare at its most vicious level, and the raw natural forces which challenged them daily out on the open sea or on the land of this isolated island. The chief and the village council of elders were respected at the highest level. They expected it from all the villagers or outsiders who crossed into their domain.

The younger men of the village hadn't been invited to the welcoming kava ceremony nor would they until I was formally invited to stay by the Chief and his elders. The chief would be held responsible by the village for my actions if I was invited to stay longer than the next market boat trip back to the main island in four days.

By custom, I started the ceremony in the long ceremonial bure with its varnished log-beamed thatched roof. It was decorated with tapa cloth, a handcraft of the island. Its inside walls were thin, young, sun-dried bamboo reeds woven intricately into panels. Its swept hard dirt floor was covered with tightly woven, beautifully patterned reed mats. No nails or inorganic material had been used in the ceremonial bure's construction. Its four thick, tropical hardwood ancient corner posts probably rested on the skeletons of four captured warriors. They had probably been buried alive under each corner post during its construction in cannibal days to support the structure for eternity. This practice allowed the captured warriors to die honorably instead of being cooked in an oven and eaten. They were this island's main source of protein along with the wild boar before the arrival of the cow and horse.

This big, ancient bure was a national monument to the perfection of Fijian village craftsmanship and their handsome strong architecture. Hand-carved, polished, antique hardwood war clubs decorated its walls. Shell beaded strands covered its windows. The giant kava bowl was three feet in diameter. It had been carved from the trunk of a single hardwood tree. A large tapa cloth tapestry depicted old abstract designs from the vision of its village artisan painters. A hollow log drum sat off to the left of the group. It was clearly still used to convene the village for emergency or ceremonial occasions. Twenty sacred large ivory whale's teeth or tabuas hung in a row on their handwoven rope straps on the edges of the giant tapa cloth backdrop behind the great chief.

This was an old, rich, proud traditional village. I sat cross-legged in its boardroom, ready to chant my best stuff, or it was the village sailboat one way on a no return trip Wednesday morning; weather permitting. I had to measure up in the next 30 minutes of ceremony. Even then, I would only get a couple of days of sightseeing if I failed under the watchful eyes of my assigned village host. He was about to be assigned by the chief. The ceremony was really a play within a play to save face. If my performance was a disaster, or my fate already predetermined, then I was on a 3-day, 4-night package cruise plan village vacation.

I opened my ammo box at my side. I took out a bundle of special southern Lau island group kava which Dr. Joe had given me. This was Fiji's most highly sought-after kava. It was scarce and expensive. Most of this species was exported to the USA to be put into tranquilizers by the big drug companies. This batch was the best of the best and these northern islanders had mostly only heard stories about it in their province.

I presented it to the village chief. I chanted the traditional words of presentation and identified the origin of the kava, which registered on the blank-faced chief and his elders with only a telltale tightening of their lips. Their tongues tensed in anticipation of its taste and narcotic effect on their minds. Premium kava cooled and numbed lips and tongues instantly.

The chief accepted the cheesecloth wrapped bundle of primo kava. He handed it to the village elder to his immediate left. The elder sniffed it. He opened the cloth and put the tiny, powerful bundle of sun-dried roots in a stone bowl. He began pounding it into powder with a stone mortar by hand in a rhythmic beat. The chief and his boys chanted a thank you litany a thousand years old, in pure island village dialect.

I could sense the warrior ghosts moving under the corner poles. They were prepared to enter the room with their cold fury of evil. The great chief and his elders went into a high gear, staccato chant to ward them off.

After it was pounded into a fine dry powder, the yagona, or kava, was placed in a porous cheesecloth wrap and handed back to the chief. His duty was to squeeze it in the water of the kava bowl. The water was in a thin walled, village handmade fired red clay pot. He used it to pour the spring water into the kava bowl. The cool water leached the kava into the bowl. It left only its soggy organic dregs behind in the cheesecloth sack. In minutes, the bowl of kava was a dark gray. It was ready to drink.

By custom, the guest always drank first. Then he passed the bowl back to the chief who drank. Then each elder drank. The chief served everyone but himself. He was the ranking person who faced the bowl and drank from its cup. However, the elders exerted power over the chief collectively. Chiefs were paramount in Fiji, therefore, chosen from royal children. They did not rule only by lineage and nomenclature.

The council of elders selected a new chief from a pool of royal pretenders in each village and province at the death of an old chief. Paramount ascension to chiefhood was for life. However, timely resignation was expected and demanded as senility approached. Also, continued abuse of power often resulted in fatal hunting or fishing accidents. Chiefs depended on perceived power, which was absolute, but also communal. The men behind the chief were the village enforcers and its board of directors. The missing witch doctor was the hit man and final counselor, if needed.

The chief served me. I took the worn hand carved coconut shell brown cup from his hand. I drank the kava in the traditional one gulp. Its effect was narcotic. It lethally numbed my tongue, and I had to make my life's most important speech in five minutes. I thanked the chief politely in Fijian and then passed the common cup back. We would all drink from it one man at a time. The chief drank next. He ceremonially thanked me for the powerful kava, and then he served his elders who all liked the stuff. It was like doing pot from a private drawer in Maui, Hawaii. I was off to a good start if I could move my numbed tongue and control my mildly hallucinating mind. The last elder drank. He passed the cup back to the chief. We all sat cross legged on the hand-woven reed mats. They waited for me to make the expected ceremonial request speech.

I paused for a moment. It forced the room to focus on me and let the kava's effect strengthen. Just as the silence was on the verge of being uneasy in the deadly quiet ceremonial bure lit by silent traditional whale oil fueled lanterns, I spoke in Fijian national dialect:

"I am Cooper, a Peace Corps volunteer living near the village of Nakanaka on the coast of the province of Nagoga, from the state of Colorado in the USA...your friend during the great war against the Japanese. I have lived for almost three years among the Fijian village people, working with them to create the Valley Co-op which markets their crops including potatoes, watermelon, banana, passionfruit, and broomcorn."

There was murmur after the word "potatoes". It seemed my mild fame had preceded me here by way of the Fiji national short wave ban reports on the incident. This was a good sign. I continued:

"I have worked very hard with the people of my province to strengthen their co-op before independence, so they can chart their own course after the Great White Queen comes from England and returns Fiji to the rule of the Council of Chiefs through the Parliament of All People."

This was a bit of a lie; I knew most rural Fijians naively thought the Council of Chiefs was going to govern the country. They had little working knowledge of the new Parliament or of its legislative power to make law. I continued:

"My work with the Fijian people as a guest of your country is nearing completion. I must soon travel in the great silver bird from Nadi to the Polynesian island kingdom of Hawaii, a province of the USA, and finally, to my state of Colorado and the village of Telluride."

I had grown up on a ranch, but no Fijian understood the concept, because all land was communally owned. No traditional Fijian would ever live outside of the village for any reason, except exile which meant death. I always picked the nearest town to the ranch. Telluride was a dilapidated, down at the collar mining town of peeling paint Victorians, miner shacks and rotting, wooden fronted old west buildings. This white lie pleased Fijian villagers since I would have been an exiled man if I lived on a ranch. Animals, plants, and spirits lived in the woods outside villages in Fiji, not people.

"A great tragedy happened when a Fijian co-worker was murdered in the capital city of Suva three months ago."

Everyone murmured. They collectively made a mental note to have this fact checked on the next trip to the Nadi market on the main island on Wednesday. That's how the bamboo wireless worked. An islander's mainland relative at the Nadi market would know the Fiji Times newspaper details of Patipati's murder with the two Peace Corps volunteers.

"While the Valley Co-op's new crops are replanted after the great wind, I have come to surf the famous blue reef. Also, I wish to rest on your island to regain my strength before the long journey to my village over the great blue water."

None of these village elders had ever been on a jet liner to the USA, so their sense of the great journey was historic time, not jet age time. These Fijians always rested before their long trips by sailboat from isolated island group to island group, so my request was logical. The surfboard lying skeg up on the matted floor behind me corroborated my alibi. I did not mention my desire to walk the fire pit and enter the Land of the Dead Chiefs. They would not understand this request since they did not know me or my power yet. The right time would come for each of these requests.

"I want to present the chief with a special gift given to me by the prime minister. This gift is for the honor of requesting to stay in your village through the next full moon, and to surf the sacred blue reef whose waves come from the Antarctic Sea at the South Pole, the home of the Ice Gods."

On rare occasions, an iceberg floated into extreme southern Fijian waters. It caused panic as a sign of hostility from the gods to the south, especially when a village boat was sunk in the night crossing. I read the chief's face and he knew there was more to my story than he could perceive. He knew I was about to put him on the ropes. I had done it expertly and by the book, ceremonially by custom.

"The great whale's tooth of the High Chief of the Council of Chiefs shall remain forever in this bure on this island as a memory of my visit. It is my clan's gift to the village."

I whipped out the engraved, initialed small whale's tooth. It was about 50 years old. It had belonged to the prime minister. I handed it to the chief. He could barely hold it he was so excited. It was like handing a U.S. mint gold bar to a banker to pay a debt. This was the most prized and sacred object in traditional Fiji. The chief held it in his old, tough, callused hands.

"I request you assign me a bure to be housed as a guest. I will contribute money to the household during my stay. Permit me to surf the blue reef and leave on the first boat after the night of the full moon."

This was the trick pitch. I hoped to slide past the chief in his kava narcotic fueled frenzy over the sacred whale's tooth. If I left on the first sailboat after the full moon to the main island, then I had to be present for the firewalk on the day of the full moon. If I left on full moon, they could send me on the last boat before the firewalk.

The chief's words in his response to me were critical. I listened, as did the elders who mulled the request. The chief paused. He waited for an elder to voice opposition. That was their right, and one did. He seemed to understand my trick wording. He spoke in their obscure, ancient village dialect. He thought I would not understand it. I heard the words "moon" and "fire" discussed but understood no other words even as I searched my mind's past conversations with my Fijian language instructor Aki in

Hawaii. The chief paused again. He asked why I wanted to stay past the night of the full moon.

I lied a little again. I said, "The big surf on the blue reef often comes during the high tides of the full moon days. I want to ride the legendary surf. It is the biggest on earth if the Ice Gods are angry in the Antarctic Sea."

The chief paused again, and no one spoke. He held the balance of power. His duty by custom was to accommodate a generous guest in the Peace Corps service of his country while protecting his villagers from the intrusion and potential danger of a stranger. Seventy years of grace, courage, wisdom, and power focused on the request. His decree was final. The bure was silent, and he was backed by the enforcers behind him. Their young warrior minions were waiting outside to enforce the edict.

The chief looked at the sacred whale's tooth which was magnificent. Then he looked past me at the triple stringer, nose, and tail piece Greg Knoll big wave cannon. I had brought it from an Aussie friend in Sigatoka. He had bought it from a Pan Am pilot who won it in a poker game in Honolulu. The pilot brought it to Fiji to surf the main island's inner reef shore break. While drunk at the Sky Lodge Hotel, he stupidly sold it to my friend for $50.00 Fijian and a chance for a roll in the hay with his half-Chinese, half-Indian, exotic party girlfriend. The pilot passed out too early to complete the last half of the deal.

The chief spoke: "We accept your gift to our village and welcome you here. You may stay till the first market boat past the full moon. You may surf the blue reef alone. No villager may surf with you. No villager may attempt to save you from the blue reef if you fall on the great waves that strike our island and carve endlessly the high bluff for our village on the sleeping volcano. You will stay with Eli at the bure named Kennedy for your fallen heroic president. He sailed Fiji's water in his war canoe. Eli shall be your guide in our village. He is the son of Lilalila at my right, cousin of Alu, who is in Lautoka for a fortnight. Eli has a good wife and a young girl child. You shall contribute 10 Fijian dollars to his household. You may hunt and fish with our people. You shall attend the Methodist church on Sunday, a day you cannot surf or hunt. Consult Eli before leaving the village. You are now the village's guest."

My victory was conditional as I was now under practical house arrest. Except for the three activities prescribed, I had to ask Eli, a man of no rank but probably being groomed to be an elder when his father died, for permission to do anything. This included talking to the village's unmarried women who had been put off limits by omission. I had been assigned to a house with a baby girl, while no village house girl had been assigned to me.

The Kennedy connection was intriguing, but probably a coincidence. Fijians named their bures. They painted the name inside the headboard of the main door frame of the formal entrance at the front of the house. Many Fijians still thought Kennedy's PT-Boat had been based in Fiji, which was not true. He had been hugely popular in Fiji when he was President of the USA.

I might have gotten Eli for his house name as an honor, but more likely, it was a test for him. If I screwed up under his watch, his ascendancy to elderhood took a dive. His ascent had already been weakened by the birth of a girl as his first child. He would be on guard duty day and night since my supervision was his only job for the next month. The chief had let me stay, but he was extremely wary. I could not by custom approach him directly again. All requests had to go through Eli, a young unranked man in the village. The chief smiled and chanted my formal invitation with the village elders. Then he called for the drum to summon Eli and the younger men to sample the special Lau kava...

My long-legged horse suddenly dodged left. The wild boar hunt was underway as he galloped faster to catch the horses suddenly accelerating ahead of him. I concentrated as palm fronds whizzed by my eyes like sharp-edged knives. The dogs barked loudly about 1,000 yards upslope to the east. They were on the scent of a wild boar. Hunting season opened. I balanced my six-foot bamboo spear in my right hand. My knees and thighs dug into my horse's flanks. The dangerous chase began over the rocky grass covered flank of the ancient dormant volcano.

CHAPTER THIRTY-NINE

THE WILD BOAR

The dogs barked louder as we galloped out of the thick low bush of the volcano's mildly sloping windward base. The horses were knee-high in wild grass on what appeared to be an abandoned cattle plantation. The land had been cleared of the thick, tropical bush in the past decade but was no longer grazed.

Ventures came and went in Fiji as various foreign speculative groups tried to farm or ranch paradise. This one had collapsed, probably because of the poor transportation between the Island of Fire and the main island's capital city of Suva. Also, the villagers tended to kill a cow or two for each sacred or special occasion. This practice wiped out the profit in the deal for the investors who had leased the land from the village. They also hired the villagers as cheap cowboys to herd the cattle. Unfortunately for the investors, the cows couldn't swim the ocean to market and the cowboys ate the herd without regard to profit margins or return on investment. A village near my house had eaten a $20,000 prize Texas breeding bull as a Christmas feast, which it rustled from Fiji's National Tropical Agricultural Station.

We galloped full speed across this 2-3,000-acre grass field. I followed the mongrel village dogs 100 yards ahead chasing a mature wild boar. He had been surprised in the open meadow. We rapidly closed at an angle as the two lead riders moved to cut the pig off before he could reach his brushy home turf. There he could make the chase extremely dangerous as well as miserable. So with luck, they would intercept the boar. He was a five- or six-year old male with 10-inch tusks. He was 200 yards from the edge of the thick bush. The leaders rode to turn him back toward the five of us who were now charging with bamboo spears in our right hands behind the wall of 15 or so village hunting dogs. Village dogs lived two or three years, and their deaths were often violent while boar hunting.

My horse galloped at full speed. It was dangerous riding with no saddle and a rotting leather bridle. The 1,200-pound animal galloped full speed toward the wild boar behind the dog pack. He was sure-footed, but one misstep into a hidden cattle hoof hole in the high brown grass meant that I would be launched like an Atlas rocket into space.

Suddenly, the two lead riders cut off the wild boar. He turned back toward the wall of dogs rather than face their bamboo spears as they wheeled their horses in chase. Eli, my keeper, and official host, rode at the head of our spear point of galloping lancers. We were now spreading out to form a 50-yard-long picket line to block the boar's escape. The boar, whose sight was keen and whose sense of smell was legendary, probably saw Eli on point. The wild boar sped toward the dog pack that charged pell-mell toward him, barking madly. Danger lurked everywhere.

The boar met the dogs at full speed. He lowered his head, and a black and white spotted mongrel hound was almost ripped in half. The wild boar tossed him 15 feet into the air. His hindquarters were paralyzed instantly as the boar's tusks broke the dog's back. I had heard stories about these kamikaze wild boar attacks. I had never faced one at close range. Four or five of the larger dogs went for his throat simultaneously as the two trailing horsemen jabbed at his hindquarters with their bamboo spears. They attempted to paralyze his rear legs and render him helpless for a kill. They missed on both jabs. The spears grazed his well-muscled flanks. They cut his coat, leaving bloody gashes that only enraged him. He gored another village dog through its heart, killing it instantly.

The two trailing horsemen semi-circled and quickly closed again for the kill. Eli's rapidly charging horse suddenly hit a deep hidden cow hoof hole. Eli's body cartwheeled into the air as the horse's leg snapped and the horse came to a standstill in three strides. Its left lower front leg and hoof shot off at a wild angle as it stood helpless, in shock. Eli landed headfirst and disappeared into the deep grass to the uphill slope side of the dogs.

The enraged, wounded wild boar who had just killed a third dog went straight at Eli's fallen horse. It leapt into the air and speared it through the heart. It killed the horse in one bold stroke. The horse fell to its side. The horse's blood spurted into the air like a small oil well gusher in west Texas, splattering the dogs and boar as they madly fought each other in a wild frenzy.

Eli suddenly rose and stood in the waist-high grass. It was a bad decision. The boar saw him 50 feet away. It turned and tossed another dog into the air. It charged from a standing start like a drag racer. I had been riding to Eli's upslope flank. I had the only fast intercept line which could reach the boar before he charged into Eli and killed him. The two horsemen chasing him from the rear had split at the dead horse. They had to pass straight through our irregular picket line of dogs and horses to avoid a collision. There was not enough room for them to wheel their horses. They flashed through the line of four riders at high speed. Then they started to slow and cut left and right respectively to cover our flanks. The advancing line of hunters raced toward the boar with the dog pack in hot pursuit. Eli stood erect, dazed, staring in shock from his fall in a frozen trance. The boar narrowed the gap to ten yards.

I spurred my horse bare footed and clenched my spear. I aimed it to hit the furious wild boar in mid-air as he leapt to gore Eli through the heart with his two razor-sharp 10-inch tusks. The barking dogs were only a yard behind him. If I missed my target as I charged between Eli and the wild boar, he would shred my right calf to the bone and probably sever an artery in my leg. That meant sure death on the isolated windward side of the dormant volcano on the Island of Fire. If I reined in my horse and cut behind Eli and gambled on a perfectly perpendicular, more difficult spear thrust and missed, Eli was dead. The wild boar would tear him in half as he stood slightly unconscious, partially blinded by the low morning sun.

I pivoted the horse to the hard right and downslope. I cut between Eli and the charging boar. The boar was now airborne. I set my spear almost perpendicular to the horse's flank. The boar hit the bamboo spear full force. He grotesquely impaled himself on it in the air. The momentum of his jump carried him, with the spear impaled in his throat, into the right flank of my horse behind my thigh. I sped past Eli, letting my spear drop at the last moment.

The boar's violent impact had almost toppled my horse, but he found his footing at the last possible moment. The boar's lowered tusks had only nicked his thick winter coat. The wild boar bounced backwards with the bamboo spear in his throat. The pack of village dogs pinned him to the ground in seconds. The other riders thrust their sharp-tipped bamboo spears into his heart. They pinned his hindquarters to the ground only a few feet from Eli, who lay sprawled in the high grass. Eli had been knocked down again when my left knee grazed his chin as my horse sped past him at full speed.

I reined in my horse 50 yards downslope. I took a deep breath. I checked my horse's bleeding right flank six inches behind my bared right calf and feet. This had not been fun, and my body was on full alert from a massive adrenaline rush at the moment of the spear thrust. The only spear I had thrown before today, was my high school track and field team's javelin. I had been a high hurdler. I had tossed the javelin infrequently on boring spring practice days between wind sprints.

I reined my horse to a complete stop. I surveyed the scene. Eli lay spread eagle on his back, but he had raised his head, so he was still alive. Three dogs were dead. Their bodies were strewn grotesquely in the high African hybrid Savannah grass. The village dog pack was at bay, but blood spattered with minor wounds.

Eli's horse lay dead in a bed of bloody brown grass. Five mounted hunters surrounded the wild boar. Their spears were in his flanks, heart, and throat along with mine. My spear's shaft had been broken in half by its impact with the ground after the boar bounced off my horse. Otherwise, it was just another day in paradise as the Pacific Ocean sparkled deep blue a mile away with the white puffy clouds which had formed over the long dormant volcano crater in a crystal clear blue sky.

The village was on the opposite side of the volcano's crater. No other living thing moved in my sightline. No sail or ship broke the ocean horizon. No airliner broke the blue skyline. No sound, except for the breathing of the hunters, horses and dogs broke the silence of the dead, except the rustle of the high Savannah grass in the light, trade wind breeze. The sun drenched my khaki shorts-only clad body with heat and energy. My muscles unclenched from the charge downslope to the deadly confrontation with the wild heroic boar.

No one moved. No one shouted as the mounted hunters loosened the tension on their bamboo spears. They backed their horses away from the dead boar who would soon be roasted in an underground oven to feast the village to celebrate my visit. Life was as pure black and white as it ever gets for a few moments.

Seven men, six horses, 12 or so village dogs rested together spent from war on the side of a sleeping volcano in the center of a grassy field cleared by forgotten fools in the middle of the Pacific Ocean. If I could have vaporized myself at that moment, I might have done so. The bond of mind and purpose were one. The feeling of satisfaction was total.

Then the village hunters raised their bloody tipped bamboo spears. They cheered, and they chanted in unison. It was an ancient Fijian hunt chant. It had been composed on the dark continent. The chant swept across the high Savannah grass, borne by the wind. I joined them in the chant because I knew its words in my heart.

It was the same chant conceived in a castle in the north of Europe legions ago before my ancestors crossed from Normandy to Britain in 1066. It was exactly the same as the Fijian chant that had traveled by dugout canoe from Africa to this small island. We all knew the chant. It was imprinted on our subconscious memory. It was about life, death, celebration for the tribe's welfare. I screamed the chant into the air. The wind blew it across the vast stretches of the South Pacific where a man's life was no more than a cork floating in this great pool of blue ocean water.

I spurred my horse. I rode back slowly to the small group of horse-mounted spearman, feeling the midday sun burn into my back. I chanted with the bronze-black Pacific island warriors, at the top of my lungs. I was happy to be alive but sure I was in a dream. It seemed to me the metaphysical dream world had completely replaced the world of daily realism. I rode slowly across the vast expanse of brown Savannah grass on the fertile slopes of the dormant volcano.

I had become the Ute Indian. I had switched my dream world with my reality world. I would need to find a guide to return. I had no need to hurry and no need for fear. I wanted to enjoy the voluntary exchange and live in the dream world. Hopefully, a guide would appear to return me to the real world. If the guide didn't appear, I would round into the edges of the dream world. I would float in this Savannah grass waving in the soft trade wind on the windward side of the sleeping volcano in paradise for all eternity.

CHAPTER FORTY

THE COOKOUT

The wild boar was two feet underground as it cooked in a traditional Fijian earth oven. Earlier, some of the younger men in the village dug a pit about four feet deep. It was big enough for the pig. Plus, it had room for the addition of cassava roots which were tasteless giant turnips. Creek rocks and volcanic rocks had been heated in a bonfire in the pit until they were white hot. The wild boar had been gutted, but otherwise left intact with head, feet, and tail. When the rocks were white hot, they were placed with large wooden tongs into the bottom of the earthen pit. They were covered with a thick layer of green banana leaves. Next, the boar and the cassava were placed in the pit and covered by additional banana leaves. Then, finally, a couple feet of earth were added to seal the village's dinner in the oven to bake for six hours. I had watched as the wild boar was carefully lowered into the pit onto the bed of succulent banana leaves.

I had helped dig the pit and the hard labor had felt good in the island's fresh tropical breeze. We all had shoveled light, rich black volcanic soil in rhythm to a Fijian chant which made the work seem easier. It took four men about 30 minutes to dig the pit on the edge of the village near the bluff. The pit overlooked the lagoon where the village's inter-island sail-boat was docked.

Eli rested in the Kennedy bure. He was still recovering from his fall. He lay on an inch-thick pile of woven mats with a knotted wet cotton sulu across his forehead. His wife kneeled nearby to tend him. He clearly had suffered a bad concussion, but the Island of Fire had no doctor or nurse. The witch doctor, Alu, was still away. The home remedy was sleep until the dizziness ended. I gave him two of my Darvon pills from the Peace Corps standard issue first-aid kit which was in the aluminum ammo box. I hoped they would help his concussion.

I had once played an entire second half of a college fraternity intra-mural touch football game with a broken rib. I was aided only by Darvon and Jack Daniels. I told Eli to mix a little kava with the Darvon and he would mend quickly.

The wild boar went into the underground pit at mid-afternoon. The feast time was planned for well after dark. I decided to walk to the western end of the bluff and watch the sunset. I stopped to check on Eli, who was asleep. I got some ganja or pot from the ammo box. I didn't smoke much ganja, but I needed a treat after the wild boar hunt, coupled with a beau-tiful sunset over the deep blue Pacific Ocean. I wanted to cool-out with nature and wait for the feast.

I concealed the Fiji grown ganja and rolling papers in a Johnson and Johnson band-aid tin that my mom had sent me to augment the doctor-lev-el first-aid kit the Peace Corps supplied. Mom's little surprises always helped, even if their eventual use was not what she had intended. Rolling papers were readily available in Fiji. Most villagers bought tobacco at the marketplace and rolled their own cigarettes like cowboys.

Village Fijians rarely used band-aids, so I knew anyone in Eli's family who snooped through the ammo box would not find the ganja. I didn't know all the village rules. I didn't know if these villagers smoked any pot. They were isolated from day-to-day contacts with the Indian Hindu population on the main island. Many of the Valley Fijian villagers in my province grew ganja for extra cash and secretly smoked it.

I slipped the band-aid box out of the ammo kit without waking the heavily drugged Eli. I walked bare footed out of the bure's men's side door which was open. The late afternoon sun was weakening in strength. A light cool ocean breeze continued to break the brutally humid tropical heat of Fiji's nearing rainy summer season which was November through April in the Southern Hemisphere. It was still technically a month away. I knew I wouldn't miss the rainy season after I left Fiji, but it was the only thing I wouldn't miss.

I walked from Eli's bure, which was on the northern edge of the village, to the western side of the village. I said, "bula" or hello to the playing, small nude children as I crossed the village common. Most of the adult male villagers were taking a late afternoon nap while waiting for the feast. It was high tide and the reef fishing had been completed for the day. The women had gathered firewood for the next morning's fires. They had carried water for the feast from a spring near the village. It ran year-round except in extremely dry winter periods.

The location of this historically reliable spring actually determined the village site, not the south facing lagoon. The lagoon provided fresh fish daily, but it was a poorly protected harbor. Water was extremely precious on this small windward island. Even though it usually received 100 inches of rain annually, no large-scale storage system existed to collect water.

Five minutes beyond the village perimeter, I found a private spot in a small palm grove to view the sunset and smoke a joint. I rolled the joint on cheap coarse New Zealand cigarette paper. I wished for some fine Zippo paper from the USA. It was still about an hour before dusk. I pulled slowly on the joint and let flashes of jumbled thoughts race through my mind. I shielded my eyes from the western sun with a Pan Am visor I carried for these occasions. One of their pilots had given it to a volunteer. He traded it to me for some surfboard wax.

Flashes of Patipati lying dead in Suva co-mingled with flashes of the wild boar bearing down on Eli and me. Had the gods sent a message for me to back off or was the boar just part of the test on the Island of Fire... Flashes of Dianne boarding the Pan Am jet were jumbled with the chaotic scene at the Nadi Sky Lodge Hotel. It had seemed completely random at the time. Then came the incident on the wild boar hunt. Were they connected to the dream world of my life on these dangerously mystifying magical Fijian islands? During one week, I had been shot at by a stranger and charged by a wild boar. Dianne had left Fiji convinced I was the target, not Patipati in Suva. The dream state had suddenly become extremely dangerous I wished Patipati was present to guide me on the Island of Fire, but that clearly had not been his karma or his destiny. I shuffled through my thoughts. I heard only the light breeze through the palm trees on the bluff. The faraway voices of children playing on the village common were muffled. Occasionally, a large high tide wave broke hard enough against the base of the bluff's cliff below to shatter the silence and accent a thought. The fresh ocean-charged, ionized air drifted up after each one of the crashes. The air recharged my lungs with fresh energy. The surf was getting big as the sun dropped. Big sets rolled into the lagoon from the south. The surf built without warning.

One thought began to dominate the other thoughts. Eli owed me a favor big time. He would be my vehicle to the chief and the witch doctor, Alu, when he returned, to let me walk the fire pit. I had saved his life. While it was still his assigned job to watch me for the village, he would have to honor my request to ask the chief for a pow-wow to discuss my walk through the fire pit. The plan steadied my nerves. It revealed a logic by the gods for the sudden chaos of the wild boar hunt which was a normally routine event for the village hunters. My keeper had evolved into my blocking back. I had to make my most important move soon. I had to train with the men who were chosen to walk the hot fire pit at the next full moon.

The ganja drifted through my mind in less paranoid waves as the puzzle solved itself. The sun dropped behind a thin cloud bank hanging off the west horizon of the island. It lit up the sky in a spectrum of colors whose red, pink, purple and orange hues exploded like a bomb. This was the real magic of the islands. The grace, courage and dazzling multi-colored displays of its sunsets tranquilized its inhabitants and froze them in time and place forever. No picture, no laser, no art object in the world came close to these nightly light shows in Fiji's western Pacific sky. I had become an addict of the magic moments which lasted for ten to twenty minutes over the Pacific Ocean as the orange fire ball sank through light late-winter cloud layers. The sunsets saturated the retina until it begged for mercy. This sunset fix had locked me into the Island of Fire with a finality. I suspected its dawn would unspool my destiny.

The mauve-orange ball dropped out of the lowest layer of the cloud bank. It disappeared into the dark blue sea. It was extinguished in a spark of dull red-orange as the Fijian sea gods rested it for the night.

I walked alone in the twilight. I heard the village beginning to stir for the feast which was still a couple of hours away. Women were grouping in cooking bures to prepare side dishes for the feast. They would serve the men in the village's ceremonial houses. Everyone else would eat in selected bures throughout the village. The women were preparing fresh reef fishes boiled in coconut and onions, charcoaled Pacific lobster, and prawn or Pacific shrimp in boiled coconut milk. They were also preparing pitchers of fresh passionfruit and pineapple juice to drink.

The youngest children had already been fed. They would be asleep by the time the feast started. The older children were now rounding up the younger children for their mid-week bath in the island's only winter stream. It emptied into the ocean at the base of the eastern bluff. A bath consisted of a swim in the brackish fresh-water pool with homemade village soap. The Methodist missionaries had done one job well. They had taught the village women to make strong soap.

I needed a bath, so I followed the line of younger children with their sibling teenage guardians down a path east of the village. I was still high from the ganja. I did not want to start drinking kava with the men two hours before dinner. At the rate these island men tossed down bowls of kava, I would be bloated by feast time.

A bath would feel good and a swim would be relaxing. The east trail was the one I had climbed on arrival to the village from the lagoon. A third of the way down the bluff, it branched to the left for a half-mile. Eventually, the group arrived at the base of a small waterfall with a pool. Apparently, we weren't walking all the way down to the lagoon tonight. We had stopped for a shower in the waterfall which was normally down to a trickle at the end of the dry winter season. It had been recharged by the typhoon's heavy rains.

A teenage boy carried a flaming torch ahead of me. He pushed it into the mud at the edge of the shallow pool as light for the 20 or so younger village kids. The oldest teenagers had stayed in the village to help prepare the feast or pound the kava for the elders who had gathered in the chief's house.

In the flickering torch light, the nude bodies of the happily chattering younger children provided a living Matisse painting of unspoiled form, beauty, and innocence. The preteen children herded their young brothers, sisters, and cousins through the cascading waterfall. They soaped them down with crude white rectangular bars of village homemade soap. An older boy, Ito, beckoned me to join them. I stripped off my shirt but left on my khaki shorts. This was the missionary instilled custom practiced by older men who bathed or swam in the presence of younger female children.

I waded into the pool. I felt the warm, sun heated island water up to my ankles. I stepped under the cascading waterfall into nature's shower. The waterfall felt cool in the warm, tropical night air. It washed away a week's grime, sweat and dirt. I tried some of the lye soap which stung. It removed another layer of dirt as it opened up my pores. My whole body breathed again as the ionized, cascading cool water invigorated my spirit.

The younger village kids laughed and played. They talked to me in the national Fijian dialect they had learned in the village school. The older kids tried out their English, which they studied from the fourth grade until they finished sixth grade. Only a few children were chosen by parental rank or intellect to board for high school on the main island. I enjoyed the half-hour pre-feast shower with these outer-island Fijian children. Their world had not been interrupted by the call of adulthood or the rapid westernization of Fiji's main island. I hoped they would not turn it into a cheap resort someday for Australian, New Zealand, and eventually, American, and Japanese tour groups.

I wished I could freeze time for these kids, but Captain Cook, Gauguin, and Pan Am had opened their paradise. Tears came to my eyes as they taught me a song the village children sang while bathing in the flickering torchlit waterfall of a faded British crown colony.

CHAPTER FORTY-ONE

THE FEAST

The village log drums called the chief and his elders to the feast from their kava binge in the men's ceremonial story-telling bure at the edge of the village. I was at the boar pit. I watched Eli, who had miraculously risen from his mats, and the younger men extract the boar from the underground oven. They brushed the dirt from the upper layer of the baked banana leaves. The succulent smell of roast boar wafted through the warm night air. It was a smell I had first encountered in Hawaii during Peace Corps training. It was always magical, and my mouth watered.

The best meal in the world was earthen pit roasted Pacific wild boar. This one was special, because only a half-day earlier, its 10-inch tusks had missed my lower leg by inches. I anticipated enjoying eating every bit of my portion of the wild boar.

The aroma of the wild boar strengthened as it was lifted from the pit. A village teenage boy took my hand. He said the chief had summoned me to join him at the village ceremonial bure to feast with the other hunters and the village men. The teenage boy led me away from the pit, holding my hand, as was the custom in Fiji among men. Warriors in dress sulus often walked hand in hand down the capital city thoroughfares in

Suva. This often shocked uptight Aussie, New Zealand, American and even European tourists. It had taken me a year of living in Fiji to become accustomed to this cultural trait.

We moved swiftly through the village. We passed the blazing kerosene lanterns in the bures. Groups of women finalized their dishes to present to the chief and his fellow diners. I was led to the front formal entrance of the village's ceremonial bure. I kicked off my flip-flops by custom as I entered. No living human being, male or female was permitted to wear shoes by custom into a Fijian bure. Fijians rarely wore leather sandals in the rural villages. The thought of wearing them inside a house or bure had never been considered in the entire history of the country.

The long bure's reed matted floor had been covered with a long, hand loomed white cotton tablecloth. In rural Fiji, bures had no furniture. All meals were served on a long cotton tablecloth laid across the central mat covered floor. Diners sat cross-legged and shoulder to shoulder around it. There was no silverware; Fijians used their right hand to eat. They picked up food and drank soup from a coconut bowl. Large enamel tin dinner plates sat at each place for the village men who were eating with the chief. No places were set at the head or ends of the long rectangular tablecloth. The chief would sit in the center of one side. The most important guest would sit directly across from him. This made conversation easy during dinner. The villagers concentrated on eating first, with important conversation saved until after dinner, when more kava was consumed.

I arrived as the chief entered through the front door of the bure. The tall well-muscled boy led me to a place across from the chief. Warriors scrambled to their cross-legged positions around the table. Their places were predetermined by rank and custom.

As soon as we all were seated in the flickering semi-dark, lantern lit room, gaily feast dressed bright, floral, cotton sulued women began entering through the opposite women's side door. The first wave carried glasses and pitchers of passionfruit juice. They scooted on their knees, torso's upright, to the tablecloth. They presented the chief with the fruit juice made with cool fresh spring water. It had been stored in shaded clay waterpots.

Women were prohibited by custom from standing or walking upright in the ceremonial bure in the presence of the seated chief and village men. They scooted about quickly on their knees. They also always worked by custom behind the men. The women were not by custom allowed to eat

with the men. When they weren't serving or ferrying food, they knelt silently around the walls at the edges of the bure's single large room. They
waited silently for their next task. No words were spoken as they served
the feast by custom. They learned to serve feasts during girlhood.

The chief's older wife was the manager of this feast. It was a major celebration. She directed ten older wives of the elders in the bure.
They brought tin pots of hot, fresh reef fish in coconut milk, steaming
prawns, eggplant, and platters of sliced roast wild boar to the cloth
table. They served each man separately. They started always with the
chief when a new dish was presented. I was served second because I
was the honored guest.

A legion of younger wives and older teenage girls ferried dishes, food,
and clean tin plates to the women's side door of the bure while the ten older women inside constantly replenished our plates. They served the chief's
feast with dignity, grace and precision. This Fijian custom made the American college educated, liberated feminist Peace Corps women volunteers
crazy. Some had left Fiji rather than eat with the women daily and during
feasts in villages which enforced the custom strictly. In the urban areas of
the main island, this practice was fading, except during ceremonial Fijian
events. On the Island of Fire, custom and tradition still strictly ruled.

The meal was one of the best of my young life. The wild boar was succulent, delicious, and tender. The fresh reef fish boiled in coconut milk and
Fiji onions was five-star. The steamed prawns and charcoaled Pacific lobster blended with the boar perfectly. Steamed eggplant also cooked vaca
lola with coconut milk and the cassava or the African potato, provided
veggie carbohydrates for an over-the-top meal.

I washed it all down with glass after glass of fresh, cool, passionfruit
juice. I stopped eating when I couldn't force down another mouthful.
Conversation had been functionally sparse as everyone devoured the
wild boar, the specialty of the evening. Seafood was the everyday village staple. I had plenty of lobster and prawn while the chief and the men
concentrated on the wild boar.

Fijians had no desserts, so after the main course of the dinner was
complete, conversation began as the men stretched out prone on the mats
with their heads resting on carved wooden headrests. Later, the kava bowl
would reappear, along with tobacco and rolling papers or packages of Fiji
cigarettes. Then story time always commenced again.

Everyone rested for twenty minutes. Then the chief called the men to their cross-legged positions in an oblong circle. The ten women had quickly cleared the long ceremonial bure. They ate the remains of the feast in their bures laced with village gossip.

The younger men brought the kava bowl to the ceremonial bure from the chief's bure. Bowls of kava started to circulate rapidly. The chief called on Eli to tell the story of the hunt to the 'isas' (or approval sighs) of the other men. The chief, by custom, formally put Eli into my debt. This story ensured that the other village elders knew of my bravery during the hunt. I had saved Eli from the boar's vicious assault which could have killed or maimed him for life.

Men had died hunting wild boar for the village. Men and women had also been killed reef fishing when sharks attacked. Gathering food was still dangerous on this island, only a couple of hours by speed boat from the international airport at Nadi. The contrasts in the third world were stark and sometimes maddening. Although people were killed in car accidents going to the grocery store at home, somehow it seemed to be a different kind of danger when the Fijian daily routine still called for personal risk to eat.

Eli finished his story with a flourish of his hands. He showed how my horsemanship had blocked the boar's wild attack. Good Fijian story tellers used their hands constantly. They painted a picture of motion to accompany their work. I secretly hoped television never came to these islands, but I knew the Japanese would never allow this market to escape. Fiji's story time bonding would suffer.

I had for three years enjoyed the best story tellers in the world. Their tongues and hands wove the intricate tales of current and legendary historical deeds. The stories lifted the village men from the routine existence of life each night. The stories thrust me into the world of danger, humor, tragedy, and myth. I was in a circle of warriors in a long bure with the yellow light of flickering lanterns in a place where the earth was still untamed.

At the end of Eli's story, the chief, by custom, asked me to add to the story. I spoke in national dialect. A man next to the chief translated for some of the elderly village men. They only spoke the provincial and village dialects. This gave the story an interesting reverie. I explained the game of polo in my country which had taught me the horsemanship I had used to hunt.

Several of the men had heard of the game. One remembered the British army had a polo field at the Nadi military barracks early in the century.

A Royal Lancer horse cavalry unit had been stationed in Fiji's western province of Viti Levu during a period of Fijian political unrest. They had heard stories from their fathers or grandfathers of watching the soldiers hit a small ball with a long stick on a grassy field near the site of the present international airport. The English women watched while Fijian house-girls held umbrellas over their heads in the hot tropical afternoon sun.

Their fathers had marveled at the speed of the horses and the precision of the riders. They wondered why such skill was used to chase and hit a ball instead of hunt the wild boar. The boar lived in the bush near the Nadi barracks. I didn't have a good answer for them. I said the game was a favorite of the American army's cavalry units which fought the Indians in the American west. It was later played on big southwestern cattle ranches as a social activity.

The game, I added, sharpened a fighter's or rancher's riding skills. The position of the horse by a foot or so often meant life or death. They all understood my explanation of polo. Eli was proof, sitting next to the chief, aided only by Darvon and kava, instead of being prepared for burial the next day.

It had been a great hunt. Its story would become a village legend until the imposition of western communications technology and its related media wiped out the village story tellers. The Fijians' future had been decided by the World Bank to work as hotel laborers and taxi drivers.

I hoped these people of enormous goodwill, great native intelligence and athletic ability would live on their semi-remote island and hunt wild boar until the end of the planet. I knew in my heart my very presence was a siren warning change. Neither the warrior wild boar hunters, the American Peace Corps volunteers, nor British Cavalry polo players were part of Fiji's future. The village wild boar hunters were destined to be bartenders, waiters, and glorified bus boys. Perhaps tonight the Sea God would keep the sun and it would not rise from the ocean tomorrow. Then these brilliant warriors would remain frozen in time as a memorial to when the earth and mankind were young, with survival and adventure as friends.

This feast and story session ended early for me. At sunrise, I planned to scout the most legendary winter surf in the Southern Pacific. I could hear the surf building. I intended to test my own survival in an adventure I had fantasized about since arriving in Fiji. This village would be my witness or my undertaker.

CHAPTER FORTY-TWO

LET'S GO SURFING NOW

At sunrise, the village roosters began to crow. The women built the early morning wood fires for tea. I was up already. Low tide was only two hours away. I could hear the big surf pounding on the rocky beach below the bluff. The Island of Fire had Fiji's most unique and dangerous surfing beach. The island lay west and north of the main island of Viti Levu in an open ocean channel that ran unbroken to Antarctica.

The island's barrier reef also had a wide, unbroken opening which faced due south at the entrance to its shallow lagoon. This unique combination meant waves rolled north uninterrupted several thousand miles to the Island of Fire. Their centers were channeled through the wide reef opening. They rose over a shallow lagoon bottom like giants. They broke onto the narrow beach below the thousand-foot bluff which they had created over a millennium of time. It was the end of winter in Antarctica. The last great storms were sending giant waves north to Fiji as ice walls plunged into the sea.

Most of the monster waves died helplessly on Fiji's outer barrier reefs far to the south. Occasionally, rogue wave sets made it through to the Island of Fire. These rogue waves surpassed any wave in the world in form and power, according to Fijian legend. I had first heard the legends from the Fijian story tellers in the late-night kava sessions of my province's villages.

They said waves like mountains had struck the Island of Fire 500 years ago. They birthed the great bluff in one day.

The concave bluff channeled the prevailing easterly winds as they whipped around the island. If the trade winds were strong, they helped hold up the giant waves. This produced a sheer cliff of surf which broke at the last moment before it slammed into the base of the bluff with its rocky, narrow coral beach.

This made surfing the Island of Fire's lagoon dangerous, if not impossible. My mission was to scout the lagoon's big breaks and find an escape route off its walls of water.

Since the morning of the hunt, larger and larger sets of waves had been crashing into the bluff below the village and the wind was howling, so surf time had arrived. It was the end of the fabled wave sets from the south for a year. I had heard one first-hand account about these legendary waves from Patipati's cousin. His village's fishing boat had been sunk while on a wedding trip to the Island of Fire when a rogue set of waves roared in one August afternoon. He reported them to be higher than the boat's mast. They smashed into the 40-foot, island-made, motor-sailer, which was on open anchor and drove it into the lava rock bluff destroying it in minutes. This rogue wave set had struck without warning on a winter day when the break in the lagoon was a routine rolling 3-5 feet.

Most Fijian sailors apparently feared this lagoon in the winter and avoided it. Only the Island of Fire's sail powered freighter braved it during the winter season. It was sheltered in a concrete berth at the extreme eastern edge of the lagoon. The berth was built by the U.S. Navy Seabees during World War II for a PT-Boat base to protect the northwestern flank of the allied air base at Nadi which later became the international airport. The Seabees had chosen their site well. They had poured a thick solid concrete pen. Thirty years later the small PT-Boat pen sheltered the island's sail powered freighter winter after winter. Although rogue waves rumored higher than its mast had crashed across the island's barrier reef, the village had never lost its boat.

To my knowledge, no surfer had ever attempted the Island of Fire's big surf. I suspected an Aussie eventually would. They were already drifting into Fiji's remote southern beaches in the winter. Sooner or later, one would hear about the Island of Fire. Only their historic racism and therefore lack of Fijian language ability had saved this virgin surfing secret.

I walked down the steep path to the lagoon, carrying my surfboard. Eli followed with four village teenage boys. They had come, I suspected, to recover my body if I smacked into the jagged black lava rock bluff. The rest of the village was eating breakfast. After breakfast, the villagers would wander over to the bluff at low tide to view the event from box seats a thousand feet overhead.

No attempt had been made to dissuade me from this early morning mission, nor would the chief try. Athletic endeavor, like war, was sacred in Fiji. Participants were expected to endure the consequences. Fiji regularly produced the best rugby team in the world from a population base of 100,000 males. A year ago, I had seen the Fijians defeat the British Lions in the national stadium for the World Rugby Championship. The Fijians had played mostly bare footed against the elite English team and won. Fijian teams won at rugby from the village to the national level because the players were willing to be buried on the field. This gave them a psychological edge over their more seasoned, better trained and better coached western opponents.

Athletics was like war to Fijian men. Once a man made the decision to play, he was expected to play all out. If I wanted to surf the lagoon and die in the attempt, it was my business. In Fiji, I would die with honor. There would be no vain attempt to rescue me and risk other men's lives. If I failed, I suffered the consequences. Eli and the boys would collect my body, if they could find it once the giant waves subsided.

They would sit neither in judgment nor disdain at my attempt. They wished me neither success nor failure. They would only care that I enjoyed the moment, that I was brave, was tested, and defeated my personal demons. They would enjoy and appreciate the athleticism of the act and celebrate it in story and legend, whatever the outcome. Someday, one of the village boys who watched me would try it, also, when he had access to a fiberglass surfboard.

I continued the half-hour walking descent off the bluff to the eastern lagoon. This would bring the group to the PT-Boat dock for my paddle out to the reef entrance. I reflected on my life and understood why this hour had arrived. I needed to break physically from the western world. Then I could break mentally from it to walk the fire pit in search of Patipati's killer and enter the Land of the Dead Chiefs to answer a riddle.

A ride down the face of a monster rogue wave would make the physical break final. After the ride, I knew I would live in two worlds. The first, my new physical reality, and the other, a dream state to voyage through the bleak landscape of the last stages of the industrial revolution. I planned to return to my natural spirit state on the face of a giant wave. I hoped the angry Antarctic Ice God who sent the large icebergs into Fiji's waters had not sounded a false alarm.

Eli and the teenage boys chanted a fishing song as they walked. It was their most appropriate choice for the occasion since they didn't know *LITTLE SURFER GIRL* by the Beach Boys. As I walked, I prayed to the Octopus God who protected my province's coastal waters from the Shark God who ruled the Island of Fire's waters.

Long ago in a legendary battle between the coastal village warriors of my province and the Lau warriors of the smaller eastern outer islands who attacked them in their outrigger war canoes, the Octopus God had risen from the ocean floor. The Octopus God rose to the ocean surface to strangle the sharks who traveled and protected the Lau warriors in their outrigger canoes. The Lau warriors fought to subjugate the southern coast of Fiji's main island of Viti Levu after they conquered the eastern coast.

The great Southern Pacific octopus, often six feet in height, is the only known force in the South Seas that can kill a shark. On the fateful day of the battle of the outrigger canoes, the giant octopi rose en masse to kill the Lau allied sharks. The sharks were circling the battling outriggers to eat the fallen warriors of my province. To avoid the massacre of his subjects, the Shark God promised forever to harm no warrior from my province when he traveled or swam in the ocean.

I had been made an honorary chief in my province, so I prayed to the Octopus God to protect me from the sharks. Large sharks often surfed the waves through the Island of Fire lagoon's wide south face entrance to feed on the tasty schools of brightly colored fish inside the reef. It was tough enough to surf big waves. If a shark broke your line, it would be impossible.

We descended the last bend in the steep trail at the eastern end of the bluff which was 100 feet above the ocean. I saw the waves and they were giants. The set rolling across the center of the lagoon was 20 feet high. It was being held up by a 25 mph-plus trade wind that hooked around the concave bluff. It was channeled back to mid-lagoon with enough force to stall the wave's break until almost at shoreline.

It was low tide. The big waves sucked the water 100 yards out into the lagoon. They exposed a rock-strewn coral floor all the way out from the bluff's narrow beach. If a big wave ground me into the lagoon's floor, I feared there would be nothing left but skin shards on the coral coated volcanic rock lagoon bottom. The bluff itself was weathered, exposed, jagged, volcanic lava rock which had been pounded for eons by the ocean. If a wave slapped me into it, my body could be impaled.

The slope of the walls of the pure blue Pacific waves were perfect. Like a siren, they called me into the lagoon. I had hoped to scout on a smaller day. I walked along the narrow path behind Eli with the village boys trailing. We quickly reached the abandoned PT-Boat pen and the village sail powered freighter. It rocked on 3-foot swells in its concrete nest at the extreme east end of the lagoon where the incoming waves dropped to 10 feet because they crossed the convex outer reef that guarded the lagoon. Only the waves that came directly down the pipe of the lagoon's due south face wide central opening were big. They were unimpeded by the island's barrier reef.

On most days, I would have been happy to surf the smaller well-formed 10-foot waves of the eastern lagoon to show off for the always admiring Fijians. It was not one of those surf and show times of past winter Fiji days on the main island's southern beaches. This was my personal OK Corral. It was time to paddle out during the two-hour low tide turnaround which would intensify the waves' height. They would roll unimpeded across the shallow floor of the rocky lagoon and crash into the sheer bluff.

I stripped off my Earth Day tee-shirt on the end of the concrete pier of the PT-Boat pen. I pulled a tube of Vaseline out of my shorts pocket. I rubbed the Vaseline on my legs and under my eyes to protect me from water logging. I then took the blackened burnt end of a stick from my pocket. I wet it and charcoaled around my eyes. I looked like a raccoon. This would help break the glare off the water as the sun moved east to due south. I needed to see the home of the giant wave sets. I would paddle on my surfboard in my khaki shorts. From my other pocket, I pulled out what was left of my wax. I rubbed down the 10-foot surfboard; I needed my footing on the steep blue walls of the waves.

I tossed the wax and Vaseline to Eli for safekeeping. I said goodbye to him and the village boys. I jumped off the concrete pier into the surging water some five feet below. Eli lowered the thick fiberglass coated triple stringer nose and tail piece, 10-foot blue Greg Knoll surfboard to me. It was a big gun made for the big waves. It was very different from the 7-foot Hobie I used on the southern Fiji beaches near Sigatoka.

With a splash, the long, heavy fiberglass board hit the water. I scrambled aboard to paddle diagonally out toward the lagoon's entrance while there was a break in the wave action. I quickly went up and over some five or six-foot swells. I ducked under a 10-foot early breaking wave at mid-lagoon. I was being sucked out in the ebbing tide. It was easy paddling to the east center part of the mile-wide lagoon. Then I rested. I sat up on my board and faced the incoming swells. I quickly glanced up to the top of the bluff where the entire village had gathered for the show. I prayed to the Octopus God for a good one.

I stayed parked to watch the next big set pass down the pipe to the west. I wanted to find a safe exit point from the right breaking waves. Ten minutes later, a set of three 15-20 footers boomed down the pipe in formation. I paddled up and over 10-foot lead swells inside the reef. The tunneled trade wind held the wave faces up until they broke virtually against the bluff. However, the curl provided a tunnel I could ride only to the east and exit. I had to be on the last wave of the set and be prepared to jog down the narrow rocky beach quickly toward the PT-Boat pen a quarter mile away.

The decision was easy, and my plan was set. I paddled toward the center of the opening in the lagoon's reef to wait for the perfect set of waves. I might get only one big wave chance. I had to surf perfectly a half-mile across a sheer blue wall of water. Then I had to shoot a water cave for 100 yards and drop out into 5-foot shore break. Finally, I had to run for my life down a very narrow ribbon of rocky, coral-strewn beach with a 20-pound surfboard. I had to make cover at the PT-Boat pen before another big set of waves broke against the volcanic rock bluff.

The line between courage and suicide had always been thin. Today it was stretched to the limit. I paddled fast to a new position in the outer swells. They were 20 feet as I rode up and over the first one. It crossed into the lagoon's opening. Then I saw it looming on the horizon. It was a half-mile behind the next 20-foot swell.

It was a small tidal wave. It was going to be at least 50 feet high by the time it hit the middle of the lagoon's entrance. It was the biggest wave I had ever seen. It was moving toward me at a high rate of speed. It was icy dark blue and had been born in some traumatic event thousands of miles south in Antarctica. Perhaps an entire glacier edge had splashed into the Antarctic Ocean during the spring thaw. Its birthplace didn't matter. I was cornered in the corral by an ice blue stallion. The rogue wave hurled toward me. My only escape was to ride it. The tidal wave would already be cresting as it reached the lagoon entrance. There was no way to ride up and over it. I paddled madly out of the lagoon entrance toward its forming crest for the long ride into the lagoon's bluff beach.

It was easy to paddle because all the ocean water was being sucked out of the lagoon. Its floor was almost bare to the reef. Reef fish went by me out to the sea like speed boats. I could see the bottom as I paddled. Then I began to climb the monster wall straight into the sky at five feet a second. At its peak, I wheeled the long heavy surfboard toward the watching village on the bluff. I flattened my body against the rough waxed fiberglass surface. I accelerated with rapid arm paddles.

I was suddenly almost 50 feet above the lagoon floor. I moved 10 miles an hour as I stood up on the nose of my surfboard. I looked off the high dive. In one milli-moment, I chose between an easy, relaxed fall to my death or the explosive, gut wrenching ride to hell off the right face of this monster wave.

I cut right perfectly and dropped in on the deep wave face. I saw the ugly dorsal fin of a large white shark make the turn 10 feet under me. The surf gods must just have wanted to see if I was still awake. The big board accelerated. I maneuvered my strong, wet, slippery feet to keep it stable on the wall of the monster wave. I rocketed across its face, dropping a foot or so every 10 feet in my quest for the pure white light of life.

I glanced up as the wave towered high above me. It foamed at the top. Then it started to fold as it reached the lee of bluffs a hundred yards from the narrow black beach. I rocketed into the ice blue walled water cave of the tidal wave's curl. I reached out and touched its translucent blue walls with my hands for balance. I screamed through the pale filtered light of the water cave. I was closely pursued by a 3-foot dorsal fin attached to a white hulk beneath the wave's surface. We were both surfing for a personal best.

I figured I would lose this killer at the shoreline because he couldn't walk. Until then, I hoped my Greg Knoll surfboard was faster. Then the translucent light disappeared at the end of the long blue water tube. My heart stopped. I crouched and sped blindly toward where it had been. I suddenly realized the steep vertical wall of the bluff had cast a dark shadow over the end of the tube. I was 50 feet from blasting through it. A second later, I burst into daylight. I dropped into a dangerous 6-foot lip of the roaring white water. I heard my board scrape the beach.

I jumped free of the board. I pulled it from the foaming surf and ran onto the rocky shoreline only 10 feet from the bluff. I ran as fast as I could toward the gray concrete hulk of the PT-Boat pen. I heard the explosive crash of the monster wave into the center of the bluff a quarter mile behind me. I heard rocks falling into the ocean with thunderous splashes.

I glanced occasionally over my right shoulder to watch for the incoming action. I trotted full speed with the heavy long surfboard under my left arm. The coral shards and rocks tore at my bare tough-skinned feet. Their bottoms had been hardened from three barefoot years in Fiji. Both feet started bleeding. I slowed to a walk, in pain. One hundred yards from safety, I saw the first wave of another giant set. I knew unless I dropped the surfboard, I was dead. I ditched it with great reluctance. Although we had fought with great valor together, there was no other choice.

I heard the heavy board drop onto the rocky beach. I tried to sprint barefooted, ignoring the pain and remembering my high school track drills. I ran full speed, gasping for air. Exhausted, I reached the safety of the PT-Boat pen. I turned and watched a 30-foot wave smash the surfboard into the bluff. The wave broke it in half on a protruding lava rock. The monster slaying surfboard was dead. Then, I saw the battered carcass of a 20-foot Great White shark in the foaming white surf a quarter mile down the beach. The white shark rode the monster tidal wave all the way into the deadly bluff. He had tried to kill me.

The Octopus God had honored his deal with the warriors from my province. I watched with reverence as the dead white shark's body was battered into the bluff and bloodied with each new breaking wave. I turned and collapsed into Eli's arms. All the strength suddenly left my cold body. I blacked out from hypothermic exhaustion and pain.

I regained consciousness minutes later lying on the wet concrete pier in the sun next to the island's sail powered freighter. Eli and the village boys stared at me. I groggily sat up slowly. They held both of my hands in a Fijian expression of their appreciation of the wave ride. A warrior's physical touch was very important in Fiji where words were saved for stories. As I wiped the salt from my eyes, I saw the Fijian villagers still watching from the center of the bluff. They chanted a victory song.

The log drum thundered, sending the news of my ride throughout the village. The 'vulagi' Peace Corps volunteer had ridden the great tidal wave. He had lived and saw the sun again. His feat would live in village legend for a thousand years. I listened as the log drums beat their message to the Fijian gods. I realized I was still alive in the dream world after the great ride through the lagoon on the ice blue monster wave from the South Pole.

I had crossed a major life divide. I had left the threat of the disruption of my physical world behind me forever. The rest of the month would be metaphysical.

CHAPTER FORTY-THREE
THE DAY AFTER THE NEXT MORNING

I woke up at dawn the next morning and my feet still throbbed painfully from the run across the rocky coral beach. Both of them were taped in gauze from my first-aid kit and soaked in septic cream. Coral cuts could be deadly, and they became infected quickly. They often led to the amputation of feet or limbs if not treated properly. During the first day of Peace Corps training in Hawaii, we were drilled on the treatment of coral cuts and tropical infections in general.

I had a scar as big as a quarter from an infected blister on my ankle. It had gone untreated too long during my first month in Fiji. The infection had almost reached bone before the provincial doctor stopped it. In tropical Fiji, deadly bacteria seemed to flourish everywhere in the humid paradise. I knew it would be a week before my feet healed, so it was time to read a book and maybe help teach English at the village school. Action adventure was sidelined.

I had brought a copy of Stranger in a Strange Land to the island. I sipped my morning tea in the bright light of the open bure side door. I began to read the book which was red hot among the PCVs in Fiji. The tattered copy had been through five hands before it was traded for my used copy of Catch-22. Milo Mindbender had been my literary hero of the last decade. I would have recruited him for the Valley Co-op staff. I wanted him to replace me when I departed Fiji. Reading had always been one of my favorite passions, so I read hoping the morning would pass quickly and quietly.

At one o'clock, several chapters into the book, I decided to take a break. I pulled out an old pair of rotting, sun bleached white, Converse basketball lowtop sneakers from my ammo box. I left them untied after I carefully pulled them over my bandaged feet. I had met the village school headmaster at the feast. He had asked me to drop by the school and meet the new English teacher. She had just moved to the Island of Fire from Suva where she had attended the University of the South Pacific. Since most Peace Corps volunteers in Fiji taught English in schools, he wanted to utilize my English skills while I was on the island.

The school compound was at the east end of the village. It was about 100 yards from the perimeter of the bures. It was a tropical colonial style white painted wood building three classrooms long. The classrooms opened onto a tin-roofed porch. It was one of two wooden buildings on the island. The other was the medical commissary which was visited by a Fijian-trained doctor one week every other month. The school's tin roof also served as a water collector for four concrete underground cisterns. They stored emergency drinking water for the village in periods of long winter drought.

In Fiji, if a house had a metal roof, then drainpipes were added which channeled the run-off water to a concrete cistern or round aluminum above ground storage tank. Many tropical leeward islands went up to six months without rain. This always amazed people who assumed a country whose annual mean rainfall was 200 inches always had plenty of water. It also amazed me because I once saw it rain 16 inches in Suva on the windward side in four hours.

The classes were grouped in pairs. I walked to the room marked 5/6 where the older children learned English. It was usually taught in the afternoon. I entered the open door and introduced myself to a pretty 22-23-year-old, tall, part-Polynesian female Fijian teacher. She could have been a model in the U.S.

I hadn't thought about women in a week. The sight of this attractive teacher startled me. She spoke to me in perfect Lauian, the national dialect of Fiji. I assumed she was from one of the outer eastern islands near Tonga where the Fijians who were Melanesian and the Tongans who were Polynesian regularly intermarried. All Fijian teachers trained at government expense had to do four years of assigned national service before they could return home to teach. She clearly had been posted here to improve the island's school. I guessed also, to listen or spy for the royal family and the prime minister, who were from Lau.

I explained that the headmaster, Vula, had asked me to assist her in teaching English while I was on the island. She addressed me in perfect Oxford English. She clearly had been taught at the elite capital city girls boarding school. She said my help would be appreciated, but I was not to teach American slang to the children. The British colonial civil service and the English educated Fijians loved the American spirit but deplored our murder of the king's language. The Aussies and New Zealanders were also held in contempt for their English dialect.

I immediately enjoyed my assignment to help this beautiful young princess from Lau. She dutifully worked on a backwater island to educate kids who were mostly bound to gold mine or hotel jobs at the beach resorts near Nadi. I hoped to get invited to dinner with her in one of the senior teacher's bures. The teachers' bures semi-circled the school, forming a private compound. It was also fenced off to keep the village cattle from wandering through and destroying the teachers' demonstration vegetable gardens.

All Fijian teachers throughout the country grew demonstration gardens. This program encouraged the villagers to be more industrious and to grow a wider range of veggies. These gardens also ensured the teachers ate well and could barter for village fish and meat. Of course, their labor force was free—it was the older school children. No football practice in the afternoon for these sixth graders. They weeded and hoed the school veggie garden.

I worked to make 100 or so flashcards of key English words with a black magic marker. I had brought the marker in my ammo case. She fortunately had a supply or 3x5 index cards. They were always in short supply in Fijian schools. Many Peace Corps teachers spent half of their meager salaries on school supplies to help their village pupils progress. I admired their dedication and thought it would be fun spending a couple of hours a day at the island school. The flashcards were always popular, according to my volunteer teacher friends.

After an hour's work, I had my flashcard set ready. She assigned six sixth graders who were studying for the national secondary school exam to accompany me to the veranda. I drilled them with the flash cards while she worked on reading with the eight fifth graders.

The six uniformed, bare-footed 12-year-olds followed me out the door. They sat down cross-legged facing me on the stone floored porch of the school in the shade. I already had their respect. The school had been dismissed to watch the big wave surfing. The four girls wore the usual green cotton school dresses. They had been designed by the Methodist missionaries in the late 1800s when clothes were introduced to Fiji's villages. The missionaries thought, logically, if the girls wore dresses in school, they would wear them in the villages after they graduated. Most island village women still went topless and only wore sulus from the waist down. Traditions were hard to break.

The boys wore khaki shorts, and both of them had rare white cotton shirts. Their families were prosperous if they had shirts. The PCV teachers were always buying a shirt for a poor Fijian village schoolboy. I would happily have gone to school in shorts without a shirt at age 12, but the grass was always greener on the other side of the fence.

I remembered my mom once made me a shirt on her new Singer sewing machine. I would have gladly donated it to a grade schoolboy in Fiji if I had been aware of their need. All their uniforms were hand sewn on the foot-pedal Singer sewing machines. Every married woman in Fiji possessed one to manufacture their family's cotton clothing. The missionary wives had taught the Fiji women to sew and they were world class. These village women bought cotton print or muslin cloth with the money they earned at the Nadi marketplace. They sewed daily. The machines zinged from the village bures.

My first flashcards for these bright-eyed, smiling kids were SURF, then BOYS, then BEACH. They loved my word choices. I linked them together in the Beach Boys song *LITTLE SURFER GIRL*. Fijians loved to sing, so it made teaching them English words easier when they could learn a song. My goal was to teach these kids the entire new Beach Boys album. I had memorized it before I left the main island. This would shock village visitors on some future day. The kids would be singing *LITTLE SURFER GIRL* in perfect American English while they played on the village common.

After an hour on the veranda with the sixth graders, Ella, their teacher, came out. She dismissed the group to afternoon gardening. I excused myself. I said I would return tomorrow, "same time, same station." And she reiterated "No American slang in my classroom please, Mister Cooper."

I headed back to the village. I walked tenderly on my bandaged feet. I hoped she was watching. I couldn't garden on my crippled feet to continue our conversation, but I hoped to gain her attention during my daily school visits. She was absolutely the most beautiful Fijian woman I had met. I was also intrigued by her posting on the Island of Fire. Why wasn't she already married to an emerging royal family member who was being groomed for a top government post. Maybe she would tell me and maybe she wouldn't. Now, it was time for a nap before dinner, and then it was more reading by Coleman lantern light while my feet continued to heal.

CHAPTER FORTY-FOUR

THE FIREWALKING DEAL

A week drifted by quickly. I read Stranger in a Strange Land twice. I taught English every afternoon for two hours, and then helped garden for another hour. After my second day, I had been invited to have four o'clock tea with the headmaster, Ella, and the other teachers. I listened to an educated version of the village gossip. Since all three teachers were from other provinces, they didn't hesitate to dish the villagers in a polite way. PCVs throughout Fiji had used the schoolhouse tea gossip to protect their flanks in the judgmental villages.

By Friday, I had ascertained the Great Chief was in the declining years of his power. He had no real successor. His closest pals were too old to ascend the throne. He didn't trust Eli's generation yet, which had extensive contact with the outside world. Their judgment was colored by colonialism and tourism. The chief's father had been a cannibal. He still had one foot firmly in the past. Like the historic war Chief Ouray of the Colorado Utes, he knew it was all over for the old purist traditional way. He wanted to control his island's integration into modern Fiji. Because of the Island of Fire's proximity to the international airport, western and Asian developer scammers were already nibbling at the island. They had approached the government Native Land Trust Board in Suva to lease the island's pristine, protected eastern white sand beaches for hotel development. The developers looked upon the village as a cheap labor source to be exploited at their convenience.

The power behind the throne was Alu, the master of the firewalking. He was a 20th generation witch doctor who traced his lineage back to the long boats from Africa. His adopted daughter was the fabled Woman of Fire. I had not seen or met her, which was odd after 10 days in the village. No one would talk about her publicly or privately on or off the record.

This deepened the mystery and increased the danger signals. Every time I had hit a total wall of silence in Fiji, there was a witch doctor involved. Extreme danger always lurked behind that wall and I knew to proceed with caution. I had observed perfectly healthy villagers in the prime of their lives be cursed by a witch doctor. It was usually for some perceived crime against a chief of the village or the witch doctor. One I had known well, died within a month. This village was famous for the black magic of its ability to firewalk, and the iconoclastic isolation of its chief and elders. The fact that the government had no daily operated outpost here was significant. The island's teachers lived in virtual exile in the school compound next to the village.

The Island of Fire had produced no native teachers of its own. This was a significant chink in its armor. This chink gave me a channel of information that was closed otherwise. The opinion of the teachers was that firewalking was not a harmless phenom whose primary future was a national tourist attraction. It was rooted in the village's thousand-year-old transfer of knowledge from the dark continent. It was grounded in psychotic control rooted in sexual taboos by successive witch doctors. It was deadly and the headmaster had seen two men burn to death in the pits. These deaths went unreported to the Fiji colonial government and the newspapers. There were no photographs, so there was no evidence. It was like the secret war in Laos—it didn't exist, but it did.

Firewalking was not touch football on the White House lawn with the Secret Service as cheerleaders and the president's sister-in-law as referee. This was Joe Kennedy vs. the Italian mob for bootleg liquor rights. Strong men were gutted and left in the shore break to die. The witch doctor and the chief controlled the village society from top to bottom with the monthly firewalks. They could burn an enemy or a male pretender to power to death in an instant. How the Woman of Fire fit into the power scheme was the missing piece of the puzzle. Either the teachers didn't know, or they weren't talking to a PCV about their intelligence on this matter. It was a Fijian family secret, and it loomed like a comet in my future, if my instincts were right. I had to walk the fire pit to complete my mission on the Island of Fire.

I limped home on my rapidly healing feet, thanks to Johnson and Johnson technology. I plotted timing my request to Eli to firewalk. It had to be this week. The headmaster had said the next group of men would enter the Master of Fire's bure and start the two-week training period on Monday and stay there until the full moon.

Ella, the young Lau teacher, had not given me an opening, although she seemed attracted to me, so another mystery shrouded my brain. It convinced me she was a royal family spy, not a bored beautiful Fiji teacher-to-be. Otherwise, her skirt might have been easier to lift in the bush after a gardening session. She was definitely more than met the eye. I wondered if the chief and the witch doctor were on to her.

She seemed to have no local boyfriend, even though the village males all had sailor's eyes developed during a thousand years of natural selection at sea in the South Pacific. They had sailor's appetites, too. They balanced their risky profession with skirt-chasing, dark rum, and kava. The U.S. Navy had nothing on these bronzed South Pacific he-men who were the secret favorites among the Pan Am stewardesses who chose a walk on the wild side during sailing forays out of the Sky Lodge Hotel in Nadi.

By the time I reached the bure, I decided after dinner, and before Eli and I went to the chief's bure to drink kava, was the time to make my play. That gave Eli two days to bring the chief around. It only gave the witch doctor, Alu, one day to lobby against my request. He was not returning from Nadi until the Saturday night market boat docked, according to the school gossip. I thought maybe he was cursing an airplane or rental car in Nadi. His absence gave me some advantage in an away from home game.

No Peace Corps volunteer had ever walked the fire pit. This would be an experience vicariously shared by my colleagues throughout the country. It would enhance the Corps in the eyes of the Fijians. It would add extra protection against the Peace Corps' enemies who were surfacing daily to destroy it as Fiji's independence neared. The prevailing mood among the potential power grabbers was to evict American kids with the British.

Certain reactionary forces in Fiji had already moved for more economic or personal power in the vacuum being left by the hasty British retreat.
The capital city gang didn't want wide-eyed American kids advising villagers and provincial chiefs. They planned to consolidate their political
power bases for future profit.

The firewalk would shock these interests and further bind the Peace
Corps to the hearts of the rural Fijian villagers it served so well. After Eli's
wife served us dinner and retreated to the cooking bure to nurse the baby, I
planned to make my request. Then he would have to talk to the chief at the
start of the kava session. Eli owed his life to me. He could not refuse this
request, even though he was my keeper and the chief's spy. I would give
him the last of my special kava for the occasion. It would put everyone in
a good mood while they considered the deal.

A college friend's father had told me to always buy good Scotch for
special business occasions with the movers and shakers. I approached
the open door. I saw the small cotton tablecloth being set for dinner.
My place was across from Eli every night. I hoped lobster was on the
menu since Eli's wife had been reef diving with the village women in
the morning. Pacific lobster sauteed in coconut milk with sweet tropical
onions was the perfect meal for this conversation. My mouth watered as
I entered the men's side door and took my seat cross-legged across from
Eli's empty place.

CHAPTER FORTY-FIVE

THE CHIEF'S DECISION

Eli and I were pounding the last of my ultra-magic kava in a stone bowl at the chief's bure. Dinner had gone well at Eli's bure, although he was shocked (if Fijian's were really ever shocked).

I had said, "I want to walk the fire pit."

He asked me why I wanted to walk the fire pit. I told him it was to clear my mind to help solve the murder of my Fijian warrior friend, Patipati. I couldn't have lied to him and then attempted to walk the fire pit. I knew the witch doctor, Alu, would intercept any impure thought and use it to destroy me if he desired. However, I didn't tell Eli all the details of the murder scene which apparently had not reached this semi-isolated island yet.

The government and the Peace Corps had also done a good job of controlling the facts that were released to the press to protect tourism. No one knew the sexual details of the killing except those who were admitted to the crime scene. Fiji was always Fiji, so rumors in the capital had spread every explicit detail, but the Fiji Times had not published the facts on the eve of independence.

Eli had not even heard about the murders. They didn't concern him. He knew I had saved his life, so he quickly agreed that he would ask the chief on my behalf to walk the fire. It was clear though, he would not recommend to the chief enthusiastically that this was a good plan.

He said, "I have walked the fire from my 18th year. It is always difficult and always dangerous. Men are hurt and die walking the fire if their preparation is poor and if their mind is weak, or if an enemy usurps their power."

He stopped. His last phrase about enemies caught my attention. The rest was common sense. Peace Corps volunteers speculated endlessly about the physical and mental state of both the lesser-known Hindu religious firewalkers and the better known Fijian firewalkers. Hypotheses ran the gamut of callused feet from a lifetime of going barefoot, to mind control coupled with special food for the period before the walk. I had heard wooden poles burst into fire when touched to the bed of glowing hot coals and stones in the pit. The callused feet theory didn't hold much stock with me. Fire was fire. Something else was going on here. I wanted to find the answer if I could while I solved the mystery of Patipati's death.

In our conversation, I tried to draw Eli out about the enemy thing, but he avoided it. Eli also did not discuss the Master of Fire, Alu the witch doctor, or the Woman of Fire. I had already learned more gossip at the school's afternoon tea parties than Eli was willing to dispense over dinner. Clearly, the witch doctor had a lock on this village through the firewalking. His power rivaled if not exceeded that of the old chief.

Eli finished pounding the kava. I released my hold on the stone pedestal. Its mortar rings still echoed in my ears. The chief had assembled his elders and ten or so of the younger men like Eli for a Friday night story session. Many of the villagers were away at the market in Nadi or the mines. They included both his young and old wife, so he was extra bored.

After a more informal but always tediously the same kava ceremony, we started business. After a couple of fishing stories, which served as news updates on the week's reef catch, Eli took the circle.

He said, "There has been a request from a great warrior from another land"—all eyes picked up—"who rides the great waves like the white shark, who rides the horse like the wind from the Great Ocean that feeds our people. His bravery is unmatched, but now he wishes to tame the wild spirit of his mind to find the answer to the death of his friend, a member of a clan of Fiji not from this island."

Eli was brilliant. Churchill would have been a proud parent.

"He wants to see a vision in his mind, to find the path to the secret murderer of his dead warrior friend. He wants to avenge the crime for Fiji's gods. He sits with me tonight on a quest from the great land of the Eastern Pacific. He requests to walk the fire at the full moon and to be the first of the Peace Corps volunteers to have this honor."

Eli paused as the kava cup was passed to him. He drank it in a loud gulp. The chief went white. He now looked like my grandfather with a tan. The blood rushed from his brow to his stomach. Only his short cropped curly white hair identified him as a Fijian villager instead of a colored bank clerk in the capital city. He stalled for even a rudimentary response. He looked to the right where the witch doctor or Master of Fire, Alu, should have been to instantly kill my request. He signaled for a fresh round of kava. This would take five minutes to serve if he ritualized it to the max. He stalled like a football coach running dead ball plays.

Eli sat cross-legged, expressionless, and waited as the cup made the rounds. The chief served each man as was his right. He chanted to the max. Everyone else just sat in rigid amazement and stared blankly at the kava bowl. Even the elders wanted no part of this decision. No one knew which way the wind would blow with the witch doctor, Alu, in Nadi.

At the end of the kava round the chief announced a bladder break. Everyone scrambled out to find a coconut tree to pee on. The kava went through bladders like near beer. The men peeing on the village coconut tree trunks for a thousand years had probably evolved the indestructible batch that lived in Fiji. Actually the nitrates in human pee are good fertilizer in poor, sandy soils.

The chief disappeared, but not into a grove of palm trees. He entered a bure next door. I followed him silently and found a coconut palm as close to the bure as possible without being obvious. I stalled my pee as long as possible. I heard a young Fijian woman's voice reply to the chief in a chanted, ritualized ancient dialect. It was like the old African war chants I had heard the old women sing in my province. It was eerie. I could not understand a word, but the great chief's reply was in village dialect. It was respectful and bordered on submissive.

I had never heard a Fijian Chief use this tone with a woman of any rank. This included a wife, even if she was a princess, not a commoner.

My pee ended. I walked back toward the chief's bure believing I had heard the voice of the mysterious Woman of Fire.

I had definitely encountered a pure strain of ancient witchcraft and black magic practiced on the long boats and transported to Fiji a thousand years ago. It had been preserved on this remote, poor dry island with its poorly protected lagoon and rocky shoreline. Few other Fijians visited here, so no outsider witch doctors had mutated the village practices and rituals.

My heartbeat quickened. My stomach muscles tightened. I started to re-enter the chief's ceremonial bure men's side door. I was also startled that the female voice had caused sexual arousal which was not common after drinking strong kava. Like alcohol, lots of kava produced impotence or the 'limp dick' syndrome. The western rodeo cowboys at home applied this term to dudes who dared to cross into their turf without consent.

A minute or so later, the chief entered the bure. I could see in the orange kerosene lantern light his color was back. He sat. The chief, to everyone's amazement, ordered another round of the ultra-special Lau kava. Everyone had figured he would hoard it for himself and for the elders after the obligatory early rounds with the thirsty younger men of the village.

The last of the Lau kava put everyone in a festive mood, in spite of Eli's request for me to walk the fire pit. Five more minutes passed as my heartbeat intensified from the strong narcotic kava. My mouth was paralyzed. No one had spoken, except ceremonially. They wouldn't, because the chief, by Fiji's Roberts Rules of Order, controlled the floor. It was clearly not open for debate or consultation.

He spoke in dialect—not to me but to Eli, my sponsor and keeper: "I have watched the courage of the great white warrior from America. He surfed the mighty wave from the land of Ice Mountains that hunt our people on long voyages to the south. I have seen the White Shark God try to destroy this mighty warrior when called to our lagoon by a voice of evil. I have seen this warrior understand and use the power of the Octopus God given to him when he was made a chief by the Great Southern Chief Kavula, who is paramount in power among the never defeated Mountain River warriors of Fiji who fear the tide and the reef, their enemy in battle."

Eli translated. I was not surprised at the chief's perceptions. The defeat of the 20-foot white shark through the use of the gods and magic had impressed him, but not the athletic hell ride through the stormy lagoon. Great young warriors were expected to perform great physical feats or die. This improved the species by not passing on their defective genes to children and grandchildren. No weak people were needed or wanted here where the life of the community was precarious daily. It was cruel and stark natural selection. It worked well here where nature was still king of the day.

The chief had expected me to beat the wave but not kill the white shark. He had given me a key clue and a chance to back down now. I could still leave alive on the Wednesday market boat. The white shark had been called by an enemy to destroy me. I had bested the shark with my head. I had called on the magic of my province from the most legendary battle of ancient southern Fiji. It saved the proud, fiercely independent mountain people who had never been conquered from rule by the fierce, well-traveled, well-armed outer island warriors. They used their outrigger canoes like the Vikings used their longboats to raid and conquer most of Fiji.

The chief knew my enemy was humiliated and angry by his defeat. Most of the elders had probably perceived this along with the chief. This is why the witch doctor, Alu, remained near Nadi in the village of Lautoka, the western provincial capital for Viti Levu's Fijians. Alu had called the shark to destroy me after hearing of my arrival at the village through a spy. The chief's power had increased as long as the American warrior remained in the village with Eli, a retainer of the chief. Alu reasoned the chief might use this white warrior's knowledge in their life long game of chess. They balanced the power of politics and power of magic to preserve the village.

The chief was willing to let me go unharmed. He had benefited from the witch doctor's failed first move. The victory would help him for a year or two in the village. It brought the chief closer, with honor, to the Land of the Dead Chiefs. Then his choice for the village's next chief would have to confront the hidden, ancient black magic power. The chief could not help me further if I continued my quest to walk the fire. My failure could hurt him, the villagers, and his search for a successor who could balance Alu and the Woman of Fire if she succeeded Alu.

The chief continued: "The body of the Great White Shark lies rotting at the bottom of the high bluff which protects our people from the sea. No man can touch it. The Sea Gods will leave only its bones and teeth for our village. The power of the Walk of Fire is special to our people. It protects us from our enemies by providing us magic that no other village in the kingdom of Fiji has been granted by the Gods. It has kept the vulagi white man, and red man, Hindu, from our shores. No Pacific enemy has subjugated this village, although we sit in alliance with the great paramount chief of the western province in council at Lautoka."

"The great warrior has proven his skill by defeating the white shark. I cannot deny his request to walk the fire of my people as requested by Eli, a strong young warrior of our village whose clan's god granted him an additional life."

The chief trumped the witch doctor in absentia with the white shark number. He still did not address my wave ride. The chief also rebuked Eli for putting himself in the position to have to make the request for me.

Eli's star had fallen. He knew it as his gaze dropped to his knees. His star would only rise again if my quest to firewalk succeeded. If my walk failed, the absent witch doctor, Alu, and the mysterious Woman of Fire would bury him at the next full moon after my firewalk. I had given him his life back on one day with luck and horsemanship. I had taken it from him again at this kava session. Even if I left the island, this request had made him a marked man coming on the heels of the dead white shark. The witch doctor, Alu, would take his revenge on Eli, probably sooner rather than later, to restore the balance of power with the chief. Eli's death by curse or fire would reduce my visit to only the memory of the great wave ride. That was no more than good Hollywood stunt work in the eyes of the power players on the Island of Fire in this ancient metaphysical ballet.

I called for a round of kava. It was my right as a warrior guest. I continued to think, barely hearing the chanted formalities. The fresh kava was prepared by Eli's father and distributed a cup at a time. The chief had accepted my request in Alu's absence. He left it to me to end the contest. He wouldn't block the request if I persisted.

I had saved a valuable warrior and potential chief of the village. I had ridden the tidal wave and destroyed the white shark. I reeked with power and spirit. He didn't want to displease the Fijian gods whose position was still unclear to him. My pursuit of a Fijian warrior friend's secret murderer was a valiant and honored duty.

Being an American and a Peace Corps Volunteer was trendy, even in this remote village. Many of its elders had fought with the U.S. Navy as 'pilots' in Fiji waters for the PT-Boats which attacked and sank Japanese submarines and shipping off the coast of Fiji. Several Island of Fire village sailors had died when the American PT-Boats were blown out of the sea by the superior firepower of the Japanese submarines, aircraft, and destroyers.

The chief waited for the last two cups of kava to be served. If I spoke, I was gone on the Wednesday boat. I would suffer no loss of face and be a local surfing legend forever. If I remained silent, then Eli's request stood approved. It had been accepted by not being 'denied' by the chief in the vacuum of power created by the dead white shark and the witch doctor, Alu's continued absence. The irony was the witch doctor, my enemy, was the Master of Fire. He would have to train me for the ceremony to walk the fire pit. It was a death sentence in the chief's mind. The witch doctor controlled the knowledge I needed to succeed.

The man next to Eli finished his kava. He passed the cup back to me. I had served him last after I called for the round. The chief then served me a cup of kava since no man could serve his own kava. I felt the familiar cool taste of the drug from the root of the yogona plant. It rushed numbingly through my mouth and down my throat.

I sat next to Eli. All eyes were silently fixed on me. I emptied the hollow, well-worn, polished coconut cup into my mouth in the traditional one gulp. I set it down in front of the kava bowl. I had ten seconds to speak or the chief would call the next story teller to Eli's right. My tongue was numbed by the narcotic power of the kava, but my mind made the decision as the image of Patipati's face burst into it. We wanted to walk the fire pit in two weeks at the full moon, live or die. If I died, we would be in the spirit world together, forever friends.

I barely heard the chief call the next story teller. I heard the sighs from the elders whose very essence of being had just been put into play for the first time in decades. They knew the witch doctor, Alu. They believed he would kill me without remorse to regain his edge in the power game with the chief as his father had before him with the chief's father and his grandfather before him with the chief's grandfather. They didn't personally want to watch me die in the fire pit. After the wild ride in the surf, they simply believed magic was magic and young warriors were young warriors, and unless the gods intervened, the outcome was already decided.

Only the possible intervention by a powerful Fijian god on my behalf would keep their interest for the next two weeks. Alu, against me in his home village, was a no contest game to them. I had used my province's power to kill the Great White Shark. That had been impressive, but they assumed I didn't understand the next level of magic. I could not call the gods to rescue me from the fire pit and Alu's evil black magic unless I was on a divine mission. A thousand years of black magic had to be pushed aside in a legendary walk across the fire pit for me to live.

The chief and the elders would wait patiently for the expected outcome. Some of them secretly would look for a sign from the universe of power shifting in this isolated tight village on the high bluff of the flawed lagoon in the middle of the deep blue Southern Pacific Ocean.

CHAPTER FORTY-SIX

THE RULES OF THE ROAD

I woke up when the first village roosters crowed on Monday morning. I drank tea and ate with Eli's family. After breakfast, he led me to the Firewalker's bure where I would live and eat for the next two weeks until I walked the fire pit. I thought, a little sadly as I walked across the village common, watching the uniformed children walk toward the school compound, that this might be my final adventure.

Eli said I would be joining six other men in the bure who would walk the fire at the full moon. All six of them had firewalked before. I would be the only novice. He worried my language problems with the village dialect and the absence of another novice firewalker would damage my chances for a successful walk.

The Master of Fire, Alu, had returned to the village by the market boat late Saturday night. After he learned that I had elected myself to the hot walk of fame, he had chosen only very experienced walkers for the next show. He had moved his first chessman quickly, signaling our match had begun.

Eli had been alarmed when he returned to the bure to tell me the names of the chosen warriors. None of them were from Eli's clan, the chief's family, or the boar hunt group. None of them owed me or my village allies anything. They were the hand-picked centurions of the witch doctor, Alu, who assumed his principle public role as Master of Fire for the next two weeks. He was my principle instructor.

I entered the bure with hope. I knew I would receive no charity, although even the witch doctor could not defy Fiji's custom, its gods, and the great chief totally. Alu knew to ignore Fijian custom in the treatment of an invited village guest, especially a courageous warrior, opened the door for retribution from the gods. Not even the Methodist god could save a villager regardless of rank from an angry Fijian god.

The other six men had arrived at the bure before Eli said goodbye. He handed me a sleeping mat. I had left my ammo box with him, plus letters to my mom, Anne, Dianne, and the Peace Corps staff in Suva. Eli touched my hand in a show of support. Then he disappeared silently. His life rode on the outcome of my walk. He had helped me all he could as a warrior. He had to remain passive during training for the firewalk.

I ducked through the bure's formal door. I entered its only room where we would live for two weeks. Eli had explained the basic firewalk training rules to me because of my poor command of the village dialect.

He had said, "Sleep only in the Bure of Fire. Drink no kava for the two-week period. Have sex with no woman for that period, regardless of temptations."

Patipati's warning on this rule re-emerged from the recesses of my mind.

"Eat only food prepared for the Bure of Fire for the other men or do not eat. Drink no tea or coffee, but only water from the spring brought to the bure. Walk the lagoon's coral stone strewn beach at low tide in the high sun each day. Walk it slowly. Concentrate on each step. Block out all physical pain with the roar of the breaking waves. Concentrate on the beat of breaking waves because in the fire pit you concentrate only on the chanting of the Master of Fire and the village women."

These were important rules. He said I would learn others.

Finally, he added, "Wear no sandals or shirt until after the firewalk. Wear a new sulu," which he presented me for all occasions including sleep.

Clearly discipline, pure body and mind control were key, with light physical training. The sex taboo was already in effect since my attempts to connect with the schoolteacher, Ella, had failed. The unmarried village girls remained dangerous land mines in the current environment. Only

Anne aroused my sexual appetite in a dream or a thought.

The only items I brought to the bure were rolled in my mat. They were a toothbrush, a towel, soap and a new paperback book to read, For Whom the Bell Tolls. I suspected the days and nights would drag during firewalk training.

The six Fijian village men, three of whom I recognized from the chief's kava sessions, and three who were total strangers, were already seated cross-legged in a semi-circle. Their mats were rolled tightly behind them. They talked among themselves in relaxed dialect about village gossip. The most famous was Levulevu, a massive retired national all-star rugby player who limped slightly. Training for firewalking was routine here, although I was an unknown in their equation.

I sat cross-legged at the right end of the semicircle. I assumed we were waiting for the Master of Fire. I listened to the conversation. It was about the past Saturday's market day in Nadi. I heard there had been a minor crisis when the U.S. Air Force had been asked to leave Nadi over a shooting incident at the Sky Lodge. It had been resolved by agreeing to have two Fijian army officers live with the Air Force detachment to assist them in the future with community liaison. The villagers seemed to think this was a good assignment. The American Air Force had fast planes and cheap beer.

They included me in their discussion by asking me questions about riding the monster wave. Apparently, they had no knowledge they were part of a stacked deck. They exhibited no overt hostility toward my inclusion in the group of firewalkers. I answered their questions about surfing. The politics of the firewalk was not in this group's plane of reasoning. These younger village men were carrying out an assigned duty, like their fathers and grandfathers. It was two weeks out of routine working and sailing village life. It also gave them a chance to dry out from the nightly kava sessions. They were used to long, inter-island sailing trips in the company of men, so no sex for two weeks at sea was routine.

Just as I was about to explain how a modern fiberglass surfboard floated, in walked Alu, the Master of Fire. He was dressed in an ancient, braided grass skirt sulu, bare-chested with red paint on his black-bronze face. He carried a short leather whip, an antique carved hardwood war club, and wore full ceremonial garb, including whalebone bracelets, shark's teeth necklace, and gold armlets. His entrance signaled serious business and class started.

The six village men rose and dropped to one knee in respect, a gesture usually reserved only for a chief when he walked into a bure. I rose, following their lead, showing no sign of disrespect to the witch doctor, or signaling that I had deduced his game plan. Disrespect or independence gained me nothing, while obedience and diligence might throw him off his game plan. Until I saw his pitching selection, I wanted to be just one of the boys. I knew he intended to burn me to death, or irreparably maim me in the fire pit, which was tantamount to death. He had watched me through his village ears ride the big wave and kill the Great White Shark which he had conjured up to eat me. He instinctively knew if my feet burned and I fell into the pit, I would make no attempt to save myself. He won either way. He probably preferred the latter event since death of an inferior guest warrior in the fire pit would attract no sustained Fijian backlash at this point in history. The Brits were officially gone in two months, so he was home free with the fire pit scheme.

If he had to openly use a black magic curse to kill me, he risked the ire of the village warriors. They could question his vengeance against the guest warrior who had saved Eli's life and then rode the tidal wave. Alu still ultimately held the winning long-term hand though. He could destroy any dissident warrior in the fire pit during a future firewalk.

The Master of Fire started his chant. He danced around the bure barefooted, cleansing it of evil spirits which could disrupt our firewalk by hiding in our bodies. He sprinkled a yellow powder from a pigskin pouch on a rawhide strap which hung at his waist.

I was slightly startled when he sprinkled yellow powder on my head. He danced in front of me in rhythm to his chant. He dusted every man, then he danced by us one by one and blew the powder off our hair onto the bure's beautifully handwoven reed mats. Later, I would learn if the powder had not blown off my hair that I could not have walked the fire pit. That indicated inhabitation by the evil spirit of a relative who had died in the fire pit. I was pleased to know none of my relatives in past or present reincarnations had died in the fire pit. Scientifically, it really indicated I didn't have a sweaty scalp from sheer fear.

Alu's absolute control was the idea on display both ceremonially and mentally. The Master of Fire, a.k.a. witch doctor, was establishing his control right out of the starting gate. It was like a quarter horse jockey on the favorite at Riudosa Downs, New Mexico, in the All-American Futurity. My mom took me to it every 4th of July after my dad died in a polo accident. One year a horse from a neighboring Paradox Valley ranch in Colorado won the race. I got to stay an extra day in Riudosa, New Mexico instead of returning to rope and brand calves.

The Master of Fire chanted. He did intricate dance steps in his grass beaded skirt. His loincloth flashed under its wild swings. The Methodist missionaries had done such a good job that even the Master of Fire wore a loincloth to cover his genitals under his native garb on ceremonial occasions. Only in a few late-night Kava fueled dance ceremonies at Chief Kavula's village with the old bare-breasted women chanting the cannibal war chants had I seen the warriors swing bare dicks and balls under their finely woven and beaded grass skirts. It still stirred up the old ladies like in the days of old legends.

These village dances reminded me of spring frat parties. The brothers got drunk and danced to Otis Redding in chinos without underwear to impress the sorority girls. The girls wore flowered-cotton print dresses that clung to their nipples and pelvises as they sweated during the dances in crowded, airless fraternity house basements. Paganism existed in all societies. Only the rule of law kept it underground and late at night.

The rhythm of the chant to the beat of the Master of Fire's bare feet on the hard, mat-covered floor loosed demons in my body and soul. Clearly, I thought, rhythm was a key to walking the fire pit. Some hidden rhythm in nature chanted by the women guided the firewalkers across the fire pit in a sequence that defied the BTU energy of the heat. It was psychic, I knew, perfected by trial and error over a thousand years. It was like surfing the monster wave. The power was in your mind, not your body.

Hundreds of hours of learning the rhythm of smaller waves had brought me to the Zen place that produced the ride from hell down the face of the 50-foot monster in the lagoon. An inner, barely understood rhythm guided me mechanically through the danger as long as I didn't let my head put on the brakes and block it. I had learned the first lesson today which the Fijian village men knew instinctively. It was to listen to the rhythm of the fire and the chant. Also, I needed to block out all thoughts during the firewalk.

After the Master of Fire completed our ritual cleansing for the next full moon firewalk, he sat down across from us. He was a little out of breath at 60 years of age, but still in great physical shape with powerful arm and leg muscles, a short bull neck, large bronze-black face with a flat nose and solid chin. He was a product of genetic perfection at the village level.

The witch doctors received the pick of the province's common-born village girls for marriage, and vice versa for the Fijian women witch doctors. They doctored the female and male children from birth. They operated with the maximum of inside genetic information. They chose mates for physical strength, handsomeness, and brains. They knew the latter was the key to their professional survival and unchallenged power.

Fijian witch doctors were the mental keepers of the medical, psychic, and spiritual secrets of the village. They were also astrologers and healers. Their knowledge of herbs and remedies was legendary. The western anthropologists were still trying to pick their minds. Their use of 'bones' to throw a curse was real and frightening. They took human life without remorse, even though the colonial government and the Methodist Church were both convinced witchcraft was not practiced in Fiji. In reality every village had a witch doctor who could be readily identified after a week in the village by anyone except the honeymoon couples who came to Fiji to fuck in the shore break on deserted white sand beaches.

Witch doctors were very active in Fiji and they secretly practiced their craft daily. Their ancient rivalry with the village and provincial paramount chiefs never ceased. Many Peace Corps volunteers became unwitting pawns in this game. The most infamous case recently had been a volunteer on an isolated western outer island village. He left Fiji in a straightjacket with a Peace Corps staff doctor bound for a psychiatric ward in Bethesda, Maryland. The Peace Corps made him officially one of the disappeared and no inquiry by his friends still in Fiji had produced a statement of his well-being. His curse had been potent and when coupled with the extreme isolation of the village, perhaps life-ending.

Witch doctors carried tropical mushroom powders in their dried gourds for the chiefs. The Fijian chiefs were the Green Bay Packer coaches of the South Pacific's most legendary warrior cannibals. They knew their profession well. There was no doubt in my mind the Master of Fire, Alu, was the quarterback of the Fiji League. His warriors and only his warriors walked the fire pit.

I tuned in for his story about the history of firewalking (he spoke in the national dialect for my sake). It was a great con. In the ancient days there had been a war between the Island of Fire and a northern village on the main island of Viti Levu. The chief and his warriors from the Island of Fire captured a prince from the enemy village. They held him prisoner in the slave bure. They fattened him to be cooked in an earth oven and eaten, as all high-ranking captured warriors were by custom to preserve their honor. Before being roasted in the oven, the prince was being fattened with fresh sea turtle meat, plentiful in Fiji.

The prince claimed a magic power. He was seen speaking often to invisible small men like the leprechauns of Ireland by his captors in his bure. All efforts to negotiate his release failed. He was eventually led to the oven. It was fired with logs. He was sealed in it and cooked by the victorious Island of Fire warriors. When the villagers opened the oven, the prince was alive. It blew everyone's mind, including the witch doctor and chief. They needed a quick deal with the prince to keep their power. The warriors planned to revolt and follow this now more powerful magical leader.

The chief had the prince brought to the ceremonial bure. He offered to exchange the prince's freedom for the secret. The prince knew a good deal. He told the chief about little men who put their bodies between him and the hot oven walls. They protected him from the heat and saved his life. He did not give the chief and witch doctor all his secret power until they released him safely. He gave all the warriors on the Island of Fire the little men as slaves forever to carry their feet across the hot coals of the fire pit. They had to obey certain rules which he based upon his captivity, like no sex or kava, and eat special food like sea turtle meat.

The chief made the deal, but the prince feared for his safety. To ensure he was not drowned on the way home, he refused to tell anyone but the witch doctor the secret of calling the little men until he was safely on the main island of Viti Levu near his village. The chief wanted him gone, dead or alive, from the Island of Fire which was named for its volcano. He called his sailors reluctantly and sent his rival, the witch doctor, to deliver the prince back to his village safely. He forever doomed himself and his chiefly successors to the power of the successive witch doctors. They alone could call the little men for the firewalks, only they knew the prince's secret.

The little men story was cute. Mankind will never know if the prince happened to get a sauna on a rare Fiji low humidity day, or if he practiced a form of Tibetan mind over body temperature control or if he had a pre-arranged deal with the witch doctor. Notwithstanding the legend, I wasn't going to totally rely on the Master of Fire to call the little men on my behalf. If he called them to honor my deal with the chief, my bunch of elves might be timid, sick, or inexperienced. I could not be sure of equal treatment and the village of fire didn't have a civil rights officer. I might get Edsels, not BMWs.

I was planning to concentrate fiercely. I planned to copy the exact behavior of the other six men. I planned to listen for every bit of information and focus on the firewalk like final exams with no roll in the hay at the school compound on a slow training night. There would be no kava on a hot day, and I would eat only food brought to the bure which the other men tasted first. I planned to eat only from the common plates in case the witch doctor tried to poison or weaken me with mushroom potions. I planned to walk the hot coral beach at low tide, barefooted, and listen to the rhythm of the ocean waves in place of the village women's chants.

The Master of Fire listed the rules. I discerned little from his deliberate village dialect, but I picked up key phrases like: no sex, no kava, eat only turtle meat, drink pure water, and sleep well.

Eli's crib sheet had helped me. He had completely paid his debt to me in his own mind for saving his life during the wild boar hunt. The burden had shifted to me to walk the fire. I needed to unravel the mystery of Patipati's untimely, but I suspected not accidental, murder. Hopefully, the clue was still stored in my subconscious mind, waiting to be dislodged when manmade camouflage was stripped away by the firewalk. This quest for Patipati and only his quest would sustain me until the full moon shootout on the Island of Fire.

CHAPTER FORTY-SEVEN

THE BIG TIME HIKE

The preparation of the fire pit on the village common was under way. In just a few days, I had to walk the fire. It had been a slow, dull two weeks in the men's dorm with the exception of the Master of Fire's perfectly timed tricks. The troops I had been assigned to walk the fire with were on routine 'carrier' training mission. They whiled away their days playing Bones, a village gambling game. It was Fiji's version of the card game, Hearts. They played with a frayed deck of cards that was clearly marked. They did not walk on the hot, rocky coral beach at high noon. They abstained from kava, which did impress me since most of these guys normally drank a half-quart a day The no sex taboo was real, and no wives or girlfriends appeared at night or during the day. I was pleasantly surprised again by their discipline.

The food was three star, but mine stopped arriving on a separate tin plate after the Master of Fire observed I only ate off the common platters. If my food was segregated in any way, I ignored it. There clearly had been a food poisoning plan and I had blocked it. Alu had probably powdered my food with potions that could have toasted me on or before the firewalk. College history had taught me too many popes had been poisoned in the

Vatican game for me to fall for this trick. After three years in Fiji, I knew well that all the witch doctors dabbled in deadly herbal or coral poison, sedatives and mildly disabling narcotics. It had been fun to watch the Master of Fire's reaction when I only ate food from plates the other six men had sampled first. He couldn't poison them all to weaken me. After three days, he surrendered, and we moved on to more deadly games.

The walk on the beach each day strengthened my healing feet bottoms. It helped me concentrate. I paced my walks by listening to the rhythm of the ocean break on the lagoon's outer reef. Occasionally, I found pieces of my battered Greg Knoll surfboard. I saved a small blue chunk for my scrapbook. I gave the other battered pieces to the village kids. They believed the same small men who lifted the firewalkers' feet across the hot coals, also held up the surfboard. That explained why it didn't sink when I rode the tidal wave. I almost believed in the small men.

A volunteer friend of mine's surfboard had been destroyed when he stopped at a southern coastal village on the main island for lunch. He left his surfboard on the beach where he had been surfing. When he returned after lunch, the village kids had peeled the thin fiberglass veneer off the Styrofoam sheet of flotation to look for the little men. He basically had a throwaway cooler instead of a $300 Hobie surfboard to take back to his home village.

The rotting white shark had gradually disappeared. The sea birds had cleaned it to the bone and jawline. Its skeleton still lay gruesomely on the beach against the bluff where it had washed ashore. No one had collected the shark's teeth, which was highly unusual since they were favored for necklaces by the island's warriors. Clearly, every villager knew this shark's mission. They wanted no part of its teeth's karma unless and until I walked the fire, or I was buried in the ground. No one wanted to affront the witch doctor, Alu, by wearing new shiny white shark teeth around the village while I was still alive on the rock.

I missed my two-hour trips to the village school each day, but I didn't want a mental diversion or sexual temptation at this point. I hoped to connect with the young teacher, Ella, on the way out of town at the firewalkers' feast, if I attended.

At the end of the first week after my routine had been established, I was a half-mile down the beach on my low tide walk. I heard a scream from the water. I turned and looked toward the reef. I saw a solo young village woman who seemed to be tangled in her reef fish net. She was drowning. I dove into the ocean. I swam quickly toward her, letting the outgoing tide do most of the work. I reached her about 200 yards out in the lagoon. She disappeared under water. I dove to rescue her. In clear blue lagoon water near the east reef, I saw the cause of her problem.

Her fishing net was caught on a jagged piece of reef coral. Her foot was twisted in it, when a swell surged in toward shore at the low tide, she became submerged. She had also lost her diving sulu in the process. She was completely nude. Her young lithe body was highlighted by large, brown breasts and elongated nipples in the clear, warm ocean water. Her wet black triangle exposed her opening as she struggled with her free leg. I surfaced for air. I quickly dived again. I released the entangled net from the coral head. This move allowed her to float free to the surface. The net still dangled from her foot.

I swam up to the surface. I unwrapped the net from her foot as I ascended. I accidentally brushed her thighs and breasts in the process. We both bobbed to the surface. She suddenly tugged down on my wet khaki shorts. They were off in a second since they were not belted. She grabbed my dick with her other hand. She pumped it fiercely as she dove forcefully and pulled me under water. I anchored my feet in the loose sand while I held my breath, confused by her aggressive act.

I was not amused. I had stupidly swum into a trap set by the witch doctor, Alu. She was one of his students or relatives. I belatedly realized an island village girl could not have tangled herself in a reef fishing net in shallow water. She had incredibly well-developed lungs from free diving since early childhood. She could stay underwater for minutes at a time. She could have held her breath and easily untangled the net from the coral. Also, they never dove or fished alone, for safety and companionship.

My dick, which had not been touched by a female in weeks was throbbing. It was ready to explode in a premature ejaculation of high school drive-in proportions. She firmly stroked it and I bounced into her breasts. If I failed to break her grip, she could stay underwater three-plus minutes. She swam side to side effortlessly to elude my off-balance grasps for her arm. A swell came in suddenly breaking my tip-toe connection with the sandy bottom.

If I ejaculated, the firewalk was over. I would have to quit the training or risk the firewalk with fatally broken concentration. I knew if I broke the sex taboo, that precise psychological thought would hit my brain halfway across the fire pit. It would end my life. Paranoia 101 was at work here. I knew no man could break a taboo and survive the fire pit.

She was skilled at her job. She probably had trained at the mines where quick hand jobs were performed by some of the teenage girls for Nadi market shopping money while their older, unmarried sisters did the real thing for bigger bucks. I was going to come in 10 seconds. I had to figure out an escape plan. Then I remembered the Fijian taboo on anal sex. It was absolutely taboo because of the tropical island group's large, deadly bacterial population. I floated toward her. I faked enjoyment of her strokes as a deception. I concentrated hard on holding my breath. I reached under her black triangle. I jabbed my finger not into her vagina as she expected when she opened her thighs, but in her ocean water lubricated anal sphincter.

She was extremely shocked and startled at my blatant breaking of a taboo. She reflexively released my penis to pull my index finger away. I was free. I started to swim away. I pivoted my back to her. I swam full speed toward shore before she could regroup. I was close to orgasm, but once free of her warm hand, the cool ocean water saved the day.

She didn't quit swimming after me until I reached waist deep water. She was crying as she waded nude onto the empty beach. She ran toward the old PT-Boat dock, still crying hysterically. She would receive a severe physical beating from Alu for her failure. I had seen women beaten badly in the Fijian villages for perceived sexual affairs, or a perceived failure of duty. They unfairly had no appeal to anyone and only a near death incident would bring a routine police inquiry.

Her beating would allegedly be for losing a valuable fishing net. Only she would know it was for the failure to seduce me to wipe out my firewalk or force me to walk having broken the sex taboo. If the Master of Fire were really angry, he would also curse her. He might make her barren for life, therefore undesirable for marriage. That act would condemn her to a life of prostitution at the mine or the sugarcane port of Laulaka. The tramp freighter crews paid a Fijian dollar to fuck Fijian dock whores while Fijian village day laborers loaded the 112-pound sacks of raw sugar for shipment to the U.S. and Britain, Fiji's biggest traditional sugar customers.

I morbidly hoped I would see a slightly bruised girl in the village, because I feared for her life. There was no help for her on the witch doctor's home turf. I feared my walk of fire was starting to take a high toll. Eli was already on the line, and an unknown teenage girl was now in jeopardy. If the casualties continued to mount, I would have to pull the plug on Pati-pati's mission to stop a massacre of innocent villagers by the witch doctor. Worse case, I might have to kill the Master of Fire to stop the game, even if it risked hard jail time for me in Fiji or death at his warriors' hands.

No British court would convict a Peace Corps volunteer of the premed-itated murder of a witch doctor if he was tried before independence. Alu was on a mission to wipe me out at any cost. I was ready to get gun slinger tough if necessary. I was a native of the wild west.

My khaki shorts washed in on the next breaking wave. It was luck. Their pockets were filled with air. I pulled on the wet shorts. I continued my daily walk on the hot black lava rock and broken coral-strewn beach. I visualized my walk across the fire pit.

Each day I walked the coral strewn reef. Each step further toughening my feet after three years of wearing flip-flops and walking bare footed everywhere in Fiji. Each day I felt more confident I could walk the fire. Patipati's face blazed in my mind. I walked and walked the lonely narrow south beach of the Island of Fire, 10,000 miles from home.

Afternoons were spent with the other men. We did cleansing rituals and chants for the firewalk. Sometimes the Master of Fire attended. I learned the dance-like steps from the men. We practiced them over and over across the bure's matted floor which was the approximate length of the fire pit. They practiced with me, out of respect to me. They still didn't seem to know about the witch doctor's agenda of dirty tricks.

I kept waiting for the Woman of Fire to appear. She hadn't appeared and no one mentioned her. She didn't seem to exist except for the voice I had heard a week ago. I knew I had heard the soft husky Fijian female voice the night the chief disappeared into the witch doctor's bure.

Two nights before the firewalk, I slept in my sulu near the edge of the bure's side wall on a hot night. I started having a wildly erotic dream about Anne. I sometimes had erotic dreams and ejaculated in my sleep if I abstained from sex. It had been a normal occurrence in early teenage boy-hood, but it had stopped in high school on the weekend drive-in movie cir-cuit when my date performed at least a hand job per movie. I had figured this might happen in firewalk training. I had already mentally consigned it to the masturbation camp, not the female sexual activity camp.

The dream progressed as Anne moved into one of her left leg behind her neck over her shoulder, right leg around my back Tantric yoga positions.

Her Hindu instructor had taught her well. I mounted her. Then a warm breast bounced into my open mouth. That was impossible in her yoga position. My subconscious brought me back to the dream world of the dark bure. I struggled awake from deep sleep. I heard a footstep strike the floor near the bure's side women's door. The next footstep hit the ground outside. Then there were no footsteps, just silence.

I could see no one in the dark bure. The moon was behind heavy cloud cover. The sounds of all six sleeping and snoring men filled the room. Who had the mysterious visitor been and had she been attempting to bring me to orgasm in my sleep? Had Alu launched a night attack or was my imagination in overdrive as the firewalk approached.

My hand groped over the sleeping mat instinctively. I felt what seemed to be a cool, small, fine soft gold earring next to my thigh. I slipped it into my nearby khaki shorts pocket for safe keeping until my next beach walk. I did not sleep the rest of the night. I was like Daniel Boone on guard duty for a wagon train crossing the Cumberland Gap in Cherokee country or Kit Carson defending Taos against Ute raiders.

The next day when I walked the beach at low tide, I stopped. I looked at the gold ring which was smaller than the looped gold earrings the Fijian village women sometimes wore pierced through their earlobes, even though the Methodist missionaries had banned the practice. A tiny blood stain on the thin fine gold ring looked fresh. It was a mystery, and it was scary. I decided no more deep sleep until the firewalk was complete, and as a precaution, I would wear my khaki shorts under my sulu at night for extra protection.

The witch doctor, Alu, would apparently stop at nothing to sabotage my walk and break my growing confidence which he observed daily. The sex angle seemed to be his last line of attack, and it had failed completely. The fire pit was near completion as I watched from the bure window. I wondered if another surprise attack would occur tonight. It was the last night before the high noon firewalk on the village common.

It might be just another routine night for me, or it might be my final night on earth. The gods held all the cards. I reconsidered my plan to stay awake all night because a tired, weakened mind and body might win the battle for my foe. However, if I slept all night, my foe might attack again with no time for me to recover mentally. It was a dilemma as the west sun started to set before the last sea turtle meat dinner of the final night before the rapidly approaching firewalk.

CHAPTER FORTY-EIGHT
WALK THE FIRE, BABY

Sun-up woke the village roosters. Sun-up was seven hours before the firewalk. The men ate no breakfast and drank no tea. They drank only fresh cool water delivered directly from the spring in clay urns. I didn't trust the jugs of water, so it was abstinence for me until after I firewalked. I had slept in two hour stretches during the night. I had carefully positioned my sleeping mat in the center of the room away from the bure's doors and windows. I slept between two of the other village men. I had worn my khaki shorts under my sulu to avoid a surprise attack. I even sewed a loop of thread across the zipper of my fly. It was a final precaution I took after my final pee against a palm tree before bedtime.

The night was routine. Apparently, Alu's next trick, if it occurred, would be in the fire pit. Maybe I had passed a secret test and the witch doctor, Alu, would cease fire and treat me like the other firewalkers. Not a likely scenario, I thought, but hope sprang eternal at 25 years of age, so I silently prayed for peace.

After visualizing my walk across the burning coals and meditating an hour, I walked around the bure to get limber. Then, I went outside on the still-dewy, dark-green, thick grass of the village common to stretch my legs. Next, I returned to the bure and assembled the traditional garb for the firewalk. It included a woven grass skirt, cow leather breast plate, assorted armlets, and anklets. This was the same garb I had seen the fire-walkers wear at the well-attended cruise ship sponsored walks in Suva. There they were paid in hard Fijian dollars to entertain the tourists on a South Pacific cruise.

I was worried that the braided dry grass skirt might burst into flames in a second if it hit the burning coals or hot rocks. I wondered if a fire-walker had survived a thousand-foot dive from the bluff into the lagoon in a flaming grass skirt. I made very sure my grass skirt was at my knee line. I adjusted its rope belt high on my waist. I wished it was like Anne's Australian miniskirts, but no cross-dressing was allowed for the firewalk.

I had planned to not view the fire pit until it was time to walk it. I scout-ed the firewalk I had attended in Suva a year before when the Island of Fire's villagers had performed for a cruise ship crowd to earn money for their school. The pit had been approximately 30 feet long, eight feet wide and about a foot deep. It consisted of hard, softball-size rocks which were heated by a wood fire all night. They were hot enough to cause paper to blaze at touch. When the firewalkers were ready to walk, a villager raked the hot wood coals evenly with the white glowing rocks. This procedure formed a smooth bright white gray bed of super-heated rocks and wood coals for the firewalkers.

There were no distracting low temperature bright orange flames, but only super-hot wood coals and rocks which ignited everything they touched, except the firewalkers. A tourist had given them her French de-signer duty free scarf. She had not believed the firewalkers' flaming paper demonstration. She watched her scarf go up in flames instantly and the crowd was convinced.

The rock and the embers were deadly hot. The Fijian firewalking was not an illusion or magic trick. Novices by tradition walked last, I hoped for some quick cooling.

Walking immediately ahead of me was Levulevu. He was the retired former Fijian all-star rugby player. His left knee had been damaged play-ing against the British Lions in the legendary Suva stadium upset. This had slowed his fabled speed forever since there were no NFL quality knee sur-geons at any price in Fiji. Career-ending rugby injuries were very final in Fiji. Levulevu now walked the fire with a limp for applause on Saturdays instead of playing before thousands of screaming fans at the provincial rugby matches in Nadi.

I felt honored to walk after such a famous Fijian athlete. He had helped me often in the two weeks of training because he had admired my surfing, even though I didn't play rugby. He also knew and had played with Jeff, my Nadi Peace Corps friend who had been a football player in college in the Big Ten. Jeff had made the Fijian national team as an alternate after two brilliant years of play for the western province's team. The jock club network had worked, and Levulevu promised to block for me in the pit. I planned to memorize his big footprints and planned to follow in them when called to walk after him.

Morning sped by too quickly and suddenly it was high noon. I passed up 'Bones' and finished Hemingway. At noon, the Master of Fire arrived. He eyeballed us and danced around. He chanted in his usual costume for formal firewalking related occasions. He chased away any leftover evil spirits. Then he led us in a conga line to the pit. It had been built dead center in the village common where 400 or so ceremonially dressed Fijian villagers of all ages had gathered for the event. I was the only full moon guest.

The Great Chief welcomed his villagers, then the firewalkers. Then he and the Master of Fire, Alu, who was not firewalking, exchanged well-rehearsed formal greetings with special kava. The ancient hallow wooden drums conveyed their message. The ceremonially dressed, bare breasted women, young and old, began chanting while they danced in place.

The Master of Fire had an old steel British made garden rake with a long wood handle. He began to even out the hot wood coals and rocks into a smooth bed for the firewalkers. He was precise and ceremonial at the same time. He made each move of the rake stylistically attractive to the eye. His motion hypnotized the watchers and calmed the firewalkers.

After a couple of minutes, the fire pit was ready. He signaled the first walker to action as the women's deafening chanting increased to the drum beat. There was no need to burn hankies or paper bags here. A group of young village teenage future firewalkers had tended the fire's rock bed of burning wood all night and all morning.

Faster than I expected, the first walker stepped to the pit's edge, paused for 10 seconds, and then walked across it in ten long, quick, rhythmic steps. He arrived safely at the pit's exit to the approval of the village. He had displaced a small group of stones in the pit's center so the Master of Fire, Alu, expertly re-raked the pit like a dealer in a Las Vegas casino re-shuffles blackjack decks after each hand.

The women's chanting grew louder again, and their breasts bounced freely. The next village firewalker was signaled to the pit's edge. My stomach tightened. I tried not to hyperventilate. I fought for control of my breathing using a yoga meditation Anne had taught me. I felt my dia-phragm begin to function. I concentrated on the cooler outside air as it en-tered my nostrils and then the hotter inside air as it exited my nostrils. As I did this, I closed my eyes and focused on my third eye, not the fire pit. I did not want to see Alu. I did not want to watch another walker until Levulevu.

I had trained hard for two full weeks with no sex, no kava, and pounds of sea turtle meat. My feet had been reconditioned by the walks on the hot rocks and sharp coral on the lagoon's beach. I hoped there would be no physical foot shock when I hit the rough hot rocks and coals. I wouldn't feel the heat if I blocked it from my mind on the way across the pit. Mind control over matter was the issue. I had plenty of the good little strong men on my side, since I didn't need them in the long Greg Knoll surfboard anymore. In fact, I had a surplus of little men. After the firewalk, I wanted off this island fast if I solved Patipati's murder.

I silently counted the firewalkers with my eyes closed tightly. They went singly in order at Alu's voice command. About three minutes later, I heard Levulevu called to approach the pit. I opened my eyes just as he stepped into the fire. He took two long steps...and his rugby dam-aged knee collapsed suddenly. Unexpectedly, he went face down into the flames. He struggled to rise on his hands. He could not because he had been blinded by the fall. Then, he unexpectedly quit moving. He lay dead still. He silently burned to death in shame in the pit. Mercifully, he was totally unconscious, and he died after a long minute. No village man moved to save him, and the women never stopped chanting as he burned to death in the pit.

After it was certain he was dead and not maimed, and his spirit no longer suffered as a human being, the Master of Fire, Alu, called for help-ers. Four young men with long hardwood poles appeared. They rolled his scorched, sickening, blistered body off the pit into the green grass and onto a sacred ancient Fijian made leather ceremonial burial stretcher. It had appeared instantly, too. The smell of burning flesh was pungent. The sight was horrifying. Levulevu's entire face was missing. The act of letting him burn to death honorably had been kind in the Fijian village's world ideal.

Levulevu, a great warrior athlete, had failed his firewalk test. It was better for him to die voluntarily in the fire pit than be a maimed beggar for the rest of his life. Maybe, I thought, the all-foreseeing Fijian gods had saved him from a collapsed knee on the deck of a sailboat in an ocean storm when other villagers' lives would have been endangered. The Fijian gods had acted in the pit. The village would mourn and miss him. He had died honorably, a national sports hero. He would live in village legend forever.

I remained calm and a surreal sense surrounded me. I finally understood the firewalking game completely. The pit destroyed the physically or mentally weak males for whatever the village's needs or the god's reasons. It was a form of natural selection practiced by these strong, proud, independent Fijian island people who had my full respect.

The Master of Fire re-raked the pit. The women started chanting again. I walked directly into the pit. I did not wait to be called by my enemy, Alu. I don't even remember how many rhythmic steps I made. I did not feel the burning embers under each of my footsteps, only the heat from the glowing pit as it rose around my cool body. My searing eyes focused on Eli who waited for me at the fire pit's exit like an airport beacon light. The village chant accented each step as some subconscious skill blocked the heat from the soles of my feet. Blue light filled my third eye.

I crossed the fire pit without fear or a care in the world to the chanting of the village women. I collapsed two steps out of the pit. I fell on the grassy tropical soft ground. I rolled over and stared straight into the sun. My mind was completely blank...

I went still frame by still frame through the events of my life the morning of Patipati's death. The single frames stopped suddenly as I left the Banana Cafe. I saw clearly from my point of view one of V.J. Singh's small delivery trucks, with a driver, driving down from Laulau Heights. It drove quickly past my Land Rover and the Banana Cafe. Its driver was the thug shotgun rider of the baked potato truck.

I deduced there was no reason in the world that V.J. Singh's small delivery truck should have been coming from a wealthy Suva colonial residential neighborhood at breakfast time. The thug driving also knew Patipati and me by sight. I knew, at that moment, V.J. Singh had plotted the murder of Patipati as the enlarged still frame of the truck and the driver's face froze in my mind forever . . .

Suddenly, a voice reached my inner consciousness. Eli's hands helped me rise from the lush grass carpet of the village common. His hand shielded my eyes from the overhead noon tropical sun. I blinked my eyes open, turning off my mind's film projector.

I had walked the fire pit and I had survived it. The bottoms of my feet were tender with sunburn degree blisters, but they worked fine. I had cleared my mind of all the murder's inconsistent facts. I had seen the photo that it had stored. It had been stored to be retrieved and utilized to solve the murder. Patipati's spirit had guided me once again. Levulevu had saved my life with his death by revealing the secret of the fire pit.

There were no little men, only nine or ten rhythmic, quick, confident steps across the fire pit. My brain had shut down my sensory system completely. My physical body had functioned perfectly. Firewalking was an incredible natural survival device to preserve the isolated island's village and its balance of political power. I knew it would disappear fifty years to the day the first beach hotel opened on the Island of Fire.

I had one more trip to make and that was to the Land of the Dead Chiefs on Monday after the feast for the firewalkers. Sunday was the Methodist day of rest. On Monday, the great chief would grant me my trip to the Land of the Dead Chiefs as my last act on the Island of Fire.

CHAPTER FORTY-NINE

IF IT'S MONDAY IT MUST BE THE LAND OF THE DEAD CHIEFS

The "Kava of Death" started to blur my vision. The Great Chief of the Island of Fire, my new paramount ally, chanted in rhythm. It was very ancient and so chilling it could have only traveled on the long boats that carried the ancient ones and their boars from Africa across the Indian Ocean to Fiji. The chorus of old women behind him rhythmically swayed as their bare breasts bounced to their more and more hysterically paced chants. They were calling for the Dead Chiefs to open the gate for me to enter the Chief's land to avenge Patipati's death.

My eyes blurred again. I tried to focus on the crudely painted letters KENNEDY above the door frame of the bure of Eli. He was the front runner to be the next chief of the Island of Fire. The women danced bare breasted with grass skirts from the waist down. They moved to the beat of the old log drum. The great chief motioned for me to take the last bowl of the 'Kava of Death'.

I sat cross-legged facing the chief. My right hand lifted the sacred carved stone cup to my lips. The cool, soothing 'Kava of Death' pulsed across my tongue. The women danced closer to me. They circled and their full breasts began to smother my face in an explosion of brown nipples and black-bronze flesh.

The female breasts that had given me life as an infant were now beginning to suffocate me. The 'Kava of Death' numbed my entire body. The kava had paralyzed my central nervous system. I could not move. I stopped breathing. My spirit flew toward the open bure door toward the Land of the Dead Chiefs.

I existed no longer on the metaphysical plane of the Island of Fire, although my body still lay motionless on the finely-woven reed mats before the great chief. The women, still chanting, squatted over me. They painted my body with a white coconut paste, the Food of Life. They prepared to hurl my spirit through the gate into the Land of the Dead Chiefs.

They coated both sides of my body with coconut paste, Fiji's universal food. They painted red lines from my heart to my ears with a water-based clay dye. This represented the Mother Earth from which knowledge sprang to feed man. My ears would hear the Fable of the Dead Chiefs and confirm the identity of Patipati's murderer.

The drums beat faster. The great chief chanted with Alu (who now, after the firewalk, respected my warrior and chiefly powers). The women and Alu, the witch doctor, began to empty my body of all fluids. I had to enter the trance-like state of death necessary for the spirit's journey. They would leave only enough blood in my body to ensure my spirit's return to Eli's house.

I could not feel my body. My spirit flew toward the gate. Alu called the mysterious Woman of Fire. She appeared suddenly and poured a vial of potion into my throat. It released my spirit from my body completely. I saw a black implosion in my third eye which hurled me through the gate to the Land of the Dead Chiefs. I traveled through a long, dark, cold, underground river cave with no light. I emerged. I sat cross-legged face to face with the Gatekeeper, the great-great-grandfather of Patipati. He was my guide. He lived in the Spirit World's Ocean of the Universe.

I asked, "Is it V.J. Singh who killed the great warrior, Patipati, who was away from his village under my command?"

He remained silent. His silence confirmed that V.J. Singh had murdered Patipati. I remembered well Patipati's instructions that silence to any question in the Land of the Dead Chiefs meant 'yes'.

The circle was complete. The knot of revenge was tied.

I then asked, "Did Lee Harvey Oswald kill John Kennedy, my land's late president, a great chief and founder of the Peace Corps?"

He spoke, the fable he chanted in Fijian translated roughly into this story: "In your land, in the year 1962, there were three great living chiefs. They all coveted each of the other chief's power. The most public great chief was your young President Kennedy, a man of great courage and idealism but from a flawed clan of Irish bootleggers and gangsters. His father had murdered, stolen and bribed to help him gain the highest position among the chiefs of your land."

"In your land, there was also a very powerful, secretly dying great chief whose name was Sam Rayburn. He wanted his province's chief, Lyndon Johnson, to inhabit the great white bure. He wanted this to occur before he died. He was angry at Kennedy's father for blocking his ally's, Johnson's, succession to power. Chief Rayburn was also blinded by his allegiance to his province. He constantly warred to advance the position of this province in your land.

"His other ally was a powerful, guileless CIA warrior Allen Dulles. Dulles, a traditional Yankee warrior, was a willing ally. He hated the upstart Irish thugs around John Kennedy and his father. He vowed, secretly, to return a legitimate king to the great white bure."

"Your land's third great chief, Earl Warren, had no warriors. He could only act in judgment of the other great chiefs. In your land, Cooper, as in Fiji, only a great chief can murder another great chief. Lee Harvey Oswald was a commoner. This is all I know."

He looked away. "So, young warrior of fire, return to your land through the gate of the Land of the Dead Chiefs."

He disappeared in a flash of pure white light. My throat felt the constant drip of the sweet, lactic taste of human milk. It was like an IV It continued until my eyes slowly opened and focused. I saw the blurred letters KENNEDY above the door frame of the house of Eli. The village's log drum began to thunder again. I realized my body was levitated. It did not touch the floor mat. I was motionless with no feeling or physical sense of being alive.

The women massed behind the great chief. The familiar chant of the past hour continued floating into the night air. From a side door, I saw the spirit form of the Woman of Fire enter. She was dressed only in a sulu that dropped off her full, soft breasts, touching the floor. Her long black hair flowed over each shoulder and glistened in the lantern light.

As she approached me, the great chief led the village women and drummers out through the bure's Kennedy door. I was alone with the Woman of Fire. The ghostly figure of the Woman of Fire was silhouetted in the low orange light of an ancient whale oil lantern. With her left hand, she reached up to her right breast. She dropped her black cotton sulu in a single motion. She revealed her beautiful, tall nude body. It was highlighted by a long pencil-thin strip of curly black pubic hair. Her opening was rimmed with glimmering gold rings. Her right hand emerged from behind her back. I saw the blade of a razor sharp, ancient Fijian stone war knife.

She approached my levitated body which remained motionless. It was still completely without feeling. I saw and I heard but could not move or feel.

She spoke in Fijian, "You have returned from the Land of the Dead Chiefs, a journey few warriors survive. The trip is allowed only once in a lifetime when granted. Attempt a return for any reason and my knife will find your heart."

Then the Woman of Fire fed me a potion. The motion of physical life returned. I slowly sank to the matted floor while my coconut-paste encrusted white body glowed orange in the low light of the lantern in a house named Kennedy on the Island of Fire in the middle of the Pacific Ocean.

Fiji's dream world was out of control. I knew it was time to return to America. I definitely did not want to ever return to the Land of the Dead Chiefs during my present lifetime. My eyes focused on the nude bronze-black body of the Woman of Fire silhouetted in the low orange light.

I felt fear as my earth senses started to return after the journey to the Land of the Dead Chiefs. I continued to focus on the nude, lithe body of the Woman of Fire. It still shocked me.

She squatted over my body. She scraped off the dried white coconut paste, and my pores breathed again. I saw her vaginal lips and she had been pierced in a way practiced in East Africa a thousand years ago. She had experienced the ritual of female piercing. Her vaginal lips were enlarged. They exposed the pink interior of her canal. She had an abnormally enlarged exposed clitoris. She had small pure fine gold rings pierced around the edge of her lips. These fine gold rings matched the one I had found in the firewalker bure by my sleeping mat. I finally knew it was the Woman of Fire who had been in the firewalkers' bure the night of the sexual dream before my firewalk.

She chanted as she scraped off the hard, matted, chalky dried coconut milk with the stone war knife. I still could not feel or move my penis. She scraped the last of the matted coconut paste from my body.

She started a new chant. Terror then panic struck my 25-year-old brain and Anne's yoga breathing meditation did not produce internal calm. Her dark canal's rim of gold ringlets began to circle me in slow motion as the fine gold rings tinkled like bells. A strange sexual arousal began sending rockets of tiny sharp feeling through my earth body. The swirl and sound of the gold rings glinted in the orange whale oil lantern light. My spirit returned from the dream world and rejoined my body. I lost consciousness again.

I awoke again on Tuesday morning. I lay on a sleeping mat in Eli's bure in a sulu covered with a light cotton blanket. Eli and his wife smiled. They handed me a cup of hot tea and a bowl of fresh passionfruit. My stay on the Island of Fire was over. I knew I would sail tomorrow on the Wednesday market boat with the villagers to Nadi market.

I had survived my dangerous ordeals physically intact. I would carry a great secret back to my country about the murder of our young president. I had one more stop to make in Fiji and it was in Suva. I had to settle a score for Patipati, my dead friend. I planned to arrive in Suva on Thursday night. I preferred to strike without warning or delay. I did not want the news of my firewalk to precede me to the capital city. It might alert my enemies and the Peace Corps staff would speed my exit.

The Hindus like V.J. Singh knew the power of firewalking. I'd witnessed their version of it at valley weddings. This walk would bring more public fame. I needed to move fast before the story spread from the Nadi market or the mines to the capital city press. It was hard news that a PCV had walked the fire pit.

Even if I was still weak from the firewalk and the journey to the Land of the Dead Chiefs, I had to sail Wednesday. Then I planned to drive northeast to Suva on Kings Road around Viti Levu alone. My arrival in Suva would be after dark and secret. The plan was complete in my mind.

I sat up alert. I spoke to Eli, his wife and baby girl. These were my first human words in 24 hours.

I spent the rest of the day eating, napping, and saying goodbye to the villagers. I walked over to the school. I wanted to help Ella in the school garden on my last day and say goodbye. Fresh air felt wonderful.

As I arrived on the school's porch, Ella walked from her classroom. She asked me to help her in the school veggie garden. I followed her, surprised. A strong trade wind gust lifted her sulu above her broad, brown, bare hips exposing the tip of her magic black triangle. She did not pull her sulu down as she slowly walked into the bush past the garden.

CHAPTER FIFTY
SUVA, THE FINAL DAY

After I had recovered the Land Rover from its hideout, I headed north. Then I drove southeast around Viti Levu's lightly traveled rain-forested coast to avoid detection during my trip. I had driven into the capital city from the north east. It was the opposite direction from my usual south eastern route. It was late dusk when I arrived in Suva.

I had stopped for one night at an isolated, rotting, wood-framed, dull white, English colonial hotel an hour northeast of the boat landing. I rented a private single room for $5.00 Fijian. I needed to shower, eat, and get 12 hours of uninterrupted sleep. The splendid isolation of this empty roadside hotel was perfect. It had been built in some forgotten era of Fiji history, probably during mineral prospecting times. Its colonial British hotel dinner after home cooked meals tasted horrible. I missed the fresh, organic island food I had eaten daily. The hotel fare filled only the void in my stomach from the long boat ride on the calm ocean, but hotel sleep was refreshing and worry-free.

I woke up completely focused on my mission in Suva. After a better hearty English breakfast, I drove toward the capital city through the rain-forested, always muddy roads of the island's eastern side. It was slow traveling but uneventful. The summer's first torrential rains came in late morning. I had slipped unobserved into the capital city. I parked the easily recognizable co-op Land Rover on the edge of the main downtown area near the eastern side of the Parliament building. I traveled on foot. I took only the good luck red coral stick, a remnant of the infamous 50-triple-C mud flap, and a yellow slicker in my canvas briefcase. I also had reached up under the driver's seat and put the Polaroid of Dianne in my cotton shirt pocket for good luck.

I darted quickly into a narrow back street of the run-down crumbling downtown wholesale district. It was mostly 100-year-old stone warehouses with store fronts. Two blocks into this mostly Hindu-Chinese merchant enclave, I found V.J. Singh's half-block deep sprawling store and warehouse. The store's lights were out for the night, but his counting office on the second floor had lights burning. He was personally doing his books for the day. After he finished the daily tally, I had heard his Chinese mistress was brought by a personal driver-bodyguard for her nightly visit. Later the driver would deliver V.J. Singh home to the wife and kids in Upper Laulau Heights, after they dropped his visitor off. I waited and watched the store from the dark shadows of the alley behind another store for about a half-hour. His black Australian General Motors sedan showed up with the thug driver Patipati and I met on the Suva road and Singh's mistress. She was a half-Chinese, half-Fijian teenage girl who should have been an international model. She went up the back stairs. The driver walked down the street toward the Banana Cafe for dinner. The cafe stayed open late for sailors.

I knew about this nightly passion play because Dr. Joe ate at the Banana Cafe most nights. He had followed the thug driver back to V.J. Singh's one night. Dr. Joe kept an eye on V.J. Singh's habits because of the wholesale kava trade. Dr. Joe was not above blackmail. He had attended Harvard Business School.

As soon as the driver left for dinner, I slipped down the alley. I crawled under the high, Aussie-built American style sedan. It looked like a big four-door Chevy Impala in the USA. I had worked part-time for one summer at a Malibu, California gas station to pay my rent while surfing during a college break. I had learned to do a light brake job. I slipped my tiny steel file from my khaki shorts pocket. I had used the file to smooth out the newly patched dings on my surfboard. I went to work on the copper tube brake lines. I filed deep grooves on all four brake lines. The grooves were not deep enough to cause them to leak in the alley. I did not want them noticed by the thug driver.

V.J. Singh lived on the highest ridge line in the wealthy section of Lau-lau Heights. He had city light views. The first major pressure on the brakes on the steep downhill trip to Suva center, after pounding through Suva's rainy season potholes in a couple of days, would avenge Patipati's murder.

There was no reason to go to the police about my sighting of the V.J. Singh delivery truck the morning of the murders. It was too circumstantial for the Fiji Police. Patipati was dead. He could not corroborate our encounter with the thug driver and his shotgun rider on the coastal mountain road. V.J. Singh's driver would claim he lost control of the burned potato truck which had been routinely overloaded. He would claim he jumped to save his life. This was a fairly common occurrence in Fiji's badly maintained muddy mountain roads. V.J. Singh's trucks delivered everywhere in the capital city. The thug driver would have a falsified delivery report for his trip to Laulau Heights on the murder day and as a back-up, his boss lived there.

If I hadn't walked the fire, Patipati's murder would have been the perfect crime, but I had walked the fire and survived. Early each morning, V.J. Singh and his driver descended the steep, narrow road from the peak of Laulau Heights to the warehouse at sea level. They had just run out of routine trips in the shiny Australian sedan.

I peeked out from under the black sedan into the dark alley. I saw no one. I crawled out. I was ready to disappear into the shadows like a ninja. I stopped. I took a piece of the battered mudflap of the girl with the 50-tri-ple-C tits out of my canvas briefcase. I stuck it under the rear bumper, out of sight. It was a good luck piece for Patipati and me. Next, I opened the unlocked door. I slipped the red coral stick and the baked Polaroid of Di-anne's private parts under the front bench seat and secured it under a coil spring. If the police found them, it would perpetrate the capital city sex cult theory. Then, I slipped out of the narrow unlit street unnoticed.

I walked the four blocks on dark back streets past the national market toward the main customs shed. I wanted to say goodbye to Dr. Joe, but his office lights were already out when I arrived. I was saddened; I knew I would never see him again. Since I knew where he hid the spare key, I let myself into his office. I turned on the first electric light I had used in a month. I left him an undated note:

> *Dr. Joe,*
>
> *Thanks for all your help. I could never have run the Valley Co-op without your numbers crunching and annual reports. Send this year's report to the Co-op Minister and Ratu Kavula. Please sign it for me.*
>
> *I hope I meet you in my next life. I surfed the 50-foot wave. I walked the fire. I have to escape from Fiji, so I'm going on the Saturday Pan Am flight. Sell my share of the Wine Co-op if you can and please give the money to the National TB Hospital in Patipati's name.*
>
> *Best Regards, Cooper*
> *PS.—Burn this note.*

Dr. Joe had been my principal Peace Corps Volunteer ally in the dream world.

I resisted an urge to cruise the capital city disco one last time. It was not the time to be high profile in Suva after the brake job. I was sad. I would miss the independence ceremonies. I had stayed an extra year in the Peace Corps to help Fiji's economic transition. It was better to be out of sight and out of mind if V.J. Singh tanked at full speed.

With independence only a month away, the police would have no time to investigate an apparent auto accident or follow leads if they discovered the cut brake lines. Rumors were rampant in Suva that full scale Fijian uprisings were coming after independence. One rumor was that the murder of all Hindu and Muslim Indians would occur one night after independence.

Fiji's police and military forces were being deployed to keep the country peaceful. They had to minimize the settling of old scores as the British rulers pulled out after the Union Jack came down in England's last crown colony of any consequence. Modern English colonial empire history was ending in Fiji, not with a bang, but a thud as the third world moved in different rhythms after World War II.

I headed over to the little hotel where I had the Potato War massage. I checked into a cheap room under Tab's name for $2.00 Fijian. I knocked on my masseuse's room door. I wanted a bath and massage, especially for my feet which were still pink and tender. A Filipino sailor answered the door. He looked at me dumbly.

Suva was transient like all port cities. It seemed no one ever lived in the same box very long. During my three years in the valley, no Fijian had moved in or out of a bure I visited in 10 villages up and down the Sigatoka River except for burial. A family member had always been at home for verbal messages. Some families had inhabited the same village home sites for 500-plus years.

I went back to my room. I slept soundly another eight hours. I awoke early. I walked a back route to the Peace Corps office. I met with the country director who wanted to know why I hadn't been to work at the Valley Co-op in a month. I said I had been surfing.

He said, "You're a bad apple, Cooper, and a bad influence on the other Peace Corps volunteers in Fiji. You're out of here on Saturday's Pan Am flight to Hawaii straight through to the mainland. Don't come back—and I've heard, by the way, that you can't from an Indian friend who clears the embassy and Peace Corps equipment through customs. Also, the Co-op Department sent a senior officer down to Sigatoka to take charge of the Valley Co-op during your absence."

"The Peace Corps has been relieved of staffing it. I've deducted the cost of the Polaroid camera you borrowed for the Valley Co-op, which is U.S. government property, from your back pay. Goodbye."

This was mostly good news. The co-op was ready to fly or crash-land with Fijian management. Tears came to my eyes, though. I had been relieved unceremoniously of command. I couldn't hand my polished steel sword to Patipati who I had groomed for the top job for three years.

Tab had departed Fiji, and pre-independence fighting had probably already broken out for the control of the Handicraft Co-op. The tourists would continue to push the prices higher with each cruise ship and Pan Am Boeing 747 that arrived in Fiji, filled with vacationers. Dr. Joe would depart after Independence and the kava market would be vulnerable again to lucrative Christmas market corner plays by the capital city Hindu wholesale crowd. I hoped the new co-op officer, who was probably from another province, could lead Chief Kavula's valley farmer's in peaceful tobacco negotiations a year from now.

The bell had tolled for me. It was time for paradise found and about to be lost to find its own beat again, without neo-colonial Peace Corps provided administrators like me, Tab, and Dr. Joe. No matter how lofty our ideas and how fair our refereeing, we weren't blood Fijians. I picked

up my one-way Pan Am ticket, back pay, and termination papers from the
latest Washington GS-5 receptionist. She didn't even know my name. She
probably had never even heard of Patipati or Tab. I walked out of the front
door of the Suva Peace Corps Headquarters office forever.

The drive across the southern coast was beautiful. The bright sun reflected off the ocean. On the mountain stretch of highway, I stopped briefly
to view the burned-out wreck of the bandit potato truck at the bottom of
the deep rain-forested gorge. It was a memorial to the potato war. It would
rust away and be covered by vines in its rain forest grave.

CHAPTER FIFTY-ONE

ANNE

The escape from Suva was complete. I crossed the final southern central mountain pass. I started the steep, dry descent into the southwestern windward side of Viti Levu. I was about 20 minutes from Anne's beach hotel. I hadn't seen or talked to her in almost 30 days, except through ESP while on the Island of Fire.

For the first time in three years, Dianne was gone from my life completely. I missed her like an old friend who had moved away. Lately, it was always Anne, the Aussie girl-woman who rode the typhoon with me, I thought about.

My left brain said to me: Drive past the hotel and be free of her, Cooper. Leave Fiji completely, forever. The typhoon day was a moment— dangerous, beautiful, brave—but only a moment. She belongs to the Southern Pacific winds, deserts, and beaches. You belong to the North American Rocky Mountains, its mesas, and big skies. Your fates touched for a moment to save another life, but that is all that happened. You cannot return to Fiji, probably forever, but certainly while the prime minister is alive. It will tear your heart out if she stays in Fiji and you cannot see her. Pass the entrance to the hotel. Drive to Sigatoka and pack, then visit the bure of Chief Kavula...

This argument was compelling. After the Island of Fire, much emotion had exited my mind. The Woman of Fire had restored my sexuality but not my desire. The experience had been too bright, its heat too hot, death too near too much of the time. Ella had failed to arouse me.

I maneuvered the Land Rover through the ascending and downhill blind corners with the grace of a ballerina on center stage. We were one for this last leg of this final trip. We had logged many miles and careened through many adventures together. Better, I thought, to meditate on the driving, be one with the machine, and forget Anne.

The sign for the hotel came at the Land Rover like a bolt of lightning in the early afternoon southwestern Fiji blue sky. I was a hundred yards from the turn. I floored the Land Rover at 60 mph, foot on the accelerator, my heart stopped cold like ice, almost not breathing. At fifty yards even my breathing stopped, and my life was in suspension. My blood was frozen and my whole body was cold. Twenty-five yards and I touched the brake pedal. I drifted toward a slow turn down the hotel main road. New air entered my nostrils. It restarted my heart and sent life back into my body.

I sped down the main entrance road. I breathed again. As it forked to Anne's house, I hoped she was home resting in the early afternoon heat while she relaxed before the hotel's busy dinner period. I turned my Land Rover slowly and saw her veranda.

She was surrounded by a hammock, rocking slowly under a ceiling fan. Only her head was above the wide, bright blue and red-stripped cotton pouch. She looked straight at the Land Rover, her eyes wide open and round with joy.

I braked the Land Rover to an easy stop. I cut the engine. I leaped out the door, unable to speak and barely able to order my feet into motion. She smiled but did not speak or stop rocking as I approached her. I was silent and smiling as our spirits touched again. I crossed the freshly macheted, lush, summer dark green grass. My flip-flopped feet glided like a runner at the end of a marathon. My heart was in deep rhythm with my breath. I was alert but tired. I was joyful but sad to see the finish line near the end of my Fiji experience.

I ran to the wooden steps. I felt the vitality of youth take control of my body. My blood rushed through my body with fresh energy for every cell. I walked toward the hammock. She stared at me, smiled, and then closed her eyes.

I approached the hammock's edge. Her flowered red sulu was open to allow the sun to touch her body as she meditated. Her hands were on her flat, firm breasts, her diamond nipples hard, her stomach taut, her left leg raised slightly. She was the same tauntingly beautiful, tanned dark brown, lithe girl from the outback with whom I had survived the greatest typhoon in modern Fijian history. She said nothing. She moved only her fingers. They continued to stimulate her breasts softly. Her eyes and mouth were closed. Her breathing was controlled, yoga style.

Her mind was my mind, and my mind was her mind. I dropped my khaki shorts and pulled off my shirt in the hot afternoon sunlight. She had led me from the Suva road where she had stationed her spirit to watch. She knew I would pass after the full moon. Her spirit had entered me at the turn. It had given me back my sexual sensuality. Her sentry spirit had guarded the road each day, watching for me.

The handwoven cotton hammock was wide and strong. I climbed over its low side. I entered Anne in one motion. She was already wet when I filled her to the tip of her womb. Then she began a low, throaty chant. Her hands released her breasts and cupped the back of my head at the neckline. Her canal contracted in ringlets, igniting my spirit. Her chants increased in pace, timed to her contractions, which brought us to a total and complete orgasm together. I felt the sentinel spirit leave my body and enter her womb. Her chant turned to words. I held her tightly. Her hands were now on my lower back.

Anne said, "My spirit had watched the road since full moon to bring you to me when your Land Rover passed this place. If you had not passed by the next full moon, I would know you were dead, eaten by the great white shark that came to the hotel's coastal reef after you were here last. Your enemy called the shark, so I gave it my portion of Patipati's spirit which was still in my body from the day of the typhoon.

"I swam into the surf and directed his spirit to enter the shark. I sent it to the Island of Fire so you could destroy it, or it would search for you forever with its curse. The white shark accepted the spirit. It swam away from me even as I bled in the water from the full moon cycle. Now, I know you have killed the white shark and walked the great fire. I hope you have avenged Patipati's murder so his spirit can be reborn again to live a complete life and die naturally and become a warrior spirit to protect his village in its forests forever."

Then she ran her hands over my hips and over my thighs.

"You have made a journey to the Land of the Dead Chiefs that my Aboriginal grandmother told me about in my former world in the Australian outback. You can make this trip only once, I know. Since I know you have come from Suva, I am sure Patipati's death has been avenged. Your private thoughts also tell me that from the Land of the Dead Chiefs, you have learned a great secret which you now must take to your land. Your spirit will not rest until the secret has been released and the land cleansed of its blood.

"I will join you in your land in time, because our spirits were melded into one forever by the great storm. Your spirit is now one-half me and one-half you, and mine the same. The great wind blew them together on the bridge. They cannot be separated by death. Together, they are greater than the whole, their fused weld impossible to break. I know you cannot return to Fiji, because Ratu Sili stayed at the hotel with your Fijian replacement. I heard them talk about the deal you made to save the potato crop.

"They did not know about our relationship, so they spoke openly while they ate in the hotel dining room. They are allied with a V.J. Singh, as you probably know. They plan to exploit the Valley Co-op's farmers once you are gone. You probably know this and have already made plans to neutralize them."

I did not comment. She did not need to know the details of my trip to Suva the previous day.

"I feel your sperm in my canal. It is active, and that is good. The Woman of Fire, I know by legend, has returned you well to me. We will wait to make a child in the snowy winter in your land by the great, white-peaked mountains. You must not enter me again until that time or we will make a child here, half each from our fused spirits. I would carry it to term alone, unprotected by a warrior chief. You must go now from me and the hammock and my egg of the child who will be born in the mountains of Colorado.

"I know you have come from Suva. Your enemies will follow your tracks until you leave by the great silver bird. They must not know you were with me today. Only my old, blind housekeeper is here, so you are safe. My dead husband picked her so she could hear us, but never see us. Also, she does not understand English, only Fijian. She cannot betray the secret of your stop. You have not spoken, and you will not."

I was stunned but knew this warrior-spirited woman was wise beyond her age. I withdrew from her. I felt her warmth ebb as the tropical air replaced it. I rose from the hammock to dress. I had to continue my trip to Sigatoka to close out this chapter of my life in the Islands of Paradise.

She said, "Hand me the vial on the rattan table."

I did. She took it. She raised her thighs, knees in the air, arched her back and inserted it deep into her vagina. She chanted and removed it, empty.

"This will kill your sperm. It is an herbal remedy of my grandmother used by the Aborigine women on the desert when they must keep moving and it is too dangerous to bear a child of the wind."

I was startled by her sudden action, but it made sense. I wondered what was in the vial but couldn't speak or ask. I pulled on my khaki shorts and my shirt. I felt the prevailing trade winds in my face.

She said, "Go with the wind now. You are safe as long as you leave Fiji before the trades stop blowing tomorrow at sunset. Sleep in the safety of Kavula's bure with his warriors tonight. Leave tomorrow on the Pan Am flight east. Tell no one of your stop here. There must be no connection between us again until I reach the safety of the great white mountains in your land of Colorado.

"Send for me when you are ready. Each Sunday night, I will meditate when the sun drops into the sea to the west. I will do a Tantric yoga sexual meditation, my tongue against my upper lip, my right forefinger rubbing my clitoris. There is a nerve which connects them. This will cause me to orgasm in the sunset's colorful hues.

"When the sun rises from the sea in the east, it will bring my pleasure at sunrise, wherever you are. In this manner, the sexual, sensual nature of our spirits will be revitalized until our bodies join again. Go with God, boy-warrior. Always be brave until I am with you again in the cold, white snow by the desert."

She began to cry in a low, controlled chant from her diaphragm. I folded the sulu across her nude body without touching her. Then I turned as she closed her eyes, with tears on her cheeks. I leapt from the veranda.

I opened the Land Rover door and climbed into it. I planned to leave no tracks on this final day in Fiji, like Ute Indians moving from the Colorado mountains in fall to their Utal desert winter camp.

The Land Rover barked into life. The old, blind Fijian housekeeper came to the door. She carried a large clay pot of water in her hands for Anne to cleanse herself. It was the custom after a Fijian village woman had sex. I backed out of the yard. I saw the old woman stop at the edge of the hammock and they began to chant. She began to cleanse Anne who swayed gently in the breeze.

They disappeared as the Land Rover spun around. I exited Anne's driveway onto the main hotel road which would take me to the coast road for the 18-mile ride along the Coral Coast to Sigatoka without the typhoon's death riding over my shoulder on this trip.

I was alone with my spirit, blown by the trade winds and guided by the love of the girl-woman from the great Australian outback. I could hear her chants in the wind. They whistled through the Land Rover's open vents. They merged with the harmonic tones of my spirit as the coast road from the capital city disappeared rapidly, forever, under the wheels of my gray horse.

CHAPTER FIFTY-TWO
GOODBYE, CHIEF KAVULA

I timed my entrance to say goodbye at the Sigatoka co-op's headquarters office to be at 4:30 Friday. Everybody was ready to leave for the hotel bar across the street. I walked to the hotel with the staff and bought B.J., Raja and the three office workers a round of drinks. They were non-committal about their new Fijian Co-op Department boss from Suva. I didn't push for information because their fate was with him.

Beer tasted strange. I had abstained for a month from the western world's drugs. I barely finished two beers. They clouded my purified mind in a strange blocking manner. I shook hands all-around. I said goodbye forever to these clerks who collected the money, kept the books, did the government paperwork, and ran the back offices for me while I managed the Valley Co-op. They were the dedicated, unsung heroes of old-world colonial commerce. After two rounds, I said my thanks and final goodbyes.

The drive to Chief Kavula's village was an easy half-hour on the now dark coast road. A lantern was lit in his bure. I parked the Land Rover. I walked through the side men's door, carrying a small bundle of kava I had brought from the Island of Fire. He was finishing dinner with his old wife. He was happy to see me. She left to beat the village log drum and call the elders and village men together. The potato warriors were called to their last council with me.

I didn't have to tell my warrior friends I was leaving Fiji. I didn't have to tell them Patipati's death had been avenged. They had already heard from Nadi by way of Sigatoka market gossip that I had walked the fire and entered the Land of the Dead Chiefs. They instinctively knew I had gone to the Island of Fire to avenge Patipati's death. They believed I would not leave Fiji until I had performed my duty to my fallen warrior friend.

They had even heard I had come from the east to Sigatoka, therefore from the capital city, because two of the village women had been at the bus stop when I crossed the pontoon bridge in the gray co-op Land Rover to say goodbye at co-op headquarters. They had expected my visit, but not tonight. They were only surprised by my early arrival.

The kava ceremony was simple, low key, and elegant. Since I had given them no warning, there was no province-wide feast and ceremonial departure dancing. That meant five cows, a hundred chickens, five goats and half the village reef fish population were spared to feed them during the summer. They needed their food supplies to help celebrate the week-long independence feast. It would strain the province's thin food supply after the storm.

After the kava ceremony was completed, the old chief presented me a whale's tooth. It was to guide me to my home village safely, even though he knew it was illegal to take out of Fiji. This magic would protect me during my travel home from my enemies.

After more rounds of kava, my turn came to tell a story. I told one about a young warrior of ancient times who rode an outrigger long boat in the great waves from the south. He walked the fire, saw a vision, and avenged the death of a fallen warrior from his village before the sun descended from the western sky and took him for a ride into the night stars.

Tears came to the corners of old Chief Kavula's eyes. We drank kava round after round until midnight. I slept on a mat in the chief's bure at his feet. Before the first village rooster crow, I woke. I placed the new co-op Polaroid camera by the chief's feet and left before first light. Chief Kavula slept silently as I departed. I knew I would never see him again.

I dropped the Land Rover off at the co-op building. I dropped its keys and my headquarters' door key through a mail slot. I walked across to the hotel tourist taxi stand. I was a civilian again for the first time in three years.

I caught a taxi to Nadi Airport for half fare. It was going empty one way to meet the Pan Am incoming Saturday flight from Sydney. I opened my eyes only briefly during the trip to see the sugar cane rimmed southern beaches as we sped along.

Check-in was easy and quick, and strangely efficient. Leaving was always faster, it seemed, than arriving. The customs officers stamped my passport 'no return, exit only, Fiji'. The prime minister's deal was final as they entered a handwritten notation next to my name in a leather-bound customs log.

I walked to the departure lounge. I ignored the duty-free shop, tears in my eyes. I had no one to share the moment with at the strangely clean, sterile, modern international airport. It was time to leave. I had left no tracks. Chief Kavula and his warriors would not talk to the colonial police authorities before independence day. After independence, they were back in control of Fiji again.

The national Hindu radio station blared from the speakers at the Indian owned duty-free shops to attract travelers' attention. Just as I started to walk to the boarding gate for my Pan Am flight, I heard a news announcer call an alert for a special bulletin from Suva. The Indian shopkeepers all froze because of the country's pre-independence jitters.

I understood a little Hindi from the Valley Co-op meetings. I listened. I understood only a few key words from the radio bulletin before I turned and boarded the Hawaii-bound plane. They were "driver," "V.J. Singh," "two dead," "explosion," "fire," and "sex cult."

The gods had worked their magic through my earth body today. Patipati had entered the spirit world for rebirth. As the great silver jet took off into the late afternoon Fiji sunset, I left paradise and its dream world forever.

Ni Sa Moce

(Goodbye)

A LOOK AT TELLURIDE TOP OF THE WORLD (THE NEW WEST, BOOK TWO)

Pull on boot cut jeans, strap on spurs and lever a bullet into a saddle rifle for a Four Corners adventure centered in the smoldering stewpot of Telluride.

In the late 1970s, Cooper Stuart has returned to his sprawling historic mountain family ranch near Telluride. His widowed mother is managing the ranch with ever increasing bank loans while the Ajax Ski Company is determined to rule Telluride's future.

After a hundred years, the gold and silver mines are playing out – the Ajax Ski Company owner made a fortune in the postwar uranium boom near Telluride.

Bear Spirit, a Ute Indian Vietnam helicopter pilot and Indian Water Right's activist throws in with Cooper on the YBarC. Judy rides the range with Cooper on her champion barrel racing horse and Adrianna, descended from centuries of Spanish gold mining witches, also joins to help save the YBarC 's rangeland and water rights from the forces that would destroy one of the Americas' most remote and beautiful places.

AVAILABLE JUNE 2021

ABOUT THE AUTHOR

Tom Tatum is an author and accomplished film and TV producer/director. He is the founder of Tatum Communications, inc., which has produced, directed, and written over 400 TV, documentaries, video segments, VHS/DVD's, commercials, and Motion Pictures. Tatum's work has been seen by a worldwide audience and includes notable titles like Double High, Winners Take All and Greenpeace's Greatest Hits. Tatum Video's indy action/extreme sports program library spans 40 years and is one of the largest in the world.

Currently, Tatum operates his Ute Peak Ranch in New Mexico, and is "lead sled dog" on many multi-million-dollar solar projects via his company Ute Peak Solar, Inc. An avid advanced skier, he is married to well-known Colorado and Taos, New Mexico artist, Kathryn Tatum.